ASSASSIN

Assassin

A Makedde Vanderwall Thriller

Tara Moss

OPEN ROAD
INTEGRATED MEDIA
NEW YORK

ISBN: 978-1-5040-9911-0

This edition published in 2025 by Open Road Integrated Media, Inc.
180 Maiden Lane
New York, NY 10038
www.openroadmedia.com

For the readers

ASSASSIN

PROLOGUE

It's illuminating to know what you're worth dead.

The woman stared at the figure displayed on the computer screen before her, then cast her gaze back to the open balcony, blind for the moment to the domes and spires piercing the dawn Spanish skies, blind to the pigeons flying past, the movement of cloud and light, blind to everything save for the six deadly digits imprinted on her mind. The balcony shutter doors were thrown open to the world, allowing a cool breeze into the sterile, masculine apartment. Carrer de Bertrellans and the gothic quarter beyond were still sleeping. She had an instinct to reach out and close the doors, shut herself in. But that was foolish. Eventually they would find her here.

500,000 Euros.

The woman knew death could be cheap. Plenty of assassins would kill for one tenth of that price, and others would—and have—killed for much less. For a car spot. For a pair of sneakers. She should perhaps be flattered by the lofty price tag, but the people who wanted her dead would not be set back by half a million Euros. They could pass off the expense as fuel for their private jet or perhaps the annual budget for the floral arrangements in their city offices and their various extravagant homes. That kind of money was nothing to them, and paying for death was nothing to them either. This was not the first time they had spent large to have her out of their lives. And so here she was, hiding out in the Spartan and heavily secured apartment of a hired killer halfway across the world, seeing her life condensed to a harrowed digital photograph, some vital statistics and that six-figure price.

This is what my life has come to, she thought.

No one could plan for this. Not really. She had tried to mentally and physically prepare for this moment for weeks, had in fact monitored communications such as these precisely for this purpose—connecting the dots one by one until she had hacked into the network her would-be killer was connected to, a series of electronic signals and communications exchanged online. In today's world, if you knew the right people, removing someone was as simple as pressing "send." Money and instructions sent remotely. It was the language of the modern assassin—cold and virtual on one end, and all too bloody and real on the other. Now, just as she'd feared, those who wanted her dead had stopped trying to reach the paid assassin they'd sent for her: they realised he had failed. While her family back home and her former lover in Australia worried about her whereabouts, perhaps assuming she was dead, her pursuers were taking no chances on letting her live. They'd put out a wider net. Killers from all over would hunt her down. These were hard financial times, and there would be plenty of interest in a half-million-Euro score for a mere woman of no political interest and relatively little notoriety. She would be considered easy pickings. An easy kill.

The reflex of fear was soon replaced with another, more useful emotion.

Rage.

The woman looked at the photograph beneath the price. She still bore some resemblance to the image: too much. The photograph of her was around a year old. The original was candid shot, capturing her in a rush of movement, body blurred with action, running barefoot across the lawn of the palatial Cavanagh mansion in an elegant evening gown split daringly to the thigh. In stark focus and blown white by the camera flash, thick blonde hair flew back from her startled face; her eyes were wild. This image had been splashed across the papers at the time. Her presence at Damien Cavanagh's extravagant thirtieth birthday had been a small scandal. They'd cropped the image. Focused on the face.

She had been running for her life when that photo was taken.

She hadn't stopped since.

The woman ran a surprisingly steady hand over her long, dyed-brown locks. She turned from the screen and closed the laptop with one hand.

Deep down, she'd known this day would come.

CHAPTER 1

When faced with a homicidal psychopath, particularly an intelligent and sadistic one, standard police work just wasn't enough.

Unlike the visionary or mission-oriented mass murderer, the psychopathic serial killer does not end his reign of terror after one horrible, orgiastic spasm of violence, but waits in the shadows for his next victim. He does not turn his weapon on himself. He has no conscience. There will be no regret, no guilty confession. Intelligent psychopaths see to it that they leave no trail—no witnesses, no fingerprints and, increasingly, no DNA traces. The killer isn't the husband, the boyfriend, the ex, the victim's loved one, like the sad majority of homicides. There are no informants to mine, no obvious, traceable motives to follow. The serial killer is the violent stranger who doesn't kill for money, for personal gain, for romantic jealousy, for any normal motive. Without sheer luck, or a mind that understands his, he can't be traced or predicted or stopped.

Federal Agent Andrew Flynn tried to remind himself of those facts as he stood before his team of rookie profilers, nursing a mild hangover and a much more vicious and distracting malaise. When he was not neck-deep in the unsavoury details and brain-searingly violent images of fresh cases—sadistic serial rapists, killers who tortured the elderly, the weak, the vulnerable—his days with the Australian Federal Police now concerned training up a small team of people who, like him, would come in to join the dots that good investigative techniques simply didn't cover. Bright up-and-comers not yet scarred by the field. Young things who still naïvely thought they wanted this job, wanted *his* job. Banal settings: airless briefing rooms and impersonal hotel rooms and freaked-out country cops wondering how it could have happened to them, how this horror could have visited their nice little town. Cardboard boxes full of horrific crime-scene photographs telling horrific stories he knew could have no happy endings.

Andrew Flynn stood before a whiteboard covered in bloody images. He closed his eyes for a moment, lids sticking from fatigue. The room smelled of strong drip coffee, disinfectant and sweat. The fluorescent lights hummed. "Okay. Worthington case," he said, indicating the board. "As discussed yesterday. You all studied the file last night. What can you tell me about our killer? Gender?"

"Male," Patel answered.

It was an obvious call, and certainly one America's NCAVC—National Center for the Analysis of Violent Crime—PROFILER "robot" computer program would choose. Serial killers and rapists were almost invariably male. Australia had not yet had a known female offender of that type; and worldwide there was only really one woman in recent memory who fit the most narrow description of a serial killer.

The US prostitute Aileen Wournos had been quite singular in being a lone multiple killer, unrelated to her victims and, some argued, sexually motivated, though her profession obviously muddied those waters. Most female killers murdered children in their care, or were "black widows" who poisoned husbands for insurance, neither of which patterns matched what had happened to Mr. Worthington.

"Our perp needed power to move the body to the dump site," Patel concluded.

"Yes," Andy confirmed. "Strength would be needed to move the body, and yes, statistical likelihood indicates same." Profiling was, at times, a matter of maths.

"And the semen found," Leighton Gerard said. Gerard was overconfident and disruptive but well trained. Not his favourite member of the new national profiling unit. Andy had agonised over his inclusion.

"Correct. Though it may not belong to the killer. Semen was motile, but that only proves recent sexual activity." They could not rule out the possibility that the victim was involved in an intimate homosexual relationship, unknown to his wife. It was too early to rule out any possibility, no matter how remote. "Type?" Andy asked next. There was silence. It was a question not so easily answered.

"Visionary? Mission-oriented? Hedonistic? Power- or control-oriented?" The four classifications commonly assigned to serial killers. "Each of you *did* review this file last night?" he asked impatiently, with unnecessary sarcasm and edge to his voice. On hearing his own hostility he realised his head had not stopped throbbing since he'd woken on his couch at six. He slipped a hand into the pocket of his dark blue suit and popped two Panadol from their foil, turned from the group, and chucked the pills back with a sip of coffee that looked—and tasted—like crude oil. Then he asked the question again. "Type?"

Federal Agent Dana Harrison spoke up. "Not visionary," she said, and Andy thought, *Finally*. Harrison was a bright and eager member of the team. She was part of a new generation of officers fast-tracked by academic qualifications, having won a scholar-ship to study Investigative Psychology with David Canter in the UK after graduating with top marks with an MA in Psych and PhD in Forensic Psych. Out of the half-dozen members of this newly formed federal Serial Violent Crime Profiling unit—SVCP—she was the youngest and least experienced, but the most impressively academically qualified and arguably the most switched on. She was also in her late twenties and possessed an unconventional beauty that Andy sometimes found himself distracted by—full mouth, warm chocolate eyes, light brunette hair pulled back into a severe ponytail.

"Good. Why not?" he asked her for the benefit of the group.

"Visionary killers often see visions or hear voices telling them to kill. This looks like the work of a psychopath, not a psychotic," she said. "It's too organised. Also, in relation to the sex of the offender, the victim was strong and physically active so it would have taken some strength to subdue him."

"Good," Andy answered and tore his eyes from her. "What's an example of an organised killer? What makes them different?" he asked the room.

"Well, the Stiletto Killer," someone answered. "The case you worked on. He was organised."

It was Agent Patel again. He was dark, heavy-set and middle-aged, and at his words a tiny, fragile thing in Andy's chest fluttered and curled up, wounded. The same fragile thing he'd been drinking to placate most evenings. Andy took a steady sip of coffee to mask the jolt he felt. By the time he put the cup down, he was again empty of emotion.

Patel was right. The Stiletto Killer had been organised. He'd left a trail of slaughtered women on the streets of Sydney before Flynn had figured him out, pegged his methods, his motives and his identity . . . and brought him in only minutes before he claimed another victim. That narrow victory was what had put him here, in this room in front of these officers. After years of Andy working his way up, his superiors had recognised his aptitude for this kind of work. He had been sent to hone his skills with the best at the Quantico FBI Academy in Virginia in the USA, where profiling and the infamous behavioural sciences unit were born in the 1970s, and where the term "serial killer" was first coined. Andy's talent for understanding psychopaths and homicidal madmen was a combination of natural ability, exhaustive study, overseas training and personal experience. Very personal. He'd single-handedly cracked two serious serial sex-crime cases, and most importantly one of Australia's biggest and most widely known serial murder cases, "The Stiletto Murders."

But the cost . . .

These officers thought of the case as Andy's triumph and they generally forgot about the finer details. How one of the victims had been Andy's ex-wife. How his former girlfriend had been strung up on a bed, sliced by the madman's scalpel. How he'd very nearly lost her, too. People who knew better wouldn't bring up memories like that in polite company, not if they were normal. But these people, here in Canberra, were not focused on niceties. They had not been there when Andy had suffered those losses, working that case. The victims were just details in a case file. Names and statistics. It had to be that way or you'd go mad in this line of work. If they knew about the personal connection for Andy, as some of them must, they filed it away somewhere as irrelevant to their task. Andy had grown almost used to discussing the famous case with the emotional distance of a robot. Though there were times, like this morning, when he found himself unprepared.

"Aren't all psychopaths pretty much classified as 'organised'?"

someone added. The words drifted past Andy's ears as his mind continued to wheel and turn, looking for something to hit on.

He felt Dana's eyes on him.

"Not necessarily," Andy replied, vaguely but also correctly.

His mind had wandered to unhelpful places. He locked eyes with Dana. *Harrison.* The look of curiosity and concern in her large brown eyes brought him back. She was like that. She noticed when he was distracted, when that fragile thing in him ached and writhed. She was empathetic. It was part of what made her suited to profiling, and unsuited as well, he feared.

"So, if this is not the work of a visionary killer, then what is our probable type?" Andy asked.

"Hedonistic?" It was Peters.

Andy nodded. "Type unknown, but possibly hedonistic." Someone who killed for excitement and arousal. "We've seen something like this before, with a murder in . . ." He looked to the file notes. "An unsolved murder in Berrima eighteen months ago that may be linked—details are in your updates files—though the post-mortem wounds are considerably more advanced in the Worthington case. Why does the killer remove the flesh from these areas?" He pointed to the victim's cheeks. "Ideas?"

"Um, to disfigure—"

"No," Andy said, cutting Gerard off. "Blunt force disfigures. Fists. Boots. Hammers. It's fast; it's passionate. But this is surgical, isn't it? Precise."

"To keep as souvenirs?"

"Better," Andy said.

The Stiletto Killer had kept souvenirs. He'd been a shoe fetishist. A foot fetishist. They'd found stiletto shoes in his bedroom in the small apartment he had shared with his elderly mother. They'd also found individual toes and even an entire foot, preserved in formalin, amongst other body parts. But the Stiletto Killer was dead now. It was over. Had been for more than a year. So why had he been on his mind so much lately?

The answer was obvious. It was because of Makedde Vanderwall. It was because she was still missing.

Mak.

Andy's phone vibrated in his pocket. He slid it out, recognised the number, put it back. His shoulders rose, along with the urge for a drink. *Makedde.* His every muscle and fibre heavy with an emotional weight he could not unburden, he glanced helplessly at the white, round clock at the end of the room. It was nine-forty-five. Too early to take a break. Too early to deal with all that phone call would stir up.

Focus.

Andy's phone rang again. He felt it vibrate in his pocket for a few seconds before he looked. It was the same international number. "I have to get this," he finally said, relenting. "Harrison, take over." She stood and swallowed. "Brief the group, please," he told her, indicating the file. He left the room. It was better he was out of there, but he regretted that he'd called on Harrison twice. It was foolish.

He shouldn't treat her any different from the rest.

Flynn made his way down the blindingly overlit corridor to his office and closed the door behind him. As swiftly and instinctively as a smoker whips out a cigarette, he opened the bottom drawer of his desk, pulled out a seven-hundred-millilitre Johnnie Walker and sipped a shot straight from the bottle. It felt reassuring in his hands, and the whisky-burn in the back of his throat was both familiar and necessary. It was only one sip. *One.* He recapped and replaced the bottle, closed the drawer and straightened up. Then he put in a call.

"Mr. Vanderwall. I'm sorry I missed you."

"Have there been any updates?" Les Vanderwall was straight to the point, his voice punctuated by tiny cries of static across the twelve and a half thousand kilometres between them.

"Not on our end," Andy admitted, that small creature in his chest squirming again. They'd had this conversation before. "You know I'm not involved with the investigation."

Les Vanderwall was a retired Canadian detective inspector. His thirty-year-old daughter, Makedde, had flown to Paris pursuing an Australian private investigation case and had not been seen since. It had been nearly two months, and he and Flynn feared the worst. Mak and Andy had been in an intimate relationship. She'd moved to Canberra and lived with him for seven months in the house he still lived in now and, though she had left Andy a couple of weeks before departing for Paris and he'd had nothing to do with her decision to go, he felt somehow responsible. Les Vanderwall felt Andy was responsible, too. You didn't have to be a profiler to pick that up.

"But you *know* what's going on," Les insisted. He was making his daughter's whereabouts Andy's problem, though Mak, even when she was in love with Andy, would not be influenced by him on even the most minor issue. She was her own woman. Had been from the moment he met her.

"I stay across things as best I can," Andy replied reluctantly. "But there's not much to stay across at the moment." He didn't want to say the trail was cold, though clearly it was. They needed something fresh to resuscitate the case and lord knew there were many who didn't want it resuscitated at all. It didn't help that she wasn't an Australian citizen and that she'd last been seen on French soil.

The line was quiet for a while, and Andy wondered what was on the older man's mind.

"And you'd tell me if you heard anything from her. No matter what."

"Yes. You know that," Andy snapped. "You don't even need to ask, do you?" His temper flared like kindling.

God, I wish I had heard from her. Heard anything. Even a "Fuck you, Andy."

There was a long pause and the line came up in static again while both men considered what next to say.

The past several months had been some of Andy's worst. When he'd returned from a stint of training at the FBI Academy in Quantico to find that his live-in girlfriend had made good on her plainly stated promise to leave, he'd not been in the best frame of mind. Mak hadn't left a note. She hadn't wanted him to pursue her, or even talk to her, not until they'd had some "time to heal." But of course he'd come straight to Sydney once he'd found the house empty. His efforts amounted to too little, too late, their intense relationship damaged by his constant absences, and now that she was out there somewhere, presumably in Paris, alive or dead, it hardly surprised him that she would not contact *him*—especially as it seemed another young man had flown out to join her there. He'd come to accept that. It had been hard. But he'd accepted it. Mak and this young man with whom she'd become involved had both fallen off the radar after hitting Paris, which led credence to the idea that Mak simply didn't want to be found.

But her employer, Marian Wendell, had not heard from her since she broke the missing person's case she was in Europe to solve. The subject of her investigation, Adam Hart, had been returned safely to his worried mother's arms in Australia. Mak had personally seen him off at Charles de Gaulle airport. The Mak Andy knew, the woman who had been pushing so hard to get her career off the ground, would have felt it prudent to accept the new cases that were coming in on the back of that success. It was an opportunity to establish herself in the industry. Instead, according to Marian Wendell, the work had been pouring in for her and she had to keep telling her clients that Mak was on leave. And most telling of all, Mak's father, Leslie, had not heard from her. Their relationship had always been a strong one. Mak loved her father deeply. She'd lost her mother to cancer and her widowed father was the only parent she had. Now even Mr. Vanderwall had taken to calling Andy to find out what had happened to his own daughter, and Andy had precisely nothing to offer.

It was eating away at him from the inside. A cancer of a different kind.

"What about that family?" Les Vanderwall said, deliberately not mentioning their name.

Les was referring to the wealthy and influential Cavanagh family. A year or so earlier the body of a Thai national had been found callously disposed of in a dumpster in Sydney. The girl had been young: no older than fifteen. The victim was tied back to Damien Cavanagh, the sole heir to the Cavanagh billions, after a mobile-phone video surfaced that allegedly showed him with the girl in a bedroom around the time of or shortly after her fatal overdose. Damien, who at thirty was at least twice the age of the victim, appeared to have paid to have sex with her, and then caused her death, possibly by accident. Yet his identification in the grainy video was called into question and the case against him stalled. It was not so easy to nail the sole heir to one of Australia's biggest fortunes.

But Makedde wouldn't let it go.

She got hold of the video and managed to identify a rare Brett Whiteley painting in the footage, a painting the Cavanagh family was known to own. Thanks to her dogged efforts, including crashing Damien Cavanagh's thirtieth-birthday celebrations to find the room where the painting had been hung,

DNA material relevant to the case was found at the family's Point Piper mansion. Had it been anyone else, charges would have been laid. But Damien Cavanagh had his family to protect him, and protect him they did.

And then more bodies started turning up.

The girl responsible for taking the grainy video of Damien Cavanagh happened to get herself murdered in a supposedly unrelated incident. And another girl who'd seen the video died of a drug overdose. A close friend of Damien's turned up dead around the same time that blame for the Thai girl's death was focused on him. An alleged suicide. He'd been a party boy. An easy scapegoat for the unfolding scandal, Andy figured.

The Cavanaghs, via their impressive legal team, denied any knowledge of the Thai girl, despite the video that allegedly showed Damien with her and the very solid DNA linking her death to a room in the Cavanagh house. No, it was all Simon Aston, Damien's friend, now conveniently dead. He was to blame. He'd brought her there. He was the one in the video—though it did not look like him at all. He'd accidentally administered the fatal dose and his alleged suicide was the result of remorse for what he'd done. The Thai girl's presence in Australia was linked back to a grim, underage sex-trafficking racket, but before further investigation could be done, the couple responsible for her arrival in Australia also turned up dead. Not suicide this time. Those two were hacked to pieces. The Cavanaghs had since been tentatively linked with an organised-crime ring out of Queensland, but as far as Andy knew, that trail had also gone cold.

In all the mess Makedde had ended up at the top of the Cavanaghs' hate list for her ongoing role in trying to bring justice for the girl and the victims of the subsequent cover-up. And now she had gone missing. Those who crossed the

Cavanaghs had a habit of turning up dead, and Andy hoped to hell Mak had not already joined that growing list. Damien Cavanagh, and his father, stank of some kind of involvement in her disappearance, but it was not something anyone could yet prove. And not a lot of people were keen to connect those dots either. It was professionally and politically dangerous territory. Andy wanted to believe they would be brought down eventually, but it would take time and a lot of very careful investigation and political manoeuvring. None of which Andy was personally in a position to perform. And none of which was related to his job here in Canberra with the new SVCP unit.

"Mr. Vanderwall," Andy began patiently, "you know I'm not involved—"

"Of course I bloody well know you aren't involved in the case. But you *know*. What are their chances? Is there any traction? I mean, are they bringing Jack in for questioning at least?"

Jack Cavanagh. The patriarch.

It was not a small thing to bring Jack Cavanagh into the station for questioning. Not a small thing at all. He was one of Australia's wealthiest and most high-profile business people. He had friends in high places. The press would be all over it. And he would crush the homicide squad if they made even the most tentative move on him. Crush them. Careers would be ended. No, Andy doubted very much that was on the cards any time soon.

"It doesn't look good. They are doing the best they can, but there is a lot of pressure to abandon the case against him."

Corruption. Perverting the course of justice. Murder. If they could just get him on something. Something he couldn't weasel his way out of.

"I wish I had something to tell you. She seems to have disappeared without a trace. They've been dealing with the French police. You know what the French police are like. Can you imagine? But as I understand it, there's nothing. She left the hotel and wasn't seen again. No sign of a struggle there. She just walked out and didn't return . . ."

This simple fact was killing Andy. It was killing both of them.

He looked at the closed drawer and imagined the bottle in his hands again. *Just another little sip.*

"They sent us the belongings they found in her room," Les finally said.

That's what this was about then. It meant the police were finished with them.

"There's not much there. She didn't leave her purse or passport behind, or her camera, unfortunately. She left clothes, toiletries and her suitcase, though. Things I doubt she would just discard."

Andy nodded to himself and swallowed. He didn't know what to say. No, Mak was not the type to abandon clothes in a hotel room in Paris. Nor was she the type to run off without settling the bill. There were many unconventional things about Mak, but lawlessness was not one of them. She'd been through a lot, more than any woman or man should have to endure, but at heart she was a nice, law-abiding Canadian. The daughter of a cop, no less. Not innocent exactly, but she was nowhere near irresponsible. He didn't buy for one second that she'd done a runner on a hotel of her own volition.

Something had happened to her. Something terrible.

CHAPTER 2

The filthy mattress on the floor of the cellar had been her home for an immeasurable stretch of time, and now she sat on it with an unlit cigarette dangling from her parched lips, her bare ankle straining against a heavy cuff secured to the wall by a chain—an ankle crusted with the dried blood of superficial abrasions.

From where the metal had cut into her.

The woman had woken here, on this damp mattress, drugged. It had taken some time to become lucid. She had been held prisoner in this dank prison for days, but how long exactly? With no light, no windows, she could not count the days—the weeks?

Stale water.

Cold TV dinners. A cat's water-bowl.

The metal cuff. Grating.

And darkness. So many hours of cool, silent darkness.

The woman did not smoke, but a match, a single match for lighting her cigarette, held her only grim hope for survival.

Her captor had given the cigarette to her and was watching now. Watching it in her lips. She looked up into his dark eyes and, as he handed her the tiny box of matches, she said, *Thank you.*

Thank. You.

Thank. You.

Yes.

All thanks for the cigarette, sir.

A cigarette. The final request before death. And for Makedde Vanderwall, a final chance. She fumbled with the matches.

I'm lonely. Lonely. Lonely.

And then her captor is close, so close, towering over her with his hulking body. So large. Too strong to fight. But close enough to smell is close enough to kill. *I want you*, she whispered, pulling the clothing from her shoulders, inviting him, licking his ear, running her tongue across the scarred, repulsive cheek of the professional killer who was her captor, her warden, her abductor.

His belt buckle dragged along the stone floor. His hands. On her.

His rough flesh. Against her. His desire. Pressing.

His sickening penetration.

But the key and the match—these two things held her freedom. *The key and the match. The key* . . . She could do it. If she could just survive this. Do what she had to do. And then, she had it, the key, the match, the flame—blue and nearly invisible at first, then rising in magnificent amber, dancing across the mattress, across his shirt, his hair. A blaze, beautiful, vengeful and horrific.

Eat fire, fucker.

Makedde Vanderwall woke to the sound of a single piercing scream. She could smell smoke and burning flesh—the sickening mix of cooking skin and hair, like sulphur and seared meat. She sat up violently and looked around her, blinking, her body a tangle of adrenaline and fear. For a moment she was unsure whether the scream had been her own.

Yes. You were screaming. Again.

Though Mak had been sure of the smoke, the air was clean, her lungs clear. There was no fire. She was in bed, the early light coming in past the shutters over the balcony. It was another nightmare. Her subconscious was still in that dank cellar in the French countryside, but the rest of her was in the bedroom of Luther Hand, the hired assassin who had been her captor. The man she had burned alive.

Mak's face was slick with sweat and her stomach felt dangerously queasy. She stifled a gag, and quickly realised there was more. *No*, she thought as she pulled the bed covers off and ran through the spinning dark for the nearby toilet, a hand over her mouth. She had just made it inside the black-tiled cubicle when her stomach emptied itself through her fingers. There wasn't much there, but she managed to aim what there was at the open toilet. With a ferociousness that surprised her, she gagged and choked until the feeling passed, then sat back on her heels, disgusted. She flushed, closed the lid, wiped her mouth. Cold water felt good on her hands, growing warmer as the pipes woke. She washed her hands and kept the tap running so she could splash her face. *Dammit.* Face wet and eyes half closed, she stepped across the narrow hallway to the bathroom and flicked the light on. A bottle of spring water sat next to the sink and she used it to rinse her mouth and brush her teeth once, twice. Still, the acid taste remained. Her eyes strayed to the small bottle of Chanel No. 5 on the toiletries shelf. She gave the top two quick squeezes and the air filled with the distinctive, musky floral scent. She brushed her teeth again.

Perhaps unsurprisingly, the nightmares had become worse since she'd found the order for her death. What would happen if a second of Cavanagh's hired killers got hold of her? What horrors awaited her? And all because she wanted justice for the things the Cavanaghs had done, the people they'd had killed for their own gain.

Justice is dead.

Mak leaned on the rim of the sink with both hands and looked into the mirror, where a slim, naked woman with bone-straight black hair greeted her. The light cast unflattering shadows, accentuating the jut of her collarbone and the contours of new, lean muscle. She'd been exercising using the dumbbells and chin-up bar she'd found in the man's apartment—push-ups, tricep dips, pull-ups—and her thin arms appeared uncharacteristically ropey and tight. Her breasts were full and round, but beneath them were the first signs of increasingly taut abdominal muscles and the hint of ribs. The soft taper of her hips had been reduced to angles and hipbones, something she had not seen in her mirror since her early days as a fashion model over a decade earlier. She'd dropped a dress size, maybe more. Mak preferred her softer, curvier self, but weight was sliding off her like water. *It's stress*, she told herself. She'd have to fight to keep weight on, to stay fit. She needed her strength. Displeased, Mak leaned in, tilted her head down and pressed her clean fingers to the part in her hair. A pale band of dark blonde roots already showed through. In only another week it would be obvious, the part giving the unsettling effect of a bald stripe. She'd need to dye her hair again. She had resisted the urge to give herself a short chop, such was the identifying flag that had been her once blonde mane. But long hair provided some semblance of cover, she had decided; and, after it had been dyed and chemically straightened, she felt it bore no resemblance to her former style. The black hair hung like a curtain, casting new shadows on the angles of her high cheekbones and falling straight and shiny past her freshly muscled shoulders, contrasting with fair, unblemished skin.

Unblemished, except in the places where she had scars.

The thin, raised cicatrices weren't obvious unless you knew where to look. Unless you knew what they meant.

That Mak had managed to turn the tables on her would-be assassin might have given her some sense of satisfaction were she in a movie. Instead, it only filled her with numbness. She'd sacrificed a great deal of herself to get him in a vulnerable position down in that cellar out in the remote French countryside, that makeshift prison where she'd been kept for days. She'd sacrificed so much to live. There were things she couldn't undo, couldn't un-know. The man named Luther Hand would not be coming back here, would not be coming for her, could never touch her again. But there would be others to take his place. There was no doubt of that. With a half-million-Euro price on her head she didn't dare stay in one spot for long now. She hoped the contract had been put out to international freelancers only because the Cavanaghs did not know whether she was alive at all. What easier way to tie up the loose ends than demand her dead body for a price? Perhaps she really had successfully disappeared? Perhaps this was a last-ditch effort to wipe the earth clean of her? A desperate move? Now that this new price was on her head, it felt like the woman marked for death could not possibly be her, and in some ways the inconveniently living woman they sought to erase was *not* her, in fact no longer existed at all. She was now a woman without a name, without a life, without a home. She'd tried to imagine starting again. She'd changed her appearance, was learning Spanish from books and CDs, trying to get the accent right. On good days she'd toyed with the idea of a new life, dared to dream of somehow putting all the violence and death behind her. But they wouldn't allow that.

Mak? Are you still in there?

She stared down her own feverishly bright, hollowed-out

eyes and barely recognised what she saw. The arrangement of her even features and her tall, feminine build meant she was still beautiful, despite the weight loss, the terrors, but she was visibly *haunted* as well. She carried a new darkness. Mak had once read about a study where rapists and sex-murderers were given the plain, black-and-white headshots of a number of women. They were asked to choose which ones they would target. Each of the men picked the same ones. Why? It was something in the eyes, they said. A disturbing thought. Mak pondered what it was in her that had made her a psycho-magnet for so much of the past five years.

Unsettled, she turned away and flicked off the light.

Makedde padded back through the dark and crawled into bed, pulling the covers up high. She rolled to one side, paused and then rolled over again. After a minute her pale, sinewy right arm strayed from the sheets to pull the laptop towards her on the bedside table. She flicked open the lid with one finger, the screen coming to life to illuminate the corner of the bed in a soft, alien glow. Could she get any more sleep? She scanned the dim room: the bedroom of Luther Hand, the man she could not shake from her nightmares.

Wrong.

Everything is so fucking wrong.

Mak had lain low here for weeks now, and as if by osmosis she felt she was absorbing Luther's invisibility, his separation from the world. Part of her was even beginning to relate to the dead assassin.

The one-bedroom apartment had seemed almost unused when Mak first arrived, holding her gun and jumping at every shadow. She'd learned many things as a private investigator—how to dig up information, how to hack the most basic passwords, how to pick locks. Arriving here, double-checking the address she'd found on Luther's laptop, she'd been afraid she would have to put her less-than-perfect lock-picking skills to use. But the last key she tried on his keychain had fit the main lock like a puzzle piece, despite looking, at first glance, like a key for a vehicle of some sort. Another fit the dead bolt. She'd let herself in and set off a screeching alarm system, but the little lock and unlock symbols on the key soon proved the solution to that problem. With a simple press of the button the alarm went silent and she was in, sheltered, his Glock shaking in her hand and his home at her disposal. The ease with which she'd entered this inconspicuous fourth-floor apartment and its ability to hide her from the outside world had seemed like an omen of some kind.

And just like that this had become her temporary home. For weeks she couldn't stand the sight of another person, didn't feel safe even on La Rambla under cover of evening darkness in the busiest crowd of innocent tourists. But this secure cave had bought her time. And Mak had needed time. Time to recover. Time to learn about her would-be killer. Time to plan.

She was not sure how long it had been since Luther had last used the apartment. The air had been stale, the fridge empty. There'd been only a few supplies in the cupboards and the microwave had the manufacturer's plastic wrap still across it. There'd been no personal items in the apartment at all and she wondered if Luther Hand had even left his fingerprints behind. What he had left, though, were clear indications of a man obsessed with security. The balcony doors were covered over with slatted metal shutters made to look like a modern designer addition rather than the security device they were. And he had a small cache of weapons, a fake ID and a few thousand dollars in various currencies stored in a hidden compartment under a loose board beneath the kitchen cupboards. It was secreted so cleverly it had taken her ten full days to discover it. He had a Peugeot in a car spot in the alley outside. She'd checked it and found a sniper's kit in the boot. It was not as large as the assassin's kit he had been travelling with when he'd abducted her in France. Outside the farmhouse she'd found a black Mercedes packed with cash, jewels, a similar sniper kit and smaller weapons including a Glock, which had fallen out of the glove box along with four fake passports. The jewels and cash, she presumed, were the spoils of some recent job.

But most importantly, she'd found this very helpful laptop in a briefcase in the car. It had proved at least as practical as the cash. She'd mined it to find the address of this apartment. According to the collection of title deeds he had filed away, Luther's lethal trade had bought him a lot of bolt holes in major cities like this—one in Mumbai, another in Moscow and even one in Sydney. And the laptop identified her attacker as Luther Hand. He had other IDs, but Luther was the name he'd used back in the cellar where he'd kept her prisoner for over a week. It was the name she knew him by. The name that haunted her nightmares.

Luther Hand.

Mak had torched the Mercedes from the farmhouse and kept the rest. She had his Barcelona apartment now—purchased under the name of Pedro Blanco, which matched one of the false passports from the Merc—his local car, his weapons and at least a fraction of his riches. Mining his computer had been easy. She'd hacked into it as an "administrator," using a technique she'd learned while getting her private investigator licence, and she'd successfully searched and prodded its digital treasures, finding addresses and phone numbers, the title deeds under his various false IDs, vague references to locations and marks, bookmarked news articles about Makedde and the Cavanagh family. She'd also uncovered some cryptic references to what she suspected were bank accounts or codes for bank transactions. He'd made some attempts at coding his files, though clearly he never anticipated someone getting as close as Mak was now.

And Mak had found photographs of herself on Luther's laptop.

There were photographs of other people as well. Candid shots like hers, the subjects clearly unaware they were being photographed.

She'd checked their names online, to see what she could find:

VLADIMIR GORKESKY. RUSSIAN NATIONAL. MISSING, PRESUMED DEAD.

SUSAN FALLUMA. TURKISH NATIONAL. FOUND SHOT IN THE HEAD IN HER HOME.

NICOLAS SANTER. BRITISH NATIONAL. MISSING, PRESUMED DEAD.

Nicolas Santer's disappearance appeared to be the most recent, not counting Mak's own. It was a big deal back in London, if the online news was anything to go by. Santer had pissed someone off and had fled with a lot of wealth that was not his own. Luther had got rid of him, just as he had got rid of the others.

They were all marks. They were all dead. Except Mak.

The assassin had kept notes on his grim work and those who hired him for it. She'd found communications with agents he referred to with single letters. Encrypted emails. Encrypted files. It wasn't all spelled out, exactly, but it was there. The numbered sequences would be territory codes or bank accounts or phone sequences; the letters indicated names. She'd searched online for matches, but hadn't found any yet. A professional could, though. A forensic technician could. This little laptop could, perhaps, seal the fate of the Cavanaghs. Here was an electronic trail that led back to them. A real forensic trail—she was sure of it. If she could find a way, she would get it to the police, or to the media. Someone she could entrust with taking the Cavanagh family down. Someone who wouldn't give up. She had some ideas about who that would be.

Mak wanted justice for what the Cavanaghs had done. She wanted justice for their innocent victims—the unnamed Thai girl found in the dumpster, Megan Wallace who'd filmed Damien Cavanagh with the girl, and everyone else who had found themselves disposed of in the cover-up.

Especially Bogey.

She wanted justice for Bogey—her lover—the man she'd fallen in love with and who Luther had killed for no reason other than the fact he was looking for her in Paris when she was chained up in that cellar. He might have alerted police, so he was silenced.

Bogey had done nothing. He'd known nothing. He'd simply got in the way.

Makedde cast her gaze over the icons on the desktop of Luther Hand's computer as her mind came into focus. She took a sip of water, the glass clinking for an instant against Luther's loaded Glock on the bedside table. It was nearly five a.m., the computer told her. In Australia it would already be the next day. She wondered what her friends were doing, what her former lover Andy was doing. She thought of him often. Wondering. Would he, in time, forget her? Mak finished the glass and felt the cool water filter all the way down to her hollow, still upset belly. She should probably eat something.

Resigned to wakefulness, she reached for the remote and flicked on Luther's flat-screen television to CNN's news coverage, the volume low. An artificial glow filled the room, along with a reassuring murmur of her native English. She swung her long legs out of the bed again and padded to the kitchen to turn on the kettle and scoff two dry crackers in quick succession.

Andy.

She wondered what he thought had happened to her. She wondered what he would say if he knew.

Mak prepared a cup of tea, returned to the bathroom and rested it on the sink edge. The air still smelled of Chanel No. 5 and something less pleasant. She washed her hands thoroughly and arranged her tools before her. Years of modelling had taught her about the power of makeup, but now she used it not to beautify but to disguise. Though it was early in the morning and she was unlikely to encounter anyone on the streets, she felt she could not risk leaving the apartment looking too much like her former self. She tied her hair into a tight ponytail at the nape of her neck and raised a makeup brush to her dyed and shaped eyebrows. With a deft hand she darkened them further, emphasising the arch, then applied a quick coat of black mascara over her naturally blonde eyelashes. She smoothed a light layer of 30+ SPF foundation over her skin from forehead to chest, a shade or two paler than her natural complexion. She took another brush and swept a smudge of darkness under her eyes—eyes that seemed a brighter shade of blue-green with her newly black hair. The darkness under her eyelids was not flattering, but it wasn't meant to be. It gave the effect of shadow, and subtly deeper-set eyes. She painted her full lips with quick dabs of a matte, earthy lipstick. Immediately her sensual mouth appeared smaller. Finally, with a hand that shook slightly, she took her dead lover's black-rimmed spectacles and slid them on. She'd replaced the original scratched lenses with non-prescription glass. She'd already considered this was, perhaps, an overly morbid ritual, but Bogey's glasses served the dual purposes of changing her appearance in a simple but effective way, and acting as a kind of link to him. In any event, she couldn't bring herself to toss them away. This was all she had left of him.

Bogey would understand, she thought, and that's what seemed to matter.

Mak stared into the mirror and wondered what her eyes still had left to see. Transformed, she walked back to the bedroom, slipped on a sports bra and panties, track-pants and a warm, sleeveless hoodie, and tied her running shoes tight over low socks. Strapped against her ribs, where it chafed the least, was a nine-millimetre Glock. She would not leave the apartment without it.

At five-fifteen she switched off the perimeter alarm system, stepped into the narrow stairwell, turned both bolts until the apartment was secure and switched the alarm back on again. Across from her was the entrance to the only other apartment on her level. She'd watched the owner come and go a couple of times from the safety of the security peephole in Luther's door. It was an old woman—no threat. And she was never up this early.

Mak did not bother with the elevator. It was barely large enough to turn around in, and after her experience in that farm-house cellar she'd developed a strong aversion to small spaces. She preferred the stairs, and she took them now, bouncing a little on each tiled step, stopping to circle her ankles and stretch her legs at the bottom before walking out into the dark, narrow street, Carrer de Bertrellans. There was the typically European smell of urine in the streets, which always seemed to be there before the rains or street cleaners washed it away. Bags of garbage had been left out for collection overnight.

Mak strode to Santa Anna, warming up with a jog before breaking out in a solid sprint, her running shoes falling quickly and quietly on the old stone streets. The sun was not set to rise for over an hour, and the vast square in front of Barcelona's dramatic gothic thirteenth-century cathedral, Catedral de la Santa Creu I Santa Eulàlia, was empty save for flocks of pigeons. The skies glowed a midnight blue above, the moon invisible behind low cloud. As she ran briskly across the square, past the remains of first-century Roman aqueducts and city walls, and up the steps of the cathedral, she thought briefly of the tale of Saint Eulàlia, the co-patron of Barcelona to whom the cathedral was dedicated. As the story went, she was a virgin who was stripped naked in the square before a miraculous, sudden snowfall covered her to preserve her modesty. The enraged Romans then sealed her into a barrel and stuck it with sharp knives before rolling her through the streets. Her body lay entombed in the old crypt under the cathedral. Unlike modern Hollywood horror tales, chastity did not exempt young women from torture and death in Roman times, it seemed. But it did make religious martyrdom possible.

Mak pushed herself harder with every stride up the cathedral steps and along the winding streets around the impressive church, as gargoyles of horned bulls and snarling dogs and unicorns and other mythical creatures peered down at her just as they had watched other passersby for centuries.

She ran the streets, her mind puzzling over the choices before her and the tasks ahead. Mak was no martyr. She resolved to again stay in during the daylight hours, as was her custom, and spend the evening in her usual spot, practising for what inevitably was to come. But soon, she would need to break out of the security of those routines. She needed to abandon Luther's apartment. She needed to leave Barcelona.

And to do that, she had to find a new identity. *There is no luck,* she told herself. *Only preparation. Preparation is everything.*

She was nearly ready.

CHAPTER 3

Dark clouds moved over the shores of Sydney's moneyed suburb of Rose Bay, the idyllic blue water turning black and choppy. A lone outrigger canoe made its way over increasing white caps, bobbing up and down in the surf next to moored boats. Along the quiet shoreline, joggers rugged up for a sprint back, pulling on hoodies. Mothers turned designer prams around as the first cool drops of rain began to fall.

Jack Cavanagh, patriarch of one of Australia's richest and most influential families, observed the darkening autumn day from the railing of the *Rosebud*—a forty-plus-metre Oceanco Idefix yacht named in reference to Hearst, the American publishing tycoon. The light rain did not bother him, the trade-off being a moment of solitude. After a lunch of fresh seafood accompanied by a view of the Sydney Harbour Bridge designed to impress the visiting VIPs, the other men had moved inside with their host—a publishing magnate and former politician—and the striking boat had begun to make its way back towards Woollahra Sailing Club at a leisurely pace. On deck, the salty air stung Jack's eyes. He was troubled by what he perceived to be a subtle shift in the dynamic of this once welcoming guild of influential men. The host was hospitable, as always, but Cameron

Goldsworthy, the British dotcom billionaire, had seemed to distance himself from Jack in front of the others. And there had been a certain amount of whispering, he'd thought. A kind of discomfort with his presence.

Jack brought the lip of a delicate flute of champagne to his mouth and sipped. It was losing its fizz.

He sensed movement on the deck, heard footsteps; Cameron Goldsworthy appeared at his side. "I thought we ought to chat," the man said.

"Of course," Jack replied and gave a tight smile. He and Cameron had unfinished business. An unfinished business deal, to be exact. "How long are you in town?" he asked casually.

"Just a week before heading to Cannes. You?"

"Not going anywhere at the moment," Jack replied, his tired eyes watching the horizon again. He balanced his warm flute of champagne on the edge of the rail, fist wrapped around the stem.

"How's your lovely wife? What is her name again?" Cameron asked.

"Beverley's fine. And your new bride?"

"Oh, fine."

Cameron leaned against the rail and caught Jack's eye, offering a disingenuous smile with a mouth full of perfectly white cosmetic dental work. Despite being close to Jack in age, he was a man with a vernal, youthful air about him, argu-ably thanks to the influence of his third, much younger wife, Catriona, a well-known South African fashion model. Their recent lavish wedding had been covered extensively in the press. Jack and his wife, Beverley, had not been invited. It was the first clear signal that there was a problem between the two men, and that there was clearly some reason, beyond cold, hard business, for why the negotiations between them had stalled, though only six months earlier it had looked likely that one of Goldsworthy's companies would make a significant investment in Cavanagh Incorporated's transport arm. In certain ways, Cameron had the lifestyle and international reputation Jack coveted and the association would have been good not only for business reasons but for Jack's international reputation. Goldsworthy had made a lot of money during the first dotcom boom, investing in all the right places and pulling out before the crash that bankrupted so many in the nineties. He counted several Hollywood celebrities and European royals as close friends. He had his own multimillion-dollar super-yacht, twice the size of the vessel they were on today, and it popped up in all the right places throughout the year: Cannes, Monaco and in Australia for the annual Sydney to Hobart Yacht Race and accompanying billionaire social season.

Jack watched his companion warily, silently, deciding not to broach the subject of their previous business negotiations. Cameron Goldsworthy, for his part, seemed in no rush to get to this "chat" they needed to have. He put his hand out, detected the light rain and shrugged, and when he pulled a fresh cigar from a pocket in his pale blue Brioni sports jacket, a deck hand arrived out of nowhere to smile unobtrusively and to cut the cigar end for him. The deck hand offered the two men fresh champagne and caviar on blinis, both of which they refused, and then vanished as quickly as he had arrived.

Once they were alone again, Cameron leaned on the rail and casually offered his lit cigar to Jack, who shook his head.

Cameron took a leisurely puff and the aromatic smoke drifted past Jack's nose.

"I hear Beverley is in Europe," Cameron finally said. "Lovely woman, Beverley. She's been very loyal, hasn't she?"

Jack nodded, sensing something disagreeable in the tone of the haughty British accent. Beverley had decided to take a sudden holiday to Europe without him. They hadn't spoken much in the previous three weeks. It was not a welcome subject.

Cameron paused and took another puff. "Weren't you signing some big transport deal here? Some kind of a bullet train thing between . . . where was it now?"

"Between Sydney and Melbourne."

"Yes. That's it."

"It's still happening," Jack said quietly, though there'd been complications.

"I see." There was another long pause. Cameron took another drag of his cigar. "You know, I've heard some interesting things about you lately."

Jack's chest tightened. "You have, have you?"

"I have," Cameron replied. He took another puff and let the smoke out slowly, drifting on the salty air. "Very disturbing rumours. I'm sure they're not true, but if they were . . ." He shook his head. "Well, I'd be very disappointed. Something about you bullying a young private investigator. A woman."

"You hear wrong," Jack snapped.

"She was at that party you threw for Damien, wasn't she?"

"I certainly didn't invite her."

"Ah, but she was there."

The Vanderwall woman's exit from the party had been caught on camera. It was undeniable.

"In fact, I think I may have seen her," Cameron went on. "Blonde, yes? Attractive thing. An ex-model if I am right. About the same age as my Sarah." This eldest daughter from his first marriage was also the approximate age of his new wife. "Now she's missing." Cameron nodded to himself. "Seems a shame, doesn't it? She sounds like an interesting woman. I bet she'd have a lot to say."

Jack turned suddenly, forgetting his flute. It snapped at the stem and he found himself holding the narrow bowl of the broken champagne glass for a moment before tossing it into the dark waves below.

"Shame," Cameron repeated, noting the broken glass, or perhaps referring to something else entirely.

Jack faced his unwanted interrogator and crossed his arms. There were many things he wanted to say, but the fact was, Cameron was worth significantly more than Jack. He was rarely so overmatched, and the experience was deeply uncomfortable and unfamiliar. There were few people, perhaps no one in Australia, who would challenge Jack in this way, who would dare to taunt him as Cameron was. What was he getting at? Jack could feel his face becoming hot.

"Yes. This PI woman," Cameron Goldsworthy continued between puffs. "I do hope she's okay. I'm sure you're terribly concerned about her wellbeing—helping the police with their enquiries."

"Are you threatening me?" Jack blurted.

"Why? Should I be?"

Jack Cavanagh resisted the urge to raise his voice, to defend his position, to explain that Makedde Vanderwall was a nuisance, a nobody, a pest threatening to ruin everything his father had built and Jack himself had worked so hard to hold on to for his entire lifetime. He had not wanted to go after Mak or the others who had threatened him. He had been pushed into it. She wouldn't leave him and his family alone. She'd threatened his reputation, his livelihood and his son's promising future. Jack was protecting his family. Anyone would do that, wouldn't they? Wouldn't Cameron himself do what was necessary to defend himself and his loved ones? What if his precious Sarah found herself with the wrong crowd, got herself into a bit of trouble? What if some stranger, even a young woman, tried to bring his whole empire down? He'd had no choice, dammit. No choice.

It was clear that the rumours about Mak Vanderwall had been circulating amongst his peers. And how could he defend himself? He could not.

"Excuse me. I have to go," Jack said and, with nothing further to say, he left Cameron Goldsworthy and the irritating, smug look on his face. He demanded the deck hand order a water taxi to take him to shore. He'd call the host later and explain that he wasn't feeling well.

When Jack reached the fourteenth floor of his city office his secretary of many years, Joy Fregon, was absorbed in the work at her desk. She appeared surprised to see him back, but she said nothing about his abrupt departure from what should have been a relaxing afternoon on the water.

"I want no calls, no disturbances at all until Mr. White gets here," Jack insisted. He could barely contain his sense of panic.

At the mention of White's name her eyes flickered with recognition. "Yes, Mr. Cavanagh," she said.

He shut his door.

Sitting forwards tensely in his leather chair behind a massive mahogany desk hundreds of metres over the bustling Sydney business district, Jack Cavanagh fought an unsettling feeling of being trapped.

There had been times when this office was respite enough, when he'd toiled night and day here with the fever of ambition and been satisfied amongst the proud sporting memorabilia and the artworks he'd earned with hard work and business acumen— including a painting from Sidney Nolan's famous Ned Kelly series that had set Jack back over five million dollars. Seeing it, owning it, knowing he'd captured it had made him proud. The more you have the more you stand to lose, perhaps. Perhaps that was why the sight of its bold colours and iconic imagery didn't thrill him now, only made him feel worse. Or perhaps it was that another of his coveted art collection had played a role in identifying his Point Piper family home as the scene of a crime.

Yes. Jack's art collection had cost him in more ways than he could have imagined.

It's all closing in. Closing in . . .

The scandal that had started with his son Damien's questionable friends and nocturnal activities, and had spun off into countless other problems, like falling dominoes, had already cost Jack one of the biggest deals in Australian history, it seemed. The historic high-speed train system between Sydney and Melbourne, the one that Cameron Goldsworthy had mentioned, had been in the making for some time. Cavanagh Incorporated had been close to winning the contract. It had been all but officially signed when talks were put on hold. Financial shake-ups in government infrastructure were cited as the reason. Austerity measures were in place around the world, there was no doubt about that, but Australia had fared better than most countries, reliant as it was on commodity sales in the strong Asian financial markets rather than the troubled US and European markets. Financial concerns were not the real reason, he felt sure of it now. Recent speculation in the media had taken its toll on those negotiations, just as unfavourable gossip appeared to have made its way around the world, damaging Jack's reputation in ways he could not repair.

The blackness. It's closing in . . .

A feature piece one month earlier by respected investigative journalist for the *Tribune*, Richard Staples, had been the latest and most direct hit to Jack's standing. Staples's article had been the first to openly question Jack's behaviour, and was the first to publicly mention him in relation to Vanderwall's disappearance in Europe. He hadn't blamed Jack for the disappearance—not directly—but he didn't have to. The previous clashes between Vanderwall and the Cavanaghs were well known. Staples and the *Tribune* had been very careful with their implications. There was nothing Cavanagh could sue for. But it had looked bad. It had looked very bad indeed.

After Staples's story was published Beverley had departed suddenly for a holiday. Even before she'd left, their home life had become tense with all the conversations they were not having. Their troubled son. The rumours. The business deals on hold. And though his son had, for now, successfully sidestepped any blame for the girl's death, there was still speculation about an ongoing police investigation. And Cameron Goldsworthy's jibe about his marital problems had smarted most because it hinted at an unspoken truth. The events of the previous year had begun to fester. It was a cancer eating away at every part of Jack's life. His own wife had started to suspect him. He felt it. Jack's family was crumbling. Not that anyone but the likes of Cameron Goldsworthy would dare mention it. Not yet. Perhaps Jack should avoid social outings for a while. Avoid others who might be whispering about him, and privately gloating about his impending downfall . . .

There came a gentle knock on the closed door of his office, breaking Jack from his dark contemplations. Joy, his secretary, popped her head around the door.

"Mr. Cavanagh, Mr. White is here," she told him.

Jack nodded. Joy's brow was pinched. She looked concerned, but said nothing further. She'd looked concerned a lot lately—of course, Jack had been taking a lot of meetings with Mr. White lately. One did not take meetings with Mr. White unless things were serious.

After a moment Robert White, known by some as "The American," walked into the room with his head tilted slightly down. He made some polite comment to Joy, closed the door behind him and moved towards the desk. White cut a fit but unassuming figure, wearing a sports jacket and pressed slacks. His grey hair was neatly combed and his shoes did not make a sound. He always moved in a very precise manner. He was economical in his movements, Jack had noticed. White was ex-FBI. He was a consultant of sorts. He dealt with security issues for Jack.

Jack stood to greet him and the two men shook hands and exchanged courtesies. "Bob, thanks for coming. We have an issue," Jack said and sat.

The American folded himself into the chair opposite Jack, leather creaking. He waited.

"This afternoon Cameron Goldsworthy bailed me up. He said he'd heard things. He accused me of bullying Makedde Vanderwall. He mentioned her disappearance."

The American considered this with a blink and a barely perceptible nod of his head. "Goldsworthy is a bold personality," he said thoughtfully. "He does like to stir up trouble. There have been no new threats and nothing in the papers for four weeks. Private speculation is unavoidable, though, I'm afraid. Did he say anything concrete that concerned you?"

Jack shook his head. "Rumours then."

"Rumours could be enough to lose this deal outright," Jack complained, though within himself he knew the contract was lost.

"Has Damien contacted you?" Mr. White asked. Jack shook his head again.

Like Beverley, Jack's wayward son, Damien, was not in the country, but not because he was holidaying with his mother.

The last Jack had heard, his son was in Monaco and frankly Jack didn't want to think about what he was doing there. Damien had been advised not to leave the country, but he hadn't been told by a judge, and so off he'd gone. Damien was a loose cannon if ever he was and worrying about him took all of Jack's spare time and quite a bit which was not spare. At sixty-nine, he'd wanted to hand the mantle to his only child, his only son. It wasn't to be, it seemed.

"Are there any updates?"

The American shook his head. "Your son is still in Monaco, but it looks as though he may come home. I'll alert you if he makes any firm plans. In the meantime, we're keeping an eye on him."

Jack was torn between wanting his son home and wanting him to stay away, where he was less likely to cause further scandal.

"And Vanderwall?"

"There has been no sign of her, but we are looking into every possibility."

What could the silence on Makedde Vanderwall mean? Jack wondered. He was nervous that someone knew more than he did. Was she dead? Was she alive? She was supposed to have been killed in Paris, well out of the way of public scrutiny in Australia, but increasingly it appeared that might not have gone according to plan. There'd been no body found. That was good, he supposed. But Luther Hand, a man whom Jack had agonised over giving the green light to, had reportedly sent word that his mission was complete and then disappeared without asking for his remaining funds. Why would he not want the money? Jack didn't like it. There was too much that didn't make sense. He worried, too, that the police could be making connections. Connections that would be hard to shake off. His influence could only protect him for so long.

"Where would Cameron Goldsworthy hear about Vanderwall?" Jack said, though the question was rhetorical. He took a deep, ragged breath. "It's not good. It's not good . . ."

"The Staples piece was not published internationally, but I'm afraid it was widely read," The American said. And it was still on the *Tribune*'s internet site, Jack knew. Apparently nothing could be done about that.

"He's not planning anything else?"

"Richard Staples has moved on to other stories for the moment. He's currently researching a piece about the live-export trade in Indonesia," Mr. White said. Staples was now being monitored.

"Keep watching him. He . . . I just can't have him print another piece like that. And still no one has asked for the second half of the funds?" Jack said of the apparently botched attempt to have Makedde killed.

The American nodded. This information was nothing new, but it did not ease Jack's sense of being trapped. He wondered who was whispering about him, what was being said, what would happen next. And an unsettling image came into his mind again. An image that had been recurring in his nightmares. It was the image of a dinosaur sinking deeper and deeper into blackness. Into tar.

It's closing in. The blackness.

The American studied him quietly for a while, saying nothing. "If Vanderwall is alive and sets a foot in this country, we will know," he finally offered. "She won't trouble you again."

"I want . . . I want proof. I don't care how," Jack Cavanagh said. "I want proof she is dead."

CHAPTER 4

"Women kill, too."

All eyes turned to Agent Dana Harrison, the youngest member of the fledgling SVCP unit. The small group of criminal profilers was seated in the incident room on metal chairs, the whiteboard before them still grimly adorned. Their post-lunch caffeine had worn off and, until Harrison's comment, it had looked like their discussions would fall back into circular patterns of argument.

Agent Harrison sat forwards in her chair. She'd worn her brown hair down this afternoon, Agent Andy Flynn noticed, and now she tucked a lock behind her ear.

"All day we've been saying 'he,' but *women kill, too*," Harrison argued. "Think of Katherine Knight."

Katherine Knight. The woman from Aberdeen in NSW had stabbed to death, decapitated and skinned her former de facto partner, cooking parts of his body and hanging his skin from a meat hook. It was an unusual case on many levels, not least for the post-mortem treatment of the body and the gender of the killer. She had been found at the scene, sleeping off the drugs and violence of the night before, passed out on the blood-soaked bed. The mother of four was now doing time at

Silverwater as the first Australian woman to be sentenced to life without parole. Likewise, Omaima Nelson, the US–Egyptian former model who killed, cut up and cooked her new husband, frying some of his body parts in oil, had no hope of parole.

Yes, women could kill.

"She attacked her partner after sex. She had him in a vulnerable position. If the Berrima case is linked to this one, our perp could be a woman and these men could have been lured by her," Harrison concluded.

Andy smiled to himself. Dana was bright and challenging.

On this one, though, his instincts told him she was wrong. "And the DNA traces found on the body?" Patel said.

"It could have been from another encounter, as Agent Flynn said. Unlikely, but possible."

"I guess we shouldn't rule out any possibility at this stage, no matter how unlikely," Patel replied and shrugged. "Until we work up a more complete profile I recommend we focus on the unique pattern of wounds. As I said this morning, the marks don't fit with mutilation intended to obscure victim identification. In my opinion it suggests trophies. Or anthropophagy," Patel offered.

"Cannibalism," Dana Harrison said and nodded. "Jeffrey Dahmer and Albert Fish both consumed the flesh of their victims." Unlike Knight and Nelson, whose cannibalistic tastes were in question, Dahmer and Fish proved to have eaten large parts of their victims.

"In this instance we have an adult male victim," Andy said. "Thoughts?"

"Dahmer was a homosexual who suffered severe mental illness," Patel commented. "He felt he could conquer loneliness by consuming his victims so they could never leave him. Is our killer mentally ill then?"

"Have to be, really," Gerard muttered unhelpfully.

"Dahmer chose easy victims. They were from a lower socio-economic group. Our man—or woman—chooses tougher targets," Harrison said, ignoring Gerard and poring over the file. She was really relishing the role, Andy could see. "Worthington was what, a strong, fit, successful small-business owner? Hardly easy pickings. To succeed the killer must be high functioning," she argued.

Andy watched his group, their interactions, their arguments.

His mobile phone vibrated.

Mak.

His mind went immediately back to his conversation with Les Vanderwall that morning, though it was unlikely he would call again so soon.

He checked the number. This one couldn't wait.

"Carry on," he announced to the room and left his protégés to continue their discussions. He walked the bright hall and let himself into his office, closed the door, took a seat. His hand dropped down to hover near the lower drawer for a moment, a quick shot of whisky his first instinct, but he pulled it back. He'd had far too much to drink the night before and was still suffering for it. He had to work harder to keep himself under control. Since Mak had gone missing, he was finding it hard.

Andy dialled his former boss from the landline. "Inspector Kelley, it's Flynn. Sorry I missed your call."

Detective Inspector Roderick Kelley had been Andy's boss and mentor when he was working homicide for state police in NSW. Andy admired him enormously and after a few high-profile cases, most notably the Stiletto Killer case, Andy had earned Kelley's much-sought-for respect. In the most recent policing reshuffle, which included police headquarters moving to Parramatta, Kelley had been quietly offered the position of commander of the homicide squad. Andy knew he declined the position and the pay rise it would bring mostly because he preferred working cases with his team and despised the politics of the higher levels of policing. According to Andy's good friend and former police partner Detective Senior Constable Jimmy Cassimatis, Kelley was the only detective inspector in the new building to have his own office. It was clear that his old boss remained something of a legend within the NSW police. Without his recommendations Andy suspected he would not have been able to get the SVCP unit up at all.

"Flynn," the inspector replied, typically economical of speech. "The Hempsey murder we discussed last night . . ."

They'd spoken late, Andy recalled, though truthfully he didn't remember the conversation well. He'd been several hours into staring at the bottom of a whisky tumbler, which increasingly filled and emptied each evening like a tide pool after the sun set. Andy frowned and searched for the details as Kelley had presented them on the phone. *Single homicide. A woman in her thirties. The staging of the body suggested sexual sadism.* Andy had suggested that it was unlikely to be a first offence, considering the description of the wounds.

"We've found a couple of incidents in the area that fit the pattern you asked me to look for," Kelley told him. "Two sexual assault cold cases, both also in the Surry Hills and Strawberry Hills area. I think we could benefit from your perspective . . . the perspective of your unit. How soon can you get here?"

Andy felt a rush of adrenaline. "Three or four hours by car," he replied without hesitation. "Is the scene still secure? I'd like to see everything in situ."

"The body is at Glebe now." The well-known "city" morgue. "But forensics are still going through. I'll see to it they don't release the house to the family until you're finished. Come to my office first thing in the morning. And, also . . . I've been on the phone with Berrima. If you want to send a man over to look at the cold case there, they'll be receptive."

Andy nodded to himself. Kelley was on side. "That's good news." Certainly it was if the Berrima case *did* turn out to be linked to the Worthington homicide. "I have someone in mind. And I'll be bringing another member of the team for Sydney," Andy added before signing off.

"I'll see you and your man then," Kelley said and hung up. Andy leaned back in his chair. This was a small breakthrough.

Within police departments there was still some resistance to using profilers and when it was deemed necessary they often farmed out the role to academics who had never seen action, or even American FBI profilers who were flown in to assist in key international cases. A lot of state police still felt a certain bitterness when the AFP tangled with their cases, even as consultants. The new SVCP unit was not well funded or well understood by others in the law enforcement community. It was a program in its infancy—a program designed to keep resources within the police departments. Despite this undeniable advantage, it had been hard to get up and it would be far too easy to have the funding pulled. For it to work, old habits needed to change. This was part of that change, he hoped.

Andy put in a call to Berrima to arrange the details of his unit's involvement. When he returned to the incident room he found his profilers were still discussing the Worthington case. He let the team continue for a few minutes while he considered his strategy.

"The Berrima case does have several parallels," Harrison was saying. Andy watched her, letting her finish her comments before announcing his news. ". . . and not only the wounds."

When she finished speaking she turned and looked at him, and she saw the anticipation in his face. And once she did all the faces in the room turned to Andy, too. They waited for him to speak.

"I've been on the phone with New South Wales," he announced. "Patel, I'm sending you to Berrima to look at the cold case. I'm working on getting you to Benalla to examine the Worthington crime scene as well, but Victoria has been slower to come on board. If the cases are linked, you'll need to present a solid case to argue it. It crossed borders so be particularly mindful. No one wants to claim a serial killer."

There was a subdued feeling of triumph in the room and Patel seemed pleased to have been chosen for the Worthington case. "That's good news. When do I travel?"

"They're expecting you tomorrow. And Harrison," Andy continued, looking to Dana, "we will travel to Sydney this afternoon. There is a homicide there they'd like us to take a look at."

He hadn't actually seen Agent Harrison smile before, he realised, but now the corners of her mouth turned up.

"We're being let out of the cage?"

"We're being let out of the cage," Andy confirmed.

Agent Flynn found himself in the driver's seat of his Honda, outside Agent Harrison's flat, looking at his watch. It was past four. If she didn't take long, they might beat the worst of the rush-hour traffic getting out of Canberra. He'd hastily packed for one night, maybe two. Kelley had sent through preliminary details on the Hempsey homicide and information on the sexual assaults that might be linked to the case, and now Andy looked down at his laptop, which was propped open awkwardly on his thighs, heating up at the base. The crime-scene images were as disturbing as Kelley had led him to believe.

Ms Hempsey had been bound and gagged. She had cuts all over her body.

You tortured her. And you liked it.

He frowned, closed the computer and took a breath. He pulled out his phone and dialled Jimmy Cassimatis, his former police partner of over nine years. He hadn't visited for a while.

"Cassimatis," Jimmy answered.

"Jimmy. How are you?"

"Well, if it isn't the Golden Boy," he replied mockingly, recognising his friend's voice. "How am I? I'm working with a pack of fucking arseholes. That's how I am. You? How are things in the ivory tower?"

Andy laughed. "No ivory here. And no tower. And Inspector Kelley is not an arsehole."

"Not Kelley. Jesus, I'd love to still be working with Kelley. No, *Hunt* is the arsehole. If I had to deal with Kelley all day, it would be a fucking holiday," Jimmy explained.

Andy doubted that.

"This guy's fucking arrogance is driving me batshit." He'd made inspector and Jimmy was shifted under him. "Honestly, he's been inspector for two seconds and he acts like he fucking owns everyone."

Andy had heard that Hunt was after Kelley's job and now that he'd made inspector he was already gunning for a promotion to commander, too. He'd risen in the ranks with unprecedented speed since Andy's departure.

"Well, I'd be happy to swap with you," Andy lied.

That had perhaps been true only the day before, but now that the unit was finally getting some traction and he would soon be on the road with Harrison, he felt differently. Still, he did miss working homicide, particularly under Kelley. And he missed spending more time on the street, getting his hands dirty.

"Yeah, right. You don't have to deal with psychos any more; you only have to talk about them," Jimmy complained.

"Is that what they're saying? Look, I might be able to swing a visit."

"Thank Christ. Angie was starting to think you'd forgotten us."

Andy shifted in his seat. He looked to the door again. Dana was nowhere to be seen. "You know the Hempsey murder? The young woman in Surry Hills?" he said.

"Yeah. Ugly thing that is."

"It's come my way. I'm headed to Sydney now. We'll be going over it with Kelley in the morning. Looks like a potential serial crime to me," Andy explained.

"A serial killer? *Skata.* As if Sydney hasn't had enough of those." The shadow of the Stiletto Killer could still be felt. As with so many high-profile serial-killer cases, the newspapers rehashed the details any time a major crime was mentioned. Worried parents were still known to warn their daughters not to go out at night in high-heeled shoes, as if that could protect them.

"Want to stay with us?" Jimmy asked. "How about dinner tonight? Angie will be offended if you say no."

"Tonight? I don't know." He was already across most of what Kelley had sent, he supposed. The crime scene was still being analysed. "Yeah, okay. Yes to dinner, anyway. But I'll be staying at a hotel in the city." He'd stayed at the Cassimatis home plenty of times. Angie was an excellent host, but with four children in the place it wasn't somewhere to stay for work.

Movement caught his eye and Andy noticed Harrison emerge from her flat with a duffle bag slung over her shoulder. "I should go," he said and looked to the hands of his watch again. The drive would take about three hours. Maybe less if they were lucky. "See you seven-thirty—eight? Is that too late?"

"Sweet. After dinner we can lose the kids and have a beer," Jimmy said and hung up.

Andy leaned across and opened the passenger side. Agent Harrison had changed for the drive, and now she wore a brown leather jacket over a white cotton shirt and slim-fitting denim jeans. She slid inside, bringing with her the scent of her perfume, and when she turned and smiled at Andy, clutching her duffle bag in her lap, there was no denying to himself that he found her beautiful.

As soon as he realised it, his instinct was to keep her at a professional distance.

"Put that in the back," he said more gruffly than he'd intended, and that lovely, rare smile faded. "Can you read okay in the car?" he asked.

She nodded.

He looked out the windshield and turned the key in the ignition.

CHAPTER 5

On Wednesday afternoon Makedde Vanderwall strode along the labyrinthine streets of the Barri Gòtic area with a dog-eared map tucked discreetly into the pocket of her leather backpack. Even after weeks living in the area, she still occasionally found herself on undiscovered streets that twisted and turned until her inner compass was in a spin. Like Catalonian architect Antoni Gaudí's iconic Barcelona buildings, each appearing to melt and curl, there was nary a straight line in all of the old town.

Mak wore the casual garb favoured by the locals—skinny jeans, a lightweight leather jacket over a sleeveless hoodie and flat-heeled boots that were good for walking. She pulled her hoodie up, and kept her head down.

Over time she'd begun to feel less paranoid on the streets. Around every corner she'd feared another assassin, another Luther, but now she could see she was anonymous. She'd opened her eyes to the beauty here, the obvious friendliness of the locals. And everywhere in the gothic quarter there was history. The spectacular Barcelona cathedral, built on an ancient crypt. The countless museums. Medieval walkways sculpted in sandstone; wrought-iron lamps so old that they would have once lit up the night with dancing oil flames instead of the modern blink of electricity. Tapas bars overflowing with loud patrons. Stained glass. Carved signs. Well-worn stone. Gargoyles watching from above.

Many times now, Mak had wondered whether it was possible to successfully take on a new identity, to live here happily. Hers was a lonely existence, but only because she worked so hard to be invisible. The Spanish were not a solitary people. All through the night they talked and drank and danced, while Mak locked herself inside Luther's apartment, only venturing out for exercise or to buy supplies. Would she ever bring herself to forget, to move on? Could she let justice take its own course? Could she live with herself, as someone else?

She was about to find out.

Mak pulled the hood forwards on her head as she walked.

She arrived at La Rambla, the popular tree-lined pedestrian mall flanked by single lanes of traffic on both sides, that stretched about twenty blocks, from Plaça de Catalunya to the seaport. It was busy, as always, and she moved down the promenade without attracting attention, the locals engrossed in their own shopping, or selling to the tourists, and the tourists busy gawking at the architecture. The Spanish were friendly, but not aggressive, as Mak had found the Italians in Milan when she'd been modelling there. The men in Barcelona did not leer or follow her, did not pinch her bottom as she walked up the steps from the subway, or brazenly sing the praises of her female form as she passed the cafés. No, here she could remain unmolested, unharassed. Vendors smiled. Waiters were flirtatious but respectful. She was left in little doubt that she could have company if she wished, but she did not, and in time, as she'd grown more familiar with her daily routines, she'd realised that she could go about her life as invisibly as she needed to.

Despite everything, she'd begun to feel almost safe.

Mak arrived at the entrance to the famous Mercat de Sant Josep de la Boqueria, a public market that dated back to the thirteenth century. The large open-air marketplace was announced by the presence of an enormous crowd of local Catalonians and tourists, over which the oft-photographed blue, gold and red stained-glass sign hung, featuring the name of the market and an insignia: a shield below a large crown. Above the crown, a silver bat was proudly displayed, its broad wings spread. Mak wondered about the significance of the winged creature.

She stopped, took her backpack off and put it on back to front. There were many pickpockets in crowded areas like this. Once prepared, she stepped into the crowd, passing vast and impressive displays of vividly coloured fruits—perfectly formed apples, oranges, bananas, pears, lemons, avocados—and exquisite handmade chocolates shaped as tiny shells, beetles, poodles, cats or miniature replicas of the Sagrada Família. Other stalls held mountains of nuts, dried fruits or dried mushrooms behind spruikers hoping to attract the tourist Euros, instead of merely the interest of their clicking camera lenses. Mak moved past each familiar display, barely giving them a glance, and made a beeline for her favourite cheese stall further inside the market.

Today a woman with short hair manned the stall.

"*Hola. Quisiera comprar . . .*" Mak began and scanned the latest offerings. She pointed at one of the hard sheep's cheeses that looked appealing. "*Me gusta comprar un queso de oveja buena.*"

The woman lifted the cheese out of the glass case and nodded, speaking in rapid, singsong Spanish, only half of which Mak could catch. She sliced off a small sliver and handed it across. "*Buena.*"

Mak nodded in agreement, tasting the sample. It was very good. Strong and nutty in flavour. She made a sign with her index finger and thumb to indicate approximately how much she wanted. The woman placed a knife over the block and Mak stopped her.

"*Un poco*," she said and indicated a smaller amount.

The woman shifted the knife. "*¿Tanto?*"

"*Sí.*"

"*¿Algo más?*"

"*No. Es todo*," Mak replied. *No. That is all.*

She put the block of sheep's cheese in her backpack and walked to the next stall, where she bought some penne pasta, fresh tomatoes and basil. On the way out of the market, she averted her eyes from the grim displays of whole pig's ears and trotters, thick cow's tongues, tripe layered and folded like fleshy curtains, and flayed whole sheep's heads of all sizes—almost enough to make her a vegetarian again. She stopped at a popular stall that was literally overwhelmed with dozens of cured legs of *jamón*, ham, hanging from every available square inch of the display. They had particularly good *jamón serrano*, the famous dried hams, and the stall was always very busy. When the vendor was free she purchased a typical Catalan chorizo from him. He wrapped it up and she popped it in her bag and thanked him. She left the market and continued southeast down La Rambla, slinging the pack back over her shoulders once more, now heavy with her fixings for dinner.

Now, where is this place?

She wasn't quite sure what to look for. What kind of a shop would it be? Surely no one *advertised* what she was seeking to buy. Would it be a private residence, perhaps? Luther's address book did not make it entirely clear.

Only a couple of blocks down from the market, directly across from the famous Chinese dragon hanging over La Rambla, she found the entrance to Carrer de l'Hospital, a road she had not had reason to venture down before. It was still single lane, but this road was set between actual kerbs and was a little less narrow and winding, an indication of relative modernity compared with the opposite side of La Rambla, where every lane was twisting and medieval, barely able to take a car. Carrer de l'Hospital was hemmed in from the sidewalk by tall eighteenth-century terraces with flat roofs, each five or so storeys high, adorned with evenly spaced balconies of intricate wrought iron. Here, after only a few minutes, she felt a subtle change in atmosphere. Tourists came to this street, certainly—she could see several of them, and the presence of a money changer and some tiny tourist stalls indicated as much— but it seemed most foreigners did not venture too far from the attractions of La Rambla, and the area had not been gentrified. The rows of terraces grew a little more decrepit as she walked further from the main street: balconies rusted, laundry hung out in limp lines, flapping in the breeze. There was more graffiti here. Mak felt herself grow instinctively more alert to potential dangers. The area was slightly reminiscent of some of the more run-down streets of New Orleans's French Quarter, she thought. She paused as she passed a lovely square with a large church built, as per the charming, typically Spanish habit, in two distinct eras. Part original Roman church, part eighteenth century, perhaps? It had five huge archways with wrought-iron gates across the front, beneath a flat-faced façade of stonework so old it appeared to be crumbling. Next to it, a hotel appeared to have been made from what once was a convent: there was an old statue of Mary in one window.

Mak kept walking.

Then, in an area of graffiti-stained stone and increasingly dire-looking shops selling the same tired souvenirs—plastic bulls covered in bright shards of glass, T-shirts with vulgar slogans (*SPAIN* apparently the acronym of *Sex Paella Alcohol Is Needed*), red polyester flamenco dresses swaying in the breeze out front—she found the address she'd seen in Luther's contacts. Before her was a single door and a narrow shop window of dirty glass, lined with gold watches, glass costume jewellery, fake Rolexes and dusty clock radios. Deeper inside were cardboard boxes brimming with what looked to Mak like junk. A show of desperation and broken promises frozen in time and locked behind glass—wedding china, engraved anniversary gifts, vinyl records that once meant something to someone. She checked the address again and shrugged.

Could this be it?

She pushed open the door, the edge of which hit a small bell rigged to chime, and she walked over a doorstep that was worn smooth like a river stone from more than a century of use. "*¿Hola?*"

A strong, swarthy man of about five foot nine emerged from a back room, frowning. His hair was black and curly, his eyes dark. His beard was the result of at least two days' growth. He wore jeans and an unironed, collared shirt, gold rings on his fat fingers.

"*Hola. No parlo el catala,*" Mak told him. Her Catalan needed work.

"*Ingles.* English," he replied in a heavy accent. It was a comment, not a query. He looked her up and down from the tips of her motorcycle boots to the top of her dyed raven hair, eventually settling somewhere in the upper half.

She nodded, wearing her most good-natured expression, but not a smile. "Javier Rafel?" His dark eyes flickered with recognition. *Yes, it's him.* "Mr. Rafel, you come highly recommended."

"By whom?" he replied slowly, with a long gap between the two words, as if his brain was searching for both the right language and the right response for the circumstances. He hadn't decided yet what he thought of her. He moved behind his cash register, and placed his hands on a broad open book—a ledger.

Mak removed a thick wad of Euros from her satchel and calmly laid them on the table under her palm, right in the crease of the book. Between her thumb and index finger the number *100* was visible. Javier quickly took the bills from her and slid them under his ledger, then lifted the edge to count all twenty of them. His grubby hands were swift and no one would see the transaction from the street. Yup, this was her guy. He lumbered past her to the door and flipped the sign over to indicate that he was closed. "You come," he said in a gruff voice and led her to the back room he'd first emerged from. It would have been big enough for perhaps four people to stand comfortably if the space had not been filled with tatty boxes, a wooden chair and an overpoweringly large black safe, much newer and more high tech than the shopfront would lead one to expect. As it was, the two of them could barely fit in the remaining floor space. Mak was immediately on high alert. If something went wrong, there was only one exit, possibly with a time lock or other security device on it that this man could activate if he chose. If he somehow had an idea of the money he could make by capturing her, dead or alive, he would not hesitate to lock her inside.

No paranoia. Don't get paranoid.

She fought to remain composed as he closed the door, locking the two of them together into the windowless space.

Luther Hand had trapped her in that dank cellar while she was drugged and unconscious, but she was alert now. She could defend herself. She'd brought Luther's Glock, a gun she'd practised with every day. It was loaded, but the safety was on. This man could not trap her. She was more likely to kill him here in his shop, out of paranoia, then to end up at his mercy.

Her gun hand itched, and she rubbed her jeans pocket absent-mindedly.

"How long for a Euro passport?" she said in a steady voice. "It has to be fast." She had not seen her Canadian passport since Luther Hand had abducted her. She felt certain it had been burned to cinders in the French farmhouse. She had never made a move abroad without it, but her passport had been in her handbag, along with her mobile phone, all taken by Luther when he'd abducted her. They were doubtless destroyed. She had considered visiting an embassy to apply for another passport, but that would quickly put her back on the grid. Considering the reach and resources of her opponent, such a risk seemed unwise. But acquiring false identification brought its own risks. She'd wrestled with this step.

"You *policía* or something like this?" the counterfeiter asked her.

She looked him in the eye. "No," she said. *Daughter of a cop, yes. And no, he would not approve.* "I am not a cop," she confirmed, plainly and decisively. "I'm someone in need of a service, and I hear you are the best to provide it. Have I been misled?"

"This passport. It is for you, yes?" She nodded.

"I don't know . . ." He was obviously fishing for more cash. "It is difficult."

"That's two thousand I just gave you. I'll give you another eight when I have that passport in my hands, as long as you can do it quickly. But if I've been misled . . ." She frowned and put out her hand, palm up. "You can just give me my two thousand Euros back now and you won't see me again."

His eyes widened. "Let's see now," he protested quietly.

It was a good starting price. Not crazy enough to make her stand out as a fool, she figured, but good enough to show she meant business.

"Top quality. Fifteen," he said. "Five now."

Her face hardened. Luther's notes indicated this was his local counterfeit passport contact. From what she'd seen of Luther's collection of passports, the work was excellent. Or perhaps Javier handled the business end of things and someone else made the goods? Could those fat fingers really produce so exacting a product? Either way, she was sure this was the man, and she needed ID.

Mak didn't want to be taken for a pushover. "Twelve. Four now, eight later. That's all."

"Fifteen is my price."

"Fine. I'll have my money back now." She turned and moved to leave. She'd stand at his counter until he came round. She didn't like this airless room.

Javier touched her elbow and nodded his confirmation. "Two days," he said. He appeared to think for a moment. "Come on Friday around five. The shop will be closed. I will be here." She handed him an envelope containing her unsmiling passport photographs. They wouldn't let her wear the glasses in the image. She'd not been surprised, though she preferred the morphing effect of the spectacles. Without them she felt she looked just a little bit too much like Makedde Vanderwall.

"Friday," she repeated. "I'll bring the rest then." They had a deal.

Business completed for now, she stepped out onto the dirty street and took a deep breath. Two days was even faster than she'd hoped. Only two days and she would have her own identity. She could travel. She could check in to any hotel. She would be so much more unhampered. Mak wondered what had kept her from taking this step before.

Two days . . .

Javier Rafel could not believe his luck. Grinning at the

thought of all the money he would soon make, he picked up the phone and made a call.

CHAPTER 6

The Cassimatis family lived in a single-level red-brick home in Merrylands, in Sydney's west. Every centimetre of the eight-hundred-square-metre lot served a purpose. There was the house itself, fully packed with six family members, the single guest room overflowing with stored toys and rarely used gym equipment. And there was the driveway, bumper to bumper with his-and-hers family cars, and the small yard adorned with a basketball hoop, two bicycles, two tricycles, a leaf-filled inflatable kids' pool—currently out of use—and several pieces of weather-worn sporting equipment. On any given day the cars and bicycles and footsteps of varying size came and went at regular intervals, and the lights inside burned through half the night.

Tonight the family was joined around the large, circular kitchen table by their guest, Agent Andy Flynn, finishing a late dinner of steak, potatoes and peas sautéed in lashings of pepper, salt and garlic. The eldest of the four children, Dominique, was the first to leave the table after clearing his plate, followed closely by the others old enough to walk, and Jimmy, who tactlessly explained that he had to piss.

Andy found himself at the table alone with Jimmy's wife,

Angie Cassimatis, and the youngest boy, Edmond, who watched the profiler with eyes the colour of dark chocolate, drool wetting his gap-toothed mouth.

"More water?" Angie offered. She was a tough matriarch in the traditional Greek mould. She ran the household with a firm hand, got the kids to church on time and could often be found— dark cascades of curls piled on her head—cooking and designating chores like a sergeant. Somehow, with four children, she'd also found time to complete her training as a nurse.

Andy shook his head. "Thanks, Angie. That was lovely." He hadn't had a home-cooked meal in a while. He'd forgotten that full, wholesome feeling.

Angie got up and began to load dirty plates into the dishwasher with one hand while supporting the smallest Cassimatis over her shoulder. Edmond continued mutely to watch Andy from his elevated outlook, mouth open. He was sleepy.

"Let me do that," Andy protested and pushed his chair out.

"Sit!" she demanded, pointing a finger. "You are a guest here. I won't have you clearing the dishes."

This was a regular pattern whenever Andy visited, which hadn't been terribly often since he'd moved interstate. He knew Angie didn't take kindly to guests trying to help out. In time the toddler began to fuss and Angie abandoned the dishes and excused herself from the kitchen to make her way to the closest couch. "Sure I can't get you anything more? Ice cream, maybe?" she asked across the room, and in seconds she had undone her top and pulled Edmond to her breast.

"No, I'm fine. Thanks, Angie."

A soft smile spread across her face and a kind of peace seemed to settle on the house as the boy fed. Though Angie seemed unbothered by the company, Andy became self-conscious looking in her direction. He began to concentrate on the bottom of his water glass, wondering if he would ever become a father. The responsibility of parenting scared him more than a little. Maybe that was why he kept fucking things up. Despite having been married once, he'd resisted "settling down."

A toilet flushed and Jimmy returned to stand in the kitchen doorway, leaning his bulk against the frame. He was built like a teddy bear, all stomach and grin. He'd put on a few kilos since Andy had seen him last. If Andy's Achilles heel was his drink, Jimmy's was anything deep-fried, or made with chocolate. Or both. Doctors had warned him to cut back for the sake of his health, but he'd obviously been ignoring that advice lately. "Mate, wanna go somewhere for a beer?" Jimmy asked, rubbing his hands together.

"I would, but I've got an early morning," Andy replied. He pushed his chair out again and started to stand. "I'll help finish the washing up—"

"No, no," Angie protested from the living room, though he'd hoped she wouldn't hear him. "Don't touch a thing. You're a guest here," she said, though when Edmond complained she turned back to murmur sweet nothings and stroke his fine hair. "A nightcap then," Jimmy suggested. Before Andy could protest, Jimmy left him to cross to the liquor cabinet in the living room, where he poured them both a Johnnie Walker. He knew Andy would be unlikely to resist his favourite drop.

It would be rude to say no, Andy supposed. He hadn't seen his closest friend in a while.

"Get you anything, hon?" Jimmy asked his wife as he walked past her, balancing the overfilled drinks. Angie shook her head and continued to run delicate fingers over their youngest child's hair as Jimmy bent to kiss her on the forehead. Andy watched the exchange with a flicker of sadness. The breakdown of his own brief marriage to Cassandra didn't have to taint his relationships forever. Some people simply were not suited. He could have tried harder with Mak. He could have been more open. He could have taken a real chance. She wouldn't have left him then. She wouldn't have gone to Paris . . .

Jimmy returned to the kitchen and closed the door for privacy, clearly relishing the chance to talk. "I thought you'd never come by again, you dick. How about my boy?! Beautiful kid, isn't he? You haven't seen him since he was, what? Six months?" Jimmy had sent photos, but Andy hadn't found time to visit. "He just had his first birthday. They grow so fast."

"You do have a great family," Andy told him sincerely. "Four sons!" he exclaimed and flexed a flabby bicep. "Who'd have thought?"

They clinked their glasses, brought them to their lips and tipped them back. As ever, the whisky tasted good. Possibly a little too good. Andy felt his shoulders drop. This was a good idea, he decided. He'd been too tightly wound.

"So how are things with the . . . S-C-V-P?"

"SVCP," Andy corrected him.

Jimmy made a face. "Sorry."

"It's fine. Unless you factor in that I trained in an area that's rapidly losing credibility."

"*Skata*. Is it that bad?" He'd obviously heard some recent controversy.

"Depends on who you ask, I guess," Andy replied. "Criminal profiling has taken a public beating lately. It hasn't helped my case, that much is certain."

Over the years Andy had strongly associated himself with the FBI's Behavioral Science Unit (BSU) and Behavioral Analysis Unit (BAU). He'd spent a lot of time in Quantico, learning the FBI methods of profiling pioneered by Robert K Ressler and John Douglas in the seventies. It wasn't what he'd joined the police force to do, all those years earlier, but it was what unfolded for him, especially after apprehending the Stiletto Killer. Andy proved adept at homing in on the hardest killers to catch—the loners, the ones who killed randomly, who killed strangers, the sadistic ones or the psychopathic ones or the crazy ones who kept on killing until they were stopped. And the FBI program was the most promising. Now, years on, he'd staked his career on it and he could see those foundations crumbling before his eyes. There'd been some damning research released, most notably by a team of psychologists at the University of Liverpool, concluding that the FBI's celebrated methods were worthless or worse, in some cases actually impeding investigations by sending officers after the wrong suspects. And there'd been a big piece in *The New Yorker* recently, criticising John Douglas, and James Brussel before him, essentially comparing the famed profilers to astrologers and psychics. Charlatans even.

Twenty odd years after the FBI's criminal profiling methods reached critical popularity with *The Silence of the Lambs*, Andy had finally established himself as Australia's top profiler exactly when the world decided they didn't want one. What were the chances?

"Fuck, man, I'm sorry," Jimmy said and meant it. "It's not like anyone can fault what you've done, however you did it."

He might not understand Andy's process, exactly, but he was sincere. Jimmy knew how much his friend had sacrificed, personally and professionally. "I mean, you are the one who figured out Ed Brown. And that other fucker. That rapist."

"At the SVCP we use a combination of profiling methods, but . . ." Andy trailed off. *But it doesn't seem to matter. The future of the unit is uncertain.*

My future is uncertain, Andy thought.

Their conversation paused. They sipped from their drinks.

The air felt heavy.

"So what about this murder in Surry Hills?" Jimmy began. "You think it's a serial? That he'll do it again?"

Andy nodded. "Given the opportunity, yes." That was the fear. Any kind of domestic murder was a tragedy, but with a killing like this there was the very real danger that it would happen again, possibly soon, after a cooling-off period of unknown duration. Crimes like this were rare, and driven by intensely sadistic compulsions, not by the more normal motivations of greed or jealousy. Andy believed the murder of Ms. Hempsey was not the result of a personal relationship, and clearly that was Inspector Kelley's suspicion, otherwise he would not have been called in.

"So what about the husband? The boyfriend? He in the clear?"

Apparently Victoria Hempsey's boyfriend hadn't been on the scene long. He was an IT guy. No record. On the night of the murder he was with five colleagues at a popular restaurant in the city.

"The husband died some time back. So far, Kelley doesn't like the new boyfriend for it," Andy explained. "We'll see. His alibi is good. Kelley did dig up a couple of sexual assaults that might be related. It could give us more to go on, if we're lucky. Do you remember a rape in Strawberry Hills years ago? The woman who was tied up? It was quite a brutal attack."

Jimmy nodded. "The one where her shoes were stolen and we all thought it was the Stiletto Killer come back to haunt us?"

Andy flinched.

"So this might be the same guy who did the rape?" Jimmy continued, frowning and rubbing his lower lip with the side of one hand.

"Could be. The same guy struck again a year later," he said of the Graney assault.

67

Jimmy nodded to himself, paused and nursed his drink. "Sick bastard. You got DNA?"

"They found semen on the victim. They're running it for a match to the DNA from the rape cases to see if there is a link," Andy explained. "Maybe they'll get their results tomorrow, but it could take a few more days."

It wasn't like *CSI*, on which you could get DNA and solve a case in thirty minutes, minus commercials.

"Sick fuckers," Jimmy said. "I'll never understand where these arseholes come from." He tilted his head and finished most of his glass, the ice clicking against his teeth. "Another?" he offered.

To his own surprise, Andy still found himself resisting. He wanted to be sharp for Inspector Kelley in the morning. And for Dana, he realised. "No, thanks," he managed, though he knew he sounded weak. His friend raised an eyebrow, then went quiet for a while, rolling his empty tumbler from side to side on the tabletop, making wet crescents.

Something was on his mind.

"Go on," Andy prodded.

Jimmy took a breath and exhaled loudly through his nose. He seemed to consider his words carefully. "Has there been any word on . . . *her*?"

Makedde.

Andy's chest tightened at the mention of her and that thing in his chest squirmed. He shook his head. "Not a damn thing."

"I fucking hate to ask, you know, but *Jesus*. You still hearing from her dad?" Andy nodded.

"*Skata.* And he hasn't heard anything from her?"

They both knew what that meant. It meant she was likely dead. What other explanation could there be, two months on? Why stay in Europe? Why do a runner on a hotel and disappear? Unless Makedde hadn't planned it. Unless Jack Cavanagh was responsible. Before the news from Inspector Kelley, Andy had spent much of the morning making discreet enquiries about the case against Jack and Damien, a case that seemed to be going nowhere.

"Have you closed the murder of that Thai girl?" Andy asked.

"Dumpster Girl?" Jimmy said.

That was the unfortunate nickname she'd been stuck with, having been discovered in a reeking dumpster in Sydney, discarded like yesterday's trash. After a few promising leads she was still a Jane Doe, unidentified, despite having a very unusual tattoo. The police didn't know much about her, except that she was of Thai descent and had entered the country thanks to a questionable couple with links to sex trafficking, who had since been murdered. She had been sexually active and no older than fifteen. Probably somewhat younger.

"Hunt seems satisfied that her overdose was the fault of Simon Aston, that mate of Damien Cavanagh. He says he is convinced that the Cavanaghs knew nothing about her."

"You don't seem convinced."

"Are you fucking kidding me?" Jimmy slammed a fist into the table, and their glasses rattled. "If he was *anyone* except Damien Cavanagh, he'd have been brought in for questioning. He'd have been a strong fucking suspect, let me tell you. You know what his reputation is like. Everyone knows he goes for the young ones. He's a fucked-up, privileged trust-fund psychopath. That's what he is. And she was maybe twelve, maybe fourteen, and she died *in their fucking house*, that fuck-off expensive waterfront mansion of theirs. What do you think she was doing there? An illegal immigrant like that? If she was some rich Australian family's pretty white daughter, maybe somebody out there would give a shit, but no one does."

Jimmy was practically frothing. He was usually laid-back, to a fault. In over a decade of knowing him, Andy doubted he'd seen him so furious about anything before. Somewhere along the track, this case had awakened something in him.

"As it is, Simon Aston has been pegged for it," he continued. "It can't be proved, of course, but Hunt doesn't want to look further. Simon didn't exactly seem like a stand-up guy, true, but if he was still alive, I'm sure he'd have had a thing or two to say about it."

Dead men could not defend themselves.

"And it doesn't explain the video of Damien with her. A video that went missing somehow. It all stinks."

Andy had been there for the very early stages of the murder investigation, before he left for Canberra. Then Inspector Hunt had taken over. "You sound like you don't have much faith in your detective inspector," he said.

Jimmy's face darkened. "Yeah, well, you hear right."

"You think he was somehow involved in making the video disappear?"

His friend pushed himself back a touch. "I'm not saying anything. It's just . . ." He hesitated. "*Skata*. I don't know."

Andy recalled Hunt throwing up at the Stiletto Killer's flat when they'd found the trophies he had kept in his closet and under his bed. The grisly Polaroids. The body parts. Hunt had shown signs of unearned arrogance even as a constable and those tendencies had worsened. Andy had never warmed to him. In some ways he was surprised the man had been made inspector in the recent reshuffle, but apparently the powers that be liked him. All this meant Jimmy was never going to like Hunt, of course. He was sly and politic—everything Jimmy was not. And Andy's friend, though a good cop, would be a senior constable until the day he died. He was his own worst enemy. Andy had seen it time and time again.

All that was no longer Andy's problem. Andy had enough problems of his own.

"You just can't tell," Jimmy said awkwardly. He tilted his head and screwed up his face, eyes averted. "You know, Mak. She's always bloody hard to pin down. Maybe she'll just . . . show up one day."

And maybe I will *have another*, Andy decided.

He pushed his chair out, stood, opened the door and ventured into Jimmy's living room. He fixed them both a second drink.

He made it strong.

Andy Flynn finally woke with his phone alarm screaming at him in ever louder digital tones, his head foggy and sore—the familiar sensation of a hangover. He was in a stiff hotel bed at the Rydges World Square, a short drive to the scene of the Hempsey murder in Surry Hills, but a fair distance from the new police headquarters, where they were due to visit Inspector Kelley. He was distantly aware that he'd hit the snooze button several times, and now only had fifteen minutes to make his way downstairs.

At seven-forty-six he stepped out of the lift to find Dana waiting in the lobby mezzanine area, sitting in a chair beside a wall of convex glass. She was dressed in a plain, dark suit and flat shoes, her hair pulled into a tight ponytail. She was on time. Good.

"Morning," Andy muttered as he approached.

Dana looked up from the newspaper and quickly stood to greet him.

"Good morning, Agent Flynn," she said, mentioning nothing of his appearance, which he knew from brief inspection in the mirror involved prominent eye bags. His hair was still a bit damp and he doubted his quick work with the electric razor had been entirely successful. He felt seedy.

"Have you eaten?" he asked her. She nodded.

"I haven't," he said, and her face dropped.

"No? Well then. Let's get breakfast," she suggested.

"There's not much time. I'll eat in the car while you drive. Have you been to HQ?"

She frowned. "Here? No."

"I'll direct you," he said and handed her the keys to his Honda, to her evident surprise. Part of him wondered if he was still a little tipsy from Jimmy's. Inevitably, he'd stayed too late.

The drive to Parramatta involved battling traffic, something Agent Harrison proved adept at. She accelerated at every available opportunity while Andy sat strapped into his own passenger seat, consuming a passable takeaway breakfast wrap and strong coffee. He found he was glad he'd worn a dark shirt and tie that wouldn't highlight any spills.

". . . that some of the mutilation of the foot is related to the damage to the hands. I think the victim was defending herself with her hands when the blunt object was used, but these cuts to the feet . . ." Agent Harrison was saying as they flew through yet another intersection.

"You are not convinced that they are all defensive wounds?" Andy replied, his eyes pinned to the road. He'd had the same thought about the injuries.

"Some, yes. It looks likely her ankles were bound, but if so I think she broke free somehow. She kicked out at him. Maybe he even let her believe she might get away? The killer hit her again, kept her down. The toe, though, is different."

Kelley had sent a disturbing sequence of photographs from the crime scene. The body told its own story. The wounds were unique. The photographs showed a bloody nub where the victim's big right toe should have been. The other wounds could be defensive, but the toe itself? No, Andy just couldn't see how that could be the result of a struggle. More like intentional torture building up to the severed toe. Everything about it made him uneasy. It was a bit too familiar. Perhaps that was the same reason Kelley had brought him in.

"I suspect the post-mortem will confirm that all these wounds were inflicted before death. I suspect she was conscious, too, and he wanted it that way. This was all about power for him," Harrison said. She spun the wheel and accelerated again.

Yes, it was about power, Andy thought. And sadism.

Andy Flynn looked up at the tall, almost monolithic face of the NSW police headquarters building and frowned. The coffee had helped clear his head, or at least focus it, but he found himself wrestling with an ill-defined anxiety. Perhaps it was because he missed his work with homicide. Perhaps it was because he hadn't been back to Sydney since Mak had left for Paris and gone missing.

Perhaps he just needed more caffeine.

Harrison cleared her throat. Andy binned his empty coffee cup and strode up the steps into the grand glass-fronted entrance of the building, passing plain-clothed officers with chequered lanyards and swing tags and a row of colourful police recruitment posters. *Target a Great Career*, one poster declared, with a SWAT team member in full gear, pointing the muzzle of his gun. Harrison was at his side, matching him stride for stride, her footsteps echoing on the pale flagstones as they made their way through revolving doors and into the cool lobby to the reception desk. He noticed her take in the slick, spacious design, the high ceiling, the columns and six modern, oversized hanging lights with a kind of surprise. Andy often thought the place presented more like an upmarket hotel than a police head-quarters—only with a metal detector.

"Federal Agents Harrison and Flynn," Andy announced at the desk. They showed their IDs and a uniformed officer made a call to Kelley. He pushed the registration book towards them and they signed in and were given passes.

"Eighth floor. Head on up."

Andy fed his laptop case and phone through the metal detector and Harrison pulled a thin object from her handbag and presented it before pushing her things through. It was an iPad or one of those tablet things, he guessed. They gathered their gear and ascended the quiet escalator in silence. Once they were at the bank of elevators, Harrison remarked, "This was where you worked?"

Andy shook his head. "I spent most of my career with the homicide squad at the old headquarters. It was nothing like this." The College Street headquarters had been a relic. This new building was showy and open plan. Large meeting areas. Courtyards. Sleek designer furniture. In addition to the homicide squad, it also held the headquarters for the NSW firearm, sex crimes, drug, fraud, property, robbery and serious crime squads, amongst others. It presented a professional face. Something corporate.

He pressed "up" and an elevator greeted them.

Soon they were pushing through glass doors into the open-plan office of state homicide. It was quiet. Tranquil even. An empty office meant a busy squad. Many of the detectives were already out on cases and not at their desks, and those who were there tapped away at computers. The desks were modern, each L-shaped and holding a matching black computer. Grey carpets. White walls with red accents on doors and polished glass dividers. Large windows overlooked Lancer military barracks and the nearby Westfield. Strings of numbers hung down in neat rows along the ceiling, over desks, denoting the extension for each detective. It had the feeling of a library or accountancy firm, until you looked closer.

A whiteboard on one wall listed case information divided amongst six "Teams" and "Unsolved"—the unsolved homicide squad. Andy noticed that someone had drawn a rudimentary Santa Claus and a bug-eyed puppy in red erasable felt pen across the bottom of the board, at toddler height. Someone's children had visited, doubtless unaware of the grim significance of the various homicide teams' careful scrawls above.

"Andy, mate. How are you feeling this morning?" Jimmy had sauntered over, fresh from the kitchen. He held a black coffee in one hand and a glazed donut in the other, and looked as worse for wear as Andy felt. The hangover seemed not to dampen his mood, though. He eyed Agent Harrison and did a salacious eyebrow wiggle, as subtle as Benny Hill. "Who's the babe?" he whispered, not quite quietly enough, Andy feared.

Andy cast an anxious glance her way and was relieved to see that Agent Harrison was talking with some of the homicide squad members, introducing herself. Hopefully she hadn't heard. "Sorry, yeah, not supposed to talk about them that way."

"Right," Jimmy persisted and took a sip of his coffee. "I get it. But she's a bit of a hottie, come on. Look at her."

Andy managed a smile. "Her name is Dana Harrison. Agent Harrison to you. She's a PhD, Jimmy. She'll make an excellent profiler."

"So are you. . . ?" He stuck his index finger out and made a gesture for intercourse, using the donut.

"*No*," Andy answered quickly. Normally he didn't feel quite so sensitive about Jimmy's crude jokes and remarks, he realised. "No. She's part of my unit," he clarified.

Jimmy nodded. "Shame really, because—"

"*Jimmy.*"

Jimmy shut up, hopefully satisfied that he'd ridden Andy for long enough. "I'm just messin' with you. Geez, when'd you get so uptight? Fuck, things must be tense in Canberra."

"Yes," was all Andy said.

He felt eyes on him. Odd. Someone vaguely familiar was watching his arrival mutely from behind a coffee cup.

Detective Inspector Bradley Hunt.

He turned and faced him. Hunt was blond and had an oversized chin he tended to hold a little too high. Yes, that was him. "Inspector," Andy said and nodded in Hunt's direction.

"Agent."

There was a palpable tension between the two men. And Jimmy had instantly vanished when Hunt appeared, Andy noticed. Perhaps he didn't want to appear to be socialising. After a moment he reappeared at his overly cluttered desk, put his coffee cup down and took a seat. Andy thought he seemed anxious, but then he turned and made rude gestures at Hunt's back, middle finger extended.

Fuck.

Andy's former police partner had always lacked a sense of the politic. He worked hard, knew investigative work, was bright in his way, but he didn't exactly possess what one could call "leadership qualities." Andy didn't react to Jimmy's crude humour, or Hunt's odd gaze, though he was intrigued. Was there something personal between Jimmy and Hunt that he didn't know about?

"Congratulations on your promotion," Andy said and offered a closed smile.

"And you."

Andy excused himself to find Agent Harrison. She had stopped a few feet outside Inspector Kelley's door, which was next to the commander's. Kelley had a rare office in HQ, earned after nearly four decades in the force. In a way he was one of the last of the old breed still standing, and something of a legend.

Kelley's door was ajar. He was on the phone, talking in grave, familiar tones. When he hung up, Andy knocked.

"Flynn. Come on in. Bring your guy," Kelley said, not yet noticing that Andy's "guy" was not quite that.

They stepped inside and closed the door. Andy hadn't seen his former boss for well over six months. Detective Inspector Kelley was a lean, tall man with the posture and hard fitness of a soldier. He stood momentarily to acknowledge his AFP visitors, his hands laced behind his back and sleeves rolled up to show muscled forearms. His silver hair had turned that little bit whiter, but the slate-grey eyes were as sharp as ever. *He never seems to age*, Andy thought, *he only grows harder.*

Kelley's office walls were adorned with certificates. Bachelor of Policing. A certificate from the Humane Society. Diplomas from Charles Sturt University. Alphabetised black binders were set up in rows along his shelves, next to filing cabinets. Across one wall on a low shelf were several framed images. One was of a young boy whose face Andy recognised. It was an unsolved homicide case Kelley still hadn't dropped. Most officers had one—a case that haunted them until retirement, and beyond.

"Please, sit down."

"Inspector Kelley, this is Agent Dana Harrison. Harrison has an MA in Psych and PhD in Forensic Psych. She studied with David Canter in the UK. She's part of our SVCP unit," Andy said, by way of introduction.

"It's a pleasure to meet you, sir," Harrison told Kelley, crossing her legs and sitting forwards. Kelley didn't offer his hand and she didn't push the issue by offering hers.

The inspector gave her a quick appraisal and a respectful nod of acknowledgement, and quickly got down to business.

"Thank you both for coming. As you've seen, we have one of your sadists on our hands," he said.

Your sadists. Already, they were Andy's.

"We've got two serious unsolved sexual assaults that fit the pattern you suggested," Kelley continued and slid the complete files across.

"Plotsky and Graney," Andy said.

Kelley tapped the first of the two folders. "The Plotsky case is four years old. Kim Plotsky left her local pub in Strawberry Hills, alone, to walk home. She says she was pulled down into an alley, beaten and raped by a stranger. Locals heard her cries for help. She was found with her arms still bound, with a broken nose. She'd been drinking heavily and couldn't give any description except that her attacker was white. The rapist stole her shoes."

There it was again, the Stiletto Killer reference Jimmy had mentioned. Andy frowned. Agent Harrison watched him, also no doubt making the connection.

And the toe. The perp cut off the same toe, didn't he? Andy thought. *Yes. The big right toe. The same one the Stiletto Killer severed before you found Mak in that awful cabin. The one the surgeons reattached.*

"I didn't see anything in the file about Victoria Hempsey having shoes taken. Do we suspect he stole them?" Andy managed in a deceptively neutral voice.

"She was attacked in her flat. It's impossible to know what she had been wearing or what might be missing," Kelley replied. "She was found barefoot."

Andy had certainly noticed.

"The second reported case was twelve or so months later. Victim, Yvette Graney. Again, she left a bar alone to get a taxi and was dragged into an alley, this time off Crown Street in Surry Hills."

"That's near Ms. Hempsey's house," Harrison ventured.

"Yes. Graney was tied up, beaten and raped. The attacker broke her nose, pummelled her till she was black and blue. Again, no witnesses. He took her shoes, but this time he took her purse and jacket as well. She wasn't left tied up like the previous case, but she said he'd used handcuffs during the attack. The two cases were linked by DNA, so we know our perp is the same. Full details are in the database."

"There were no good suspects at the time?"

Kelley shook his head. "Nothing that stuck. You remember Deller?"

Andy did. He was an officer Andy had worked with at one time.

"He handled the Plotsky and Graney cases. He might be able to tell you more. He moved to Tasmania with his wife last year. I've got his details for you."

Andy nodded.

Kelley looked from Andy to Dana, and something hard flickered behind his eyes. "You two go to the Hempsey place. Tell me what you think. This fucking bastard . . . Sorry," he said, looking to Dana.

"He's a fucking bastard, sir," she fired back without hesitation.

Kelley nodded, relaxing. "This bastard tortured the woman. It wasn't enough to rape her and kill her. You've got all the access you want for Strike Force Pawn. Anything that helps close this one fast."

Strike Force Pawn. The names were computer generated and some of them were odd, Andy thought.

"I have arranged your access to Eagle Eye," Kelley continued. The *Eagle i* investigational management system. It was a police database where all the resources, statements, victimology, investigation log and exhibits for the strike force were electronically filed. He would be able to see everything related to the case and each update as it was uploaded.

Andy took the details and thanked him.

Kelley led them out of his office. "You know Detective Mahoney? She'll take you through the scene."

Karen Mahoney was waiting, and the sight of her gave Andy an unexpected kick in the guts.

She was a close friend of Mak's.

"Hi, Andy," she said and put out her freckled hand. She was in her late twenties or early thirties. Her corkscrew red hair was tied back into a clip, and there was something changed about her face, Andy thought. Something in the eyes. The past two months appeared to have taken a toll. They shook hands, eyes locked on to one another for a brief moment. A flicker behind the eyes was enough to communicate their shared grief about Mak.

"You guys wanna go in your own car?" Mahoney asked, releasing Andy's hand.

He nodded. "Yeah."

The late Victoria Hempsey had owned an attractive 1880s Victorian terrace on a tree-lined street in Surry Hills, just a block from a small grassy park with children's play swings. It had recently been painted slate grey to contrast with the white filigree ironwork garlanding the entrance and the shallow upper balcony. The front door was a mere two steps from the footpath and, as on each of the row of terraces to either side, the lower windows were barred like a prison's. Although the trendy bars, boutiques and eateries of Crown Street were a short walk away, the area was no stranger to police attention, housing as it did a dramatic cross-section of residents from families and well-to-do creatives to drug addicts and "troubled youths."

Today a tall, fair-haired junior police officer was installed on the quiet street at the front of Victoria Hempsey's terrace, guarding the scene of the homicide to preserve the chain of evidence.

"Agents Flynn and Harrison, this is Constable Hans Reichhold. One of our finest," Mahoney said and elbowed him gently.

The constable cracked only the slightest smile and logged their names and time of entry on his notepad. He'd been waiting for them. They would likely be the last ones through before forensics finished up, cleaning services came and the premises was released to Ms. Hempsey's bereaved family.

Mahoney ducked under crime-scene tape marking the outer perimeter and stepped up to the front door. "Forensics are basically done processing the scene. They'll be back in an hour to take everything," she said. She bent under a second tape and stepped over the threshold of the terrace, followed by Flynn and Harrison. She closed the door behind them.

Though the body was gone, they were being given uninterrupted time, at least.

Andy nodded. He paused to take in the entry. "Not a bad place," Harrison said, walking through.

Inside, the terrace had high ceilings and white walls adorned with colourful, unsigned paintings, perhaps do-it-yourself or bought from the local markets. A large, chocolate leather couch was covered in multicoloured throws. Art books were stacked on the floor. Cut flowers had begun wilting in a glass vase on a low, wooden coffee table, next to expensive photography books. Hempsey had been working for a small ad agency, Andy recalled. The rear of the terrace had been renovated to open onto a small, terracotta-tiled courtyard, decorated with pot plants and a small, modern fountain. A wicker sun lounge.

Balinese carvings. Tibetan flags. Ferns and hydrangeas. It was an inner-city oasis.

Andy walked around a circular wooden kitchen table set with shells and garden flowers in jam jars, his interest caught by a corkboard decorated with cards and photographs stuck with pins. He stood before it, looking from image to image. Here he could see the elements of the victim's life that had brought her the most joy. The grin of a young niece. An older couple posing before the Eiffel Tower. A gathering of women holding beer mugs at a resort in Bali, skin tanned and glossy. One image seemed to bring her to life most: Ms. Hempsey in a white gown embellished with tiny beads and ribbons of lace, her eyes nearly shut with the strength of a bright, toothy laugh. The arms of her late husband circled her waist, the two of them caught in a moment of joy, bathed in orbs of sunspots. *Victoria Hempsey.* A daughter. An aunt. A sister. A wife. She had been widowed at only thirty-two. Her late husband, Peter Groth, had died in an automobile accident eighteen months earlier, in the path of a drunk driver running a red light on a Thursday night in Newtown.

The pair had shared the unlucky gene.

Andy turned from the corkboard to see that Mahoney was leaning in the entryway, letting them make their observations uninterrupted. Agent Harrison was staring at the heavily blood-stained hardwood floor near the back windows. She looked a little pale.

"You been to a lot of crime scenes?" he asked Harrison quietly, walking over and stepping clear of the yellow plastic cards, like upright Scrabble tiles, marking out the exhibits of interest—smears of blood, the smudgy remnants of finger-printing powder, the place where discarded panties had been discovered.

Agent Harrison shook her head. "He tied her up here on the floor, near the window," she said. "That's not very private."

The room was familiar from the crime-scene photographs, but it always looked different live. Andy squinted, looking from the dark stains to the large window, recalling the position of the body, the state of her when she'd been found after some bastard had assaulted her and bled her out.

Andy opened the doors that led onto the walled courtyard, and stood in the doorway as the humid Sydney air hit him like a cloud. Harrison walked past him to step outside. He followed, watching her. She took a deep breath and looked around, adjusting her ponytail with an efficient, distinctly feminine movement of her delicate hands. The fountain was turned off. Weeds crept up between the terracotta tiles. The air was still. Andy looked up. The back of the terraces in the next street encroached onto the little courtyard, throwing the rear half into shade. Windows peered down on them.

"Did I remember that the curtains were open?" Harrison asked.

"The victim is gone, but everything else should be unchanged," he told her, observing that the curtains, which were a light cream colour and made of some kind of gauzy fabric, were tied back on one side and pulled partially back on the other. He hoped to hell nothing had been altered. Forensics had left their mark. He could see the smudgy residue of white Lanconide and dark carbon fingerprinting powders on various surfaces. The murder weapon, or weapons, had not been left at the scene, but several sets of latent prints not belonging to the victim had been recovered. And the crucial DNA—the semen. It would take another two or three days to be analysed.

"The curtains were open?" he shouted to Mahoney.

The detective sauntered over and leaned in the doorway.

"Yeah, they were open," she replied. "ISRAPS will take another few days, but I've got video." ISRAPS, the Interactive Scene Recording and Presentation System, allowed for a three-hundred-sixty-degree, high-definition view of the crime scene, with the ability to zoom in and out on any details. It was a new visual technology, like something out of *Blade Runner*. It could take a week to process.

"Got a copy of the video for you." Mahoney handed the DVD disc to Andy with a cheeky smile, as though it were a box of chocolates. They closed the outer door and came inside. Andy propped his laptop open on the coffee table and slid the disc into the side. Harrison hovered nearby.

"Shall I?" Detective Mahoney said and pressed "play" on Andy's laptop. She fast-forwarded to the footage of Victoria Hempsey's body at the scene, recorded to show what the officers had found. He asked her to freeze the frame.

Victoria.

What he saw was a stark contrast to the vital, smiling woman on the corkboard. What the video showed was lifeless flesh—abused, tortured and utterly dehumanised. Exposed. Staged for maximum humiliation and shock. The perpetrator had arranged her dead, naked body with the legs open, the arms pulled behind her back to thrust her bare chest upwards. Bra pulled down. Undies torn open and thrown to one side. There were ligature marks around her ankles and wrists, though the attacker had taken the ties off her ankles to pose her for whoever was to later discover her—her sister, who would need a lot of therapy to deal with what she'd seen. The blood on the floor was heavy because the killer had beaten and tortured his victim before her death. Her face was puffy and bruised, one eye nearly swollen over. Victoria had suffered numerous super-ficial cuts and the loss of an entire toe, which was not consistent with the defensive wounds on her hands and feet. At some point she had broken free of her killer, but she hadn't got away. He'd hit her repeatedly with some blunt object and got her back down.

And she did not get to her feet again.

There had been no forced entry to the terrace. It was possible Victoria knew her killer.

Andy stood quietly, watching as Mahoney fast-forwarded again, stopping at various points of interest in the crime-scene video. Harrison asked her to stop and rewind a few times, taking notes. Once they'd covered the entire scene and the body of the deceased was being bagged—paper bags and rolls of tape wrapped around her hands and head to preserve any evidence—he'd had enough, though that final disturbing visual stayed in his mind. Her vulnerable body, faceless.

Harrison had her arms tightly crossed, he noticed.

Andy left the two women to make his way back to the courtyard, pushing the door open and squinting at the sunlight. This time the humid air felt like a relief. Felt necessary. After some time Agent Harrison joined him.

"Do you think the killer wanted to be discovered? Got a thrill from the risk?" Harrison suggested, gazing back through the glass at the bloody floor inside.

Andy shook his head. "He didn't want to be caught. He wanted his work to be *seen*. He may have even pulled the curtains back before he departed, to show off."

She frowned, her brow pinching.

No, Victoria Hempsey's killer was not in the least bit ashamed of what he'd done. He didn't want to be caught. He didn't want to be stopped. And given the opportunity, he would do it again. Andy turned from the bloodstains visible through the glass and peered up at the windows behind them, pointing with one finger. "I want to speak with every one of those neighbours. Today."

CHAPTER 7

Fausto Martinez Villanueva took a seat at the Café de l'Opera at a small round table near the window. The old establishment was a showcase of neo-classical architecture and 1920s art nouveau. The glass-and-wood exterior was formed of soft curves, and the interior featured swirling motifs and the figures of elegant nineteenth-century women with long dresses and parasols etched into decorative mirrors surrounded by star-shaped studs.

A waiter approached his table, wearing a formal black bow tie, vest and pants, and crisp white shirt.

"*Café solo*," he said.

"*Sí, senyor*," the waiter replied and disappeared.

Fausto looked at his watch. It was still a little under one hour before Javier Rafel was due to arrive at his shop on nearby Carrer de l'Hospital. There was still time. He sipped his coffee slowly, watching the crowds pass on La Rambla. The shops were closed for the public holiday, but the tourists were out in full force, with their backpacks and cameras and bad T-shirts, the street vendors selling them expensive sodas and Gaudí postcards. The McDonald's was overflowing, he noticed.

Discreetly, Fausto popped two Adderall with the final sip of his coffee, and then ordered a second *café solo* from the waiter.

The hit of adrenaline pulsed through him, wiring him for the work ahead. This familiar habit gave him the necessary edge, and he needed the energy after making the drive from Seville to Barcelona in just under ten hours. Flying in would have incurred certain risks. It was better that no one could confirm he was in town. He did not wish to be traced by tickets or credit cards or anything else that would place him in Barcelona on this day. Not with his business here.

His business was a woman.

Though still young, Fausto had ended twenty-one lives. But he had not killed a woman before. The traditionalist in him resisted the idea—or perhaps it was the romantic in him?—but the sheer weight of Euros at stake more than ameliorated his guilt. Everyone died. It was a fact of living. This woman was a person like any other. An adult and therefore fair game. The only difference was that by the end of the day she would be dead and Fausto would be considerably the richer for it. Anyone with that high a price on her head was going to get hit by someone. It may as well be him.

Fausto, like many in the game, had noticed the half-million-Euro offering for her neat execution. But where to find her? Weeks had passed, and he had almost forgotten about her when Javier Rafel contacted him. The well-known counterfeiter wanted a twenty per cent finder's fee for his troubles, which was steep considering he wasn't risking anything. But that still left four hundred K for an afternoon's work. Well worth the long drive.

The woman, Makedde Vanderwall, was due to return to Javier Rafel's shop for her passport at five. The fat counterfeiter had asked that she not be harassed until she left his shop. No doubt he wanted the payment for his work before she was taken. When she exited the shop, there would be plenty to distract her from Fausto's presence in the crowd. The timing of her visit to Javier's shop had been carefully chosen.

When she emerged, Fausto would be ready.

"Bogey," Makedde Vanderwall whispered.

Bogey.

Mak rolled over and breathed in Bogey's dark, musky hair. She kissed his ambrosial mouth—the sculpted cupid's bow of the upper lip and sensual fullness of his pillow-like lower lip. His candied tongue. His warm skin, illustrated with ink in lines and shapes to trace with an appreciative finger.

Yes.

Her lover was returned to her, in her arms and in her mouth and inside her. And even from within layers of her sleep the familiarity of his touch brought a tear to Makedde's tightly shut eyes.

Bogey Mortimer.

She tilted her face to the white ceiling, arched her back. Her fingers caressed the clean bed sheets, fingertip to cotton. Shafts of sunlight lit her body as she pulled the sheets from her thighs, feeling his touch, or at least a touch she felt was his.

And then like every dream of him for the past two months, her tears of joy at Bogey's return transformed swiftly to tears of horror. This was a brutal evolution of the subconscious, an inevitable nightmare that was somewhat more vivid and detailed than the brief erotic dream that had preceded it. A recent memory replayed perennially in the hours when her conscious mind let go: Bogey's lips were cold and Makedde kissed them with finality, despair, revulsion. His body was no longer responsive, sensual and warm. It was heavy and exanimate, a bundle of flesh and bone, reeking of death and the pungent stench of rotting flowers. She was no longer in her lover's bed: she was alone with him in the French countryside, struggling to pull his heavy corpse up by the arms to the edge of the shallow grave she'd dug for him. Shaking, fingers raw, she gave one last effort and got him over the edge.

She dropped him and he hit the dirt below her with a dull thud, and did not flinch.

Bogey.

Mak did not know how long she stood there, weeping, her fingers bleeding. She'd wrapped herself in her lover's leather jacket to battle the chill night air, but it was little comfort. The jacket was speckled with his blood. Mak had thought she'd finally gone mad, holding herself against the dawn light and watching his inert body in that dirty hole. His legs twisted. His chest unmoving. How long had she stood there, transfixed with horror? He was a young man, dead before thirty. And why? Because he'd loved Mak, if only for a short time. She'd loved him. In a way it was her fault. She'd encouraged him to visit her in Europe. But how could she have known what would unfold? Bogey deserved better than to be killed by a brutal stranger and buried in a makeshift grave, his loved ones cursed never to know what had become of him. He deserved better, but there it was. The world cared nothing for justice.

In her nightmares, it was all the same. Mak buried him again and again. There was his body, cold and vulnerable in death.

There was the grave, the smell of fresh dirt. It was Bogey in there, and yet it was not. And now with the first shovelful of dirt that fell she felt herself pull away, back to the cellar where she'd spent so many cold days and nights alone, wondering about her own death, reduced to drinking water from a cat's bowl and trying, like a dog, to break the chain that bound her.

The cellar where she had given too much of herself in order to survive.

The cellar that had changed her forever.

Always, her dreams brought her back to that unspeakable place. The grating metal cuff was around her ankle once more, the damned cuff of a convict or circus animal. In her fevered sleep she reached down and tried to soothe the torn flesh of her ankle beneath the unyielding metal of the cuff, some small part of her still naïvely hoping for a saviour—hoping that Bogey would find her.

Not knowing he was already dead.

Makedde Vanderwall woke from her siesta feeling disoriented and unrested. She remembered snatches of her nightmare, and she tried to block them out. The memories were not welcome. The sun was high. An hour had passed, perhaps two.

Through the metal slats over the window, streams of sunlight had come to rest on the bed where the sheets were twisted around her. Her bare legs were exposed, warm and sunlit. After only a short time in Spain Mak had recalled the importance of the traditional afternoon rest. Many businesses closed in the afternoons for the siesta. The locals took their evening meals very late. The many children's parks in every suburb were still full at nine, and it was not uncommon to see locals walking prams well after sundown, hours after North American and Australian children would have been put to bed. Darkness was good for her anonymity and she embraced the early hours here, and the late ones. It was better to get into the rhythm of the locals, when she could. And sometimes, if she was lucky, she was spared her more vicious nightmares during the daily rest.

But not today.

Mak looked at the clock and noted that her alarm was set to go off in only one minute. She switched it off, sat up and stretched. This was an important afternoon and she'd wanted to be calm and rested. If she was not entirely rested, at least she could do her best to be calm. Mak made her way to the kitchen to flick on the cappuccino machine, which gurgled and hissed as it began to warm up. In the bathroom she brushed her teeth and rubbed damp fingertips over her eyelids, where mascara had streaked during her nap. Her eyes were red, as if she might have been crying.

She needed that coffee.

The counterfeiter, Javier Rafel, had asked her to come to his shop at five. As she prepared her afternoon coffee, determined to go about each step with equanimity—grinding the beans, packing the grip firmly, steaming the milk—she realised once again that her impending return to his shop filled her with anxiety. She had not felt comfortable in the man's presence, but she supposed that was hardly surprising. He did, after all, create false documents for a living. He was criminal by trade and Mak was the daughter of a cop. Given her upbringing, she could be forgiven for finding the exchange uncomfortable. There was something else as well, she suspected, some other level of dread pushing at the edges of her subconscious, but it did not bear examination. She simply had to go to him and get her passport. She didn't have to like the man.

Thirty minutes later, dressed in a sleeveless hoodie and jeans, with large sunglasses covering her eyes, Mak strode down the broad, sunlit promenade of La Rambla, bobbing and weaving between visiting tourists. The air was filled with the sounds of honking cars and chatter in Catalan, Spanish, Italian, French and occasional snatches of British English. The shops along La Rambla on either side were closed, their grubby, graffitied metal shutters locked down, providing a somewhat less aesthetic than usual view of the famous thoroughfare. But the city seemed much busier than usual. The long weekend had brought hordes of visitors from all over Europe. Had this been

America, she suspected the obligations of a key religious public holiday could not hope to outweigh the capitalist possibilities of so many keen visitors. The shops would have been open from dawn to dusk for the influx of holiday cash.

Though the shops and markets were closed, the restaurants were overflowing, and the tatty stalls along the promenade were operating, still selling their cheap bags with BARCELONA! written on every square inch, their plastic flamenco dancers, their fridge magnets and their rolls of postcards and greeting cards plastered with images of Gaudí's most photogenic work: Park Güell, Casa Mila, Casa Batiló, Palau Güell, Colònia Güell. Her eyes fell on a striking image of his famous church, the Sagrada Família, with its towering spires and exterior that seemed to melt, or rise from the ground like alien stalagmites, a building as iconic and controversial as any in the world, started in 1882 and still unfinished more than eight decades after its creator's death.

She blinked.

When she'd been ill, Bogey had given her a card with an image of the Sagrada Família on the front. They'd talked about Gaudí in their short time together. Bogey was very interested in design. He had never been to Barcelona or seen the celebrated Sagrada Família but wanted very much to go. They'd wanted to see it together. After Paris.

It was the same card, she realised. That man was selling the same card Bogey had given her.

Makedde looked away and continued walking, head down, grateful for the sunglasses that shielded her eyes from the crowd. The lenses slowly filled with tears as she walked. She'd dared to sit in the park in front of the Sagrada Família one evening as the sun set, two weeks after first arriving in Barcelona and breaking into Luther's apartment. She'd sat on the bench until the sky was black. Alone. Numb. Unable to process all that had happened.

Bogey is dead. That life is over now.

Mak walked on, and as she approached the intersection of Carrer de l'Hospital she noticed chequered blue-and-white police cars and uniformed officers blocking the way. The street that ran along La Rambla on this side was free of vehicles. That was unusual. The traffic normally ran both ways, a single lane travelling south to the port on the west side of La Rambla and one running north on the east. This side was blocked off. Now she came around the corner of the street and paused. She lifted the sunglasses from her cheeks, wiped under her eyes and put the glasses back on again.

What is this?

Crowds of people filled the sidewalks on both sides of the single-lane street, packed shoulder to shoulder, several deep. Excited faces. Bodies shifting from foot to foot. There was a palpable anticipation in the air. Many people had cameras slung around their necks. They held their backpacks and purses protectively at their stomachs to avoid the prying fingers of pickpockets, or perhaps simply because of the crush. Small children sat on shoulders. The balconies of the apartments and hostels on either side were four or five storeys high and filled with spectators.

Good Friday. There would be some kind of Semana Santa— Holy Week—parade, she guessed.

It took some effort to weave her way through the thick crowd, past the closed shops. She passed the old church she'd seen before, but saw no indication of what was drawing people to the area. They were not filing in to pray, but were instead standing outside, watching for something, or someone.

When Mak arrived at Javier's shop she found the metal shutter half shut. She ducked under it and straightened in the shadows on the other side, then stepped over his well-worn step, feeling tense. Inside, Javier was waiting for her. He spotted her and put down the silver spoon he was polishing.

"You have the money?" he said gruffly.

Mak stood in the centre of the small, cluttered pawnshop. With the shutter partially closed it was dark. It felt even more claustrophobic than before.

She nodded to him. "*Si.* I have your money."

Javier left the counter heaped with someone's discarded silverware to pull the shutter down outside his door yet further. Watching him shut her in caused her stomach to twist, and she wondered fleetingly if they were alone in the shop.

"You come," he said and jerked his dark head in the direction of the back room. He led her to the small space that had alarmed her before, carrying the little polishing cloth in his thick, unwashed fingers. She followed him. In that tiny, cluttered room nothing had changed. No one else was there. Before saying another word, he shut the door.

Mak licked her lips. There was something in his eyes she did not trust. *Something.* But then, it had been there from the beginning, hadn't it? Did he seem more nervous than before? He would not look her in the eye.

Just pay him and get out of here.

"Do you have it?" she asked him impatiently. Javier nodded and paused.

A rope of tension slowly twisted inside her. "May I see it?" she said.

He took his time washing his hands in a toilet basin, not using enough soap or effort to clean the stained nail beds, then he searched lazily through packages on top of a filing cabinet.

Finally—mercifully—he handed her a manila envelope. She could feel the passport inside and, when she pulled it from its paper, she saw with some relief that it was just what she had ordered. He'd used the photograph she'd provided and the finished product looked authentic at a glance. She gestured to a small magnifier, the kind that was sometimes called a "loop" in the modelling industry, which sat on the edge of a nearby box. Javier passed it to her so that she could examine the European passport in minute detail. Her face, framed by a curtain of black hair, sat next to the name of a stranger. His work was extremely good. She couldn't fault it.

Outside she heard a sudden, muffled roar of applause. She jerked her head around and listened. Something was happening on the street.

With her passport now in hand, an even stronger sense of claustrophobia came over her. She twitched. Javier nodded and she handed him his money in two thick envelopes. He counted it with irritating leisure while her eyes flitted about the room. I need to get the fuck out of here. Finally, she turned and went for the door herself, eager to get back onto the busy, narrow street, into the relative safety of the crowd of strangers. She wanted desperately to get away from the swarthy man and his untrustworthy eyes. To her relief, Javier held his ground in the small, awful room, leaving her to let herself out.

"*Gracias,*" she muttered and left him.

I have it.

Mak stepped out of the shop and pulled the metal shutter back up with a jerk. The street was even busier than before and she found herself pressed against the front of the shop.

There came a drumbeat, perhaps from a marching band she could not see. In response the crowd went up in thunderous applause again. She felt the urge to run, or to climb up, but there was nowhere to go. With effort she pressed through, gaining only a few feet, but then she stopped as two mounted guards pushed their way onto the street in front and the crowd leaped back. There was one white stallion and one black, and the guards wore beautiful uniforms, plumes of feathers atop their helmets. The crowd continued to back away, wary of the hooves. Behind the horses were two cleaners in green uniforms, holding brooms and pails, and more uniformed police. The police were clearing a path for someone, pushing the crowd back with open hands. Bodies pressed against her.

She looked left, looked right.

The shutter began to close behind her.

The Australian woman—or was she American?—emerged from Javier's shop, stooping to get under the metal shutter.

She straightened and frowned, finding herself at the edge of the crowd. Hundreds more had arrived while she was inside. The shutter began to close behind her.

Yes. It is her.

Makedde Vanderwall looked like her photograph—tall and pale, with a slim build and long hair. He'd seen photographs of her looking like Claudia Schiffer, with blonde locks many women from his hometown would envy, but now she had black hair that did not suit her. She was still attractive, though. Today she was wearing jeans and a hooded top with oversized black sunglasses, evidently trying to blend in as much as she could, which wasn't a lot. She was somewhat taller than Fausto and, with her height and bone structure, she stuck out in the busy crowd. She pulled her hood up, but it only made her more visible.

He could see Javier's legs as the counterfeiter pulled the roller door down. Javier's work was done. He had his money from her—he'd doubtless charged her a lot before sending her out to her death—and he'd brought her to precisely the right place at the right time. Now the rest was up to Fausto.

There were many *policía* managing the crowd of spectators for the Semana Santa Good Friday procession, but that did not worry him. They were focused entirely on the procession, as was everyone else, including the woman. Their job was to keep the Cofradías, the brotherhoods, safe. The crowds in his hometown of Seville were yet bigger. That was where his mother would be, praying with the rest of the family. But Fausto was here for something else entirely. This crowd would permit him to get far closer to the woman than he could otherwise manage without arousing her suspicion.

Fausto moved in, foot by foot, keeping his face tilted in the same direction as everyone else, towards the direction of the church. He would not take her too close to Javier's shop, if he could avoid it. The counterfeiter would be unhappy with blood on his doorstep. The woman was looking around earnestly, clearly wanting to escape. If she found an opening, she might move quickly. She was only two metres away now, but the crowd was a thick wall between them. He wanted to get closer.

The stiletto was tucked up his sleeve, the blade waiting.

A drumbeat and a plume of incense.

The crushing crowd was unyielding, all the watchers facing the church, straining forwards to see some important person or event. They anticipated some sort of procession, from what Makedde could tell. The mounted guards had cleared a path in the street and now waited for the others. She shook her head. Surely Javier would have known this was not an ideal time to come and go from his shop? The streets were packed. It could take her some time to escape the area.

A band began to play. There was movement ahead.

Finally, Mak could make out the centre of the crowd's focus.

She gaped.

Tall black cones became visible above the heads outside the church. They moved and swayed between the assembled bodies. She blinked and looked again. The cones were hoods, and they had eyes. She could now see a steady stream of figures, swathed entirely in black, wearing long robes and tall pointed hoods completely covering their faces, with only round holes cut out for the eyes. They were sombre, silent, their formal walk accompanied by the processional music. From what she could see, each black figure held aloft an ornate staff of gold and silver, or tapestries decorated with images of Jesus. One figure held a large gilded crucifix, his hands cased in black gloves. The faceless spectres moved slowly into the street, single file. The crowd cheered. On every balcony of the hostel and from every terrace, people pressed against the railings, clapping or taking photographs.

Mak gawked, unused to the spectacle.

Each pointed hood was four feet high, perhaps taller, in some cases seemingly as tall as the person wearing it. These dark figures brought to mind the notorious Ku Klux Klan, or a team of medieval executioners. But no. They were the Nazarenos. The hooded penitents. In some part of her memory she recalled having read about them. She knew these processions were a centuries-old ritual in places like Seville and Granada, but they walked in Barcelona, too, it seemed. This was the Catholic brotherhood taking part in the traditional procession of Semana Santa. She could see that they were still filing out of the large medieval church she'd noticed earlier. Drummers beat their snares, marching between the penitents. It was odd. Spectacular. Mak pushed forwards to get a closer look. Yes. There were more of these hooded men with their hidden faces, these ones dressed in white. Another pulse of excitement went through the crowd and a second cloud of incense filled the air as a giant, gilded float emerged out of the arched entrance. A life-sized statue of a stooping Jesus appeared, his inert body appearing to be weighed down by an enormous cross strapped to his back. All around him the ornate golden float was decorated with angels and hundreds of fresh blood-red roses. It looked very heavy as it moved unsteadily into the crowd, shifting back and forth with the sway of the human bodies holding it up almost invisibly from underneath.

"*. . . No puc veure!*"

Mak was tapped on the arm and turned to find a small, middle-aged Catholic woman articulating angrily with her hands. She was clearly complaining about Mak's height.

"*No puc veure!*" she repeated, hands waving around above her. *I can't see!*

Mak put her palms in the air and shrugged. There was nowhere for her to go. She was as hemmed in as everyone else and it hardly seemed fair to pick on her, as she wasn't as tall as the children on parents' shoulders dotting the crowd. She bent down a bit at the knees and was promptly pushed sideways by another group jostling for a better position.

She felt a sharp stabbing pain in her side. A camera lens. It jolted her out of her awe.

Time to get out of here.

Clutching her valuable new passport tightly, Mak began to push through the sea of people. Thankfully, nearly everyone was shorter than she was, apart from the odd English or German tourist, so she could see the scene clearly. It was impossible to cross the street ahead now, she noticed. The Nazarenos were filing down the centre, walking slowly, carrying their staffs. She would not dare run between them. Crowd barriers and uniformed police blocked some areas, arms extended, barking orders. Getting back to La Rambla could prove difficult. She could not go back the way she had arrived. She had to fight through the other way, against the crowd, past Javier's shop and into the back streets where the crowds would be thinner. She didn't know the streets on this side of La Rambla, but she could circle back somehow, she was sure. Determined, she pushed against the throng, inch by inch, the crowd pouring into every gap of available space like water. Some yelled at her again for blocking their view and finally, Mak relented, stooping down to half her height and holding her hands in front of her like a surfer diving under a wave.

Minutes later Mak broke out of the excited crowd, stood up to her full height again and looked back at the mad spectacle. The gilded float was moving up the street to further cheers and adoration, followed by still more hooded penitents, this time in red garb to indicate another brotherhood, the points of their hoods sitting up far above the crowd. It was quite a sight. All eyes were on them, showing Mak nothing but the back of thousands of people's heads—except for a couple of faces that looked at her from the crowd. Two men. Watching her. The older one turned around again, but the closest was moving her way, still several metres back in the thick swamp of people. He looked frustrated. He, too, was trying to get out, she supposed.

Mak turned and she half strode, half sprinted up the street to an alley alongside a series of medieval-looking buildings, where she was quite surprised to catch a glimpse of a small courtyard full of dog kennels and cats, beyond wire fencing. Soon she was on the parallel street, Carrer del Carme, moving at a quick pace past an incredible set of double doors emblazoned with the pop-art painted face of a Chinese woman with scarlet hair, beneath the name *Rita Rouge*, and the exotic, filigreed El Indio building on the opposite side. La Rambla itself was still crowded by the time she reached it, but here, finally, she could breathe. She'd never seen the city so busy. She crossed the street, dodging between cabs, and cut down a narrow, curved street on the other side, barely wide enough for a car, making her way towards home.

I have my passport. I have it.

It was such a relief to make it out of there. And the crowd!

It had been chaos.

She stopped.

Another procession was filing down Santa Ana. She spotted the huge float of a crowned Virgin Mary moving past, flanked in front and behind by more Nazarenos, this time wearing white robes and tall green velvet pointed hoods. The virgin herself moved stiffly through the crowd atop her rectangular, golden float, surrounded by hundreds of white, dripping candles, the float shaking slowly from side to side, shifting like a boat on the tide. From her angle Mak could see dozens of pairs of feet underneath, walking it along.

She'd have to go the other way.

Makedde doubled back, arriving at a plaza she recognised, and finally she got onto Carrer de Bertrellans—her street— entering from the other side. She was relieved to be near the car, which was parked in a rental space across the alley. It might take some time to get out of the centre of the city, but then she would be on the open road. Free. She pulled the graffitied metal shutters open with a screech, a plume of filth rising into the air. *Se Alquila Plaza De Parking*, the sign above her said. The Peugeot was there in the darkness of the tiny parking rental spot, amongst a dozen other small-to mid-sized European cars. This was Luther's local wheels. Luther's spot. She'd already packed it with his things—things she needed for the evening's work. *Yes, Luther has been unwittingly generous*, she thought darkly.

In minutes Mak was driving down the narrow lane, headed for the square, moving at an agonisingly slow pace as she waited for pedestrians to pass. *Strange.* A man was at the end of her street, watching her, she thought. From his flushed cheeks he looked like he'd been running, though he had his hands in his pockets. Her inner alarm bells went off. But then she blinked and he was gone. Was that the man from the crowd outside the church? No. It couldn't be.

Feeling overly paranoid, she accelerated again before slowing for another group. Someone brushed against the car and she frowned. Only another block and she would be on the main street.

Yes. The open road would be a relief.

CHAPTER 8

Makedde Vanderwall felt a glimmer of optimism, the first she'd had in months.

She drove out of the city under a sky ablaze with a spectacular red sunset, her long dyed hair whipping bare, muscled shoulders. Luther's car was a convertible and Mak was enjoying driving with the hardtop down once she was out of town and away from prying eyes. This was the most human she'd felt since Paris: alone on the road with no one to fear.

The roads had opened up, the people of Barcelona having completed their travels for now. The religious amongst them were praying at their preferred place of worship while the heathens enjoyed the spoils of the public holiday with plenty of rabbit-shaped chocolates and home-made food. The freeway was dotted with the occasional car as she passed huge tracts of flat industrial land at Barcelona's outskirts. Warehouses. Car factories. Rows of depressing low-income housing stood like filthy concrete dominoes, damp laundry hanging precariously from every window. The large Barcelona airport looked uncharacteristically quiet as she passed. A single plane circled above.

Barely forty minutes after she'd crawled into the car, an increasingly barren Spanish countryside flew past her on one side, the

Iberian Sea on the other. Finally here she allowed herself a smile, buoyed by her success in gaining an identity. It was as if she'd passed some important test. For so small a document her false passport seemed to offer grand possibilities. A new life even. Would she live in Spain as Ms. Cruz? Perhaps she would open a bank account in this new name. Get a credit card? Blend into the crowd instead of hiding away during the daylight hours?

For a while, perhaps?

Just until Jack and Damien Cavanagh were properly investigated and it was safe for the woman called Makedde Vanderwall to return to the world she'd known before. Canada. Australia even. Eventually she would go back, but for that to happen, a trial would need to bring the Cavanaghs down, and this far away from Australia, it was hard to know if the case against them was progressing at all. After an initial flurry of articles about tentative links between the Cavanagh empire and a Queensland organised-crime ring, the news sites had gone quiet. Even the respected Sydney investigative journalist Richard Staples, who had been the most high-profile voice calling into question the Cavanaghs' reputation, had moved on to other stories—the live-export trade debacle, with more horrific images coming to light of Australian livestock being tortured in overseas abattoirs. Then there was the ongoing fracking debate between oil companies, environmentalists and farmers. Yes, there were plenty of pressing issues to distract from Jack Cavanagh and his troubled son. The major transport deal the Cavanaghs were looking to secure had been put on hold, by all accounts, but the larger questions of corruption and criminal enterprise had simply fallen away, and the public seemed not to care. How was that possible? In a very real way, she felt her survival depended on the outcome of the investigation into the Cavanaghs. In the meantime, her life was one of uncertainty. And loneliness.

Dad.

Again she considered her decision not to contact her father. Could she perhaps send him some sign? Some indication that she was alive? A secret code—but what? She missed him in ways she had never before experienced, as if a key part of her had been amputated. But while the price was still on her head she would have to be very careful whom she spoke to. And her own father, with all of his law enforcement contacts and his tendency to expect that he could control situations, was capable of a fatal error in judgement—particularly because of his strong emotional connection to her. Emotions clouded judgement. Mak had no doubt that her father would want to personally see to it that Jack Cavanagh went down. He would get himself dangerously tangled in the mess that her life had become.

No.

She could see only three cars on the road as she neared her turn-off. Makedde pushed her foot down on the accelerator and her vision blurred, the distant cars behind her reflecting in her rear-view mirror and fragmenting out into whirling spots, her fleeting sensation of happiness already strangled. Beneath her dark glasses, a warm tear gathered at her lashes and blew back with the wind. She blinked the moisture away and focused on the road. A new identity did not change who she was. It just made her a bit more mobile. It did not mean she could see her family. Not yet. That could endanger them. But what she could do was prepare for the challenges and dangers to come, just as she had been doing for weeks, just as she would do now. Mak pulled off the main highway, making her way past an open-cut mine and down a little-used gravel track towards an area of bushes, the wheels of the car kicking up dirt. She pressed a button on the key fob and the hardtop raised itself and began closing over her. This area, about an hour outside Barcelona proper, was unmarred by man-made structures save for a single old, dilapidated house, once a cottage or small farmhouse perhaps, but now little more than a sun-bleached fireplace and one remaining stone wall, the rest torn apart by time. Mak parked on the gravel across from the old cottage, next to an area of dense thicket, pulled the hand-brake, popped the boot and climbed out of the car. It was a hard-worn, well-loved Peugeot Cabriolet. She'd found it to be reliable enough for the driving she had to do and importantly, the boot was adequate for Luther's kit, which was undoubtedly why he'd purchased it in the first place. So far, she'd only driven to and from this isolated location, but perhaps under the cover of Ms. Cruz, she could now travel around Europe? And why not? She'd lived here when she was modelling, but with Luther's cash she would not have to worry about paying the bills for a while. If she was careful and stayed out of the major cities, she could travel safely under her new identity.

She secured her hair in a ponytail, pushed her sunglasses up on her head and bent over the open rear boot.

Makedde spent some time considering the options before her.

It was not her favourite weapon, but after mounting a fore-grip she was becoming reasonably adept with Luther's polymer-constructed Heckler & Koch Universale Maschinenpistole UMP 9 submachine gun, which he'd seen fit to accessorise with a laser sight. She'd taken to practising with the weapon in the two-round burst trigger configuration, though she was still far more accurate with his nine-millimetre Glock, which was on her person at all times. Perhaps it was unsurprising she was so much better with the Glock, considering the submachine gun's violent kick—the butt often left a faint reddish bruise on the inside of her right shoulder after too many shots.

Mak cocked her head, looked at the other options in Luther's kit.

When she had discovered the price on her head, she had deemed it necessary to step up her training and found this location, perfect because of its isolation and a grouping of trees and thick bushes that provided some cover. There was no one nearby to hear her, and it was unlikely she would find herself with unwanted company. For the previous few weeks she'd spent most early evenings here. She used six empty red cans of Estrella Damm for makeshift targets and practised shooting them off the skeletal remains of the cottage using the Glock at close and middle-range distances, and the submachine gun, set for double-shot action, at greater distances. She had to stay fresh, fit and prepared if she was to survive any potential encounter with the mercenaries Cavanagh's hit money attracted, she reasoned. And sunset was a good time for target practice, the lengthening shadows challenging her keen, 20/20 vision.

The Glock and UMP will do tonight, she decided.

She would set up her makeshift targets and work on her aim until it became too dark to see, then make the drive home and head up to the apartment to prepare her dinner with the fresh ingredients she'd bought.

And then, she'd have some important decisions to make. Like what to do with Ms. Cruz.

Finally he had the woman, Makedde Vanderwall. He'd been separated from her in the crowd, and he'd had to give chase. Somehow she'd escaped him, but he'd found her again, and now successfully tracked her using the magnetic device he'd attached to her vehicle as she'd passed him in Carrer de Bertrellans.

She was having car trouble.

Fausto Martinez Villanueva watched his target as she was bent over the boot of her car, searching for tools. In the slowly failing light he observed the attractive shape of her figure, the taper of her long legs encased in tight jeans, the thick, dark hair tied in a ponytail. She could have been a fashion model, he reckoned. In another scenario, perhaps at the café on La Rambla, he would hope to catch her eye, but not here. Here he waited in a protective thicket of bushes while she searched in her car. He wondered whether she would even know how to change her tyre? Doubtful. He'd caught up with her signal, and followed her down the highway at a safe distance, eventually tracing the plumes of dirt she left in her wake on this small road. When she stopped her vehicle to change the tyre or check the oil, no doubt realising she was lost, he'd continued on foot.

She was only metres away now, unaware she was watched.

These kinds of women, always thinking themselves so independent, he thought and shook his head. After a shaky start, his job could not have been made easier for him.

Bent over the boot, Mak finished loading the magazine of fresh nine-millimetre rounds into the Glock, checked that the safety was on, and slid the handgun and a spare magazine into the waistband of her jeans. She slung the tactical strap of the UMP over her shoulder, shut the boot and straightened.

Cologne?

Somehow, the distinctly man-made odour of cheap cologne was on the breeze, drifting right under her nose. It wafted past her, wrong and out of place here in every way. A second later it was gone, but already gooseflesh had come up on the back of her neck.

Someone.

A rustle of branches.

Someone is here.

The world shifted, her senses sharpened instantly, and all

thoughts left her except the most crucial and basic survival instincts. Mak threw herself to the ground next to the car. A bullet whizzed by her so close she could actually hear its progress through the air next to her head, and that's when she knew without a doubt that it was real. It was *happening*. It had all started again as she'd feared, as she'd known it would. She was being hunted.

Mak landed next to the left rear wheel on her knees and forearms, and scrambled forwards as a second shot thudded into the tyre, causing it to leak with a faint hiss. She crawled along the side of the car on her hands and knees, not even registering the sharp edges of the gravel, and pulled the driver's door open with one hand just as a third shot pierced the small right rear window of the Peugeot, sending small cubes of broken safety glass into the car. Crouched on the ground with her back to the body of the car, she pulled the handgun out of her waistband and waited. The disturbed bushes had sounded close. Really damn close.

Silence.

Her heart hammered as she waited for another noise. In the far distance she heard traffic on the freeway. Birds squawked overhead, disturbed by the gunshots. She thought fleetingly of getting under the car for protection, but that would only trap her. She'd been seen and there was no cover here that would aid her. She needed to check her environment, use all her senses. She could bolt for the bushes, but she felt sure she would be hunted down until one of them was dead. The keys were in the ignition. She could try to drive away, but there was no guarantee she would get far. A decent shooter would take out the other tyres.

Slow down. Calm now. Calm.

Where had the sound come from? Behind the car. Southwest,

where the breeze was coming from. That's why the rear right window had been hit. It meant the car was between them for now.

Mak willed her heart back to a normal pace. *One beat. Two beats. Three.* She'd been in dangerous situations before—too many to think about—and the key was always a clear head. She had to be unemotional. Whoever was trying to kill her was after the money offered for her head. She'd known this would happen. He, or she, would be utterly unemotional about killing her. She had to be utterly unemotional about killing them. She wasn't going to be a sitting duck for anyone. Not today. Not ever. Whoever was after her could not be given a second chance. Perhaps twenty seconds had passed since the first shot. Not wanting to give her attacker more time to reposition himself— yes, *him*: that cologne—she took the chance of pulling herself inside the car. This action was met with the thunderous crash of the entire rear window being shattered with two closely timed shots. She covered her face as glass showered down.

Mak stayed low across the seats, Glock in front of her.

Southwest.

She shifted over crunching cubes of safety glass and pressed the button on the key fob in the ignition to automatically retract the Peugeot's hardtop. Obediently, it swung up behind her like a shield. A sixth shot from her attacker fired uselessly into solid metal as the car hummed and worked, the parts separating and folding up. She had twenty seconds. Stretched across the seats, Mak pulled the submachine gun off her shoulder, switched it to fully automatic trigger mode and flicked off the safety. There had been six single shots now, reasonably well aimed. Her attacker might be good, but she was almost certainly more heavily armed.

"I give up! *Me entrego!*" she yelled over the whirring sound as the hardtop pulled away. "*No me tire!*" *Don't shoot.*

In response there was the faintest sound of movement in the thicket and, just as the hardtop disappeared into the body of the car, Mak rose up on the front seats and mercilessly sprayed the bushes behind the car with lead, her hips braced against the windshield as the recoil bucked. The thirty-round magazine emptied in a wide arc from one side of the car to the other at the rate of six hundred and fifty rounds per minute, the sound deafening in the quiet evening air, branches torn to shreds and hot bullet casings falling to the leather seats at Makedde's feet. When the weapon was spent, Mak threw herself back down into the car and discarded the UMP in exchange for the loaded Glock.

She took a breath, then sat up between the leather seats, looking down the back of the car through the weapon's sights.

No shots.

After a minute she sat a little higher. Several metres back from the car and to the right, the bushes had been disturbed. She saw movement. "Reveal yourself!" she yelled. "Or I'll fire again!"

A groan.

Mak stepped cautiously from the car, keeping the Glock out in front of her with both hands.

"Step out from the bushes! Surrender! *Entrega!*" she demanded.

Mak reached the bushes and found him—a lone man, now sprawled awkwardly in the sharp branches and shot up beyond repair. He wore a dark T-shirt and torn leather jacket with slacks. No bulletproof vest. The would-be mercenary could have been in his twenties or his fifties; it was hard to tell in his broken condition. His brown eyes rolled back into his head and then forwards again, focusing on her with a childlike fear. He opened his mouth to speak, revealing busted teeth. Blood oozed from a bullet wound in his cheek. He gurgled and spat, the grim sounds unintelligible in any language. He was armed with a switchblade and a single handgun, or had been before his wrist was shattered by gunfire. He'd come to this party with the wrong accessories, it seemed.

Makedde pushed the branches back with her boots and leaned in close. She considered it a mercy when she placed the tip of Luther's gun in the centre of the man's forehead and pulled the trigger.

CHAPTER 9

Though it was after six, the Sydney humidity had not eased off. It was hotter than usual for the time of year. The afternoon sun had heated up the streets of Surry Hills like a greenhouse, caught within a white veil of cloud, and it held even now, as the shadows grew longer.

Agent Andy Flynn stood in the courtyard area of one of Victoria's next-door neighbours, feeling weary, a line of sweat snaking down from his temple.

"So you didn't hear anything unusual on Wednesday evening?" Detective Karen Mahoney pressed.

Mahoney was grilling the professional couple who rented the place. The terrace was fashionable inside, even if the exterior was run-down, which was typical for much of the area. They'd been living there for six years and seemed genuinely disturbed by the fate of their neighbour, who they hadn't known particularly well. Their upper rear windows looked sideways onto Victoria's courtyard, but the scene of her murder was not visible from their home. And here, in the courtyard, the walls were too high to see over into Victoria's space.

Andy wanted to move on.

"No. I mean, I often have the music going when I get home from work," the man named Blake was saying.

"Or the TV. We might have been watching TV," his partner, Stephen, piped up. The two men held hands, distressed.

"Do you recall what you were doing between five and nine?" That was when the sister had found her.

The older of the two, Stephen, screwed up his face. "Wednesday right? I think I was working a bit late. I got home around seven, maybe a little later? Then we ate some takeaway and watched *Drive*."

"With Ryan Gosling?" Mahoney said. They nodded enthusiastically.

"It was a DVD," Stephen said. "We had no idea what was happening next door. No idea."

It was far too early to know what information might prove crucial to the investigation, but Flynn felt eager to get moving. The day was wasting, and now that it was getting late, surely some of the residents they'd missed earlier would be returning home. There was one house in particular he was keen to get to. "Be sure to tell us if you remember anything else," Mahoney said and handed over her card.

They were led to the front door and when they stepped out into the street, they found someone waiting.

"Detective Flynn."

Pat Goodacre. You are kidding me.

"Who is. . . ?" Harrison muttered.

"Media. Don't say anything," Andy warned.

Pat Goodacre had been on his case since the Stiletto Murders. She'd got quite a few column inches out of that horror. It was years later, but she looked the same—wielding her tape recorder and flashing her pearly whites. She was too bloody good at her job. He wondered who'd tipped her off.

"Detective Flynn—"

"There is no Detective Flynn here," he said with satisfying sarcasm.

She paused and cocked her head. "*Federal Agent* Flynn. Sorry. So, what do we have here?"

"Nothing for you, Pat."

"I doubt that very much. You know what I say: the story is wherever you are. You are where the story is. And now that you are federal, well, that makes this very interesting."

It was not always good for information like that to get out. For the public—the killer in particular—to know who was watching. A profiler. Federal interest.

"How do you hope to catch Victoria Hempsey's killer?" she asked.

Voodoo, he wanted to say. *I'll get him with voodoo*. If he heard that word one more time in relation to his line of work, he would go mad.

"Is it true that the boyfriend is a person of interest?"

He shook his head. "I can't answer your questions, Pat. You know I'd love to," he lied. Andy placed his hands in his pockets and put on his best professional face. He had to be careful with Goodacre, he reminded himself. Bad press for him was bad press for the SVCP unit. He couldn't afford that. "We should get back to—"

"Do the police have reason to believe a serial killer is at work. . . ?"

He didn't answer, and she tried a different tack. "Do you know the whereabouts of your girlfriend, Makedde Vanderwall? Is she presumed dead?"

Mak. Dead.

That fragile thing squirmed in his chest.

"She's not my—" He caught himself. The blood was pumping

so hard in his ears he thought he'd go deaf. *Mak.* He took a breath. "I have nothing for you. Sorry. If you want something, you'll have to try the media unit."

Andy turned and strode away from the journalist while she continued to pummel him with questions he would not answer. Harrison kept quiet and followed him while Mahoney reiterated that Goodacre needed to see the media unit for any information.

Who the hell tipped her off?

On narrow Davoren Lane the still air felt stifling. Having thrown Goodacre off, Andy stepped up to the door of the fourth house the three of them had visited in this twisting Surry Hills back street. His suit jacket was slung over one arm. He swallowed.

"You okay?" Harrison asked him quietly. He only nodded.

Before them was a small, plain semi, the brickwork painted cream and peeling in places. Weeds crept up the step.

Mahoney arrived without a word, not mentioning the exchange with Goodacre. The questions about Mak would have rattled her, too. For a moment the three of them stood and looked at each other wordlessly, sensing this was the stop they'd been building up to—the home directly behind that of the murder victim, Victoria Hempsey.

Mahoney knocked.

They waited, listening to the inner-city soundtrack. At the end of the lane they could see the long-weekend traffic crawling past on nearby Albion Street, where crowds of pedestrians slunk past in low-rise jeans and spiky hair, holding vintage handbags and takeaway coffees. Next door, where they had interviewed a couple for nearly an hour earlier in the day, someone shut a window on the unseasonable heat and pulled the blinds closed.

There was movement inside the small semi and after several long minutes a man opened the door. He was pale and thin, dressed in denim jeans and a tatty T-shirt with a logo too worn to read. He wore a red baseball cap low over his eyes. Though it was already late afternoon, he looked as if he had been sleeping.

"Officers Mahoney, Flynn and Harrison." They flashed their IDs. "You live here?"

He nodded.

"Mr. John Dayle?"

Beneath the red cap, the eyes went from face to face, taking them in. "Uh, that's me," he said.

"We're just canvassing the area and we were wondering if we could ask you some questions about Victoria Hempsey. She lived behind you," Detective Karen Mahoney said.

The thin man scratched his nose and nodded his consent. "I saw you today, coming round to the neighbours." He nodded again. "So, do the cops have anything? Any leads?"

Andy watched him.

"I'm afraid we can't tell you that, but rest assured we are doing our best," Mahoney said smoothly and gave him a pleasant, closed-mouth smile.

"That's good. I mean, she was a nice lady. Not that I knew her really, but she seemed nice," he said and pulled the edge of his baseball cap. He was nervous, Andy thought, but so were the other neighbours they'd spoken to. No one liked talking about murder. Not when it was so close to home.

"May we come in?" Andy asked.

"Um, sure, yeah." The man lifted his cap on one side and scratched his head underneath.

They stepped inside and Andy closed the door behind them, not quite letting the latch shut all the way. He instinctively slid his hand over his Glock, unclipping the holster. The blinds were closed in the dimly lit, narrow house. The air felt damp. Dishes were piled haphazardly in the sink. Light glowed in the kitchen, and from a bare bulb hanging over the steep staircase, which they climbed in single file. Discarded clothes were strewn about the lounge/office setup at the top of the stairs. There was a couch along one wall and a computer desk in a corner, heaped with opened mail and magazines, and a bowl of half-eaten cereal.

"The cops were here yesterday, asking questions," he said.

"Sorry to bother you again. We do need to speak to all the neighbours as a matter of routine," Harrison said.

It wasn't routine. Mahoney had taken them through the notes from the first round of interviews. There was nothing out of the ordinary. But Andy wanted to eyeball the neighbours. Especially the one in this house.

"I'm just getting ready for work," Dayle explained. "This won't take long."

"How well did you know Victoria Hempsey?" Andy asked, feeling a creeping tension. He found himself standing on alert, listening for every sound, watching for every movement.

Dayle shook his head in response. "Uh, I didn't know her at all really, like I told the cops yesterday."

"But she seemed nice?" Harrison pressed.

"Yeah, I mean, from the look of her. She wasn't, uh, loud or anything."

"You never met?"

He hesitated. "Nah, I don't think so. I was aware of her, 'course."

"Did you see or hear anything out of the ordinary on Wednesday evening?" Andy asked him. "Any sounds? Shouting? Any unusual activity?"

"Uh, the police spoke to me already about that. Like I said

before, I've been working a lot. And when I'm not working I'm sleeping. I take pills so I sleep heavy. So yeah, I didn't see or hear nothing unusual. Sorry I can't be of more help." Dayle took a couple of steps backwards and looked around, his eyes searching for something.

"You suffer from insomnia?"

"Yeah, sometimes. They gave me pills for it."

Andy nodded to Harrison, giving her a significant look, and she picked up the conversation, asking Dayle about his work while Andy walked to the window by his cluttered computer desk and pulled the blinds up. The semi was positioned directly behind Victoria Hempsey's terrace. From the window Andy could see right down into the courtyard where they'd stood earlier, and into the glass window and about a third of the living area beyond: the floorboards where Victoria had been slaughtered.

You staged her. For yourself.

So you could see her there.

He dropped the blinds and turned. "Been here long?" Andy asked when Dayle had finished responding to Harrison's general questions, which he'd answered with almost exactly the same phrases he'd given the officers who'd first interviewed him the day before.

"Uh, four years or so," he answered.

"Do you like it? Nice neighbourhood?" Harrison said, working to take the increasing tension out of the room.

Dayle nodded, seeming to relax a touch. "Yeah. I like it here."

"We've heard reports of a vagrant with a long beard who might have been hanging around Ms. Hempsey's home in the week or so before her murder. Did you see anyone like that, Mr. Dayle?" Andy asked.

Dayle paused and then nodded. "Yeah. Yeah, I seen someone like that." He brought a finger to his chin.

"With a blue jacket? That zips up?" Andy asked, motioning to an imaginary zipper at his neck.

Dayle nodded again. "Exactly. That's it. I remember him. He was hanging around a bit. Looked kind of suspicious."

"Do you remember anything else about the man?" Detective Mahoney piped in. "Anything at all? Any detail could be important."

Dayle crossed his arms and looked down. "No. No, that's all I remember—he had a beard and a blue jacket. I didn't think anything of it until . . . you know. I mean, now you mention it, maybe I should have called it in?"

"Thank you, Mr. Dayle, you've been very helpful," Andy said. "We won't take any more of your time. Do let us know if you see the man in the blue jacket again, day or night. We're very keen to speak to him." They all trooped back down the stairs and Andy took a few steps towards the front door. "Do you know if your neighbour might be in? We're trying to speak to everyone we can."

"Uh, I don't really know them. A Chinese couple, I think. They might be in." He shrugged.

Harrison closed her notepad, clearly realising that Andy had what he wanted. If she was keen to ask more questions, she didn't let on.

"Thanks again for your time," Mahoney said. "If you think of anything else, please don't hesitate to call." She followed Andy and Harrison to the front door and they stepped outside. Dayle closed the door behind them and they walked up the lane, not looking back. They didn't speak until they reached Andy's car, parked on Foveaux Street.

"The guy in the blue jacket was bullshit. You wanted us out

of there," Mahoney said, standing on the footpath outside his Honda.

Andy nodded.

"You figure it's him, don't you?" she said.

Andy nodded again and leaned against his car, jaw tight. He got out his phone and called Inspector Kelley.

"It's Flynn. I want to know everything about John Dayle."

CHAPTER 10

"John Allan Dayle, thirty-three years old."

Detective Inspector Kelley pushed a driver's licence image across the table towards Agents Flynn and Harrison. HQ was quiet, most of the officers having left to enjoy what little was left of Good Friday. But Kelley had not budged. There was no rest for the wicked, or those who sought to catch them.

Andy looked at the image. It was the man they'd met—Victoria Hempsey's neighbour. "He works as a dish pig at one of the restaurants in Surry Hills," he said, looking at the face, the eyes, and remembering the feeling he'd had in the narrow house. "His place is directly behind Victoria Hempsey's terrace. He said he's been living there for four years."

"You think they crossed paths," Kelley said.

"I think he could see everything Victoria Hempsey did," Andy replied. "His windows look right into hers. And her courtyard."

Kelley nodded and drummed his fingers on the desk top, thinking. He took a breath. "Deller remembers him."

Andy sat forwards. This was getting interesting.

"I caught him on the phone after you called," Kelley explained. "Three years ago he interviewed a John Dayle about the Graney rape. Same guy. He was the key suspect."

Dana's eyes widened. Andy nodded for his old boss to continue.

"He had been working as a kitchen hand that evening, and was later spotted at a bar, the White Cockatoo, the same bar where Graney was drinking."

Andy knew the one. It was one of the few pubs along the popular Crown Street strip that hadn't been revamped in recent years. And it was close to Hempsey's terrace. "Did the victim give a description? Could she ID him?"

"She described a thin, Caucasian male in his late twenties or early thirties as the man who attacked her."

"Dayle fits that description," Dana noted. So did half of Surry Hills, but the coincidence of his being interviewed for the earlier rape was too much to dismiss.

"The guy claimed he hadn't noticed Graney at the bar, despite the fact that they were there at the same time. He said that he went home solo after having a beer. He was living alone at the time and there were no witnesses to corroborate his story." Kelley sat back in his chair and folded his arms. "This is where we have a problem . . ." he said. "Dayle agreed to a line-up. Graney picked someone different, a filler, so he was released."

Identity parades could be key in breaking cases, and quite accurate if correct procedures were followed, but still, victims of violent attacks were sometimes too traumatised to make good eyewitnesses, particularly if the attack took place at night. The reliability of eyewitness testimony had been the subject of Mak's PhD thesis, Andy recalled suddenly, and he felt his throat tighten.

"The next day, Graney thought she'd made a mistake, but by then it was too late," Kelley went on. "Obviously the credibility of any subsequent ID she made would get shot down in court. And Dayle had a good alibi for the attack on Kim Plotsky. A friend from overseas—a Pom, I think—said he'd spent the night with him in his flat, on the couch. Said he couldn't have left without him knowing. You'll find the statement is in the file. When the DNA came up as a match between the two rape cases, and he had a strong alibi, that was it. He was cleared as a suspect. End of story. Deller will be able to tell you more."

Friends can lie. And friends from overseas quickly become hard to track down, Andy thought. If Dayle was guilty and he was cleared of two violent rapes because of a flawed alibi and a failed identity parade, it was James Reason's "Swiss cheese" model of error gone wrong. Human systems—in this case, investigative processes—were like Swiss cheese, with the holes in the cheese representing potential flaws. More than one layer is often enough to catch the error—a perp falls through one hole but is caught with the next piece—but if the hole in the next piece happens to line up, there is an error once more, and the perp walks. Dayle is accused by one person, but the identity parade fails. DNA links the crime to another, for which he has an alibi, and that's it, there is no way to pin him down for either. He's free to attack again, and in this case, perhaps escalate to murder.

Andy wasn't sure what to think. "If it was him, he was pretty cocky to agree to a line-up."

"Unless he knew she couldn't ID him for some reason," Dana suggested.

A dark alley at night. A broken nose.

"It's by no means unheard of," Kelley said.

Dana crossed her legs. "There's been nothing similar in the past three years?" she said.

Kelley shook his head. "Not that we know of."

"Did Dayle move for a while? Maybe to visit the friend overseas?"

"He didn't leave the country."

And they knew he hadn't done time. Yet it would be uncharacteristic for that type of offender to stop for so long. Sexual sadists were notorious recidivists. That left another disturbing possibility. *He has advanced*, Andy thought. If Dayle was guilty, he might have got better at covering his tracks. A startlingly high percentage of rapes went unreported and perhaps after being brought in for questioning he'd moved on to another MO that couldn't be so easily linked to Plotsky and Graney. Until Victoria Hempsey.

"So, maybe this John Dayle fits your profile," Kelley said. "But we don't have anything on him."

"Do we bring him in for questioning? Or do you think he'll get spooked?" Dana asked.

Andy frowned. The man they'd spoken to was excited by the visit from the police. Nervous, yes. But would he get spooked? "I want a warrant as soon as possible to search his house before he gets rid of any possible evidence. Clothing belonging to the victim . . . or shoes. The sooner we get in there the better."

Kelley rubbed his chin. "Until we can establish what belongings may be missing, and unless someone has seen Dayle with those belongings, no magistrate will go for it, Flynn. Dayle has no priors. We have no successful link to the sexual assaults, if they are even related to the murder. He's her neighbour, that's it. You've got to get me more than that."

Andy recalled the feeling he'd had in the narrow semi. He wanted to search it, but Kelley was right. While he might have reasonable grounds to *suspect* Dayle's home had evidence linking him to Hempsey's murder, he had to have reasonable grounds to *believe* it, in order for the application to be successful. As it was, a magistrate would be unlikely to allow it, and a second application could be more difficult to get approved once one had already been rejected.

"And if we get a DNA match with the homicide case to the semen samples taken from the two rape cases, we won't have anything to convince a magistrate unless we can cast doubt on the alibi for the Plotsky case," Dana suggested. "This John Dayle didn't give a sample three years ago, correct?"

Kelley shook his head. "He wasn't charged, so no."

As with all offenders charged with a serious indictable offence carrying five or more years imprisonment, Dayle, if it had got that far, would have been fingerprinted and a buccal swab would have been taken.

"And there was no court order?" Dana asked. Sometimes investigators were successful in obtaining court orders to make a suspect give a sample.

Again, Kelley shook his head. "Not after the identification debacle. Let's get hold of this alibi of his and check the story again."

"I recommend you put him under twenty-four-hour surveillance ASAP," Andy urged. "If this is the man who attacked Plotsky and Graney and he's escalated to murder, he's highly dangerous and may attack again at any time. Killing a neighbour is reckless," he reasoned. "We can't be sure there will be a cooling-off period. And though we were as careful as we could be this afternoon, a second police visit might have spooked him—he may try to dispose of evidence. If he does, we have to catch him in the act."

Kelley leaned his elbows on his desk and rubbed his temples. He clearly didn't want to waste limited police resources tailing the wrong guy. He looked up. "You like him for it?" he asked Andy, with his hard, direct gaze.

Andy did not hesitate. "Yeah. I like him for it."

Kelley nodded. "All right. I'll get a surveillance team on him ASAP. We'll see if we can catch him with any of the victim's possessions. Catch him acting suspiciously."

It was far too early to show their hand. If Dayle was their man, they would need to handle each step of the investigation carefully. There could be no mistakes.

"Will you present for the strike force on Monday morning, first thing? Will that give you enough time?"

Andy had wondered if he would simply type up a report, or if he could speak face to face with the team. This was a good development. It was better this way.

"Yes," he said. "I'll be ready."

CHAPTER 11

Weary passengers poured off the aeroplane in sloppy lines, gripping their possessions and their passports, hair askew and perfume overloaded to mask unpleasant body odours earned by hours trapped in small chairs, thousands of kilometres above the ground in an airless cabin, eating reheated food. They walked quietly, some in a hurry, others lazily, but each too tired for talk. Announcements came and went over the PA system, and toilets flushed and sinks filled and drained in the washrooms. Some passengers gravitated towards the bright lights and advertising of the duty-free aisles, pulling out their wallets.

Mak's mouth was dry and her eyes filmy. Her legs felt tight and there was the dull ache of dehydration behind her eyes. Wearing the clothes she'd bought at Heathrow with Luther's cash—a black Burberry trench coat, jeans and black boots—she joined the hundreds of travellers filling the arrivals area, anxiously shifting from swollen foot to swollen foot. There had been no direct flights from Barcelona, and she'd been waitlisted literally at the last minute, getting to the airport hours after killing the nameless assassin in the bushes. She'd come with little more than money, her new passport, Luther's laptop and the clothes on her back. Mak had ended up on an even more roundabout route than necessary—Barcelona to Paris to London to Helsinki to Singapore to Sydney. She thought it best not to count the hours it had taken. She'd paid for a return business-class fare, in cash, much to the amazement of the woman at the ticket desk in Barcelona, so it could have been much, much worse. Mak intended to enjoy Luther's money. She'd more than earned it.

She felt peculiarly numb as she waited in line, returning to the country that had all but ruined her since she'd first visited it, roughly five years previously, for modelling work. It was a trip she'd naïvely looked forward to at the time. Her friend Cat was modelling in Sydney and really loving "the life"—the beaches, the parties. But Mak had arrived to Cat's empty apartment and everything had been spectacularly, nightmarishly wrong. Sure, Mak had found sun and work and love in Australia—the things she supposed she'd hoped to—but first and foremost she'd found heartbreak and violence and death. Yet something, or someone, had always kept her coming back.

Of course, never in her wildest nightmares had she thought she'd come back like this.

As someone else. "Passport."

The customs officer looked grim at this early hour. It was before seven in the morning, local time. Mak stepped forwards and slid her business-class boarding pass, visitor's entry card and passport across to the customs officer. Two of the female officer's tanned male colleagues were joking around behind her, and one of them broke from their hushed banter to check Mak out in a blatantly flirtatious manner. Mak smiled at him and then looked to her feet, twisting a lock of dyed hair around her finger. *I'm newly single. I'm in Australia to have a good time. I hear the men are really something*, she hoped her body language said. *I'm not committing any kind of crime. I'm not remotely dangerous.*

The woman before her remained stony-faced. "Purpose of your visit?"

"Holiday," Mak said brightly, but not too brightly. "I have friends here. Two weeks and then New Zealand before I go home." The lies came with surprising ease, as did the subtle Spanish accent. The assertion about friends, at least, was true. Not that she would likely see them. She adjusted Bogey's glasses awkwardly with her index finger and smiled again. The officer probably pegged her for the arty type, living on a trust fund. Though Mak was thirty, she'd listed "student" as her occupation. The officer lifted the new passport up and looked from the photo to Mak and back again, then swiped the passport through a machine and typed something into her keyboard. Mak felt a line of tension coil in her. Now was the moment. That passport had proved very expensive already. It had cost her thousands in Luther's blood money and very nearly her life. Or had it been a coincidence that she'd picked it up and been followed?

What would this passport cost her now?

Then, like a small miracle, the po-faced officer stamped the fresh Euro passport of a dark-haired, blue-eyed Spanish national, and wished Maria Cruz a pleasant holiday.

"Um, thank you," Mak said.

She avoided the lines at the baggage carousel, dragging the carry-on bag she'd also purchased at Heathrow, and walked out into the bright chaos of the Sydney morning.

The deed she'd found in Luther's name, on his laptop, was for an address in Sydney's inner south. It did not take long to get there by taxi from the airport.

Squinting behind sunglasses, Makedde watched the small, red-brick apartment block come into view. His was the lower left-hand side of what looked like four flats. Fresh white, looping graffiti decorated a section under a main, barred window. A thin strip of lawn at the front was overgrown with weeds and decorated with a *For Sale* sign, currently falling at a slight angle. It looked unoccupied.

Luther was off-loading the place. Or he had been.

Mak had the taxi slow as she passed it, taking in the details. The suburb of Redfern was becoming gentrified, but not this street, it seemed. She wouldn't be staying here. With its run-down feel and broken guttering, the apartment block was surprisingly out of sync with Luther's sleek Barcelona abode. There was even a series of small pot plants on the narrow porch, and a damp sofa with coiled springs escaping the tatty, flowered fabric. It seemed impossible that he would have lived here. No, she wouldn't overnight here. But she had to check it out.

With her chest feeling tight, she got the taxi driver to pull up a block away. She paid him and got out, feeling slightly conspicuous dragging the rectangular carry-on bag on its tiny wheels over the rough asphalt. The wheels made an awful noise as she walked down the sidewalk towards the address and she quickly decided to fold the handles on the bag and carry it. She was surprised, when she did, by just how noticeably stronger she was. Mind you, this was perhaps the lightest she'd ever packed. A few items of clothing, a book and a laptop. And a lot of traveller's cheques and cash hidden in every pocket. This was all Maria Cruz owned, Mak supposed, and it struck her as odd that she could comfortably carry it all with one arm. Of course there were the things of Luther's she'd kept stashed in Barcelona. She hadn't been foolish enough to bring the jewellery she'd found in his car through several international airports. The pieces were large and unusual, and she presumed they were stolen. Nor had she brought his Glock. Though now that she was exposed on this Sydney street, she felt naked without it.

Don't panic. No one is watching you.

The house next to the square block of flats looked equally still and lifeless, so she walked straight up to it, opened the squeaky iron gate at the front and ducked around the back, picking her way over dry, patchy grass. She stood her bag at the base of a dividing fence in the backyard and stepped onto it to get a glimpse of Luther's yard. It held some empty laundry lines, a turned-over bucket and similarly uneven, yellowing lawn. Against the back steps was a garden gnome sitting on its side, next to a pink, broken ornament of some kind. The scene was domestic. Neglected. Curiously female. There was no evidence that anyone had been there in recent weeks. Mak got down, took a breath, then pulled herself up with one arm with a new-found ease and hauled her case over the fence. She gently dropped it on the grass on the opposite side before pulling herself over. Her shoulder muscles felt strong, steady.

Mak landed on the other side and walked to the back door of the downstairs flat, where she went through every key on Luther's key ring twice. Nothing fit. It wouldn't be so easy as it had been in Barcelona. It took her a maddening four and a half minutes to pick the simple lock—it felt like much longer—and once the door opened she braced herself. *No alarm. Good.* She shuttled her things to the internal laundry she'd got access to and took a quick tour of the whole flat, much as her father would have done when he was still a cop, back to the wall, looking both ways. Listening. Of course all this effort was unnecessary: the place was empty and she was safe. She closed the back door.

Weird.

A woman had been living here. An older woman. The closets were empty and there were no pictures—perhaps the real-estate agent had removed them?—but though the air was stale, it still held the unmistakeable scent of faux lavender and bleach.

And everything was a bit . . . *pastel*. Pale pink carpets, flowered wallpaper weathered with age and peeling at the edges. Sad little outdated couches in previously cheery patterns. A Victorian reproduction rocking chair upholstered with balding berry velvet. *An elderly woman. Living alone. And then she died.* Mak frowned. *Had Luther been renting it out?* she wondered. He seemed quite rich from the spoils of his bloodshed, but she didn't see why he wouldn't also be a landlord. Perhaps an agent handled everything—sent the money to an account somewhere. Anonymous and easy. But why would he buy this place? Surely there would be better investments. Had he lived here at some point? That seemed impossible. It clearly wasn't where he stayed when he was in town, so it had to serve another purpose. He, like Mak, probably did not like to bring illegal, easily detected weapons through airport security checkpoints. He'd have them waiting on the other side. It was her hope that he had them waiting here.

On hands and knees, balancing on chairs or pacing the small rooms, Mak spent the next half-hour scouring every corner of the sad two-bedroom unit. She gave herself splinters pulling at floorboards. She lifted up faded pink carpet, and pushed and pulled at parts of the cramped, tile-cracked bathroom she would not have otherwise wanted to touch. There were no hidden panels, no surprises in the closets. The mouldy kitchen cupboards contained silverware and cheap dishes and no hidden drawers as the apartment had in Barcelona. But though the cupboards held no handy weapons, some had been carelessly stuffed with letters and photographs, no doubt hastily tucked away by a real-estate agent. Mak examined one framed photo from the stack. The glass was cracked.

In the photo was a matronly woman wearing a floral-printed dress and standing next to a tall, rough-looking teenage boy dressed in denim. Beneath a baseball cap the boy's face was vaguely familiar. Mak cocked her head to one side. She squinted.

Luther.

Her stomach dropped. *Luther. Luther Hand. Bogey's killer. As a boy.* To her surprise she felt she might be ill. She raced to the small bathroom and dry-heaved over the open toilet bowl. Eventually the feeling passed and she sat on her heels, breathless.

His mother lived here.

Feeling a creeping sense of unease, Mak replaced the photographs, more sure than ever that Luther's own mother had lived in the flat. And died here, too. Though she had searched with some determination, she could find nothing solid that would help her. Luther would have had to keep some kind of stash in Australia, wouldn't he? Perhaps his mother had not known about his work. Of course. He would need his hidey-hole to be accessible from the outside. Without further delay she took the torch from the kitchen and walked outside. All was quiet. Sun brightened the tiny yard and the sad unused laundry lines and forgotten garden. She scanned the outside of the building, where sunlit brick dropped off into shadow. There was a small wooden door, only sixty or seventy centimetres high, built into the brick to the side of the back step. *Access to the underside of the flat.* Mak pulled her trench coat off, left it on the step and got on her hands and knees in the dirt and dry, yellowed grass. She pulled the door open, breaking cobwebs and causing insects to scuttle about. She switched the torch on and shone the light from side to side, spotting wooden beams and foundations, and sagging cardboard boxes a few metres inside. More cobwebs.

Excellent.

She crawled across the earth floor, dirt grinding into her palms and the knees of her jeans, her lip curled up at the objectionable stench of rat droppings and damp. She passed a coil of rusted wire and an abandoned coat hanger before arriving at the first cardboard box. It held forgotten books and papers, too water-damaged for either reading or making a fire. Another cardboard box was empty, and one was heaped with more discarded hangers. She shone the light around again, seeing the square of sunlight at the other end of the building, where she'd come in, and wishing she could step back out onto the lawn. *Not yet.*

And then something caught her eye—a metal handle sticking up in the dirt near the foundations to the left of where she sat, reflecting as a small rectangle as she swung the beam over it. With a forearm and the crook of her elbow, Mak pushed the hair out of her eyes and continued, pushing aside cobwebs and shuffling on hands and knees to where the metal shone in the torchlight. The earth here was loosely packed. She put the light on its side and dug down with bare fingers, parting the dirt with her hands.

Hello.

Something metal. Something buried.

Ten minutes later Mak emerged feet first into the yard, dragging a large, locked metal toolbox, covered in dirt. She hit the fresh air with a grateful sigh, and pulled the box up to the back step. The knees of her jeans were stained dark brown and her fingers felt raw. She went inside to wash her hands in the basin and splash fresh water on her face. And then she pulled out Luther's key ring and fixed her eyes on the smallest key. The one with the rusted edge.

She sat next to the box and tried it.

Bingo.

She unlocked the metal box with a squeak of unoiled hinges. Inside was a waterproof container housing two handguns, some items she identified as the parts of a disassembled sniper rifle, various types of ammunition and a fake Australian passport Mak would find sadly useless. Beneath it was a plastic bag. She lifted it out and her heart skipped.

It was filled with neatly stacked hundred-dollar bills contained by rubber bands. She guessed there was at least fifty thousand Australian dollars there.

CHAPTER 12

The American stood in his client's lounge room, his polished leather shoes reflecting the copious sunlight in the space. It was Easter Sunday morning and Jack Cavanagh was at his weekend home in the northern suburb of Palm Beach, wearing a robe and towelling his hair off after a swim. The house was minimalist and open plan, with light pouring in through shimmering skylights and an expanse of glass sliding doors, some of which were pulled open, allowing a fresh, salty breeze to come in from the beach. Metres away, waves lapped gently at white sands.

"Bob, are you sure you wouldn't like Roberto to make you a coffee?" Jack offered again. "He's an excellent barista."

"No," The American said. He had come because he had news.

Jack Cavanagh nodded. "Let's go to my study."

They left the personal chef to make preparations for Jack's lunch, and Jack led him to the hall and up a timber staircase. They passed the quiet second-floor bedrooms and at the end of the hall arrived at Jack's study, which was furnished with a carved wooden desk, a couple of leather armchairs and a tall bookcase stocked with the biographies of prominent businessmen and politicians. A surrealist Brett Whiteley painting, recently purchased at auction, adorned the wall, and a floor-to-ceiling window overlooked a pristine stretch of beach.

"Your son is flying to Australia. He should be in the country by tomorrow," The American told his client, once the door was closed.

Jack Cavanagh was about to sit, but now he paused. His son's return would be good news in some respects, but public appearances would need to be managed very carefully. Jack frowned, then took a seat and gestured for White to do the same. The American folded himself into the chair neatly, the morning sunlight illuminating his smooth, calm face. Behind Jack, the waves continued to roll in and out, in and out.

Mr. White kept his face devoid of emotion when he added, "Also, we have a lead on Makedde Vanderwall."

He watched his client inhale sharply. "Where? In Paris? Alive?"

"Alive in Spain," he said. "But I can't confirm yet whether the information is good."

A Barcelona man, Javier Rafel, wanted money for a tip on a woman matching Makedde's description, only with dark hair. He said he did not know where she was, but had the new name she was travelling under.

"If she's alive . . ." Jack said and trailed off. The blood had visibly drained from his face.

What he didn't need to say was that if she was alive, Mak Vanderwall could have some kind of proof that the killer who had come after her, Luther Hand, had been sent on behalf of Jack Cavanagh. It would be disastrous for Cavanagh Incorporated. And for Mr. White and his professional interests.

"The information comes from a man specialising in false ID and counterfeit bonds. The woman he thinks is Makedde Vanderwall purchased a false passport from him. He'll give us the name on the passport if we pay."

"Do it," Jack demanded without hesitation.

"You should know this man is outside my usual network. His credentials are not excellent," he said. "But he has convinced me it is her."

Mr. White produced a facsimile of a passport photograph. It appeared to show an unsmiling Makedde Vanderwall with dark hair. Javier Rafel seemed to have been in contact with precisely the woman they'd been looking for. With the name on her passport The American could use his considerable contacts and Jack's financial resources to trace her. The moment Vanderwall used the passport at a border, a bank, a hotel, they'd have her.

Jack examined the image. "Pay him what he wants."

CHAPTER 13

Makedde Vanderwall slid the plastic key card into the door and it unlocked.

She stepped into the entry to the serviced apartment, awkwardly cradling the heavy metal toolbox. She pulled her case inside and closed the door behind her, shutting out the car park and outside world. The toolbox was wrapped in a towel belonging, it would seem, to the deceased mother of the man who had tried to kill her in Paris. His laptop was in its padded satchel in her carry-on bag, at her feet.

These were all of her possessions. And this impersonal apartment would be home, for the moment, at least.

Before her was a carpeted staircase leading upwards and at the sight she shrugged off the burden of her few belongings, placing the toolbox on the landing at her feet. She took the DO NOT DISTURB sign off the inside door handle and placed it outside the door, then shut the door again and locked it. With that done Mak took a breath and leaned against the wall. It was cold at her back. She had paid for one week in advance, in cash. Without a credit card the receptionist had insisted on recording her passport details for ID, so she was glad she'd had one on hand. It was increasingly hard to live without a credit card, she reflected. She'd have to organise one for Ms. Cruz.

Ms Cruz, your new home awaits.

Mak unbuttoned her trench coat and kneeled on the small landing to unwrap the pastel pink towel hiding Luther's dirty box of tricks. On instinct she reached for the smallest and most familiar of the weapons—a compact model Glock. She fitted the magazine with nine-millimetre rounds, loaded it and stuck the gun into the waistband of her jeans.

Just in case, she thought.

She straightened and padded casually up the carpeted stairs. The townhouse was quite spacious for one person. There was a full-sized kitchen near the top of the stairs and a large living room with a flat-screen television on a low-slung entertainment unit, a modern, pale beige lounge and a bookshelf that was empty save for a few brochures and tourist maps. Beyond the living room were two smallish bedrooms and a full bathroom, accessible from both. She walked through each room, checking window latches and seeing that the only decent entry and exit point was the door at the base of the stairs, where she had come in. There were none of those pesky connecting doors that would make her vulnerable to the serviced units on either side. No spots where the ground outside came near the windows. It would be hard to climb up, but if she really needed to, she could jump out without breaking a leg—if she landed right. That was good. Nearly everything in the place was a shade of white, as was the current fashion of interior design, it seemed. The space appeared comfortable but lifeless. Her shoulders dropped.

Home sweet home.

At the sight of the neatly made queen-sized bed, adorned with large, inviting, fluffed-up pillows, every one of her more than thirty hours of travel weighed on her at once.

Fifteen minutes later Mak was fast asleep, the Glock within reach.

CHAPTER 14

It was about ten o'clock in the evening local time on Easter Sunday and still sometime in the afternoon in Barcelona as Makedde Vanderwall cracked a packet of two-minute noodles into a boiling pot on the stovetop. Outside, the skies had opened up, pummelling the dark Sydney streets with heavy droplets of rain, breaking the surprisingly oppressive humidity. In the next room, the television nattered away on low volume. Mak had slept a few hours and then forced herself to wake for a proper meal and an attempt at time adjustment. If she got to bed again at midnight, she might wake at a normal hour.

Andy Flynn was on her mind.

Sometimes she still saw him in her dreams, still felt the weight of their time together. There'd once been a powerful attraction between them, such passion, but through a time of terrible upheaval. If they hadn't met at a crime scene, could things have been different? If he hadn't been recovering from a brutal divorce? If they hadn't both been nursing their own private wounds, would they have been able to avoid wounding each other? When she'd moved to Canberra to be with him they'd lived like a married couple, and that closeness seemed to cause him to close off, to shut her out, and make him reach for the bottle once more. The scars of his failed marriage to Cassandra had seemed too deep. Knowing what he'd been through, she couldn't blame him. How must it have felt when the Stiletto Killer murdered Cassandra to get at him? To try to set him up? To toy with his mind and his career? What was it like to carry that with you? That sense of being responsible for someone's murder?

Mak understood now, after Bogey.

No, she couldn't blame Andy. Things had been made impossible for them. Their relationship had crumbled, become tense. He'd been upset about her ongoing battle with the Cavanaghs and she'd ended the relationship for good reason. It had been a relief in some ways when she'd ended it.

And then she'd fallen in love with Bogey, so quickly and to such . . .

In Europe everything had been unfamiliar. But here in Sydney, in this impersonal serviced apartment, and with the comfort of her dearest friends and her former lover so painfully close, it seemed to Mak that her isolation was complete. Already the pull to her friends proved a temptation. Without her old mobile phone or address book she didn't have Karen Mahoney's number, or Loulou's or Andy's, but she could get them easily enough. The question of whether she could reach her friends was easy, but the question of whether she *should* reach them was something else altogether. Could she afford to bring her former boss Marian into this? Karen?

No.

I would put them at risk.

I would put myself at further risk.

They were better off without her.

She'd made the decision again and again. No matter how she moved the pieces around, the conclusion was the same. She had to try to remain invisible until it was safe. But how to make it safe? What were the correct steps? Increasingly, Luther's laptop seemed like the key. She had to get it to Andy—the only person she could safely entrust it to. She'd have to deliver it directly into his hands—which would bring so many other issues with it.

Mak tested the noodles with her fork. They gave under the pressure of the prongs, and she pulled one strand out of the bubbling water to taste it. Dinner was nearly ready. It wasn't much on nutrition, she knew, but it was not news to her that she was hopeless—and hopelessly impatient—when it came to all things domestic. She half suspected she would have succumbed to scurvy if not for the convenience of the Mercat de Sant Josep de la Boqueria near Luther's apartment.

What was that?

Mak had pulled a small packet of seasoning from the plastic wrappings, prepared to drop the contents in, and now she paused. Below the sound of heavy rainfall against the window and the murmurs of a car commercial in the next room, she thought she heard a sound on the staircase.

Something is wrong.

Instinctively, she dropped the packet of seasoning, grabbed the pot of water from the stove, shut the kitchen light off and crouched behind the white cupboard, her back against the wall and her heart hammering. After a beat, when she found herself cowering in the blackness of the unfamiliar kitchen, she very nearly laughed aloud. Even though she'd tried to prepare for it for weeks, the incident on the outskirts of Barcelona had shaken her deeply. Her nerves had not really recovered. Now she was flinching at shadows, at creaking floors. Ludicrous.

It's the building settling. It's your new neighbours.

But there was a second creak and a figure appeared at the top of the stairs, silhouetted in the kitchen doorway and casting a shadow across the kitchen linoleum. In the shadow, she could make out the unmistakeable shape of a gun in the figure's right hand, extended like Pinocchio's nose by a silencer. Her own gun, Luther's compact Glock, was in the living room. The filthy toolbox with the disassembled sniper rifle was there, too. *Too far.* She'd kept a gun at her side in Europe for weeks and now she was in Sydney, closer than ever to those who wanted her dead, and she'd left her gun out of reach.

There was a moment of motionless silence as the sickening reality hit home—*They know where I am. Somehow they know*—and Mak sprang up from her position and threw the hot contents of the pot at the figure, aiming at the face and head. Her intruder—a blond, black-clad Caucasian man—screamed and instinctively brought his gloved hands to his face, where hot noodles had attached themselves on his scalded skin. She swung the pot with as much force as she had, but her attacker ducked at the last second, the pot glancing off his head and the momentum throwing her past him in an awkward stumble. His gun dropped. As it hit the carpet, she fell to the ground and grabbed it, scrambling backwards on her hands and feet. She looked down at the loaded weapon for a beat and was kicked hard under the chin with blunt force.

"*AAAAGHHHHH!*" she cried, her jaw seeming to disconnect from her face. She crawled backwards down the steps, moaning, half sliding, as her attacker swung around in arcs at the top of the stairs, brandishing something gleaming and sharp.

She still had his gun. She found the trigger.

From this angle the light from the staircase illuminated the assassin fully as he stood at the top of the steps, his face crimson with fresh burns, eyes closed to slits. He had pulled a knife from his belt and he had it in a reverse grip, stabbing at the air violently with one hand, the other reaching out.

Oh God, she thought. *He's blinded. Kill him. Do it now.*

She aimed true, but foolishly closed her eyes just as she pulled the trigger.

There was a muffled thump, and a recoil that pushed her left elbow off the stair she'd been leaning on. When she opened her eyes again her attacker was down. Mak scrambled to her feet, blood trickling from the corner of her mouth, and stood over him. She trained his gun at his swollen face, but there was no need. His throat gaped from the bullet that had torn it open. There was an audible gurgle and splutter as he coughed blood and it spewed from the corners of his mouth. Soon his chest stopped moving. Slowly, a pool of darkness began to spread out into the carpet.

Get out of here, now.

The Cavanaghs had her new name and had already traced it here to this complex—to this townhouse. Somehow, it had taken them less than a day. She had no time to consider how they'd found her. Not now. Mak strapped two thick travel wallets around her waist, filled with the cash she kept on her, and the false passport she'd bought in Barcelona but was already, apparently, useless to her. She gathered the few items of clothing she now had and toiletries she could shove into plastic bags. Hastily, she took a hand towel and wiped the apartment down for fingerprints, trying to recall the areas she'd touched in her hours there. Then she pulled on her trench coat and stood over the dead body at the top of the staircase. She steeled herself. *Come on. Don't be a coward now.*

She got on her knees and patted the stranger down. His body felt firm beneath her palms, warm but lifeless. The tags were cut out of his clothing. She found no wallet. No identification. No business cards, no notes, no car keys, no phone, no clue as to who specifically had sent him—an agent, or Jack Cavanagh himself ? But she did find a spare magazine of ammunition for his weapon. *A lot of ammo to kill one civilian*, she thought. She shoved the knife and ammunition in with her toiletries and stood up again. There was no way to stage the death to look like a suicide. The stranger who had come for her had fresh burns on his face and the bullet had gone through his throat and out the other side. Mak knew that suicides didn't scald themselves before taking a gun to their throats, not dressed in black clothing without tags, in a dwelling they had no business being in. Mak didn't bother to try to retrieve the bullet. Her prints would not be on it, and ballistics could not link her to it. After a moment of indecision she wiped the gun down and left it with the body. If she used it again, it could link her to this dead man. And besides, she had Luther's Glock to protect her in future. She didn't plan on letting it leave her side again. Mak took one last look around the apartment, including under the bed for stray garments and in the bed sheets and bathroom drains for hair, turned the television off so that it wouldn't bother the neighbours and, satisfied she could do no more to distance herself from the crime scene, gathered Luther's toolbox and her small carry-on bag, stuffed messily with her things and the all-important laptop she'd risked her life to get to Australia. She stepped over the assassin's body, careful not to tread in the growing pool of blood, and made her way down the staircase to the front door.

Luther's gun was tucked in the small of her back and now she placed her things on the landing, turned the lights off, took a beat to allow her eyes to adjust, and opened the door, gun drawn. Nothing moved. The parking lot seemed motionless, except for rain hitting the glittering asphalt. She could hear cars on the main road just above the din of raindrops. She waited a beat, then dashed out of the front of the building in a crouch, hiding behind the first car, scanning the area again and then running again with a speed and strength she didn't know she possessed. Once she was a couple of blocks away, she broke into a grassy family yard and ran for the shadowy shelter of a back porch. She slid across the ground and came to a stop under the tall verandah, and sat on the damp ground with her back to the house. Utterly soaked, she slunk down and rested her head on the toolbox, her breathing rapid. Above her, in a safe and warm living room, a television was playing the very same channel she'd been watching perhaps fifteen minutes earlier, thinking she was safe.

Slowly now. Slowly. Just breathe . . .

A tear escaped. Then another.

The cover of Ms. Cruz was now useless to her. She had to go deeper. And she had to stop Jack Cavanagh before he got to her again.

CHAPTER 15

Agent Andrew Flynn sat in his hotel room in World Square, looking over case notes on scraps of paper, and searching on his laptop for anything further he could find online about Victoria Hempsey, John Dayle and Plotsky and Graney. Nearly everyone left an electronic footprint, but thus far nothing he found proved valuable. He'd been upgraded to a "suite" for his final night, though that seemed only to mean that there was a small sitting area, currently inhabited by Agent Dana Harrison, who seemed not to like sitting on chairs. She'd spent most of the previous two hours cross-legged on the floor with her iPad and the files from the case, her suit jacket hung over a chair. From time to time he watched her flick her fingers across the screen of the mysterious device and swiftly type on a keypad he could not see. He still liked written notes. Watching her made him feel old.

The remnants of a large pizza cooled on the coffee table between them. It was getting late and first thing in the morning Andy would have to brief the homicide unit's strike force on his profile of Victoria Hempsey's killer and his suspicions about John Dayle. Nothing the team had uncovered since Friday had given him any reason to reconsider his concerns about Dayle, though he'd have to be cautious about how he presented his view, so as not to seem blinded by a single suspect.

If Andy was right about him. And if he was wrong?

Andy leaned back in the hotel chair, rubbed his eyes and shut the lid on his laptop, seeing the text imprinted on the insides of his eyelids for a moment. "What were your impressions of Dayle when you met him?" he asked, swivelling the chair around to face her.

Dana looked up from her iPad. "Creepy," she said without hesitation. "I agree with you that his link to the sexual assault cases is quite a coincidence. And he seemed nervous." She shifted to face him, leaning back on her elbows and flicking her hair to one side. She licked her full lips with unconscious sensuality, and Andy swallowed.

"People tend to be nervous with the police around," he said sharply. "Beware of mistaking nervousness with guilt."

You haven't been on the beat, he was saying. *It's not like a textbook.*

Her face darkened a touch, but she said nothing. She sat forwards and cocked her head. "You told Kelley you liked him for it. You seemed pretty sure."

"Yes," he said.

He hoped he was right about Dayle. If it turned out he was wrong, he would have wasted police resources and quite possibly slowed down the hunt for the real killer. It would be a setback for the unit. He wasn't sure they could afford a setback. "For what it's worth, I agree with you," she said. "He's suspicious. You haven't changed your mind, have you?"

Andy shook his head. He had been thinking about the three-year gap between reported crimes. If Dayle was the rapist and Hempsey's killer, as he suspected, they had to consider what might have made him attack again, and kill. "He had the blinds closed over his windows, but that view would have him looking directly into Victoria Hempsey's courtyard," Andy said. "The weather has been good lately. Unseasonably warm. The victim was tanned."

"She was sunbaking out there?" Dana said and nodded. "Makes sense."

"So Dayle has been fantasising about committing another rape," he postulated. "He was spooked about how close it got in the Graney case and he's been afraid to act. Then he starts seeing Hempsey every day. Maybe she's sunbaking outside his window. Maybe she doesn't pull the blinds all the way down at night. Whatever it is, he notices her. He starts to fixate on her, starts watching her."

"So he's been fantasising for a while, planning even," Dana said.

"But like I said before, it isn't smart to kill your neighbour. It exposes him."

"So he didn't plan it. It was a crime of opportunity? He snapped, took it to the next level. Raped her and then realised he couldn't leave her as a witness?" she suggested.

It was possible. Hempsey's killer was a sexual sadist and totally without empathy for his victim. He had inflicted pain on her before death, he'd raped her and cut her as she struggled—all hallmarks of a sadistic psychopath. But not all killers were smart and despite popular belief, not all psychopaths were smart either. In reality, psychopaths with the deadly combination of high intelligence and homicidal impulse—Ted Bundy, Ed Kemper, Ed Brown—were very uncommon, and it was lack of intelligence and lack of planning that contributed to making serial killers so rare a phenomenon. Someone with a homicidal impulse who was not intelligent was more likely to be caught after the first attack, so John Dayle might have lucked out in the past, avoiding time for serious sexual assault, but if this was his first kill and he'd gone into it unplanned or without caution, they had a good chance of nailing him. He would have left evidence somewhere. No one committed the perfect murder, and certainly not without a great deal of planning. The trouble was, though the killer might have left evidence, a man like that was a ticking bomb. He could go off again at any time and they had to get him before that happened again.

They had to be smart about catching him. The moment they asked for fingerprints or a DNA sample it would give the game away. Unless they had something solid to charge him with, it was too risky.

Andy liked Dayle for the Hempsey murder. Really liked him for it.

He'd let Kelley know as much, but that wasn't enough to get them the search warrant, though warrants for telephone intercepts and internet surveillance were under way, and had possibly already come through, as the applications required only suspicion and not "belief." Inspector Kelley agreed that they should get a surveillance device into Dayle's home, but that could take time. The STIB—Special Technical Investigations Branch—was already overstretched. Likewise, the surveillance teams. It was unclear whether, or how, they would move ahead with setting up the physical surveillance Andy recommended. John Dayle might already be disposing of evidence—and the kill might have given him new confidence.

"Are we thinking the shoes taken from the rape victims were trophies?" Dana asked.

"Trophies," Andy agreed.

"And to further humiliate, perhaps? To slow down the victim's ability to get help? Taking her ID, her phone, her shoes," she reasoned.

Andy nodded again. "And the toe?"

The toe. It appeared to have been removed before death. Victoria Hempsey's feet had been severely cut in her struggles, probably kicking out at her attacker as he tied or retied her ankles. But the toe was different. The cut was hardly surgical, but it didn't fit with the pattern of the defensive wounds. That detail troubled Andy a great deal, and what he wasn't yet willing to say—was not yet willing to bring into the discussion—was the fact that the rapes had taken place soon after the media obsession with Ed Brown, who kept his victim's shoes as souvenirs, and who had also kept body parts—*toes*.

And now Victoria Hempsey is dead and her *toe is missing.*

Ed Brown was gone and the case was closed, but it was on Andy's mind constantly for a plethora of reasons, not least what Brown had done to Cassandra. And Mak's experiences at his hands—and her absence now. But he had to be cautious about making any links. Just because the Stiletto Killer was on Andy's mind didn't mean the cases were related. It would be unwise to focus on the shoes. The rapist had taken a number of things from the second victim. They didn't know whether any of Victoria Hempsey's shoes were missing. The toe could be explained by something else. Possibly.

"The toe was either lost in her struggle, or it was deliberately cut off as a form of torture," Andy said.

"But it hasn't been found, has it?"

"It is possibly a trophy also," Andy said vaguely, and hoped Dana could tell he was not willing to talk about any potential link to the Stiletto Murders just yet.

All he could do was work up a detailed profile of Dayle and recommend a strategy to the strike force. Kelley would take Flynn's advice on how to handle Dayle and the investigation, but the fact was, Andy was only a consultant on this case, not the chief investigating officer he had been in the past. In the morning he would present his offender profile to the Hempsey homicide strike force, and then he and Dana would head back to Canberra. Kelley would keep him in the loop, but ultimately it would be out of his hands.

That part wasn't easy. Not now that he thought of Ms. Hempsey as Victoria.

Not now that he'd walked through her home and seen her personal space.

Not now that it felt personal for him, too, because of the links that kept cropping up. The stolen shoes . . . the toe . . .

Dana was watching him carefully. "Are you thirsty?" she asked after a minute.

Andy was taken by surprise. "Maybe," he said, with a question in his voice. "Can I get you something, Harrison?"

"You can call me Dana," she said and stood up, and though her tone was neutral her words caused a ripple of tension. He didn't want to call her Dana. Not just at the moment. Not while she was here in his hotel room, standing before him with her hair loose around her shoulders. The old habits from his younger days were there, just waiting beneath the surface.

He could ask her out for a drink. Just something casual. They could have a few beers and see what happened next. At some point back in Canberra he had thought of that, regardless of the mistake it would be. Unprofessional. Unwise. And now he was alone with her in his hotel room and she had a look in her eyes that made him wonder if she'd thought the very same things.

Had it been dangerous to invite her to Sydney with him? She was the best for the job. He'd been convinced of that. Her or Patel, who he'd sent to Berrima instead . . .

"We could grab a drink if you like?" she suggested.

Andy was glad he'd resisted the pull of the minibar so far,

or his response would not have been so easy. "We leave early tomorrow. Be packed and ready at eight for the briefing at HQ," he found himself saying. He gave her a tight smile and flipped his computer open again, the screen glowing as it came to life once more.

Her lovely face dropped just a touch. "Of course. I didn't mean anything . . ." she responded after a beat, tilting her chin up slightly and managing a carefree pose.

"I know you didn't," he said. If he had been working with Jimmy, they would have gone for a drink.

But she wasn't Jimmy.

Dana picked up her jacket. "It's getting late. I'll, um, see you in the morning then."

He nodded, and listened as she retreated to the door and let herself out. Then he got up and pulled the chain across his door as much to keep himself in as to keep anyone out.

And he opened the minibar.

CHAPTER 16

He got on his knees and pulled out the special box under his bed. It was the most special of all the special boxes he had, and in it was a jar that had once held jam and now held something quite different. He wiped his sweaty brow and sat up and leaned against his bed, examining the prized possession through the smeared glass in his hands. His prize floated slowly in the formalin. His prize.

Victoria.

In many ways he was only now getting over the shock of having made it this far. He'd fantasised about it so long that when he'd done it he thought he might burst inside somehow. And the feeling he'd had when he'd woken the next day to find he'd got away with it was something else altogether. The police had come to him, asked about her, asked if he'd seen or heard anything unusual and then they'd simply gone away again. Somehow the sun had risen again and the world had kept turning, with him a killer. Someone with power. Someone to be feared. Someone who could command those whom he chose to command, and could pluck the chosen ones as a gardener plucks a thorny rose.

Victoria Hempsey.

She'd been his first choice. A beautiful widow with skin like milky coffee, and delicate, small feet and hands, and eyes like infinite sadness. He'd claimed her as his own and this jar was proof.

High on the thrill his prize gave him, he lovingly placed the jar back in its box, closed the lid and slid it slowly under his bed, where it sat amongst the common things—clothing and discarded shoes and his favourite magazines. And his very special boxes.

He'd finally done it and it had felt good. So fucking good. Pleasantly stirred, he clothed himself in his loose cargo pants, cupping the seam in the centre to feel the proud profile of his aroused genitals. He adjusted himself, pulled on a T-shirt and tied his sneakers on, then took the steep staircase downstairs. A baseball cap sat at the front door and he put it on and stepped out into the rain to breathe Sydney's damp night air.

Ripe with new possibility.

CHAPTER 17

It was two o'clock on Monday morning as The American, Mr. White, slipped into the serviced apartment where Makedde Vanderwall was thought to have been staying under the false name of Maria Cruz. He shut the door behind him carefully, the lock making a barely audible click. He pocketed his electronic swipe card—effective with most simple hotel-style locks like this one—and removed his wet shoes.

The apartment was noiseless and dark. He could smell something faintly burning.

He held his Beretta, the safety off, and crept soundlessly up the carpeted staircase. Near the top he made out a set of shoes, the dark soles sitting up like tiny tombstones. He moved higher, up another step, then two more, his weapon drawn, breathing softly and listening for movement in the apartment, but hearing only the relentless rain outside.

He reached the final stair.

The shoes belonged to a man in black clothing, lying on his back. He was fit and blond and dead. He lay spread-eagled on the carpet with his throat torn open. Mr. White bent and touched the wrist, though even in the low light he could see that the throat area and surrounding carpet were dark with blood. The wrist was cold. The man had been dead at least two hours.

It was the assassin code-named Geoff Rosamond. His was not the body Mr. White was expecting to find.

Outside, the rain continued to come down in sheets, drumming against the windows. Mr. White straightened slowly, breathing evenly. He held his weapon in front of him, a gloved finger resting on the trigger, and moved cautiously towards the nearest doorway, keeping his back to the wall. He entered the first bedroom with his gun extended, travelling swiftly, efficiently. In seconds he had moved around the unmade bed and pulled the closet doors open. The wire clothes hangers inside were bare. One lay on the floor, discarded. There were no suitcases. An en suite bathroom extended off the room, door ajar. He could see in the mirror reflection that the spotted shower curtain was pulled shut. He entered the space muzzle first and ripped the curtain back with one hand. Inside was a bare tub, inhabited only by a forgotten bottle of bath gel.

Mr. White stepped around the pool of blood surrounding the assassin's body as he made his way past the small kitchen, his feet inches from the man's outstretched left hand. He paused. Inside the kitchen the stovetop was on, one round element glowing red, causing the light burning smell that he had detected earlier. He stepped up to it and switched it off, and the red glow faded immediately. The living room was clear and the bed in the second bedroom was neatly made, the starched linen tucked firmly down. It had not been slept in.

There was no sign of Makedde Vanderwall.

Once Mr. White was sure he was alone, he switched on his torch and shone it down at the corpse. The assassin Mr. Rosamond was flat on his back, palms open. His face was bulging and red with burns. His eyes were closed over, swollen shut. His neck had been opened with a wide, round hole. He appeared to have been blinded, burned and shot through the throat. On the floor next to him was a gun, an upturned kitchen pot and what looked like food. Faint, evenly spaced grooves in the carpet at the top of the stairs indicated the passage of a bag of some sort. A wheeled suitcase. Rosamond wore black leather gloves on his outstretched hands. He would not have left prints in the apartment. Mr. White noticed smudges of blood on the gloved fingertips of the right hand, where he might have touched his throat briefly, hoping to stop the bleeding. The carpet around the man was soaked thickly with his blood. The body had not been moved. It had all happened here.

The American bent at the knees and frisked the dead man. No identification. No notes. No keys. No phone. Mr. White spotted a single spent bullet casing on the carpet, just beyond the wide spread of blood, and he pocketed it and the discarded gun, which he identified as a common Browning Buckmark .22 fitted with a TAC-65 suppressor.

He stood up again.

Blinded, burned and shot through the throat.

When White had not heard back from the man he'd sent for the job, he'd had to investigate. Considering what he'd found, he had to regard the possibility that Makedde Vanderwall had enlisted some heavy help. As he looked down on the dead assassin—a professional of some standing—he felt sure that Luther Hand had not contacted his agent, Madame Q, for the second half of the funds owed simply because he could not: because he, too, was dead. Somehow. That in itself was hard to believe, knowing the man's reputation. And now Geoff Rosamond was dead. Mr. White had misjudged the situation. The Spaniard, Javier Rafel, had given him good information. Maria Cruz was the identification Vanderwall had used to enter the country and to rent this apartment. But she was not operating alone. Either that, or she was considerably more formidable than he had imagined.

He frowned.

Rosamond had been ambushed, perhaps. The throat was a strange place to shoot someone. Why not use a knife? No, there had clearly been a struggle. He had entered quietly, as Mr. White had, then crept up the stairs. Vanderwall was taken by surprise. She threw the pot of boiling water at him, and someone came to her aid, removing Rosamond's weapon. There was a struggle. They aimed for the head or chest, but caught Rosamond in the throat and then it was over. They vacated the apartment, leaving nothing behind but the body and the gun, no doubt wiped of prints. The second bedroom was unused. She had enlisted a lover? Perhaps found the toughest man she could in Spain to protect her? Brought him with her? But to what end? What was her plan here? And how did that explain the disappearance of Luther Hand, who had taken her in France and contacted his agent to indicate the job was done, and she was dead?

The American looked at the swollen face. He squinted.

Vanderwall may have got lucky. Perhaps Rosamond simply slipped up. Somehow.

Or . . .

White would have to convince Cavanagh to take a bodyguard as a precaution. That would be difficult. Jack was stubborn, arrogant even. He did not like security of any kind, regarding it as a sign of weakness, of vulnerability. But Makedde Vanderwall was alive in Australia and on the move, thanks to Rosamond's unexpected failure. And she seemed to have help with her. Mr. White wondered if she would use her new ID again after this. Perhaps not. If he could not track her by the passport, he had to anticipate her next move using other methods. He would tap the phone of her ex-lover, Andrew Flynn. He was with the federal police now, which made that trickier. It would not be easy, but it could be done. Mr. White needed more manpower. More funds.

He looked down at the dead man.

Rosamond could not be discovered by police. When the cleaner came—which thankfully could be days with a serviced apartment such as this—she would find the apartment empty and clean of prints.

And with a large piece of carpet missing.

CHAPTER 18

Federal Agents Andy Flynn and Dana Harrison arrived at NSW police headquarters on time. Their bags were in the back of Andy's Honda parked across the street, ready for the return to Canberra. The drive from the hotel had been a quiet one. Andy had slept badly, as he often did before a presentation, but he'd kept his conquest of the minibar to a single round. The bottles were small, at least.

The lobby was quiet, and they showed their IDs and fed their things through the metal detector with the minimum of talk. Inside his head, Andy was rehashing every critical point he wanted to make about the Hempsey murder. He wanted to present the potential case against John Dayle, which was tricky, as they had no hard evidence as yet—no evidence at all, in fact. Fitting a psychological profile and having links to previous sexual assault cases hardly made someone guilty of murder. Criminal profiling was a tool of last resort in many ways, and that Andy felt Dayle was guilty was both a personal hunch and a prematurely formed professional opinion. Nothing more. He had to tread carefully.

Still, he was relieved Kelley had taken his advice and was trying to get a surveillance team in play. If someone else was hurt by Dayle, and he could have somehow prevented it, Andy would not be able to live with himself.

Don't go too hard on Dayle. Keep it in perspective.

Jimmy, who was not in the strike force, appeared around the glass door to the homicide squad office as Andy and Dana emerged from the elevator. He was wearing a slightly crumpled, ill-fitting suit, his shirt straining with his girth, and he smiled broadly as they entered. Andy was too focused on the task ahead to smile back. He simply touched Jimmy on the shoulder and nodded. Dana stepped away to give the two men space and Jimmy appeared about to say something, but when Inspector Kelley emerged from his office the words stopped on his lips. He lost a bit of the colour in his face.

"Is everything all right?" Andy said quietly as Kelley approached.

"Um, I've just got to speak with Kelley about something," Jimmy replied vaguely. "Later, maybe. Will I catch you before you go?" he asked.

"I don't think so. We're due back. The bags're in the car. But, if you—"

"No," Jimmy said and waved his hand. "I'll chat with you later," he insisted.

"Thanks for dinner the other night. Give my regards to Angie." Jimmy smiled and gave him a sudden swat on the back with enough force to wind him slightly. "Don't make it so long until the next visit."

"I promise."

"Good luck," his friend said and disappeared in the direction of the small kitchen.

Andy took a breath. He was terrible at personal conversations before he had to present a profile.

"Flynn. You ready?" Inspector Kelley appeared at his shoulder.

"Yes, sir."

"Come on. I'll begin."

Andy and Dana followed the inspector as he walked down a pristine hallway and pushed open a door with the words *Strike Force Pawn* handwritten in felt pen across it; inside, several men and one woman—Mak's friend Detective Karen Mahoney— were gathered. Many had their arms crossed. Some sipped coffee in Styrofoam cups from the café downstairs. Three empty chairs were available and Dana left Andy to sit next to Mahoney, near the back. The two women exchanged a few words, and Andy noticed Karen's red corkscrew hair bobbing up and down as she nodded at something Dana had said. He'd avoided looking at Dana all morning. She'd probably noticed. When Inspector Kelley spoke the room went silent. *He still has the same effect on his teams*, Andy thought. Kelley gave a brief rundown on the updates in the case—the autopsy report, which he distributed as he introduced Andy, and the good news that a surveillance team had been assigned and would begin their work as of noon that day.

Andy barely had time to be relieved by the news. He stood and thanked the inspector. It was his turn to show that Kelley's faith in him was not misplaced. "Good morning, everyone. As you know, my colleague Agent Harrison and I have been called in to consult on this case. We are part of the new Serial Violent Crime Profiling unit. The unit is made up of police officers with experience and training in this area, specifically dealing with crimes of this type. We are convinced the murder of Victoria Hempsey is not a stand-alone offence, but one the perp has escalated to and will repeat, given the opportunity."

The team sat and watched him, their arms folded. Andy felt a little part of him shrink back at the deafening silence.

"I've prepared a profile of our killer, and notes on how best to draw him out." He walked between the chairs, handing out stapled photocopies. "This is of course a general profile to be used as a tool in your investigation. It by no means overrides your work as detectives. It is a tool we hope will be helpful to the investigation."

He was keenly aware of Inspector Kelley sitting at the back of the room, hands folded in his lap. He'd done this so many times before, but with the pressure on the unit to perform, everything felt different. Or maybe it was something else. The changing dynamic of the attitude towards what he did. The dynamic that had been moving towards acceptance but had suddenly, dramatically shifted the other way. Or maybe it was something more emotional, something that the loss of Makedde had opened up in him. He felt hollow. Impotent. That niggling voice of dissent was inside him, telling him that his every word was worthless, a generalisation. Something any good detective would instinctively know. Since Makedde's disappearance, he had been battling a horrible sense that his career was utterly pointless. If he could not save Cassandra from the Stiletto Killer, could not save Makedde from whatever violence had torn her away, then what good was any of it?

Andy Flynn cleared his throat and continued. "The autopsy results are back, as the inspector mentioned. The results confirm that much of the disfiguration of the body, including the incisions and the removal of the toe, were done while the victim was alive, while she could feel it and he could hear and see her response. This point is key. Many of you saw the scene. Those who have not will by now have seen the crime-scene images. It was without question a very brutal crime, marked by sexual sadism. A person does not simply commit an act like this one day. He builds up to it. He fantasises about what he will do to his victim. He plans . . ."

Ms Hempsey's killer had raped and sodomised her with a knife, the autopsy had revealed. He had cut her skin. Had amputated a toe. All because he'd wanted to. Because he got off on it.

"Our perp targeted Ms. Hempsey intentionally," he continued, and the image of her beautiful smile came to mind, the photograph on the corkboard in her terrace. That smile and all the humanity and promise it seemed to hold. "Our perp was organised, in that he chose her and targeted her specifically. They may have been strangers, we do not know, but the victim in this case was not chosen randomly. Yet Ms. Hempsey had no history of crime or high-risk activity. She was not a sex worker or vagrant. Not an easy target. She was in many ways average. Normal. Our perp is motivated by a deep-seated hatred of women, all women. He does not differentiate by occupation or even age. He hates *all women*. He needs to dominate them. And the very real risk we are facing is that what we are seeing here," he pointed to a photo of Ms. Hempsey, dead, her flesh torn and abused, "is a sadistic offender who has only been emboldened by this escalation of his violence. He *liked this*. He liked doing this to her. And he will relive it any way he can until he takes another victim."

The officer closest to him swallowed.

"He was proud of what he did to Ms. Hempsey. He wanted to show this one off. Wanted the body to be found quickly. He believes he can get away with this and we have to prove him wrong." He put his paperwork down on the chair. "Now for demographics. He is a white male, aged between late twenties and early forties. Unmarried. We are looking for someone who lives alone and has difficulty forming lasting relationships or holding good employment."

Andy looked up. Kelley was gone. He hadn't even heard the door.

"And he'll be wearing a double-breasted jacket," one of the officers joked in a low voice.

Andy shut his eyes. Felt the room shift beneath his feet. It was a reference to Dr James Brussel, the respected Freudian and early pioneer of criminal profiling, who gave police a profile of the Mad Bomber in 1956. "And one more thing," he famously said, after giving the desperate officers his thoughts on what kind of man the prolific bomber would be. "When you catch him— and I have no doubt you will—he will be wearing a double- breasted suit. And it will be buttoned." When George Metesky was arrested one month later it was late in the day, and he was in his pyjamas. But he immediately got dressed, and emerged from his room in a double-breasted suit. Buttoned. That detail was the stuff of legends, especially after Brussel's memoirs. But it had since been alleged that the late psychologist had "cleaned up" the profile in his memoir to focus on the things he got right about the Mad Bomber, like his obsessive cleanliness and his double-breasted suit, and not the things he got wrong, like his age, background, employment status and the claim that he'd have a facial scar, which he did not.

Profiling had always brought controversy with it.

"I know some of you don't appreciate federal agents coming here to tell you how to do things," Andy said, looking over the faces in the room. "I know, because I used to be one of you. I served with Inspector Kelley for ten years."

Mahoney smiled.

"Detective Mahoney and my colleague Agent Harrison iden- tified a good potential suspect during our canvass on Friday and I'd like you all to take a look at him."

At that, Mahoney's eyebrows shot up. The other officers looked at her.

He held up the driver's licence image of Dayle. "This is John

Dayle. He is a strong suspect, regardless of the fact that he happens to fit the profile I described. He is a neighbour of the victim and could clearly see into her courtyard, where it is likely the victim spent a lot of time, possibly sunbaking. She had a sun lounge set up and she had tan lines, as you can see from the photographs." Though the tan lines were not the first thing one noticed when looking at the crime-scene images.

Andy thought of Victoria relaxing, reading a book. And Dayle watching her. Fantasising.

"He was questioned a few years back in some vicious, unsolved rapes in the Surry Hills and Strawberry Hills area. Mahoney has the details on those and will give you all that information in a moment. We recommended surveillance on John Dayle and a team was quickly put together. Dayle is a strong suspect and I believe he should be carefully watched while we investigate the possibility that he is Victoria Hempsey's killer. But in the meantime, it is too early to rule out other potential suspects. The DNA results should come back tomorrow, I've been told. Hopefully forensics will reveal more. Good luck with your investigation. Now I believe Detective Mahoney has a few words for you."

He handed the floor over to his ex-girlfriend's friend and, with his presentation done, he took a seat. Slowly the room faded, his heartbeat slowed. As Karen spoke, Makedde returned again to his thoughts.

Her memory, as ever, distracting him.

"I was wondering if I could speak with you for a moment. Uh, if I could."

Detective Inspector Kelley was at the door of his office, and now he paused, holding his briefcase. He took in Detective Jimmy Cassimatis's expression and contemplated something.

"Certainly, Cassimatis. Come in."

Jimmy followed Kelley into his office and closed the door. Kelley had taken a seat behind his desk and Jimmy sat down across from him, fidgeting. He'd never been in this office before. He hadn't had occasion to speak privately to Kelley since the reshuffle and move to the new headquarters.

"What's on your mind?"

It was a simple question. The answer, however, was not so simple.

"Look, I only wanted to talk to you because . . . well, because I have some concerns about Inspector Hunt." He said his superior's name softly, afraid of being overheard.

Kelley frowned. "Do you want to be transferred? I'm afraid I have everyone I need for my team."

"No, it's not about that. *Skata*," he said and immediately thought he should try not to swear so much. "Sorry. I mean, yes, I'd love to be on your team, as you know, but that's not why I'm here."

"Why are you here then?" Kelley's slate-grey gaze was so direct that for a moment Jimmy felt unable to speak. He was deeply uncomfortable with the situation he found himself in, and he was half motivated to simply walk out without saying another word.

"I don't know how to say this. I think Hunt may be . . ." He stopped. "Sir, I have been thinking about this a lot, and I think Bradley Hunt may have a vested interest of some kind in protecting . . . um . . ." He hesitated again, afraid of saying the name aloud, as if simply mentioning Jack Cavanagh might trigger something terrible.

Kelley sat perfectly still, his carriage upright, posture impeccable. His face had darkened a touch. The silence in the small office grew more tense with each breath. Jimmy's gaze flitted to the photos and diplomas on the walls. The binders. The carpet. And Kelley continued to wait.

"Cavanagh," he finally said. "Jack Cavanagh. I think he has

a vested interest. Bribes even. From Cavanagh himself or someone working for him."

Kelley leaned back in his chair. For a stretch of time he said nothing. "These are serious allegations."

"Oh, I know that, sir. I really know that."

Jimmy felt queasy. He'd eaten too much. He often did that when he was anxious.

"I value your opinion. And, you know I'm pretty honest. I'm not ambitious." He laughed. "Right?" It was obvious that he wasn't ambitious. Not ambitious enough, anyway. "Inspector, I came to you because I think you know that about me. There is no ulterior motive here."

"And you don't trust anyone else," Kelley reasoned.

Jimmy thought about that. Since Andy left for Canberra, yeah, that was probably true. A lot of them were good officers, honest and hard-working. He knew that. But he and Andy had worked together for nearly a decade. That level of trust was not so easy to replace.

"I can't pinpoint any one thing, but I feel the way he has steered the investigation of the death of Dumpster Girl . . . the uh, the Jane Doe from the dumpster . . . Well, I feel Damien Cavanagh should have been brought in for questioning and every time it was brought up he just shut it down. It was so automatic. It wasn't normal."

"Go on." Though he didn't say so, Jimmy got the sense that Kelley agreed with his appraisal.

"And then the other day he was getting ready for a date, straight from here. And I saw him open a drawer and put this fucking watch on. Sorry." He realised he'd sworn again. "He put a gold watch on and some Italian suit or something before he left the office, and I thought, whoa, he's come into some money."

A solid gold watch on a cop's salary? And it had seemed strange, him keeping it in a desk like that. It could have been that he wore the other one for work. That he didn't want his nice gold watch to get damaged. But Jimmy felt it was something else. He felt that Hunt had been hiding it.

"You think the Police Integrity Commission should be taking a look at this?"

Jimmy shook his head. "No. No, I just—please don't mention our conversation to anyone," Jimmy said. "I just wanted to tell you my concerns, that's all." Now that he'd said what he needed to, he felt it was all hopelessly insubstantial. "It's probably a mistake, only . . ."

"I understand. You just wanted to get it off your chest. Though Hunt clearly has more faith in you than you do in him. He asked for you to join his team."

"I know." Hunt either liked Jimmy, which seemed unlikely, or he wanted to keep an eye on him. Increasingly, it seemed like the latter.

Jimmy stood and bumped against a frame on one of Kelley's shelves. He turned quickly and caught it, apologising for himself. He stepped out of Kelley's office and closed the door behind him, shaken. He felt smaller. More anxious than before. The open-plan office of the homicide squad was quiet, some of the officers still in with Andy. But Inspector Hunt was there, at his desk.

The inspector looked up and the two men locked eyes.

It was only a second. But in that second, Jimmy thought Hunt knew everything.

CHAPTER 19

Makedde Vanderwall woke to the sound of voices and of keys rustling in a door. She opened heavy eyelids to see an unfamiliar off-white ceiling, unfamiliar rose-coloured bedding and an unfamiliar bedside clock, ornate and painted in faux gold leaf. The gaudy clock face came in and out of focus, and when she finally saw the hands clearly they told her it was one minute past ten.

Fuck.

A voice, louder now. "If you'll leave your shoes here, please.

The carpets are immaculate, as you'll see." A house inspection. On a public holiday. *Does no one take a bloody day off any more?*

When Mak had laid her head down she'd intended to wake much earlier, early enough to be out of there before the neighbourhood woke, let alone started showing itself to prospective buyers. She shuffled across the king-sized bed in a flash, leaped out from under the covers and stood on unsteady legs. She patted herself down, realising she'd slept in her jeans and T-shirt, even keeping the travel wallets on. Now her neck was stiff from the terrible, hard bed and there was a painful indent where one of the wallets had moved up her ribcage and pressed into her in her sleep. She was dishevelled and sweaty beneath her clothing, and she desperately wanted to use the shower.

There was obviously no time.

She slid the Glock into her waistband and scanned the room. At her feet was Luther's toolbox, now empty. She'd stored its valuable contents in the carry-on bag before passing out. Mak instinctively reached for the handle of the carry-on, then remembered to pull on her trench coat and her boots, which she managed to zip up with shaky hands. Discombobulated, achy and in all likelihood bruised from the death struggle at the apartment, she gathered her things around her and stood static in the rose-coloured bedroom. She looked from one door to the next, uncertain. It had been past midnight when she'd broken in and the jetlag and spent adrenaline had made her crazy with exhaustion.

The back way. That exit would be best.

With no time to be a better house guest, Mak kicked the filthy toolbox under the bed and left the master bedroom with the bed covers askew. She started towards the back door, pulling her carry-on bag along the carpet while the sounds of voices continued in the front half of the house. She caught her reflection in a hallway mirror. Her mascara had smudged and her dark hair had the look of an Amy Winehouse beehive at four a.m. after a storm.

"Hey, who are you?" a voice said and she spun around to find a shocked real-estate agent standing before her. Immaculate blonde coif. Beige suit. Small, painted mouth hanging open with dismay. Behind her were a couple of barefoot women and two men in socks, staring.

No point going out the back way now.

Mak shoved past them without a word, carrying her haul. She burst onto the street in a jog, the carry-on bag slamming against her hips with each stride. The real-estate agent would call the police, she felt sure.

I need a place to shower. Immediately.

Somewhere she could pay in cash for a few hours, and wouldn't need a credit card or ID. Somewhere safe.

If such a place still existed at all.

Really? On a Monday? Before noon?

The couple in the next room were making love—no, *fucking*—loudly. The female of the pair seemed to be vocalising in a bizarre, off-key version of scales, performing one of the worst fake orgasms Makedde had ever heard, the male apparently mute with concentration. Their bed banged against the wall, rattling the bathroom mirror with the vibrations of an earthquake tremor. Mak should not really have been surprised by the disruption, as she was in the sort of place where you could rent a room by the hour. The bed here, made up in gaudy satin sheets, interested Mak not at all, but the bathroom was a decent size and appointed with a full spa tub that had probably seen many erotic adventures but most importantly had jets. Perhaps the only patron to enjoy only the therapeutic benefits of its features, Mak had soaked herself in the big tub, the churning water easing her weary muscles. Now she scrubbed her face, a fluffy towel wrapped around her wet, clean hair, the air smelling pleasantly of bubble bath and cosmetics.

There was a final, masculine cry and the mirror stopped vibrating.

Makedde tried not to imagine the awkward post-coital scene next door as she skilfully applied a mask of moisturiser and makeup, the small, vain tasks that helped her feel more like a woman and less like a fox on the run. Groomed and recovered from her rude awakening, Mak stepped out into an alley behind Victoria Street, Kings Cross, at two o'clock in the afternoon, the bright autumn sun something of a shock after her windowless, boudoir-style hourly accommodations. Despite being raised by a detective inspector and despite being introduced to death, aged twelve, on a trip to the morgue with her father, Mak had never anticipated needing to learn about the criminal way of life. But here she was. And once you accepted in real terms that there were human beings out there willing to end your life solely for financial gain, everything changed. It was a significant shift to a different, more brutal world. Her blinkers were off. Part of her was sad about that. Another part of her was too far past it to feel the loss of innocence.

Javier Rafel ratted me out.

She had suspected it before, but now she was absolutely certain that Rafel had found out about the price on her head and sold her out to the Cavanaghs. All things considered, it was miraculous she'd got this far. After she had bought her ticket they'd had a thirty-hour jump on her while she was in the air. It was lucky someone hadn't nabbed her walking out of the airport. She would make a beeline for Canberra, she decided. The laptop was the key. The laptop had to get to Andy Flynn. She couldn't trust a courier. She couldn't trust anyone else.

And she had to remain off the police radar somehow . . . Mak walked to a second-hand clothing store on William Street, only a few blocks away, hiding behind a pair of large, dark sunglasses. She searched with no pleasure through itchy 1970s vintage sweaters and stiff polyester dresses, ultimately putting money down for an unattractive multicoloured knit beanie and poncho, and a backpack made of hemp, none of which she would have worn in her previous life even if paid. She assembled herself in the shop and emerged fifteen minutes later looking exactly like one of the local, pot-smoking backpackers. At a pharmacy next door she bought hair bleach and a henna dye, unable to decide which way to go, and as a bonus was delighted to find an array of non-prescription contact lenses. They seemed to cater to the flamboyant party crowd—red "Dracula" pupils, snake eyes and washed-out "Zombie" eyes were all options—but they also sold pairs in more natural colours. She bought some warm brown lenses and a pair of pale blue ones.

Next, she needed access to the internet. She wandered up the street, head down, hair hidden away beneath the ugly beanie, aware of the many CCTV cameras and police in the area, and slowed as she passed a shop selling phone cards and iPhones. An iPhone with its internet capabilities and maps would be handy. Sadly, she required at least one form of ID to purchase a SIM card and she couldn't risk it as Ms. Cruz, lest the GPS give away her location to the Cavanaghs like an electronic beacon.

GPS could be handy, though. Maybe handy in other ways.

It gave her an idea.

She used an internet café at the back of a convenience store on Macleay Street; though the computer looked about ten years old it worked fine, and two dollars and a few minutes later her simple search for "spy" shops brought her listings across Australia, with one store showing in a large mall only a short taxi ride away. Soon she was walking through precisely the kind of place she abhorred—a shopping centre, brimming with far too many near identical franchises peddling garments made at cut-rate cost in China and India, to be purchased by bored consumers dragging shopping bags and pushing prams on idle afternoons. This afternoon it was packed with customers of all kinds, none of whom paid her the slightest interest under her ratty hat. At a hardware store she bought flat-head and Phillips screwdrivers, a hammer, some wire cutters and insulated gloves, and then she stood, hemp backpack weighing heavily, outside the place that advertised as a "Spy Shop."

Typically, the commercial spy shop was not for real spies any more than T-shirts with the words UNDERCOVER FBI were meant for real agents. The store had large displays showing off the latest expensive surveillance equipment and locking devices, aimed at wealthy homeowners wanting to protect their cars and stereo equipment. But what Mak wanted would be much less costly. She walked in, attracting the attention of a young man in an orange polo-shirt uniform. He spun around and she smiled.

"I need a TrackALL high-quality GPS locating system with drop feature," she told him. His eyes widened slightly. "My grandmother is getting very frail and she . . . well, sometimes she does wander," she added.

He nodded and put his hands on his hips. "Yup, we do have those. Let me just check the stock in back."

A few minutes later he returned with a sealed box. "This one has a fall detector, so if she falls over you will know. It's on sale for two-ninety-nine and comes with a lithium battery pack."

She looked at the box and pressed her lips to a tight line. "So can I track it on my iPhone?"

"Definitely."

She'd have to get one after all, she decided. "Is it easy to set up?"

He nodded. "Yeah. You tech savvy?"

"Getting there," she said. "I'm sure it will be fine. I'll take two . . . just for good measure. Thank you so much. You've been very helpful." She handed over Luther's cash.

After what had been a productive start to her afternoon, it took Mak fifty excruciating minutes in the sprawling shopping complex to find the woman she was looking for; and when she finally saw her, her heart lifted.

There you are . . .

It was a Caucasian woman about Mak's own age, shopping alone. Chocolate-brown leather handbag and matching sandals. Diamond earrings, real. Self-employed and doing well, Mak guessed. She was perhaps five foot ten inches tall and her hair was long and dark, reddish brown. Makedde was seated on a bench with her increasingly heavy backpack, sipping a juice, when the woman walked by. She watched her from under her beanie and when she was a few paces ahead Mak got up, binned the juice and followed.

The complex was truly sprawling, and the woman walked at a leisurely pace through one whole level, weaving through the crowds and eventually turning into a mid-range dress shop at the end. After a beat Mak walked in behind her. A middle-aged shop assistant with dyed blonde hair and immaculate makeup clocked her and then looked away, disinterested. She didn't have that moneyed look about her. Not with her hemp and her second-hand knits. An old INXS song blared from the speakers as Mak pretended to peruse the tasteful but bland stock on offer.

"Do you have this in a ten?" the woman asked, holding up an inoffensive black dress.

"I'll check," the shop assistant answered in a flat tone, and ducked into the back. A few minutes later she returned with the dress.

Mak took a collared white shirt off a rack and examined it as the two women walked to the change rooms at the back. "Let me know if you need another size," Mak overheard the shop assistant say, and there was the click of a locking mechanism on a change-room door.

Makedde walked to the back, holding the shirt and passing a large set of floor-to-ceiling triptych mirrors. The change area was made up of six small melamine cubicles, with doors barely above Mak's shoulder height, three on each side. The tall woman was installed at the middle one against the back wall and Mak could see her dark head bent forwards as she went about the process of getting changed into the black dress she'd chosen. For her part Mak held up the shirt on its plastic hanger and gestured to the shop assistant wordlessly as she slipped herself into the neighbouring cubicle and closed the door behind her.

"Let me know if you need anything else," the assistant said mildly through the door, and walked away.

The space was perhaps less than a metre wide and the partitions did not reach the floor. Mak could see the woman's sandals, discarded, on the carpet inside her change room, one shoe flipped upside down to show its leather sole. She hung the white shirt on a peg and sat down on a small chair in the corner of her cubicle, folding her legs one over the other and clearing her mind. After perhaps two minutes she heard the change-room door next to her open as the tall woman made for the viewing mirrors.

Here we go.

Mak got on her hands and knees in the cubicle. She spotted a strap from the woman's chocolate leather handbag falling out from under a discarded pile of clothes on the chair on the far side of the adjoining fitting room.

"I don't know. Do you think it's too short?" came the woman's voice.

"You look great. It really suits you."

Mak dropped fully to the carpet, shuffled across on her back and sat up in the woman's cubicle. She pulled the handbag out and opened the zipper.

"But from the back? You don't think it shows too much?"

"Oh no. Not at all. Would you like to try the twelve?" the sales assistant said, giving her the sell.

Mak dug her hand inside. Mobile phone. Keys. Makeup.

Wallet. She pulled the wallet out and opened it. Petra Blackman. Thirty-two years old. *Perfect.* Mak grabbed the driver's licence and considered the woman's three credit cards. She took the Visa and filled the newly empty card slot with a Myer One card.

"Maybe this will be better . . ." the woman said.

Mak heard footsteps. *Fuck, fuck, fuck* . . . She rezippered the handbag, heart hammering, and replaced it on the chair. She draped the clothing back over it and in seconds she was back under the divide and in her own cubicle. The door clicked open and closed again. A dress fell to the carpet as the woman stepped into another option.

Mak stood and rearranged herself. Her face was flushed. She slid the driver's licence and credit card into her back pocket. Hopefully she had covered the theft well enough. The more time she had before the woman reported the cards missing, the better.

She walked out of the cubicle carrying the shirt.

"Aww, we didn't get to see how you looked in that. How did you go?" the sales assistant asked, unconvincingly.

"I'll think on it," Mak replied and smiled.

Oh, it is fun to be at the mall.

Jack Cavanagh stared out of the clear fourteenth-floor window of his city office, unseeing. He was seated beneath his coveted Sidney Nolan painting and his designer chandelier, gripped with ennui and a crushing sense of impotence. Before him, cognac-soaked ice cubes melted at the base of a crystal tumbler. Outside, his future was unfolding without him. He could only sit and wait.

He'd just got off the phone with Mr. White.

The operation had been unsuccessful, he was told. Mr. White never said much by phone, but it was clear that he believed Makedde Vanderwall was still in Australia, and that she was a potential threat. And now he wanted Jack to consider a personal security guard, just until she was removed as a threat.

Jack squinted.

He wondered about her. Who was this ordinary woman who had managed to single-handedly disrupt his successful business, had managed to single-handedly break the bonds of his family? Where had she come from? Where was she now? In Sydney? Nearby? What was her aim in returning to Australia?

And because of her—an ex-model, a low-level private investigator and out-of-work psychologist—The American wanted Jack to take on a personal bodyguard for the first time? He wanted Jack Cavanagh to be tailed around by some armed man, a man he would need to pay handsomely to babysit him?

It was an outrageous idea. Outrageous.

"Just think about it," Robert White had said.

Just think about it.

How had things got so bad? he wondered. When had the slide started? With the lowlife who'd tried to blackmail Jack with the video of Damien, or before then?

His mobile phone buzzed.

Jack blinked and rolled back in his chair to look at the number, his mind spinning through the possibilities. Would it be The American again? Could he have news already? A breakthrough? Or had his son, Damien, finally decided to call? He knew he was in Australia now. The American had confirmed his return.

Goldsworthy.

Jack sat up and straightened his shirt cuffs. The two men had not spoken since their exchange on the *Rosebud*. He licked his lips.

Jack looked at his watch, saw that it was already late afternoon, nearly time to head home. He picked up his phone.

"Cameron, how are you?" he said casually, his eyes fixed on the darkening cityscape outside his window.

"I'm good, Jack." There was a pause. The line wasn't particularly good. He was calling from his mobile phone and, judging from the time of day, he was still in Australia. "Look, my secretary heard from your VP twice last week. I can't do business with you, Jack," Cameron said flatly.

I can't.

Do business. With you.

Jack swallowed.

So that was it. He should not have been surprised, not after their tense exchange on the *Rosebud*. Yet Jack could not help but see this plain rejection as a new phase of his personal demise. Cameron Goldsworthy, previously a powerful ally, had given up any pretence of goodwill. If Jack was to get his business—his life—back on track, he would need to turn things around considerably.

"I'll tell him to stop contacting you," Jack Cavanagh responded in a neutral voice.

"I'd appreciate that. Take care," Cameron said coolly and hung up.

Jack found himself holding the mobile to his ear, the phone dead. He took a breath. There was a curious sting behind his eyes, but no tears came. He was numb. His index finger hooked itself around the handle of his top drawer and opened it. Inside was a packet of Cipramil—the antidepressants he refused to start taking again. And a small, silver-plated handgun.

He considered both for a moment, and closed the drawer again.

As sunset hit the neon-lit roads of Kings Cross, it was time for Mak to leave the little room she had rented. She stepped onto Victoria Street in sleek black, her newly dyed reddish-brown hair tucked under her hoodie, the trench coat tied tight around her slim waist. It was time to hit the road. All she needed now was something to hit the road with.

There were, naturally enough, a number of options to choose from.

Mak prowled Victoria Street at the Potts Point end for an old car. Not *too* old, but a model built before the early to mid-nineties, when security systems had become more sophisticated. Many cars were too newly built, and others had tiny, flashing alarm or demobiliser lights to ward her off, but because of the area, which was popular with backpackers and drifters, there were a lot of third- and fourth-hand cars and campervans parked on the street, some of which had been used by consecutive backpackers each season. Mak didn't need anything terribly high tech and fast, but she didn't want a Volkswagen van either. Too slow. Too obvious. She chose an old Holden parked at the furthest, least frequented end of the street, in part, she supposed, because it reminded her vaguely of Bogey's beautiful old car. This one wasn't restored, however. Rust had begun eating away at the blue paint over the fenders and around the headlights.

Mak put her bags on the pavement and bumped hard against the side of the car with her hip. No alarm. She looked around and, finding herself unobserved, she took the wire hanger from her room, untwisted the end and pushed the hook down between the glass window and the door. On her second try, she pulled the locking mechanism upwards, and the metal button popped up. She tossed the mangled hanger inside along with her carry-on bag and loaded backpack, closed the door and took a breath.

Right.

She took the flat-head screwdriver out of her backpack and considered it for a moment before pushing it hard into the ignition where the key should go. She used the hammer to shove it into place, ruining the old ignition housing in the process. But then, she wasn't stealing a car to be considerate.

Damn, I hope this works.

She turned the screwdriver and heard the ignition turn over. A smile spread across her face. There was no need for the gloves and wire cutters.

Not bad, she thought as she strapped herself in. *Not bad.*

She pulled out onto the road and headed for Canberra, the GPS on her new iPhone showing the way.

CHAPTER 20

Jack Cavanagh drove his emerald-green Jaguar through the gates of his waterfront mansion in Point Piper, past the high stone walls and down the circular drive, barely noticing his well-tended gardens, which were picked clean of falling leaves, or the rows of tortured willows standing like emaciated sentries, twisted on their feet and fast becoming bare in anticipation of the winter ahead.

The tall gates closed behind him and the broad garage opened, revealing two more gleaming vehicles. He pulled in smoothly between his four-wheel-drive BMW and red Enzo Ferrari, feeling dispirited and anxious. Nonetheless, he was relieved to be within his own grounds. His conversations with The American and with Cameron Goldsworthy had rattled him.

He switched off the ignition and the garage lights flickered on with a hum as he stepped out, shut the Jag and walked towards the interior door of his home, his face slack, shoulders hunched. The cleaner, Rosie, had left him some food. He hadn't tried it yet, but it was likely good. If it wasn't, he could order in. He didn't feel like going out. He didn't think he could face anyone so soon after the bad news.

Just think about it.

Jack had hired security for parties, as most people of standing did, but a personal bodyguard? Someone to follow him around for his protection? Since The American had suggested it, the possibility had vexed him. *No.* For Beverley, perhaps, but not for him. He refused to be scared by this woman, Makedde Vanderwall. It was a ridiculous notion and besides, he refused to change his lifestyle for her. It would mean she'd stolen something vital from him beyond what she had already achieved by chipping away relentlessly at his reputation.

No.

If that woman had indeed come to Australia, she had signed her own death warrant. That was all.

Jack Cavanagh pressed a fist against a button on the wall of the garage, and the roller door began to close, humming as the gears clicked over. Slowly the gardens, the tortured willows, the evening light disappeared from view. He opened the door to his house, stepped into the hall and waited for the low wail of the alarm, giving him twenty seconds to type in the security code.

As long as they get to her before she causes any more trouble, that's the main thing, he decided. He'd already come to terms with the fact that Vanderwall needed to die, that she wouldn't have it any other way. It was an ugly fact, but life was ugly sometimes. They just needed to finish what had been started. They needed to finish her and be done with it. The longer it went on, the messier it became—there was no reason for it to stretch on any longer. She was just one woman. It should not be so hard. Soon it would be done and then Jack could move on.

He could get on with turning things around. Jack Cavanagh had faced challenges before. Plenty of them. His father had built his empire up piece by piece, rising from lowly janitor to powerful businessman. The Cavanaghs were resilient men. He'd acquired that quality from his father, that determination. This was just a new kind of challenge: that was all.

In time, Richard Staples's unfortunate piece in the *Tribune* would be forgotten. He need only replace all that unflattering speculation with something solid, something positive. A high-profile donation, perhaps? *Philanthropy, yes.* Didn't Beverley have some children's hospital she wanted to help out? Or was it animals? Jack couldn't recall. The important thing was that no one had any proof of his wrongdoing. That was clear enough in Staples's article. It was a patchwork of rumours, nothing more. There was nothing that could be pinned on him: he'd made sure of that, paid handsomely for that.

And that woman, Vanderwall, wasn't even officially in the country: she'd supposedly arrived under a false identity. So she had appeared clandestinely in Australia and she could disappear clandestinely as well. Mr. White would take care of it. He always did. He'd been reliable since their very first dealings in the Middle East. And then once it was done, Beverley would come back and they would make a sizeable donation to the right cause, and they would be seen with the right people again and he could turn it all around . . .

Odd.

The sound of the alarm had not come, Jack realised. He arrived at the keypad only to discover the system was not engaged. He squinted at the screen, puzzled. He was sure he'd put it on. He always did.

Someone is in the house.

At this realisation, an electric shiver shot up the back of his neck. For one strange moment, Jack found himself frozen with fear—a sensation most unfamiliar—standing in his basement hallway with his mouth gaping open and his mobile phone gripped in one hand like a weapon.

The gun.

Jack had only ever used it once, at his sixtieth birthday party, firing it into the sky from the lawn down behind the house. It was a gift from a former police commissioner, purchased on a trip to Texas and personally engraved with Jack's name. A collector's item. Jack wasn't even sure it was still registered, wasn't sure where the bullets were. He'd displayed it in his office at one time, in a glass case. Eventually he'd put it in the drawer, a few years after the commissioner had passed on. Jack had never considered bringing the gun home or carrying it with him for any reason. Yet he'd found himself gazing at the thing not an hour earlier, as if reconsidering.

Outrageous. This is damned outrageous.

Jack had allowed the problem of Vanderwall to get to him. He'd forgotten the alarm: that was all. Or the gardener was in. Or the cleaner. Though he'd given them the day off. But that had to be it. It made Jack angry now—angry to think that all this mess was seeping further into his life, invading his thoughts, even at home, in his personal space. He shook off the feeling of fear, replacing it with a seething bitterness. Still, as he walked down the hallway of his hard-won, luxurious home, and up the staircase past his artworks and the expensive vases filled with fresh flowers, his heart pounded dangerously in his chest. And he thought about The American's words.

A personal bodyguard. Just think about it.

"Rosie?" Jack called out. "Rosie, is that you?"

Yes, it had to be the cleaner. She'd come back to finish something. That was all. Upstairs, he sensed the shift in atmosphere. The house had been lonely since Beverley's departure. But tonight something had changed. He came around the corner, into the high-ceilinged living room.

Someone is there. Someone . . .

"Hello, Father."

His son was reclining on the lounge, silhouetted by a flat horizon of water slowly turning black with the fading sunset.

Jack closed his eyes and put his hand to his chest. "Damien." He flicked on the Terzani Hugo floor light next to him and the living room was illuminated in a soft glow, the tall lamp's spindly metal legs throwing peculiar shadows up the wall. Jack had not seen his only child in weeks, and he clapped eyes on the familiar features with a mixture of intense relief and horror. He began to smile, to open his arms, but faltered. Makedde Vanderwall was in town. And Damien was, too. His son's presence might attract unwanted media attention. This was not a good time for any kind of attention.

Jack swallowed. "You're back. That's . . . good."

Damien seemed not to notice his father's conflicting emotions. He was sprawled out barefoot on the black leather lounge wearing white linen shorts and a trendy V-neck T-shirt and cardigan. In his right hand he held a tumbler filled with some deep amber liquor poured over ice. His dark hair was styled in a new way, long at the front and swept to one side. He looked tanned and fit. Jack remembered being like that—young and strong. That body could almost have been his own, once. Though Jack had never been carefree. He'd never considered himself above responsibility the way his son did.

"Where's Mother?" Damien asked, swirling the cubes in the glass.

"She's in Europe." He raised a brow.

"On holiday," Jack explained tersely. "I ran out of money."

Jack felt himself harden. *Ah. So that is your reason for returning*, he thought. Once again, he wished he and Beverley had been able to have a second child. A boy, to take over from

Jack. A girl even. Any alternative to this young man, who was now looking at his nails and appearing to pout.

"Vanderwall is here," Jack warned. "In Australia."

"Here? She's alive?" Damien said, sitting up suddenly, eyes ablaze.

Jack nodded solemnly.

"Well, for fuck's sake, Father, have her killed already. What's taking so long?"

The words, said aloud, felt like a punch in the guts. For a moment Jack's head filled with a fog of anger and defensiveness, red and vicious. He went wrong. He went so wrong with Damien. And he didn't know how it happened.

"You have no idea what I've had to do for you. You have no idea how much money—"

But clearly Damien did know what his father had done. He'd tried to have Mak killed. Unsuccessfully. He'd already docked his son's trust fund by two million dollars as a form of punishment. The American's services did not come cheaply.

"I don't want to hear another word out of you. You can stay out at the beach house," Jack said. "And keep a low profile, will you? Don't get yourself paparazzied. No parties."

From the look on his son's face, Jack knew he might as well have told him to eat his Brussels sprouts.

"*No parties*," Jack said firmly. "I mean it."

Parties were what had started this whole mess. One party in particular, where a girl—a fourteen-or fifteen-year-old girl who had no business being in the country—had died of an overdose in this very house. And though Damien denied it, Jack knew his son had had sex with her first. Had paid for that.

It was a mess.

An expensive mess.

"And I'll be getting a bodyguard . . . for you," Jack found himself saying.

Damien crossed his arms. "A *what*?"

"You heard me."

"I don't want a babysitter. Christ."

Jack ignored him. "You'll be driven out to Palm Beach tomorrow. You can stay there until this blows over."

"*Welcome home, son*," Damien muttered sarcastically under his breath. He curled his bare feet up under him and turned to look out at the water.

With nothing further to say, Jack left his thirty-year-old son on the lounge, sulking like a teenager. He walked through to the kitchen, pulled the fridge door open and examined the meal from the cleaner, Rosie, sealed under cling wrap. It was a roast, with all the trimmings. He pulled it out, heated it in the microwave and ate it in his room.

CHAPTER 21

The woman wore blood-red stiletto shoes in a shiny patent leather, the heels as sharp as needles. She was just his type— petite and curvy, with ample breasts disguised beneath a cowl- neck minidress and little dimples above her tanned knees. She had kinky hair in a mousy brown, and large, sad eyes that seemed to search for him through the slow, late-night crowd. He'd spotted her through the large window, even before she set foot in the White Cockatoo. He'd known she would come to him.

The ones in stilettos were asking for it. And the ones in the red stilettos?

They were desperate for it.

The woman looked around with an air of uncertainty, standing between the small circular tables and attracting a couple of looks. He watched her reflection in the mirror behind the bar, locked on to her signal, her vulnerability, her presence. He felt stronger with her proximity, felt like the predator he longed to be, the predator he was fast becoming after Victoria. He'd claimed one prize and he would claim another to prove to himself that he could, to prove to himself that he was as powerful as those he admired, to prove it to the world. He kept his cap tilted down, trying not to beam with the joy of seeing the lovely, lonely, perfect woman, drawn to him as if by some dark magic. Taking careful sips of Victoria Bitter, he watched her every move in the reflection between the bottles.

The woman neared him, crossing the room. She arrived just next to him and leaned forwards, flicking her hair to one side and sliding a small leather handbag onto the bar, one brown, lightly freckled forearm only inches from his wrist. His pulse jumped.

"Um . . . bartender?" she said in a voice that was timid and immediately washed away by music coming through the speakers nearby.

But *he* heard her. He heard *everything* she was saying. She had an Australian accent, but she wasn't local. He would already have noticed her if she was.

"Um, can I have a Heineken, please?" the woman said, trying again, seemingly unaware that she was being closely watched by the very man who could give her what she needed. It was her subconscious that had brought her there. Her subconscious. It was like that with all of them. It had been like that with Victoria, who'd shown herself to him again and again until he finally took her, just as she'd silently begged him to, with her high shoes and her coyly averted eyes and her brazen body. Displayed.

He shut his eyes and inhaled. He smelled cigarettes on her.

He smelled her sex.

The music changed, and he took another sip of his beer and placed it back on the bar. The bartender was filling a mug for the woman now. A large mug. It would be easy to drop a pill into it. Just a single white pill and by the end of that drink he would have her and she would get what she was asking for. He reached into his pocket.

"Hey!"

Someone was between them now, interfering. He drew a sharp breath and stayed hunched over his drink, watching in the reflection as everything around him shifted. It was a blonde woman. She was fat and sweaty, and she tapped his woman's shoulder with a manicured hand and slid in next to her, standing with her back to him; he seethed quietly, his view obliterated.

He kept his head down, breathing quickly. In his pants pocket, he unclenched his hand, let go of the little pill.

"Hey, what took you so long?" the woman in the red shoes said and embraced the blonde interloper as he sat frozen on his stool, looking at his beer and fighting violent thoughts.

"One more, please. Bartender?" the woman in the red shoes ordered, before she and her disgusting friend began an animated discussion about a band he had not heard of and would never see. He groaned—a primal sound so animal and low that no one would hear it. He removed his leather wallet, his mouth tight with anger. He found some bills, put his crumpled money on the bar and vacated his favourite stool to slide away into the night shadows. He would find her, he felt certain. He would find her.

Another night.

The man was slim and white and unremarkable, and he was walking around slowly under the harsh, colourless fluorescent lights of a convenience store; the place was lit up like a TV set in the darkness of Surry Hills. An actor in the most boring play ever conceived, he walked from aisle to aisle, listlessly, wearing camouflage pants, sneakers and a T-shirt, his every non-action artificially lit. His face was slack and he held something red in his hand. Occasionally, he scratched himself.

Senior Constable Perkins loitered outside, watching.

The man in the overlit convenience store browsed a magazine

rack near the register. He picked up the *Daily Telegraph*. Put it down. He picked up the *Tribune*, flicked through a few pages. Put it down. He picked up a *ZOO* magazine, considered the heavily endowed creature on the front—her red string bikini, her platinum hair—and put it down. Finally, he turned left and walked with agonising slowness to a humming fridge full of overpriced water and soft drinks and milk. He opened it. Pulled out a carton. Closed the door again. He shuffled towards the counter. Paused. Picked a can of soup off a shelf. Turned it over in his hands. Put it back.

Christ.

Perkins rubbed his neck.

The man abandoned the can of soup and brought his carton of milk to the counter. He fished around in his pocket. He pointed at something on the rack below the counter, spoke in a voice too low for Perkins to make out.

The man behind the counter was a young Sikh. He wore a white turban and a look of intense boredom. "It says right on it," he protested in loud, accented English and threw up his palms.

The man picked up a packet of gum and dropped it on the counter next to the milk. The Sikh rang it up on the till and the man took a while to count out his change, one coin at a time.

Perkins moved across the street, away from the store. He stopped outside a busy Japanese restaurant and watched the man exit the shop and cross the street at the zebra crossing, toting his white plastic bag. He'd bought a carton of milk and a packet of gum. Perkins would note it all down—the time, the place, the purchases.

He pulled out his phone. Dialled. "Headed your way," Perkins said. He leaned a shoulder against the side of the grubby building and flicked a spent cigarette on the ground, crushed it with his heel.

"He's still alone?" the sergeant asked down the line.

"Alone," Perkins confirmed, watching the man's back as he walked, the swinging plastic bag shifting back and forth.

If the sergeant was disappointed, he didn't let on. "Hold your post," was all he said and hung up. Perkins pocketed his phone and pulled out his Benson & Hedges. He lit another cigarette and took a long, slow drag. Next to him, a man opened the door for an attractive woman, the chatter of the restaurant spilling onto the street. The woman stepped onto the street right next to him, laughing at something her companion had said. She threw an arm around his neck and leaned in for a kiss, the back of her jacket riding up to reveal a line of flesh across her hips.

Senior Constable Perkins squinted at their embrace, took another drag and looked away.

He was part of a six-person surveillance team watching the every move of one John Allan Dayle, a person of interest in a recent homicide. Perkins had been on a number of major operations and though this was his first day on this particular gig, thus far, he was not impressed. Firstly, the guy looked pretty damn ordinary. He did not look like a serial killer.

Secondly, his house was in a very difficult location for surveillance from a vehicle because an unfamiliar car would stand out on Davoren Lane like dog's balls on a bird. They didn't have a pole camera installed, weren't sure when they'd get one, and until STIB, the Special Technical Investigations Branch, got a plant inside—which could take weeks knowing their backlog and all the bullshit with the warrants—it would mean a hell of a lot of standing around for Perkins and the rest of the team. Perkins didn't like it. The team leader, his sergeant, had hoped a neighbour would assist by letting the team set up in a room of their house, but so far they'd been knocked back. Fucking Surry Hills.

But the third and most important reason Perkins did not like this new job was simple. It was because of the feds. It was the feds who had decided on this guy, Dayle, he'd heard. A couple of federal agents from Canberra had been called in to consult on the case. "Profilers." They had fingered this Dayle guy, recommended this surveillance be done.

Perkins knew a thing or two about profiling.

He'd read the latest research debunking so-called "behavioural science" as nonsense. *Science. Fuck me.* He'd seen Malcolm Gladwell's piece in *The New Yorker* and he didn't have much time for profiler voodoo bullshit. These people weren't cops. They hadn't done a day of police work in their lives. They didn't know shit, as far as he was concerned.

Perkins finished his cigarette and flicked it on the ground.

Fucking profilers.

CHAPTER 22

The Edmund Barton building consumed a full Barton city block, framed by flat tracts of asphalt car park on two sides, hemmed in by evenly spaced government regulation trees. The building's early 1970s Seidler architecture was imposing and strange. A bunker for an alien race.

Makedde drifted past in her stolen Holden, taking in the familiar architecture of the Australian Federal Police Canberra headquarters. The bunker-like shell had vehicular access points barred by large, cylindrical posts which slid silently into the ground for all those with clearance to pass, tunnelling down into hidden subterranean parking chambers. The grid of roads surrounding the building was dotted with red AFP cars. Metal detectors were visible through the glass of the main entrance. Surveillance cameras were mounted everywhere. The open courtyard was incongruous: though it had been designed for public access, the outdoor area had been fairly unwelcoming since the AFP moved in. It possessed all the sense of freedom of a prison exercise yard, despite the presence of a small eating area with blue café umbrellas, currently closed. Makedde had sipped coffee there on occasion, under the gaze of the six storeys of interior windows, when she and

Andy had first moved to Canberra together. He'd wanted to show her off. At first.

Mak knew she was being filmed, but she cared very little. She doubted anyone would recognise her or bother to check the tape and so notice the plates of a stolen car. She was a dead girl from Canada. A nonentity. The feds had better things to do. Like nail Jack Cavanagh and his corrupt colleagues. She'd come here on emotional instinct. It was well after dark, but she half expected to see his red Honda sitting outside. He'd pulled a lot of night shifts towards the end of their relationship. She doubted that had changed. But no, his car could not be seen.

Andy.

Soon Mak was parked, suburbs away, walking through the pleasant Canberra night air on quiet sneakers. She approached the familiar house, feeling almost playful. It was a three-bedroom dwelling, and she knew the layout intimately—the exits, the floor plan and what she would likely find inside. She recognised the car out the front and as she walked past it she dipped in one smooth movement, attaching the magnetic tracking device to its underside.

Andy Flynn woke with a start. He tensed and sat up. Something had woken him. A noise? As his eyes adjusted, he saw a dark figure standing in his bedroom.

Shit. Where is my sidearm?

Andy leaped out from beneath the sheets and rolled to the floor beside his bed, crouching out of view and out of firing range of the intruder. There was a baseball bat under the bed some-where . . .

Where the FUCK did I put my sidearm?

"Andy." The voice was familiar.

The intruder stepped forwards, revealing herself to be a tall woman with a face crowned by darkness. *That face.* He couldn't believe what he was seeing.

He reached up and turned on the bedside lamp. A small, dim pool of light illuminated the room.

It is *her.*

Mak was standing near the foot of his bed—a bed they'd bought together. She was dressed in head-to-toe black, and she was wearing a hood. No, it was a wig, a dark wig. She looked quite changed, but it was unmistakeably her. As the reality set in, he found he could say nothing for almost a minute. A swell of emotion rose in his throat. He was relieved, over-joyed, confused, angry. He and Mak had tried living together here, a kind of last-ditch effort to make it work after five years of on-and-off dating. She'd moved her life to Canberra in a gesture of commitment after he landed the job of setting up the national profiling unit. But of course the new setting hadn't fixed their old problems. He'd screwed it up. Of course. When had he not screwed it up? He'd had walls up. He'd had issues. He'd had steam to blow off. This *was* her, wasn't it? This wasn't a dream? A nightmare? But if he wasn't dreaming this, then what the hell was Makedde Vanderwall doing here, in his bedroom in the middle of the night, unannounced, months after leaving him?

"You won't be needing my baseball bat," she said calmly.

It was already in his hands. A reflex. He put the bat down on the carpet at his feet and stood up to his full height. He'd been sleeping naked, he now remembered, and in the low light he thought he detected a slight grin on the face of his intruder. The lamp would have him backlit, right at crotch level. Andy took a step towards her and she threw something at him. A pair of his jeans. He held them up in front of himself with one hand. "I guess we aren't on those kinds of terms any more," he said and laughed, surprising himself. The grin remained on the woman's face for a moment, and then faded.

He pulled his jeans on slowly and did up the buttons. This was perhaps the first time Mak had helped him get dressed. "It's good to see you." An understatement. "I thought . . ." He trailed off, unwilling to describe his greatest fear aloud.

I thought you were dead.

He'd lost count of how many messages he'd left for her. "Why didn't you call me back?" he asked. "Why didn't you leave me some kind of sign? Anything?"

"Because I'm dead." She spoke slowly. The grin was nowhere to be found.

What?

She seemed vastly different from his memory of her, yet this *was* Mak. There was no broad, dazzling smile. No rush of warmth or even anger. She looked uncharacteristically pale beneath the dark hair. He didn't like the changes he saw. Nevertheless, she was still devastatingly beautiful to him. His body was already responding, despite himself. Hers was a face that had filled his thoughts and desires for years and that was not something you could just switch off. Especially now, when he was so thoroughly unprepared for her presence.

"You won't be needing this." She placed his Glock gently on the end of the bed. "I didn't want you waking up and blowing my head off."

My sidearm.

He felt his cheeks grow hot. Thank God it was only her and not some real intruder. Was he losing his touch so badly that Mak of all people could come into the house and take his gun without waking him?

"You kept your key."

She laughed, but the sound had no mirth. "I don't even have

Loulou's keys." The friend she'd stayed with in Sydney when she'd left him. "I don't have anything any more."

"Why?" he finally asked. "What happened over there?"

She walked around the bed and sat on the edge. Her shoulders slumped and he noticed she had something slung over her middle: a slim black case. "I am sorry to arrive like this, but I had to talk to you in person," she said.

"You couldn't have warned me? Let me know you are all right?" He frowned and sat next to her in the bedroom that had once been theirs.

"No," she replied flatly.

They sat together for a moment, not quite touching. "You're the only person I trust—as it turns out," she confessed softly, sounding a little surprised at that truth.

The long fingers of her left hand strayed to his, and he instinctively placed his hand over hers. It felt cool under his fingertips as he traced her knuckles, feeling her smooth skin, the familiarity of a hand he'd held so many times, a hand he'd once wanted to put a ring on. Though she was fully dressed, he was clothed only in his jeans, and with her unexpected proximity and the intimacy of the moment, he felt an urge to kiss her and pull her down onto the bed with him.

He shook his head. "Jesus, Mak, what is this? Where have you been? Paris this whole time? What happened?"

"The Cavanaghs happened."

"Tell me."

For a stretch of time he sat beside her, stunned into silence, holding her hand and listening. He listened to how she'd found Adam Hart in Paris, and sent him back to his worried mother in Australia, seeing him off at the airport. She'd planned to holiday in Paris for a while—that part pained him somewhat because seeing Paris was something he'd always wanted to do with her, but he did not interrupt. And then she told him what had happened with Luther Hand, the man who abducted her. She spoke so steadily, so evenly, it shocked him. It was as if she had practised talking about these horrible things, like she'd read them in a book and it had not really happened to her at all. But when she got to the part about the fire, she shuddered and her words stopped abruptly.

Andy held her hand speechlessly as she stared off towards the dark window. He wondered what she was seeing.

He knew not to push for more information. It was best to address the present for now. "You have to tell your father you are alive. This is killing him. He's called me every week since you went missing," he urged her.

"*Dad.*" Tears sprang from her eyes, but she stood up and wiped them away quickly. "I know. Trust me, I know. It's awful. But I can't contact him. You know how connected he is. The moment he stops agitating to find me they'll know I'm alive. They'll know that he knows, and that will put him in danger."

It was serious then. More serious even than Andy had thought.

"I can't tell him yet. Not until more time passes," she continued, her throat sounding tight.

He waited for more.

"Andy, there's a price on my head. Half a million Euros. God knows how many freelancers are after me for a chance at that kind of cash."

"Are you sure? That's a lot of money." She shot him a sobering look.

"I didn't mean to say you could be wrong, but—"

"I know it's a lot of money, Andy. Jesus, you think I don't know that? That's the problem. I know the price because I lived in Luther Hand's apartment for weeks. I watched his communications. They tried contacting him and when he didn't, I don't know, didn't give the special signal or whatever, they knew he'd failed. They put out another hit and this time it's not one killer I have to look out for—it's many. You don't know what I've been through in the past few days . . ."

She trailed off, then started again. "I know I got in too deep. You tried telling me that. You warned me I was getting . . . *obsessed* with the Cavanaghs." When Mak got a taste of injustice she just couldn't let it go. "You know the investigation you warned me about? The one I wasn't to get in the way of? Tell me what's happening. The media has been all but silent about the Cavanaghs recently."

"There is pressure on," he said.

"*Pressure?*"

"Jack Cavanagh is a heavy hitter," he explained uncomfortably.

"I've noticed that."

"There was an investigation launched by the AFP, with talk for a while about a possible link between Cavanagh's organisation and an international crime ring operating from Queensland, but . . . it's gone quiet," he regretted to add. That was all Andy had to offer: possible links that seemed to have gone nowhere. Depressing news, yet Mak's eyes had lit up.

"Queensland?" she said. "I have something for you." She slid the strap from her shoulder and opened the case. It was a small laptop. "This belonged to the man the Cavanaghs sent to kill me. Luther Hand is what he called himself—or one of the names, anyway. I believe there may be evidence here to link him back to the Cavanaghs."

"What kind of evidence? Where is Luther now?"

"Dead." Her voice was toneless.

He waited for her to explain, but she didn't.

"This has to be enough to help prosecutors get a trial over the line," she said in a hopeful voice, gesturing to the computer.

"This man, Hand, was a trained killer and highly paid. *Very* highly paid. Who else but Jack Cavanagh would pay so much to prevent me from returning to Australia alive?"

Andy frowned. Some very hard proof would be needed to take down Jack Cavanagh.

"He kept notes on his work," Mak continued, "and though I haven't been able to make sense of all of it, a forensic computer expert could. There are numbered sequences and initials that I think identify individuals he worked with, and could identify traceable payments, accounts, that sort of thing. And there are references to me and to the Cavanaghs. I had to give this to you, Andy. I couldn't trust a courier with it."

Her blue-green eyes seemed to plead with him. She appeared hopeful that the risks she'd taken to reach him would prove to be worthwhile.

"Be very careful, Andy," she warned. "If they know you have this, you could become a target. Be careful whom you trust with this."

Perhaps Jack Cavanagh had bought some influence in the NSW police force and local government. But could his tentacles really reach as far as Canberra? As far as the AFP? Just how careful would Andy have to be?

"I'm glad you brought this to me. I'm glad you knew you could trust me, Mak." He reached out to her and she let him put his hand on hers again. "Now you need to be in witness protection. We can look after you."

She pulled her hand away. "Like hell you can. I'd be a sitting duck."

"Whatever this computer has on it will be far more valuable with you as a witness," he reasoned. "You have to explain what happened and how you obtained it."

Mak gave him a joyless grin. "Really? And say what, that I killed this guy and took his laptop?"

"Yes. Tell the truth. Tell them what you told me. Tell them what you've been through."

"And you really think I'd make it to trial? How long would that be? A year? Longer? There's no way they'll let me live that long."

"We can protect you. It's a good system, Mak. It's totally separate from us, from the state cops, too. No one would know where you were."

"You wouldn't know where I was. Sure. But someone would. And all it takes is that someone wanting something—cash, a promotion, a morsel of power. Jack Cavanagh can give it to them. That's the way it is, Andy."

"There are good cops out there, Mak."

"Don't patronise me, Andy. I know most cops are honest—my own father was one—but it only takes one who isn't to get me killed."

He took her shoulders in his hands and was shocked by the way they felt: they were hard with unfamiliar muscle. "Don't give up on us, Mak. We are close to getting him."

"Close? Really. You believe that?" He didn't know what he believed.

"My faith is gone. You give this to the guys trying to nail Jack Cavanagh. I hope it helps their cause," she said and ran a hand over her hair. "I need him to pull back. He has to take the contract off my head, Andy, or I'm done. If they can't arrest the bastard soon . . . I'll . . . I'll do anything."

Mak stood up. She looked restless and he knew she was going to leave, and he couldn't bear the thought of letting her go again.

"I wish you'd been here when I got back from Quantico," he told her. "We could have worked it out."

Mak looked him in the eye and for a moment he saw the softness there again, the softness he'd once known.

"Don't follow me," was all she said. "I'll be in touch."

CHAPTER 23

Andy Flynn sat in his office at AFP headquarters, holding the computer satchel.

Mak.

Since her unexpected visit, sleep had alluded him. Her words had haunted him all night. *I woke to find myself in a cellar on a mattress, with a chain around my ankle . . .*

There came a gentle knock, and he looked up to see that a familiar face had arrived at his open door. "You wanted me?"

Nicolas Joseph. Andy had called for him.

"Please take a seat," Andy told him, motioning to a chair. Joseph was perhaps ten years Andy's junior and had a good, technical mind. Andy had got to know him over the previous eight or nine months. Since Makedde's appearance at his house the night before, Andy had been debating what to do with the laptop she'd given him. She'd clearly risked a lot to bring it to Australia and put it directly in his hands; it made sense that the computer of her would-be killer was of great value.

He drummed his fingers on the laptop case. It was the only evidence that she'd been there, in his bedroom, in the middle of the night. She'd appeared like an apparition and left as one.

"Agent Flynn?"

"I need this examined," Andy said. "We have reason to believe it holds evidence of criminal activity." He gestured to the laptop bag.

"Cool," Joseph said. "What am I looking for?"

"For evidence of a link to the Cavanaghs."

Joseph's eyebrows raised in almost cartoonish surprise. His relaxed demeanour evaporated. "You have a warrant for this, I presume."

"It doesn't belong to the Cavanaghs."

Andy watched with amusement as his colleague relaxed a touch. No one wanted to be in the firing line of the Cavanaghs' lawyers.

"It belongs to someone they were allegedly associated with. An Australian criminal who went by the name of Luther Hand," he explained. "The man is now deceased." If Mak was correct. And he had little doubt she was.

Joseph did not look a lot more relaxed with this added information. "Where did you get it?"

"A trusted source who will testify if required."

God, I hope she'll testify.

"First let's see what we have," Andy suggested. "But there is a catch. I don't want anyone knowing about it until you have it . . . what is it? Locked down. Saved on the system."

Nicolas Joseph tilted his head. He licked his lips nervously. "You are worried about—"

"Just don't worry about my worries for the moment. Put it in your system as soon as you can. Save it. I know you can do that. And don't attach it to a case until I say so. I want to know there is something on here worth . . ." Worth taking heat for.

Joseph nodded uncertainly.

"I take responsibility. The paperwork is all there," Andy

assured him. He stood and put a hand on the younger man's shoulder.

"All right." The man took the laptop case reluctantly. "I take full responsibility, Nic. Full responsibility."

"Have you opened it?" he asked.

"No."

"Good. And it was off?" He put the strap over his shoulder. "I haven't done anything to it. You won't even find my fingerprints on it."

As with anything else, it was easy to tamper with electronic evidence and destroy its value. At the Electronic Evidence Branch, Joseph would pull the hard drive out and create a "forensic image" of what was there, in a forensically sound write-protected environment, using write blockers to acquire information from the hard drive without altering or damaging anything. Andy hoped what he found proved as valuable as Mak thought it would. There was no point in getting worried about the chain of evidence yet. A good QC could argue that the evidence had not been properly procured, that they could not be sure it was legit, or hadn't been tampered with.

But for intelligence purposes, it could be worth its weight in gold.

CHAPTER 24

"It's a four-speed sports automatic. Six-cylinder engine. Less than two hundred thou on the clock. In perfect nick."

"Not perfect nick," she corrected him.

Makedde Vanderwall stood her ground in front of the frazzled car salesman. He was repeating himself now. His hair was sparse and oily, and he was as thin as the tacky wind-dancer that towered over the used-car lot, bobbing up and down, smiling maniacally and whipping its arms around. She'd started to make him uncomfortable, she could see, but she just didn't have the energy to pretend that he was doing a good job of selling her on it. She knew about the car and what she intended to pay and that was that. The standoff was over a five-year-old white Ford Falcon. No car with two hundred thousand kilometres on it was truly reliable, but it was a decent enough vehicle and most importantly it did not stand out at all. It was a terribly average car, which was just what Mak needed, and she intended to buy the thing for less than the price advertised in orange digits across its windshield.

"Well, barely a dent," the man said. "New brakes. Very reliable. It's a steal for six thousand."

He'd said the bit about the car's reliability eight times already.

"I'll give you five thousand, cash. Right now. That's my offer," Mak repeated.

He opened his mouth to try again, and responded to the look in her eyes by closing it again. He visibly calculated his commission. "Okay," he finally said, defeated.

Mak followed the thin man into his cluttered office. She filled out the paperwork using Petra Blackman's driver's licence details and placed a packet of cash on the desk. He counted it as she'd imagined he would—mouth tight with concentration and a hot gleam in his eye. Mak had decided against using Blackman's credit card before stepping onto the lot. She was not exactly cash poor and it would doubtless buy her more time with the ID. She regretted having stolen the woman's Visa card at all, now. It had been a poor, last-minute decision. When Ms. Blackman discovered that both her credit card and her driver's licence were missing she would deduce that both had been stolen, not lost. But the prospect of a stay in a decent hotel had been simply too much temptation for Mak. She'd booked herself in to the Sheraton on the Park in Sydney and given the card details for incidentals. You just couldn't check in to a decent hotel these days without plastic. At least the card shouldn't show up on the system until it was charged.

As long as this Falcon could get her down the highway okay, she would be soaking in a deep bathtub at the Sheraton and watching in-room movies in only two hours. She desperately needed the illusion of comfort, at least for a night.

"Congratulations, Ms. Blackman," the salesman said and dropped the keys into Mak's waiting palm. "You won't be disappointed."

She drove off the lot and passed the Holden she'd stolen in NSW, its interior clean of fingerprints. She wondered how long it would take before it drew some attention.

Halfway between Canberra and Sydney, Mak had to stop.

Starving.

She spotted the colossal yellow M ahead, and found herself pulling off the highway past a petrol station peopled with truckers and their huge vehicles, and into a McDonald's parking lot, despite her usual aversion to their fare. She had a hollow belly and stabbing headache. A burger and a cheap coffee chaser—with some Panadol—would get her to Sydney. She did not exactly feel like the picture of health. Food would surely help. She parked and stood in line feeling increasingly off, and exposed, as if someone was following her, which was ridiculous. Regardless, she felt better eating in the car. It was probably tiredness that made her feel almost as if she might burst into tears at any moment—which she of course would not.

There was a lot to adjust to, she supposed. Feeling a bit strange was a reasonable response.

I'm a criminal now. A criminal.

Bogey is dead because of me. And I am living off his murderer's money. Money his murderer was probably paid to kill me.

Bogey.

She'd been thinking about Bogey a lot. And her father. She wondered what her father would have thought of him.

Snap out of it.

Such thoughts were pointless. Mak checked the maps function on the iPhone she had bought using Petra Blackman's ID. She was less than halfway there. She crumpled up the greasy paper from her spent Big Mac and stuffed it in the brown paper bag. The artificial scent of car interior cleaner, which had been so overwhelming when she'd first taken the vehicle for a test drive, was now thoroughly replaced by the distinctive fast-food smell of saturated beef fat—the special ingredient of the McDonald's fry. Her stomach churned. Mak stepped out of the car, leaving the door open, and marched to the nearest bin to throw everything out. After airing the car she pulled out of the large parking lot, windows down, passing parked trucks packed with freight, and feeling full though not exactly sated, and certainly no more settled in the stomach. She soon noticed signs for the Belanglo Forest, and felt an uneasy sweat take hold, reminded of the murders of seven backpackers in the early nineties by serial killer Ivan Milat. About two decades later a teenage relative of Milat had killed a seventeen-year-old in the very same forest, using a double-sided axe. Now his life would be spent behind bars. Mak felt a touch of nausea. It was a bad place.

She sped up, and turned the radio on.

Oh God . . . No.

Mak hurriedly checked her mirrors, then swerved onto the shoulder and braked hard. She managed to whip her seat belt off and crack open the driver's door before heaving, car sick, onto the pavement on the side of the highway, losing her modest meal.

CHAPTER 25

"We have a match," Detective Inspector Kelley said.

Agent Andy Flynn was nearly at his front door. He felt wired with uneasy adrenaline, having not been able to rest since Mak's sudden, shocking arrival. The sun was down and the street lamps outside his house glowed and hummed. He had his keys in one hand and his mobile phone in the other, and as he put the key in the lock he thought, *Yes.* This was good news from Kelley. A DNA match to the two previous rape cases would solidly connect the crimes, just as Andy had suggested they were linked. They might officially start questioning Dayle's rape alibi, might see that he had lucked out in being cleared. It wasn't enough to get a court order for a DNA sample from Dayle— that would be showing their hand too early—but it might just be enough to get a warrant to search his flat, where Andy felt sure they would find evidence of his involvement in Victoria Hempsey's murder. It was a big step forwards.

"That's good news, sir," Andy said, turning the lock and entering his dark house. He closed the door and reached around for the light switch. The bulb came on over the centre of the living room, illuminating his empty couch.

"Not quite," Kelley said down the line.

"What do you mean?"

"It's a match to her boyfriend. He was there on the Wednesday afternoon, before going out for dinner."

Fuck.

Andy shut his eyes. Either the boyfriend was the killer, which Andy still found unlikely—his alibi was corroborated by several people and the crime did not fit—or the killer did not leave semen at the scene, which was out of sync with the pattern of the previous rapes. Andy locked his door and leaned back against it.

"Do you still like Dayle for it?" Kelley asked him.

Andy walked into his living room. He took a breath and placed his briefcase on the carpet. "Yeah," he said. "Yeah, I still like him for it."

"But there was no semen left by a second person."

Dayle had avoided leaving traceable DNA at the scene. That had to be the answer. "He's changed his methods," Andy argued. "He's become careful."

But there was doubt.

Agent Andrew Flynn's house in Canberra was humble and masculine. Three bedrooms. One with a queen-sized bed and small side table and a closet with a few suits and a leather jacket hanging in it, taking up one half. The other half had been empty for over two months. The second bedroom had been converted into a makeshift study he rarely used. In the living room were a curved reading lamp, a worn leather couch and his grandfather's medals in a small glass case over a wooden cabinet.

After Mak had left him he hadn't wanted to change anything. She'd taken her things, nothing more, but everything else remained the same. In a sense it was like Andy himself: a functioning object with a big chunk missing.

Makedde.

He could still hardly believe she'd shown up, without warning, in the bedroom they'd once shared. Andy had spent a lot of time trying not to think about her, and when he did he blamed himself for what had gone wrong. The fact was, he'd feared a repeat of his first marriage—he realised that now. Some part of him had feared Mak would become Cassandra. The longer they lived together the more he'd retreated from her. He could see it now. He'd loved her so desperately and he'd fucked it up.

And now look at your lives.

Terrible things had happened to Mak. She was alone and in hiding. And Andy was alone, too, watching his career implode slowly, decaying from the inside out.

She was alive, and still, he couldn't reach her.

Andy did what he always did. He buried himself in his work. Tonight his living-room floor was a kaleidoscope of fresh horrors. A boy of only ten had been murdered in a neighbouring town, strangled with a knotted blue ribbon and left in a drain, almost precisely the same way another boy had been killed and disposed of nine months previous. This was where cases like these ended up. In Andy's living room. The carpet was decorated in grim images, the small, pale bodies laid out in the final nakedness of death in a series of photographs only a homicide investigator could bear to sit amongst. He scanned the photographs once more, looked at the knots in the ribbon, and his mind drifted back to Ms. Hempsey. The news from Inspector Kelley was not good. Kelley had already been worried that the overburdened surveillance team would be pulled, and he'd told Andy as much. The commander wasn't as confident in Andy's assessment as Kelley was. Or perhaps it was that there was an immediate threat somewhere else: the team might be pressured to abandon Dayle for another, somehow more dangerous target, though that was hard to imagine.

Andy took another sip of his drink, and placed the tumbler on the carpet again.

No. They had to keep the surveillance on. *They have to. Kelley knows that.*

Kelley had a lot of pull, but those kinds of decisions were out of Andy's hands. He'd seen to that by moving here, to this lonely place, to this new challenge with the SVCP unit.

He'd seen to it that he'd end up this way, sitting in his living room alone with the dead.

Mak was at the Sheraton on the Park in Sydney, her new phone in one hand, a bottle of water in the other. She'd crawled in between the sheets, enjoying the sterile comfort and privacy of the hotel room. Even ordered room service, which she ate watching a mind-numbing television program. She'd wanted to feel human again. Safe. The illusion was partially successful. Yet Luther's Glock was always there, in her peripheral vision.

It was late when Mak pressed the call button and bit her lip. The number was already programmed in. She'd tried a few times before, but this time Andy answered in only three rings.

"Flynn," he said brusquely. "*Hi.*"

Makedde sat up in the bed, pleased he'd finally answered. She uttered that single-word greeting and let it hang for a moment, as if it had been a simple touch and she could feel him, despite the distance.

"I had to call," she continued vaguely. The urge to had seemed irresistible, but she was conflicted. She'd given him the laptop, which was what she'd come to do. She knew it was too early for results. This was something else.

"*Mak.*" The way he said her name gave her a warm shudder. "Are you okay?" he asked. "I was so relieved to see you the other night—"

"But?"

"But nothing. I was relieved. You wouldn't fucking believe how relieved," he said, the tone of his voice relaying a depth of feeling she had not heard from him in years.

She smiled; she felt a small sliver of her emotional self come back to life after months of deadness.

"In the morning I could hardly believe it had happened at all, you showing up like that. I hate not being able to contact you. I've hated that the most in the past two months, the uncertainty and not being able to contact you, not knowing if you were okay. I'm glad you called. I've been worried. More than worried. I thought something terrible had happened—"

"Something terrible did." She felt herself close again.

Luther.

"Are you still in Canberra? Can I see you?"

"No," she said flatly, almost defensively.

"If you're in Sydney, I can get there tonight. I'm consulting on a case for Inspector Kelley—the new unit is consulting on a case," he corrected himself. "Strictly speaking, my part is over, but . . ."

Always the cases, Mak thought. The cases Andy worked knew no hours, no boundaries. Violent rapists and murderers.

Psychopaths. People who needed to be stopped or they would inevitably kill again and again. She'd fallen in love with a man who shared his life with people like that. The work was hardly nine to five: she'd known that from the start. Her own father was a cop, so she understood better than most what was demanded of him. She'd seen Andy stay up literally all night on caffeine, or fly away to another town at the drop of a hat to try to put gory puzzle pieces together to halt the threat of future violence. Lives were at stake. It didn't matter if he and Mak had other plans. It didn't matter if they'd booked a holiday, if they desperately needed time together to reconnect.

There'd always been a part of Andy that Mak couldn't reach—the part of him that was in his work.

"I could stay in Sydney for a while. If you'll have me," he said. "Under whatever terms you want. I just . . . need to see you."

Mak licked her lips. She wasn't sure about telling him where she was. "Is it going well? The unit?" she asked, shifting her emotions to one side.

"Honestly? It's still early days. I have a small group of profilers working under me. Two of them are pretty strong already."

She felt a touch of pride for him. "Congratulations," she said, nodding to herself. Getting the program up had been a considerable source of stress for him when they'd been together, particularly towards the end.

"There are complications, of course, but you don't need to hear about all that."

"What's in Sydney?" she asked.

"This fucker we've been trying to nab," he blurted. "Sorry, but he's . . . well, he's a real piece of work: John Dayle." Mak thought she detected the subtle slur of Johnnie Walker in Andy's voice. It was late, after all. She guessed that Andy had been drinking and poring over cases again. She could picture it clearly—the drink in his hands, files set up in piles, crime-scene photographs spread out on the carpet.

". . . has some possible priors," Andy was saying. "Rapes. Brutal rapes. Real sick stuff. Well, he wasn't pinned down for them and that's part of the problem. And now his neighbour is murdered in her flat, with the same signature. Sadistic killing. Looks like he escalated from rape to . . . to what he did to her. We haven't been able to get a search warrant and I'm worried like hell that he's looking to kill again. I think he liked it. I think this has given him a real taste . . . I shouldn't be telling you all this. I'm sorry. I just want to see you. I've missed you so much."

"I've missed you, too, Andy," Mak admitted. His obsession with his work had driven her crazy at times, but she understood. Tonight he sounded more agitated than usual. "What's his name? John Dayle?" she said.

"I shouldn't be telling you these things."

"I want you to. You know you can tell me anything," she said.

He hesitated. "Just don't go hanging around Surry Hills at night. Promise me. Kelley is worried the surveillance on this guy is going to get pulled because of another case, so I reckon we have to press for a search warrant fast. But there has been a complication. If this magistrate doesn't give us our warrant, he'll have blood on his hands, I fear."

"That's awful."

"It is." There was a moment of silence. "I know terrible things have happened to you, Mak. I can't tell you how sorry I am. Let me help you now and you'll be safe, I promise you. You don't have to do this alone. You could be enrolled in the federal witness protection program by tomorrow."

"Federal witness protection, eh? Impressive," she said, growing cool.

"You'd be sent somewhere safe. Up north, perhaps. Somewhere that bastard can't reach you—"

"And you wouldn't be able to reach me. No one I know would be able to reach me. It wouldn't be so different from things now, would it?" *Except I wouldn't have my freedom*, Mak thought.

And if Cavanagh had insiders, and she suspected he did, then even witness protection may not be safe for her. "I don't trust it. Not yet. But I may," she said. "So there is no news yet?"

"With the laptop? No. It's with the Electronic Evidence Branch now. It will take a few days for them to go through it. Obviously they want to know where I got it. But I have a guy I can trust. He will secure it all before word is out that we have it."

"Watch yourself," she said. "Will you come forward?"

"You know I can't—yet."

"But will you? Mak?"

She'd been silent for a while. Why was she reaching out to Andy? What could he do? She'd given him the laptop as she'd planned, and now she had to go to Richard Staples, the journalist, to get the pressure back on the Cavanaghs, to get the girl's death into the public eye again. There was nothing Andy could do to help her with that. He wasn't involved with the case. Besides, he had a career to protect. Things would only get uglier before they got better. There would be casualties and she didn't want him to be one of them.

So why had she called? Maybe it was only that it helped her to feel human, having someone to talk to, someone who still clearly loved her, regardless of whether the issues between them could ever be resolved. The invisible cord that connected them was still intact, despite everything.

"I should go," she said. "I just wanted to tell you that I understand if you are angry. I do. I would be if I were you. I guessed that you thought the worst. In fact, I hoped that everyone thought the worst. I could only be safe from Jack Cavanagh if he was convinced I was dead."

And now he knows I'm not dead at all. The killer at the apartment had proved that.

"You have to believe I had no choice. I could not contact you, not anyone."

"Mak, it's okay—"

"It isn't really. I know that. But if I'd thought it was as simple as hopping on a plane and coming back here, and everything would be fine, well that's what I would have done. As it is, I had to lay low for a while. I still have to lay low." Her hands had started to shake. Emotion was taking her now.

Fuck.

"If you say that's what you had to do, I believe you," Andy told her gently down the line. She wanted to accept his help, wanted him to make it all better, but that was a fairy tale. He'd saved her life once, when the Stiletto Killer had her. This was different.

She had to do this thing alone.

"I just had to . . . um, tell you that." She looked around the hotel room, that creeping loneliness consuming her again. "I'm sorry, Andy. I have to go now."

"What's this number? It came up blocked." She didn't respond.

"Is there any way to contact you?"

"I'm truly sorry, Andy."

She hung up.

CHAPTER 26

Detective Inspector Hunt stepped off the escalator at Chinatown's Golden Century restaurant and looked around anxiously. He got himself a table at the back—white tablecloth, soy sauce and chilli in the centre—and ordered a Tsingtao. It was past midnight, but several tables were still being served. After perhaps ten minutes Robert White slid into the chair opposite, smooth as water. Hunt had only seen him in person once before. If asked to describe him, he could only say he was a Caucasian male with an American accent and neatly trimmed grey hair. Somehow, Robert White seemed completely without any other defining characteristics.

They ate prawn dumplings and sang choy bow and once the chilli crab arrived White said, "The problem we spoke about before has resurfaced. In Sydney."

Makedde Vanderwall. Hunt had been keeping an eye on customs and immigration, but nothing had come up. She must have come in on false ID.

"She set up a meeting with a journalist."

"Tell me where and when," Hunt said eagerly.

White gave him the details of the planned rendezvous. "The journalist?"

"Taken care of for now."

***

A young, startlingly thin Chinese waiter approached holding a plastic bag containing a bright coral trout. The fish stared gape-mouthed at Hunt, with round, frightened eyes. The American nodded and the waiter took it away to butcher. "She'll have her own account of things. That account can't come to light," The American explained. "You understand?" Vanderwall had clearly survived an attempt on her life in Paris and that was very bad news for Jack Cavanagh. She could not be allowed to meet with the journalist and she could not be brought into custody. That left only one other option.

"I understand," Hunt said. His heart quickened. There would be a big reward for this, if it went over well. A big reward.

"It's vital that things are taken care of at the scene, cleanly. It has to hold up to scrutiny. My client cannot be pulled in."

The trout arrived. Hunt was not comfortable with his chopsticks. He gave up on them and tucked in with a knife and fork.

"I would suggest she may be armed," The American remarked quietly, one leg folded gracefully over the other. He took a bite of fish and placed his chopsticks neatly on the corner of his plate. When he finished chewing he said, "She is perhaps dangerous. It would be advantageous if you could bring someone expendable. Can that be arranged?"

Hunt raised an eyebrow.

Expendable?

He had just the right person for the job.

CHAPTER 27

Under the tinted visor of a full-face motorcycle helmet and the armour of stiff new leathers, Mak Vanderwall prowled a maze of residential streets in Sydney's Northern Beaches. Rested after her night in a luxurious hotel bed, she now sat astride a new, satisfyingly powerful, purring Triumph Speed Triple, slipping between cars and exploring back roads.

Second, third, fourth . . .

She had become more comfortable spending Luther's blood money, she reflected as her recent purchase gleamed beneath her, unscratched and straight off the lot. *Could I be corrupted by money, as Jack Cavanagh clearly has?* she wondered. She had to admit it had felt awfully good to see the bike in the window and just walk in and lay down the cash. She'd paid half on the generous Ms. Blackman's credit card only to avoid suspicion. Drug dealers paid with a lot of paper. Drug dealers and women on the run. The torque took some getting used to and she'd spent the past few hours doing precisely that, enjoying the increased anonymity and freedom of her new transportation.

What a place, she thought as she passed a line of luxury homes in one of the more exclusive streets of Palm Beach. *What a place.* A Mercedes-Benz S-Class parked in a driveway. A dark

Aston Martin DB9. Yachts bobbed up and down lazily, sunlight reflecting on calm waters. It was a moneyed view. A view to die for, some would say. She couldn't enjoy it in the least. This was Jack Cavanagh's view. His Palm Beach house was elegantly understated. Probably designed by some famous architect. It was much smaller and less protected than his ostentatious Point Piper home. Open plan. Bedrooms on the second level. Nice stretch of beach outside. Jack wasn't there, but it was interesting to see he had recently taken on some muscle. A bodyguard or security type of some sort was milling around. A big man. Pretty young. She wondered how long he'd been on the scene.

After one last spin past, Mak took her time riding back into Sydney. After the open air of the Northern Beaches the congested traffic on the Harbour Bridge was not a welcome change. She sat in first gear, caught between bumpers, scowling as exhaust filled her nose. Lane-splitting was illegal and there were cameras everywhere. She didn't want to draw attention to herself. Sweat-soaked under her leathers, she eventually crossed into the city and rode towards Pyrmont, making her way up Harris Street, which was busy with the lunchtime crowd. She picked up a sandwich and rode on, gearing down as she reached the end of Distillery Drive. She turned down a smaller, unmarked road, gradually coming to a halt behind a concrete barrier at the back of a large construction lot, on which work had apparently been suspended for several months. Her mind was clear and calm. The meditations of the road always had that effect on her.

There were few people here. This was the raw, partially developed end of Pyrmont. Once a purely industrial area, it now featured dozens of new apartment blocks, and though Harris Street and the precincts closest to the old piers and casino were fast becoming gentrified, here, under the shadow of the M4 freeway, the gentrification factor was still absent. These streets felt all but empty of cars, let alone people. Which was perfect for her purposes.

Mak flicked out the kickstand on her new bike and set it to rest next to the concrete barrier, which hid the bike from view without impeding the path back to the road. She pulled her helmet off and walked onto the construction site, kicking up dust with her motorcycle boots. Debris had floated into the structure itself, leaves gathering in the corners of the ground-floor entry door. One presumed the global financial crisis played a role. At the front entry, Mak passed scaffolding and blue plastic tarpaulins weighed down by bricks, leaving boot prints in her wake. She had noticed the building from the raised freeway and inspected it before calling the *Tribune* journalist Mr. Staples to arrange the details of this clandestine meeting. Now that their proposed meeting time was only an hour away, Mak was at the site and pleased with her choice. The privacy of the cavernous concrete structure made it a good spot to meet someone unobserved and, though she didn't anticipate trouble, the windows and doors had not been fitted, leaving plenty of entries and exits. This was to be a grand apartment building, if it ever found funding again. There was a workman's elevator in place and a staircase without railings, and it was these stairs that she used to make her way up to the unfinished mezzanine, where her view of the apartment building's future lobby was total.

Now, where to put these?

She flipped the backpack off and pulled out a leather handbag she'd cut into and fitted with a discreet pinhole camera and directional microphone. Pete Don, her former tutor at the Australian Security Academy, had shown her how to do it. The materials were available in any common "spy" shop. Inside the handbag was a second camera, linked to her iPhone and set in a malleable lump of Plasticine, made up to be roughly the colour of concrete. She pulled out the Plasticine, unwrapped it from the cling wrap she'd stored it in, and held it up to the wall. It didn't quite match the unfinished surface of the building, she noticed, but it still blended fairly well. She left the purse in her spot on the mezzanine and, after some consideration, placed the hidden camera in the Plasticine at the base of the stairs, the lens pointing at the front entry. Her conversation with Staples on the mezzanine would be recorded; and as a security measure, she should be able to see him approach with the other camera. If he wasn't alone, she could escape unseen from the far window of the mezzanine. Or use Luther's Glock, which was tucked into the waist of her leather pants.

Confident she had the angles covered, Mak sat on an empty crate, tore into her backpack and tucked into her sandwich.

CHAPTER 28

"Flynn."

It was Inspector Kelley.

"Inspector."

There was a pause, and immediately Andy Flynn sensed that this call would not bring good news. The warrant had been rejected. He'd guessed it would.

"The warrant was rejected. The surveillance team will be pulled off as of tomorrow. They've been put onto another job." Andy sat forwards with his elbows on his desk, his eyes shut tightly. *No.* Though Kelley had foreshadowed this as a possibility, the words were a blow.

"Is there another suspect? A stronger one?" he asked.

"No."

That was little relief. If the Dayle lead proved incorrect, it would reflect badly on him and on the unit. But if Dayle was the one, the thought of him walking freely around Sydney was unthinkable. He was a ticking bomb.

"I believe you are right about him, if that's any consolation."

Kelley could be dogged in getting what he wanted. He would push for Dayle and he would keep pushing.

"But they did it, anyway," Andy said. He shook his head. "The team has been pulled off for a job the commander considers to be a more imminent threat." There was a pause. "Truthfully, I think his hand was forced. It's a matter of resources. I talked with him about it today. There's nothing more I can do about it at this stage. I'll continue to push the issue from here, but I thought I should let you know."

Andy felt his temper rise, frustration coming out of his pores and spreading through the room like a toxic vapour. This office in Canberra was not where he could do the most good, he decided. He'd made a grave error in pinning his career on criminal profiling just as the tide turned against it. And even when he could help on a case, when he was sure they had fingered the right guy, not even Inspector Kelley's support could get his recommendations carried out. Andy was truly powerless.

He held his breath for a moment, absorbed the disappointment, exhaled. "Thanks for letting me know," he said placidly.

Kelley knew full well what this meant. The risk didn't bear mentioning. They both agreed that Dayle was the prime suspect, and that whoever murdered Victoria Hempsey was sure to do it again. It was only a matter of time. But when? Next week? Next year? Police resources were finite. This sort of thing happened, especially since the global financial crisis and all the cutbacks that came with it. Police, nurses and teachers were always the first to have funding cut. Some surveillance operations brought results in only days, some in months, and some operations simply didn't get results at all. It was expensive work. Perhaps Kelley could push to get the STIB in soon to plant a device. That could prove useful. It was something.

"Thanks for your assistance with the investigation. You did some good work," Kelley said.

Andy thanked him again for the update and hung up. His office felt claustrophobic suddenly, and he opened the door with one outstretched hand.

The DNA matched the boyfriend, not the previous rapes. That was what had killed the case for surveillance. Yet if Strike Force Pawn showed their hand and brought Dayle in for questioning, there were a thousand ways he could weasel his way out again, with the knowledge they were onto him. He would have to really screw up to further incriminate himself. He'd have to confess to someone. Or hurt someone else . . .

There was a knock on the open door. "Yup," he said brusquely.

It was Agent Dana Harrison, standing in the hall outside his doorway, holding a file folder. She was looking over a ten-year-old cold case from Queensland.

"Excuse me," she offered. "Can we talk?"

"Sure."

She closed the door behind her and leaned against it.

"I just wanted to be sure that . . . we're cool," she said awkwardly. "I hope I didn't say anything to, um—"

"We're cool, Harrison."

Yes, he'd been attracted to Dana on some level, though now that he'd seen Mak there was no denying he still loved her, had never stopped hoping they'd be together again. If Dana had been interested in Andy, it was most likely because he was her mentor. He was older and experienced. Perhaps she saw in him someone she wanted to emulate, not someone she wanted to be with, and perhaps on some level she'd mixed up that admiration with something else. Harrison was a smart, talented young woman. She didn't need an affair with her superior to hang over her reputation. She was better than that. They both were. She probably would have worked it out herself, but he was glad she wouldn't have to.

"You impressed me in Sydney. I'll be recommending you in my report," he told her honestly, but her eyes continued to search him.

"Are you okay?" she asked.

"Do I not seem okay?"

She narrowed her warm brown eyes at him. Tilted her head. "Not that it's any of my business, but no."

Andy looked away and leaned back in his chair.

Mak is alive. But I can't reach her.

And Dayle . . .

"Sorry. You're right. I just heard that the surveillance has been pulled off John Dayle, so . . ."

"What?" She straightened suddenly and gripped the folder until it creased.

"Dayle is still the prime suspect, however the surveillance team was needed elsewhere," he told her. He cast his gaze over his desk and finding nothing there to comfort him, he said, "And the warrant was knocked back."

"What do you mean? I don't understand."

Andy took a deep breath. "Welcome to policing, Agent Harrison. We don't always get what we want."

Harrison flinched, apparently taken aback. "But Dayle is dangerous. He's the guy. You said so yourself," she argued, her brow pinched sharply and those chocolate eyes blazing. She was usually so measured, so cerebral about the work. He hadn't seen her angry like this before.

"Well, yes, I do believe he is guilty," he explained. "But the bottom line is we have yet to prove it . . . *They* have yet to prove it."

Andy had to stop thinking in terms of "we," he reminded himself. He and his team had consulted for the NSW homicide squad, and now their involvement was over. When Andy had agreed to leave state homicide to start this unit, he'd known he would no longer be closing cases and making arrests. The Hempsey case wasn't his case any more. And it wasn't Harrison's either.

"How can we prove it if there is no one watching him?"

"Perhaps forensics can come up with something," he muttered.

"But he hasn't submitted to a DNA test. He hasn't been finger-printed," she complained.

"Dayle has never been charged with anything and the request for a search warrant was knocked back, as we worried it would be. This sort of thing is slow going."

"But it can't be slow going. Not if he's out there, looking for fresh victims."

Harrison had been with the ACT police for barely three years before being nabbed by the AFP for this project. She wasn't experienced enough to have seen first hand how justice could sometimes go wrong, how officers could have their hands tied by a well-intentioned system built on the protection of impor-tant civil liberties. This was not the first time something like this had happened, nor would it be the last.

"Harrison, you have to let it go. It's out of our hands." She stared at him, fuming.

"Don't you have a couple days off coming up?" he asked her.

She'd been doing long hours.

"Yeah, from tomorrow," she said quietly.

"Good. You've done some excellent work. Come back after the weekend with fresh eyes. There are plenty of other cases we are needed on."

"Do you promise you'll let me know if there are any develop-ments with Dayle?"

He sighed. "There won't be, Harrison."

"But if there are?"

"I've got your mobile. Of course I'll let you know. See you next week," he said and leaned forwards on his desk again.

She turned and he watched her walk away, feeling deeply uneasy about the situation with Dayle, with Mak, with the Cavanaghs.

CHAPTER 29

Detective Jimmy Cassimatis, trapped in a persistent bored malaise, looked up from the stack of overdue paperwork on his cluttered desk at HQ only to find Detective Inspector Bradley Hunt looming over him like a dark cloud. They had barely exchanged words since Jimmy's visit to Inspector Kelley's office and this development did not improve Jimmy's outlook in the least.

"Cassimatis, you're needed," Hunt said bluntly. He did not even try to disguise his contempt for the officer in his command.

Jimmy sat up and squinted at him, wondering how to play things. "What's up?" he said, trying to sound casual.

"Someone is wanted for questioning," Hunt explained. "About additional information on the Thai girl."

Dumpster Girl. So the case wasn't quite closed, after all? Jimmy wondered fleetingly if PIC—Police Integrity Commission—was already talking about Hunt and his handling of the case. Did they have him under surveillance? Did Kelley know something about it? Was that what he'd sensed when he was in the office? That Kelley already knew something was up? Had Hunt been pushed to do more?

"Who have we got?" he asked.

"Macaylay Vanderwall."

Jimmy nearly spat. "Well, we'd all like to ask Mak a few questions, I'm sure. We planning a trip to France?"

Hunt remained stony-faced. "We have a strong lead on her whereabouts. Macaylay knows you, so we need your help to talk with her," Hunt finished.

He's pronounced her name wrong, twice. It's not Macaylay, it's Makedde. Mak. Ay. Dee. Easy. Jimmy blinked, absorbing the bizarre news. "You want my help? To bring in Makedde Vanderwall? Did everyone volunteer for that job?"

He tried chuckling, which was his usual manner of communication, but now it came out strained.

His superior, for his part, did not crack even a smirk. "She is considered armed and dangerous," he said flatly.

Jimmy's overriding thought was, *Mak is alive?*

Was this a fact? Or a rumour?

And his next thought came right out of his mouth before he censored it. "Mak Vanderwall is dangerous? *Skata.* You've got to be fuckin' shitting me."

Jimmy had seen her spread in *Sports Illustrated*, a magazine she'd posed for in her modelling days. Really, no disrespect to his best friend, Andy, but the idea of Mak armed and dangerous was an arousing one. If she was alive, it was good news. Great news. Andy would be enormously relieved. That he was still in love with her was as obvious as anything Jimmy could think of. But Mak was alive and *dangerous*? To the cops? Jimmy wasn't about to strap on the bulletproof vest.

"She allegedly entered the country on a false passport and now she's threatening to screw up an investigation by getting the press involved and spilling the beans on what she knows," Hunt continued, letting his anger show. "It's a mess. We're bringing her in."

The press?

Oh, Mak.

At this, Jimmy pushed himself back from his desk and stood. "So you're not shitting me. She's really in Australia? Does Flynn know? I thought she'd disappeared in Paris?"

"She contacted a journalist at the *Tribune*, claiming she has information. She's arranged a rendezvous for today in Sydney."

Jimmy inhaled sharply. Mak was still on the Cavanaghs' case? He'd never had the impression she was dumb—to the contrary—but she really didn't have a great sense of self-preservation, to be sure. He'd been there when she'd traced a crime scene to a room in the Cavanaghs' palatial waterfront mansion, after recognising a Brett Whiteley painting in the background of a grainy video showing the Dumpster Girl's death. If finding evidence of a crime scene in their own home didn't nail them, what could? Damien was notorious for his unsavoury activities, and now Cavanagh senior appeared to be loosely linked to a criminal ring out of Queensland, but still, they'd managed to avoid any real investigation. There'd been missing evidence; the video footage had been called into question; and it had all amounted to nothing so far. Whatever was thrown at them was easily batted away by their impressive legal team. And by Hunt. Jimmy had admitted his suspicions to Kelley, but he was no martyr. He needed his job. He had four kids to support. Mak should know by now that this obsession with bringing the Cavanaghs to justice would create nothing but ruin. It was too big for either of them. If she was alive, and wanted to stay that way, this was a poor way to go about things.

Spilling the beans . . .

And there it was again. Something that smelled wrong. What could Mak know that Hunt didn't want her to tell?

Was it related to her unexplained disappearance in Europe?

"Yeah, well, I thought that one was headed for the unsolved homicide team," Jimmy said cautiously, half joking. He searched through a drawer for a snack to take with him. If he was going to have to trawl around Sydney with Inspector Hunt, he was going to need moral support.

"What?"

"I'm just saying we don't seem in a hurry to bring Damien or Jack Cavanagh in for questioning," Jimmy said quietly, opening his trap again. "But, you know . . ."

There, a Mars Bar. He tucked in and shut the drawer with one chubby elbow.

For fuck's sake, Jimmy, just shut up.

"This isn't a kangaroo court," Hunt protested. "We have to do things by the book."

Only Hunt would throw up the term "kangaroo court." Anyone else would point out that the Cavanaghs were frighteningly powerful, with an overpaid legal team. But not Hunt. No, when Hunt spoke about it, they had to be careful not to jump to conclusions.

Interesting.

Jimmy didn't care to comment further. He'd already said too much. Instead, he nursed the open end of his chocolate bar. "Why do you need my help to bring Mak in for questioning?" he finally asked. "I mean, she's pretty cooperative, right?"

She was the daughter of a cop, after all.

Hunt clenched his oversized jaw and scowled. "Enough questions," he said darkly. "This isn't a request."

CHAPTER 30

Right on time, Makedde Vanderwall heard a car park nearby and a door slam. Richard Staples had arrived.

She'd been rereading Stephen King, and now she closed her iBook app and watched the footage from the camera on the staircase, sitting on the mezzanine, hidden by the concrete pillar. Footsteps echoed as Staples approached the building—and then stopped when he was just out of view.

Hmm.

Her camera couldn't make anyone out yet. She stood and frowned, leaning against the concrete pillar and listening. Another car could be heard. Had it parked nearby for one of the other buildings or had Staples brought someone? A photographer? She hoped not. She'd asked him to come alone. She wanted him to have the Lacie external hard drive she'd backed up with the laptop's contents, and let him do the research himself. She didn't want another story about her and the Cavanaghs. She'd seen her name and image in print enough. It was one of the reasons she had not wanted to meet in an open, public place. That and the small issue of having a price on her head. She flicked her eyes to the opposite side of the mezzanine, to the high concrete divider, beyond which was a corner window from which she could sneak out onto a high pile of earth outside, only a metre down—her planned escape point if she had to leave quietly. Just one more minute and then she'd go.

As she was contemplating her next move, a figure finally appeared on her little iPhone screen. And it was not who she was expecting at all. An overweight male dressed in sloppy jeans and an oversized shirt walked out alone into the centre of the dusty floor of the building with a distinctly familiar gait and a wry smile on his face.

"Mak? Mak, are you there?"

Holy shit.

Jimmy Cassimatis. Andy's former police partner. He was easily recognisable, even on the tiny screen.

What on earth. . . ?

Mak covered her mouth. "Maaaaaak? You here?"

Time stretched on as Jimmy walked about, irritatingly calling her name. If Staples was coming, Jimmy would ruin everything. Was Staples coming, or had he called the police? If he had, she had seriously misjudged him. Though Jimmy didn't look like he was on the job.

Had Andy sent him? How would he know where she'd be?

No, it couldn't be that . . .

"Mak? I know you are here." She watched on the screen as he moved towards the camera. "Hello, what's this?"

"Jimmy!" Mak said, reluctantly revealing herself, one palm against the filthy pillar. So her cleverly hidden camera wasn't so cleverly hidden. "*Jesus.* What are you doing here?"

He looked up, smiled and waved, taking a few paces back towards the entry, so that she was looking down on him. "Mak, it's good to see you!" he shouted up to her. "*Skata*, Andy will be so fuckin' relieved, you have no idea. He's been worried sick."

Mak winced.

"You look . . . Well, I don't know about the hair actually. Come on down, Mak."

"How did Andy know I'd be here?" Mak asked.

He paused. "I don't think he does, luv. I'm here to take you in for questioning."

"*You what?*"

He could have been kidding, he did tend towards practical jokes, but in this setting that seemed particularly unlikely. A feeling of terror rippled through her.

"Are you alone?"

"Nah," he said casually.

Fucking hell. She backed up, her hands out in front of her. "What is this?" She tried to smile back, but looked around furtively. She couldn't see anyone else, but she had heard a second car. "Jimmy, I'm just here to meet someone. I wasn't expecting you at all. Just leave me alone and I promise I'll contact you later. I'll lay it all out for you if you want."

"Can't do that, Mak. Apparently you've been a *very naughty* girl, harassing the Cavanaghs and keen to slander them, blah blah blah, and messing up an important investigation, which is why I need you to come in for questioning."

The feeling of betrayal made her stomach churn. Everything was wrong now. Everything.

Don't panic. Think.

"So you're not kidding then. Jimmy, you know that's crap. I haven't done anything to them."

Not yet, anyway . . .

"You have nothing on me," she said.

His smile faded. "Come on, Mak. Don't be like that. Don't make this difficult."

"I wonder what Andy would make of you arresting me for nothing."

"Oh, come on. No one's being arrested."

A trip to the police station would put her on the map for the very people she was trying to avoid. She didn't doubt the Cavanaghs had connections. They'd know her whereabouts in no time. On the other hand it would look bad for them if something happened to her, and there would surely be a major investigation if anything happened to her in custody. Calmly coming to headquarters with Jimmy would put a swift end to all the sneaking around and she might even be able to plead her case, come forward about the laptop backup and the reason she was in immediate, ongoing danger. She could just be upfront about what had happened. Minus the stealing and false IDs, perhaps.

"You don't have probable cause," she argued.

She thought of her father. She could call him from the station. He'd be pulling strings for her in no time. He'd be so relieved she was alive. Her hand was being forced. This wasn't how she wanted things, but maybe, just maybe it could all work out . . .

"Probable cause? You've been watching too many cop shows," Jimmy said. "Come on. It's just—"

His words were stopped dead by the ear-splitting sound of a gunshot. In a moment of unreal horror, Mak watched Andy's friend stumble backwards and fall, clutching his chest and letting out an awful, strangled cry, the sound of which echoed like the gunshot that preceded it. In seconds a man rushed in to Jimmy's side and just as Mak was set to join him on the dusty floor of the building, he called out, "She shot him! Officer down!" He spotted her and ran towards the base of the staircase, gun drawn.

It took her only a second to realise what that meant.

Two uniformed officers appeared through the doorway. One went to Jimmy's side and the other joined the first man in running up the stairs leading to the mezzanine floor. Adrenaline rushing through her, Mak bolted, snatching up her things as she went. If she made it to the other end of the mezzanine and jumped out onto the dirt, she'd still end up on the building site. There could be officers waiting there. *Dammit.* She stopped at the nearest window—a large concrete hole where a window would one day be—and she stepped up into the ledge. It was a bigger drop from here, but it would put her on the street, closer to her motorbike. She stuffed the iPhone, purse and motorcycle helmet in the backpack and zipped it up.

She looked down.

Fuck.

It was a long way. With nothing but road to catch her.

She hesitated and looked over her shoulder. The two police officers were about halfway to her, moving steadily with their guns unholstered. Watching them, Makedde let her backpack drop out the open hole of the window. It hit the asphalt behind her with a crunch.

"Freeze!"

Without further hesitation she pulled herself over the edge, her body swinging with a sickening freedom. She hung on with both hands for a moment, body dangling from the side of the building, her toes finding no purchase.

Protect your head, Mak. Keep your body loose and protect your head.

She let go.

A moment of weightlessness, eyes closed and arms crossed over her face.

And the road rose to meet her.

"What happened?"

Agent Andy Flynn was already locking his office with one hand, the phone held to his ear with one muscular shoulder. He would drive to Sydney immediately.

"It's critical," Inspector Kelley told him.

Jimmy Cassimatis was in hospital. This unexpected news topped off what had been a very bad day.

"His heart? Is it his heart?" Andy said, shaken. He grabbed his briefcase off the floor and began walking quickly down the bright hallway. Patel emerged. And Dana Harrison. They could tell by Andy's expression that something serious had happened.

"Is it his heart?"

Jimmy was always complaining about his heart medication.

Had he stopped taking it?

Dammit, Jimmy, what did you do?

"Cassimatis was shot."

God. No. At this stage, the fastest way to get back to Sydney would be by car. If he drove to the airport and tried to get the next flight out, it could delay him and only add to his frustration. Andy held a hand up, asking Harrison and Patel to wait.

"How bad is it?" Andy asked.

"I don't know yet. He's in theatre with a gunshot wound. I'm headed to the hospital now." There were noises in the background, like traffic. It sounded like Kelley was on the street.

"I'm leaving now."

"Andy, it's alleged that . . . Look, I will tell you more about it in person," Kelley said. "And I should probably tell you this in person, too, but you need to know that your ex-girlfriend Makedde Vanderwall is alive, Flynn. She's in Sydney."

How did Kelley know?

"When? How?" he asked, wondering when Kelley had discovered her.

"I have just been informed. Look, I'll give you the rest of the details when you get here."

"I'm coming over now," he said. "Was Jimmy taken to RPA or St. Vincent's?"

"St. Vincent's Public. Call me when you get here," Kelley said and hung up.

Andy noticed that he had missed a call. After learning from Kelley about the surveillance being pulled off Dayle, Andy had buried himself in the new case. He saw that the call was from Jimmy.

"Harrison, I need you to take over for now, for the rest of today. Patel, you can help. Tell the others I have to go to Sydney. It's a personal matter. I will check back in with you in a few hours."

"Is everything okay?" Harrison asked him.

He shook his head and raced down to the parking lot. When he slid into his car he stuck the key in the ignition and paused. He pulled his phone out and braced himself to hear Jimmy's message. Whatever message he'd left him before getting himself shot.

The familiar voice was captured on his phone, sounding upbeat. "Mate, you're going to love this," Jimmy said. "Your supermodel girlfriend is alive and well. Ms. *Sports Illustrated* is right here in Sydney. *I know.*" There was a nervous laugh. Always joking. Always trying to lighten the tough stuff. "Fuck, right? Look, I'm going with that prick Hunt to get her."

Inspector Hunt.

There was a pause and a crackle of static. "She's been pestering the Cavanaghs again, trying to go to the press about them. Will she ever learn? Anyway, I thought you should know. I'll call you when it's all done . . . Shall I tell her you say hi? Jesus. Does she even know you thought she was dead?"

The message ended. Andy started his car.

CHAPTER 31

Hell.

Makedde hurt all over. She'd felt this way once before, after skydiving for the first time on Vancouver Island and landing hard on unforgiving, dry ground, her technique less than perfect. Now her quads ached with the same familiar shooting pains as she stood up from the hotel bed and paced the room slowly, agitated and unable to sit still. Her left wrist was numb beneath a bundle of ice cubes wrapped in a plastic shopping bag. When she'd jumped from the mezzanine window she'd taken most of the weight of the fall evenly on her motorcycle boots before falling backwards and to the left. An impressive purple bruise was already coming up on her hip and backside. It would be black by morning. Her wrist had not fared well, but she could rotate it. No broken bones.

He's at his hotel now.

She'd been watching Andy's movements on the GPS of her iPhone. Barely sixty minutes after the incident, his car had left Canberra and started the drive to Sydney. News travelled fast. He'd driven right to St. Vincent's Public Hospital in Darlinghurst, presumably to either offer support to Jimmy as a wounded colleague, or—and Mak worried this was the sad reality—to offer Jimmy's family his condolences. Mak feared the worst.

That poor family.

Andy had driven to a location in the city, not far from where Mak was staying. The tracker on his Honda had remained stationary for the past hour. He was probably settled in for the night. Mak felt she could no longer stew alone over what had happened and his proximity drew her like a moth to the proverbial flame. She lifted the bag of ice off her wrist and rubbed the cool red skin beneath. She circled her wrist one way, then the other. Yes, it would be okay. Wincing from the tenderness of her quads, she padded to the bathroom, clad only in fresh underwear and a bra. The mirror was foggy and the floor still wet from her shower. She tossed the dripping bag of ice in the bin and wiped a space of mirror clear with one palm. *Okay. Here we go.* Grateful for the popularity of the Mardi Gras drag culture in nearby Darlinghurst, she picked up the two good-quality wigs she'd purchased in a shop on Oxford Street and held them up next to her reflection. The long, wavy red or the shaggy, streaky brunette? Perhaps the red, she decided. She pulled her damp, dyed hair back in a tight ponytail and stretched the red wig over her head with both hands, adjusting the netting and pulling the loose waves of natural-looking reddish human hair forwards over her temples.

That'll work.

Mak dressed herself in a simple T-shirt, black jeans and boots and her trench coat, and locked her room. She made her way towards Andy's car by foot, following the directions on her phone. It was in the car park of a mid-range hotel near World Square. The hotel had half-decent security; a swipe key was needed to get up to the guest floors and she felt sure they weren't about to give out his room number without permission. She would just have to try the obvious way of getting to his room, she decided. The bar was cleared of patrons on this weekday night, and Mak waited until the lobby was quiet before approaching. At this hour, only a middle-aged, well-groomed receptionist in a neat suit, tie and nametag manned the reception desk. He looked like he had been working there for some time.

"Hello," Mak said casually, leaning across cold marble. "I'm here with Andrew Flynn. It's room . . ." She trailed off. "I can't remember."

"He's a guest?" the man said.

Mak nodded and gave an impatient but friendly smile. Her eyes flicked to the clock above the desk. It was nearing ten-thirty.

"And your name, miss?"

"Cassandra," she responded, and flinched as soon as the name popped out of her mouth.

He eyed her a bit strangely as he called up to Andy's room. "Mr. Flynn, Cassandra is in the lobby. Shall I send her up?"

Oh hell. Andy wouldn't like that one bit.

A long moment passed, nothing apparently said on either side. Mak tensed. She was relieved when the receptionist finally replied, "Yes, sir. I will," into the phone and told Mak he would swipe her up. He abandoned the desk to lead her to the elevator where he used his key, hit the button for level 22 and wished her a good evening. A few minutes later Mak was on Andy's floor. The halls were quiet except for the faint sound of a television murmuring somewhere. She followed the signs to 2202, knocked and instantly heard a rustling at the door. A shadow moved across the peephole, and the door opened with the faint swoosh of hinge and carpet.

And there he was—her green-eyed ex-lover, barefoot and tall, wearing a pair of denim jeans and a black collared shirt, unbuttoned a few notches. Despite looking stressed, he struck her as incredibly handsome.

Andy clapped eyes on her eagerly. "It's risky for you to be here," he said and quickly ushered her inside. He moved past her to peer into the hotel corridor. He looked both ways and, satisfied, locked the door and slid the safety chain across. He folded his arms. "So your name is Cassandra, huh?" He looked unimpressed.

"I'm sorry, Andy. It was the first name out of my mouth. I needed you to know it was me," she explained. "Not the best choice, I agree."

He shrugged and showed her into his room. He closed the curtains, shutting out the night glow of Sydney's lights. Mak pulled off the red, wavy locks with one hand and tossed the wig on the edge of his neatly made hotel bed. She ran her fingertips over her scalp, freeing her thick hair, which was still slightly damp at the roots. His room was a decent size, with a small sitting area and a king-sized bed. A tumbler sat next to the minibar, just a scrap of amber liquid left in it. She thought she'd smelled a touch of whisky on his breath.

"Please tell me he's okay," she said.

Andy looked at her hard. Blood vessels left red, jagged lines across the whites of his eyes. There was a lot of hurt there—hurt for what was happening with Jimmy and hurt for what had gone before.

"Tell me," she demanded.

He looked away and ran a shaky hand through his thick, dark hair. "It doesn't look good."

Fuck.

"They sent me home till morning. His wife is there. He's . . . he's not even responding."

Jimmy. Not Jimmy.

If Jimmy Cassimatis was on his deathbed at St. Vincent's, thanks in part to Mak, she didn't know if she could live with herself. He was a father of four. She had lost her mother in her twenties and it had been the single most devastating event in her life to date. More than six years on, a day rarely passed when she didn't think about her mother, didn't miss her, didn't feel as much as remember clutching her warm, bloated hand in the hospital before they shut off the machine that kept her alive.

What about those four boys? The events of this day would brand them forever.

"I mean it, Mak: it's risky for you to be here. It's good that you didn't use your real name."

"It's risky for me to be anywhere," Mak replied, and on impulse, embraced Andy with both arms. She pushed her head into his firm chest and clung on tight, inhaling his scent and savouring his warmth. The weirdest thing about being off the radar and on the run was not the constant paranoia, but the loneliness, she now realised. She'd never before experienced such complete isolation. For months she hadn't spoken to the same person more than twice. She had not touched anyone, had not been touched by anyone, had not shared any of what she'd gone through. Now her ex-lover felt good, so damned good to hold, and after a moment of rigid surprise, he embraced her in return, his large hands curling around her shoulder blades to hold her close.

"I'm so sorry," she whispered softly into his chest, which rose and fell in quick succession. "It's terrible. Absolutely terrible."

"You know you are wanted for questioning," he finally said. Mak broke away and looked up at him. She thought of the officer on the floor of the construction site beside Jimmy, saying she'd shot him. "I guess I shouldn't be surprised."

How had the police known where she would be? What had happened to the journalist, Richard? Where had the shot come from? Jimmy had fallen backwards, which made her think he was shot from in front, yet the other police officers had run in from behind. So who else was there?

"Inspector Hunt has fingered you for the shooting."

Now anger overcame her sadness. "That's utter bullshit. You *know* that's utter bullshit. I wouldn't shoot Jimmy, of all people." She liked Jimmy. He was brash and even a little offensive at times, but he had a good heart. She'd grown to have real affection for him.

"But there could have been an accident," Andy rationalised.

She caught his eye and held it. "No. There was no accident. Believe me, I didn't fire that shot. I didn't fire *any shot*," she said. "I didn't even draw my gun."

"You have a gun?"

"I do," she replied. She sat on the edge of the bed, watching him.

Andy looked grim, but didn't comment. "But you didn't use it at all?"

"No," she insisted.

"Good. Ballistics can prove your gun wasn't fired. And there'd be no gunshot residue on your hands," he said, sounding hopeful.

"Not necessarily," she replied softly. Traces of gunshot residue could often be found days after firing a weapon, even after thorough hand-washing.

Andy sat down on the bed, a hand-span separating them. "Dammit," he muttered.

Mak wondered how much he'd been told. She wondered what story was being spun about what had gone down that afternoon. "Just believe I did not shoot your partner and I did not use my gun at all. It wasn't an accident either. My gun was not even visible when he was shot. No one needed to shoot anyone. That shot came out of the blue."

"Why were you both there?"

"I was supposed to meet a journalist."

He sighed. "Go on."

"Yes, it was about the Cavanaghs," she admitted, feeling the quiet anger radiate off him. They'd fought about her relentless pursuit of the Cavanaghs many times. "I have a Lacie—an external hard drive—of the contents of Luther Hand's laptop. There is a journalist for the *Tribune* who has been writing pretty freely about the Cavanagh controversy while everyone else has gone quiet. His name is Richard Staples."

"I know the name."

"I thought if anyone would write about this, he would. I arranged for him to meet me at an abandoned construction site in Pyrmont today, but he didn't show up. Jimmy did."

Andy's frown intensified. "What was he doing there?"

"That's just it. I don't have any frickin' idea what Jimmy was doing there. I didn't bring him into this at all. I hadn't seen him or spoken to him since before Paris. And . . . how did they know where to find me?"

"Well, obviously your journalist friend tipped them off."

"But why? That doesn't feel right to me. He's not been very complimentary about Jack Cavanagh. I can't imagine he would get a tip-off like this from me and just dump it without even finding out what I have. I'm not wanted by the police, as far as I am aware. Or at least I wasn't until this afternoon."

Andy thought about that. "The other option is that your communications were intercepted. Were you using a mobile?"

"I got my iPhone in a false name, but I called him from a payphone to set up the meeting. I was extra careful."

He raised his dark brows. "A false name?"

She said nothing. She wasn't going to apologise to him for breaking the law. Things had escalated way past that line.

"Okay, so perhaps *his* phone is tapped. I can see if he's caught up in any ongoing investigations," Andy reasoned.

"He has been writing about the Cavanaghs," Mak reminded him. "If his phone is not secure, it's possible it's not a legal tap." He licked his lips and stood up. Seeming distracted, he opened the minibar and poured them each a whisky from miniature bottles of Johnnie Walker. "Straight?"

"Sure," she replied. "Thanks." She accepted the tumbler and swirled the golden liquid around while he stood and downed the entire glass as though it held water.

She took a good sip and it burned the back of her throat. Her eyes stung. It was not her favourite drink, but tonight it tasted excellent.

"I've been making some discreet enquiries the past few months," Andy confessed. "There's talk of someone called 'The American.' Have you heard of him?"

"No."

He nodded. "It's a nickname of sorts for a man allegedly in the employ of Jack Cavanagh. Ex-FBI or CIA, depending on who tells you, hence the name. Very serious."

"What do we know about him?"

"That's just it. There's very little that's concrete. He keeps a low profile, if he exists at all. Even Richard Staples is unlikely to write a word about him."

"There's no one who fits his description on the Cavanagh employee database? A US citizen who is ex-FBI or CIA?" she asked.

He shook his head. "He's not officially on the Cavanagh Incorporated payroll, that much is certain. And what I've heard about 'The American' is mostly rumour. He came on the scene seven or eight years ago when one of Jack's top executives was kidnapped in the Middle East. Speculation is he has connections to the NSA, Echelon, international criminal organisations—"

"Echelon?" Mak was shocked. "You've heard of it?"

Echelon was the code name for an intelligence program run by the USA's National Security Agency and Britain's Government Communications Headquarters. It bound together signals intelligence agencies in Australia, New Zealand, Canada and the UK with the NSA to scan every single phone call and electronic exchange of every single citizen—millions upon millions of emails, SMSs, faxes—in the interests of security. Essentially, Echelon spied on the world, ostensibly to make it safer. Every one of Mak's phone calls and emails, like everyone else's, were picked up by the Geraldton facility in Western Australia and automatically sent on to the NSA to be run through something called 'The Dictionary,' to be scanned for relevant names, phone numbers and keywords of international interest—communications relating to possible terrorist activities, North Korean military plans, Pakistani nuclear development. But there had been rumours of abuse for commercial purposes, and Margaret Thatcher once allegedly used the sophisticated system to tap the mobile phone of Margaret Trudeau when her then husband Pierre Trudeau was Prime Minister. Did Jack Cavanagh have a contact who could abuse the SigInt system for him?

Gooseflesh came up on her arms. "That's bloody scary," she remarked. She considered what she could do to stay safe. "I don't think I can call you again. Someone might be watching your phone because of your connection to me, especially now that they know I am back in Australia. I wouldn't put it past these people, regardless of whether this spook, 'The American,' exists."

What had she said in her phone call to Andy? Could she have been identified from her accent? She'd have to swap her phone for another. And it would be best if she used a new name, which meant stealing again.

"If Jack has a guy like that," Andy said, "and he's willing to spend enough, there are all kinds of things to beware of. Even CCTV cameras if they have enough manpower. It'll be very hard to stay out of their way now they know you are here."

Mak and Andy were both quiet for a while. She would have to keep changing her appearance, her phone, hotel rooms. She wouldn't be able to frequent any establishments, keep any routines. And it would be unwise to be near Andy or anyone else who'd been a known associate of hers.

Andy sat on the bed beside her. "So, tell me about this gun."

"You really want to know? It's a Glock. Like yours."

"Why did you bring it for this meeting?"

"Why?" Mak laughed. She reached around and patted her lower back, feeling the Glock tucked into the waist of her jeans. "I always have it now." She could tell by his face that he hadn't noticed it when they'd embraced.

He absorbed that bit of information with displeasure. "A gun. False ID . . ."

She tilted her chin and gave him a look. "Are you quite finished?"

He pushed his glass to his lips again and, on finding it was still empty, asked her to relay what had happened at the construction site.

"I rode to the location of the meeting early," she explained. "When the journalist was supposed to arrive, Jimmy showed up, calling my name. He said he knew I was there, and that he was to bring me in for questioning. Some crap about harassing the Cavanaghs? Please. Now I'll admit I've taken a few tours past their Point Piper and Palm Beach places, but I have been quite careful."

She needed to keep tabs on Jack. She had to understand who

she was dealing with. She might have to confront him or . . . worse.

"I doubt I've been seen and I certainly haven't approached anyone." She registered Andy's obvious vexation and soldiered on with her story. "Anyway, he said I just needed to come in and it would all be cleared up. I think he really believed that could happen. Well, I wasn't about to come in. You know why. But before I could do anything, there was a gunshot and Jimmy went down. I think he took it in the chest. He fell backwards." Mak watched Andy carefully. His eyes glistened and his brows were pulled together. In her experience, he was not a man who cried. His inability to let his emotions out had frequently frustrated Mak in their time together, and here he was, his best friend shot only hours before and everything so messed up, and he was still holding it together. She supposed he thought he had to. "I had my gun, as I've said," she continued. "I came armed in case anything happened, but I didn't draw my weapon. And I certainly could not have shot him square on like that, as I was above him, on a mezzanine."

Andy appeared to snap out of his thoughts. "Where were you standing and where was he standing? Can you draw me a diagram?" he asked.

"Yes. And I can do better than that." She pulled out her iPhone. "I have some recordings. Unfortunately, they aren't very clear. I can't seem to see where the shot comes from." She set it up to play.

"Hidden cameras?" he remarked, with an air of disbelief. Perhaps he'd forgotten what she'd been taught in her Certificate III in Private Investigation. He hadn't been very enthusiastic about her becoming a PI, so she supposed it was natural that he hadn't paid a lot of attention.

"I needed a record to cover myself, and I also thought it was a good idea to see if Staples was coming alone, as he'd promised," she said matter-of-factly and started the recording. "This camera was aimed at the entryway. You can see Jimmy." They both went quiet as the footage played. She fast-forwarded until it showed Jimmy walking into the space alone. "It shows him getting shot now." Andy appeared to brace himself. When the shot rang out, the sound distorting, he remained silent. She watched his face to see if he was okay. He was. She rewound it and played it again. Jimmy was talking when the shot hit him, pushing him back.

"Where were you standing?" Andy finally said.

Mak took the hotel notepad and pen off the bedside table. "I was above, on a mezzanine, here." She made an X. "Jimmy entered from here and walked out to this spot. This is the rough area we can see on the video." She made a circle.

"Now look at this. There is someone else for a split second in the entryway. See?" She rewound the recording quite a way, and they watched again as a shadow moved over the doorway about twenty minutes before Jimmy walked in by himself. She'd missed it at the time because she was reading. Whoever it was had come quietly, and alone. Now she paused it and the shadow was freeze-framed into the shape of a tall figure.

"It took me a few times to spot this guy. I want to know who that is." She pointed at the screen. "It's not the guy who comes in to aid Jimmy. The clothing is wrong. And it isn't either of the two uniformed officers who came after me later."

"I'm pretty sure that's Brad Hunt at Jimmy's side after he goes down," Andy remarked. "A detective inspector. The one who fingered you for the shooting. I don't recognise anyone else. Who would this be?"

Mak showed him the footage from the second camera. Unfortunately, it didn't show much, but it did provide a clearer account of her dialogue. It distorted when the gunshot rang out.

"The police need this."

"Of course they do," she agreed. "I'll go in with you."

"I'm not going in."

He closed his eyes, his face contorted with frustration. "Mak. Jesus."

"No way," she said. Case closed. She'd leave if she had to. Mak had not been visibly armed. How could anyone have been aiming for her and hit Jimmy? *No.* She had to believe they had not wanted to hit her at all. They had wanted to kill Jimmy and frame her for it.

"Hunt claims you shot Jimmy in cold blood because you didn't want to come in. He says it got heated and you were angry and you shot him. He says you've been harassing the Cavanaghs and we have a duty to bring you in. Come in with me. We can sort this thing. If you didn't even fire your weapon—"

"They need only say it was a different gun. I'll have residue on my hands. I've been practising."

"Mak, you can get out. Give me the green light and I'll make sure you are looked after," he pleaded. "We can do it tonight. We can do this thing together."

She shook her head. "Witness protection? After what happened to Jimmy today?" she said, scoffing. "I don't think so. Neither of us believes that's possible now. I always thought he might have people on the inside. Now I know for sure."

The window for that option had closed when Jimmy was shot. Perhaps that was precisely *why* he was shot.

"Mak, please. You don't have to do this alone."

"Yes, I do." Makedde began gathering her things. She trusted Andy more than anyone else, but maybe that wasn't enough right now. He was still an officer and she was still a woman on the run. She suddenly felt trapped. It was a mistake to have come. This was pushing it too far.

He grabbed her hand and she shot him a look. "Okay." He backed off, palms raised.

She put her bag over her shoulder and eyed the wig on the edge of the bed.

"You don't have to go," Andy told her. "Please . . ."

She closed her eyes. A wave of panic went through her.

"Mak!"

She opened her eyes and held a finger over his lips. "Keep it down," she said and walked across to the bedside to turn the clock radio on to a rock station. The Black Keys were singing "Lonely Boy."

"Please stay for a while. We can talk about something else if you want," Andy said. "I won't try to convince you again. It's your choice."

She wanted to stay. If she could. If it was safe for a while. She didn't want to be alone. Not all the time. And if she was honest with herself, she wanted Andy, just for a while. Just for another few minutes. That would be okay, wouldn't it? Mak sat back on the bed, and let her bag drop to the floor. She watched Andy. His eyes went to the window, to the minibar, to the floor. He couldn't stay still. Soon Andy was walking back and forth, ruminating.

"I want to fix this," he finally admitted.

"And you can't. I don't want you getting wrapped up any worse in it," she told him firmly. "I'm not going into witness protection, period. And no one can know you've seen me. It's too dangerous. But you're right that the police need this footage. I can post it to someone you trust if you think that will work. Someone smart and honest."

"Kelley," Andy replied immediately. "Detective Inspector Roderick Kelley."

She knew him from Andy's time working in NSW.

"He'll want to know that Hunt's account doesn't match up with this footage. His version of events doesn't fit and that might be enough. I think Kelley's starting to suspect something isn't right. Jimmy was starting to suspect Hunt as well . . . *Is*," he corrected himself. "Jimmy *is* suspicious of Hunt."

A fresh wave of sadness went through her. "Okay," she replied. "Don't give him any idea that you know about the footage, or you'll be accused of harbouring a criminal. And it will make it harder for me to see you if I need to."

"I hope you'll need to," he said, and for a moment he looked at her with such vulnerability it took her breath away.

She placed her hand on the bed and he came to sit next to her. "I know I got in deep with all this, Andy. You tried to warn me."

Jack Cavanagh was more ruthless than she could have imagined.

Mak lay back on the bed and stared at the ceiling for a long time. Despite everything, she felt almost human for the first time in months, she realised. She was talking to someone, someone who knew her, someone who knew at least some of what she'd gone through to get here—someone she could confide in, if she could confide in any living person on earth. It was some return to her former self.

"Just tell me, why do guys like Jimmy get shot while crooked pieces of shit like Hunt and Cavanagh and like this psycho fucker Dayle keep walking around?" Andy lamented, his pain and frustration palpable. "That's all I want to know."

Mak pulled her knees up to her chest. *John Dayle.* "So you didn't get your warrant," she said quietly, feeling her mind sharpen.

"We didn't get our fucking warrant. And they pulled the

surveillance off him. They pulled the fucking surveillance off!" Andy's face screwed up as if he'd been hit. He downed another drink while she sipped hers slowly, thinking. *So there's a killer roaming the streets. Another killer preying on women for his own sadistic pleasure.* There was so little justice in the world.

It seemed to Mak that if there was a god, she was far from benevolent.

She was quiet for a long while, thoughts crystallising behind her closed eyes.

"What about the boyfriend?" Andy asked after the long stretch of silence, trying unsuccessfully to sound casual. *Ah, yes. The boyfriend.* To deflect the seriousness of his question he got up and walked to the minibar. He kept his back to her as he pulled another couple of miniature bottles from the small fridge.

"He's dead," Mak replied. "Bogey was his name."

Andy stopped and turned. "I'm . . . sorry to hear that. What happened?"

"The hit man. He happened."

Andy cracked another miniature bottle open. "These things are so effing small," he complained, emptying half of it into her tumbler. "Another?"

She nodded.

"And you're sure he is dead?"

She had a flash of Bogey's open grave. The dirt falling on his naked face. "They're both dead," she said.

Andy held their drinks. He watched her carefully, searching for signs of the emotion she found she'd run out of. She didn't have tears left for any of them. Not right now. She had reached her threshold.

"Yeah, sometimes I think I'm not such a good person to know," she said and shook her head. "I've done things you wouldn't believe, Andy," she told him. "I'm not who you thought I was. I'm not who *I* thought I was." Things between them had started at a murder scene and only got worse. Andy had been the investigating officer and Mak the grieving friend. He was going through a divorce. She was dealing with her own grief. It had always been a mess. She'd been so naïve then—so naïve compared to what she was now. She closed her eyes and inhaled deeply through her nostrils, exhaled. When she opened them again he was next to her. She accepted her tumbler and they drank together.

She leaned towards him. "I want a kiss."

His face screwed up, and for an instant his stubborn composure cleared away to reveal a deep hurt. "I want more than a kiss, Mak," he said. He slowly placed his glass on the bed cover and she leaned in to him and pressed her lips to his. A rush of pleasure and emotion came to the surface as they kissed. Mouth to mouth. Tongue to tongue. It felt fucking good to kiss him again. She dropped her empty glass and it rolled off the edge of the bed, hitting Andy's foot and landing on the hotel carpet.

"Fuck!" he exclaimed. She laughed.

Andy turned and pushed her down on the bed, propping himself up on his strong arms above her. "Think that's funny, hey?" He gently touched her face and ran his fingers back from her temples and through her dark hair while she looked up at him, liking what she saw. Instinctively, her body rose to meet his, one long leg twining around him. He lowered his face to her, his light stubble brushing her cheek. They locked together. Their problems, their history, all the things that had come between them seemed not to matter in that moment. All that mattered was that they were together, finally, right here, right now. She pulled at his buttons, opening his shirt and running her hands over his warm skin, the soft hairs of his chest. He sat up and pulled his shirt off and she did the same.

He ran eager fingers over her black bra and pushed his face into her cleavage, inhaling her. She unclipped her bra, freeing her breasts, then pulled the rest of her clothes off, tossing her jeans and underwear on the hotel-room floor. His intense green eyes took her in hungrily. When he pushed her legs open and went down on her, he looked up for a moment. They locked eyes.

"I love you, Mak."

His tongue darted out and she closed her eyes, arching her back.

Mak held her orgasm for what seemed an eternity. When it finally crashed, the pleasure rippled out like waves through her whole body, shooting up through her arms and out through her fingertips. She shuddered and sighed beneath him as he raised himself up between her legs and undid the buttons on his jeans. She felt his bare cock push at the hollow between her legs and she lifted herself and ground her hips against him, teasing. She was wet and warm, and once she could wait no longer she grabbed his buttocks and asked for what she wanted, whispering in his ear. He slid inside her inch by inch, gasping with every millimetre of progress.

"Yes . . ." she whispered with her mouth, as if her body was not already saying it louder.

They rolled to one side across the stiff hotel sheets and she pulled herself atop him, barely keeping him inside her for a moment. He held her hips as she leaned over him and inhaled the nape of his strong neck, her plump lips pressed to his stubble, smelling that masculine scent she'd always found so intoxicating—a scent like honeyed spice. Slowly, she slid her hand across his firm chest, from one nipple to the other, and pushed her hips down. He arched beneath her, body tense, impatient. She rose again until both of his hands grasped her buttocks, begging her not to move. She slowly slid back over his length, and he tilted his head back.

"Fuck."

Again and again she slid over him. He gripped her.

It was over too fast. So they began again and took their time.

CHAPTER 32

Jack Cavanagh sat at his impressive mahogany desk on the fourteenth floor of the city offices of Cavanagh Incorporated. It was late and he had not gone home.

Mr. White watched him closely, hands laced behind his back like a general. He broke from his stance to pour them each a whisky from Jack's limited edition 1960s bar cabinet. He handed Jack a drink and sat down.

"Tell me what's happening, Bob," Jack said eagerly. He'd been waiting for an update.

"There has been another development," The American told his client calmly. He only pretended to sip his drink.

As Jack nursed his whisky, Robert White outlined what had happened at the construction site, leaving out whatever incriminating details Jack did not need to know. White, "The American," had authorisation to do whatever was necessary to remove the threat, and the less his client knew about the details, the better. That had been agreed upon.

When he finished explaining what had happened, Jack's eyes were wild. "What about the cop?" he asked.

"I'm monitoring it. It's unlikely he'll pull through."

Jack nodded, seeming conflicted. "Okay. That's good, isn't it?"

"In my opinion this is a good result," White explained. "Vanderwall will get no support now. She's wanted. Any remaining credibility to her stories has been destroyed. The police don't appreciate cop killers. She'll be hunted down."

"Should we be worried about the journalist?"

"We've been watching him for a while. My opinion is that he will back off for now."

"Well, *keep* watching him," Jack urged, unnecessarily.

The American nodded. "There may be some press tomorrow about this incident with Vanderwall. It's a cop shooting, so that can't be avoided. It will work in our favour."

Jack screwed up his face. "I don't want press." He hit his fist on the desk.

The American's eyes narrowed just a touch. "You will not be mentioned, unless it is in passing. Her harassment of you is on public record. Again, unavoidable that it would be mentioned. It will work in our favour. Discrediting her is a credit to you," he explained.

He had a contact handling things with the major newspapers. Journalists tended to be poorly paid, thus only the most stubbornly ethical amongst them could resist being guided towards the "right" story using the right methods. Influence could be handled delicately, invisibly. Access. Favours. Never anything so gauche as a cheque. Most of his best journalists would not even think of themselves as having been bribed. "This will be nothing for you to worry about, I assure you," The American added.

Jack stood up and took to pacing in front of his window, drink in hand. White continued to watch him, not liking what he saw. He was using all his contacts and considerable influence to keep the situation under control, but the truth was, Jack himself seemed to be in a worrying state. Paranoid. A little erratic. After White's suggestion he'd recently hired a bodyguard, but he'd done it on his own. The man was not of White's choosing. Security was vital, but it could be handled invisibly. A bodyguard like the one Jack had chosen didn't look good. It was a problem that his client had not hired according to his recommendations. Damien Cavanagh had hired a mate to hang out at the house and *play* bodyguard: that was the reality.

"Have you heard from Beverley?" he enquired.

Beverley Cavanagh had been in Europe for several weeks. A gossip columnist had got hold of the story. It could have been innocuous—wife of Jack Cavanagh enjoys a European holiday—but it looked bad to have her travel alone while her husband was in Sydney, the subject of rumours of investigation for criminal activities, his historic transport deal on hold. It did not present the solid family front The American was hoping to see. Anything that suggested instability was bad at this point, from a professional standpoint. There were whispers that the long-standing Cavanagh marriage was in trouble.

"No," Jack said simply. He sipped his drink and stared out at the cloudless sky. The American wondered what he saw.

"Perhaps you could take a bit of time off?" he gently suggested. "Perhaps join her?"

"Do you think so?"

"It would be good to be seen together," he added. "Val d'Isère is lovely this time of year."

Jack turned, eyes downcast. "Perhaps I'll take a few days at the beach house and think it over."

"Good idea."

"Yes."

"I could arrange for more experienced security if you like. You remember I mentioned a candidate?" White ventured, still trying.

"That won't be necessary."

The American nodded. "Get some sleep. I'll let you know if there are any important developments," he said evenly.

Inside, he was already planning for contingencies. A man like White always had an escape plan. When things went wrong, they did so quickly. It appeared he was rapidly losing control of his client and he knew from experience what that could mean. Increasingly, he was of the feeling that he wanted out.

Before Cavanagh risked taking him down with him.

It was around midnight when Damien Cavanagh fetched his black Diablo from the bowels of the Cavanagh building in Sydney's CBD, having taken a frustratingly long taxi ride in from Palm Beach. Passing the security guard—who gawked when he realised who he was—Damien wondered briefly whether his father would be told he'd been there, and at what time. Obviously he was not going to just hang out at Palm Beach, like he was under house arrest. Grounded like a child. That was never going to happen. His father would know that.

Damien's car was one of only two left in the parking lot at this hour, and the only one under a protective cover. He pulled the dusty silver cover off and nodded to himself as he clapped eyes on the vehicle beneath. The alarm switched off with a chirp and he got in, ducking under the driver's door, which raised itself for him like the elegant wing of a bird. The ignition turned over easily, and minutes later the security guard was watching him with interest, and not a little jealousy, as he slunk past in the low-slung Lamborghini, paint gleaming like black enamel under the parking lot's fluorescent lights.

He pulled up outside the back door to Le Chat nightclub to find a dark-skinned, thickset man in a black T-shirt and pants guarding the door, his arms folded. He was heavily muscled and he evidently recognised Damien, or his car. He'd been expected.

The car door raised itself again and Damien stepped out,

closed the door and flicked the alarm on. The alley was tight and filthy. Music poured out of the club, the beat pounding the walls.

"Your car is good here, man," the meaty bouncer said and put his palm out, but Damien did not give him the keys. He didn't want some westie muscle-head trash taking his Diablo out for a joyride while he was inside. Fuck that. He breezed past, and the man opened the door for him at the last moment. Inside, the odour of cigar smoke filled his nose. Paul, the proprietor, appeared instantly, smiling broadly with teeth that glowed blue under the black lights.

"Good to see you. Won't you come this way?"

Damien was escorted into a small private room with plush red couches and curtains. A cheap-looking chandelier hung in the centre, and a bar lit with neon glowed in one corner, champagne bottles lined up neatly before a bevelled mirror.

He looked around, disappointed. "Where is she?" Damien asked impatiently.

"You want a drink, man? Veuve?" He clicked his fingers and gestured to a young woman in a miniskirt and short leather top. She disappeared behind a red curtain. "It's good to hear from you. It's been a while," he went on.

Damien didn't like the club owner's smile. It was a bit too easy, too try hard. "I've been away," he said vaguely and looked around the room.

It was just a tacky red square room, candle wax stuck to the gaudy carpet. Worse than he remembered.

The pink pill had really set in now. He wanted to fuck. "Where is she?"

"Have some champagne. Relax. You'll like her. Don't worry. I knew you'd like her as soon as you called . . ."

Damien didn't know this man Paul very well—he'd even

forgotten his last name—but he had some reputation in certain circles. And Damien had got desperate. Now the small talk was beginning to put him on edge. He didn't want to be jerked around. If he was going to take a chance, it had to be worth it, right? He didn't care to be manipulated. Too many drinks and the lighting too low, and you didn't know what you were getting. They could make them look younger than they really were. Some of them know the act.

In Monaco, if you know the right people, everything was easy. It was no problem. Australia irritated him. Small cities, small minds. Everyone so fucking boring and straight. He wouldn't have come back except that he'd run out of cash.

The curtains moved and an attractive blonde appeared. She held a bottle of champagne in a bucket of ice, and she smiled at him, hopeful. She set the bucket down and popped the cork, then passed him a fresh glass of champagne. Damien took it without giving her a second glance. She was not at all his type. He waited impatiently for the entertainment he'd been promised, and when she arrived, she did not disappoint. She was beautiful, small. Big brown eyes. Heart-shaped mouth. Her hair was straight and black, her skin a deep, glossy olive.

"This is Maria," Paul said. That wouldn't be her real name. "Like I said, she's new here. She doesn't speak a lot of English."

Damien smiled at her, his mind already ticking over what he wanted to do to her, and how. "What's your name? Maria?"

She just looked at him with those big eyes. "How old are you?"

She looked nervously to Paul. "Go on," he told her.

"Eighty teen," she said slowly. She was trying to say eighteen. And she was lying.

Good, he thought. *Good.*

"We want to be alone now," Damien told Paul, without looking at him.

"You've got as long as you like. I can bring you some—"

"I don't want anything. Just leave."

He heard the door close. Maria stood nervously in front of him. Perhaps Damien shouldn't have underestimated Paul. This was going to work out fine.

He heard the door open again. "Hey, I said I didn't want—"

The look in the girl's eyes told him to turn, and when he did, the words froze in his throat.

Holy shit.

The American.

His father's security man appeared through the doorway, and in a flash Damien found himself being taken forcibly by the arm away from the girl and out of the small private room of Le Chat.

"Your services will not be required," The American told Paul, who looked red-faced and panicked. He slipped him an envelope as they went past and Paul closed his hand around it.

Fuck.

Fuck, fuck, fuck, fuck, fuck.

Before he knew it, Mr. White had extracted the keys to Damien's car, and was placing him in the passenger seat. Damien was too mortified to protest.

"Put your head down," Mr. White told him as he got into the driver's side and closed the door.

"Hey, I—" he began to protest. "Put your head down *now*."

Finally he complied. He slid down in the passenger seat and bent his head low.

"Lower, please."

He shifted sideways and covered his face with his hands. "Better."

Mr. White pulled out onto Bayswater Road with Jack's son.

He immediately spotted the white car of a known paparazzi going the other way. He didn't want to be photographed driving Damien's car. He didn't want to be photographed at all. Mr. White avoided photographs and video recordings whenever possible, as a matter of habit.

"Stay down. There is paparazzi following," he informed Cavanagh Junior.

Damien took a sharp, audible breath. "Have you been watching me?" he asked.

"It is my job to look after your father's interests," he replied coolly. Of course he'd been watching him.

He shot a look to the passenger seat. Damien appeared slack-mouthed. He'd sat up again. "Stay down, please."

"You . . . He's having me spied on? You are spying on me? Hey, what happened to the bouncer guy?" he said, belatedly realising that no one had been next to his car.

"He could identify you."

"Holy shit! What did you do to him?" Damien was freaking out. Mr. White wondered what he was on. Ecstasy? Something else?

"Nothing has happened to him. He just needed to have a talk with one of my colleagues. You should know that Le Chat nightclub has CCTV cameras in every room. The toilets. And the private rooms."

Damien fell silent.

He didn't say another word on the drive back to Palm Beach.

CHAPTER 33

Ringing, ringing . . .

Andy woke with a heavy head to the irritating alarm ring of his mobile phone. He reached over to grab it off the hotel bedside table and accidentally knocked it onto the floor, where it continued to chirp and vibrate amongst his scattered clothes until it finally lay still.

Mak.

Andy sat up and observed the covers on the left side of the bed, pulled back and still showing the faint indent of a sleeping body. Had she really been there? No note. No sounds from the bathroom. He rubbed his eyes and glanced at the clock. One minute past six. He swung his legs off the bed, walked to the shower in a daze and started the water, which hit him in a cold spray at first, before warming. He stepped inside and let it pour over his face. It was far too early to ponder all that had happened the night before. That would require a lot of thinking, he knew.

First thing, coffee, he thought. Second, he had to get to the hospital and speak to someone about Jimmy's wounds. What was the trajectory of the bullet? If Mak's story checked out, and Jimmy was shot from close range or from level height and not above, how would Hunt explain that? Who was the third witness with Hunt? What did the two other officers see?

Showered and dressed in a dark blue suit that needed pressing, tie hanging loosely around his neck, Andy left his room and stalked the corridor towards the elevator.

Andy Flynn got out of his car and squinted against the increasingly intense sun, having forgotten his sunglasses in his race to leave the hotel room. He made his way to the small side entrance for the emergency department of St. Vincent's Public Hospital in Darlinghurst, pretending not to notice the press already camped on the footpath beyond the stretch of green terraced gardens, looking for a scoop. If Jimmy died, he would be the two hundred and fifty-second NSW police officer to be killed in the line of duty. Andy was not state police any more. He would be making no comments.

He passed an overweight woman in a wheelchair and a thin gentleman in a hospital gown clutching a cigarette and his IV drip outside the elevator for the car park—the sad unofficial smokers' corner. Kelley had texted him to say Jimmy was out of surgery and he could go up to ICU.

Hospitals.

Relatives were scattered around the waiting area, reading the *Daily Telegraph*, the front page facing out to show the face of his dying friend. And on the cover of the *Tribune* was another familiar face. It made him stop in his tracks.

The front page held a picture of Jimmy, but also one of Mak—golden-haired and smiling in a photograph from her modelling days.

SOCIALITE SUSPECTED IN COP SHOOTING.

Oh fuck.

One of the copies of the *Tribune* had been discarded on a chair. Andy snatched it up. There she was: Mak—Jimmy's accused shooter, the woman Andy had spent the night with. And though he now knew she was alive, he still had no way to reach her.

There'd been a time, before they'd lived together, when they would regularly leave notes for each other in the morning, after bouts of intense lovemaking. The urge to find her now, with everything going on, was almost overwhelming. Still, she'd made it clear that she was not going to frequent the same places, was not going to make it easy for herself to be found by the police or by Cavanagh's men or by anyone. He just hadn't realised that also meant *him*. He had no number for her. No address. Nothing. It had been a shock to have her in his bed and a worse shock to find her gone again, without a trace.

He flashed his badge to the triage nurse behind her bullet-proof glass, and was told to head up to the Intensive Care Unit. He knew the way. He walked the hospital corridors in a funk. Nurses passed him, some nodding hello. Carol Richardson, an ex-girlfriend he was on good terms with, worked at Prince of Wales. He wouldn't run into her here; still, some of the nurses seemed to hold Andy's gaze, he noticed, as if they knew him.

He approached the frosted-glass goldfish bowl of the ICU waiting room, with its grey carpets and red and blue chairs, beneath a crucifix.

"Andy . . ."

He whirled around. It was Angie Cassimatis. She was out of breath.

"I saw you walk in and I couldn't catch you. He's gone into surgery again," she said. Her eyes were red-ringed and large, and turned down in the corners like a sad puppy. He almost couldn't bear to look into them. "His heart hasn't been coping," she said.

Jimmy had been on Warfarin to thin his blood. That meant his internal bleeding was worse than it could have been.

"How are you? How are the boys?" he asked, putting a hand on her delicate shoulder.

"They're with my mother. They're . . . coping. I don't think Jackson understands what's happening. Edmond doesn't, of course."

"When is he due to come out?" She shook her head.

"Is there anything I can do?"

He had been distant in recent months, he knew. Geography had separated them, but worse, Andy's obsession with Mak's disappearance had separated them. In a way he'd been a poor friend of late.

She shook her head again. "Oh, Andy."

She pulled herself into his chest and wept while Andy stood helplessly.

"It's Nic, from the Electronic Evidence Branch."

Nic Joseph. "I can't really talk right now." Andy was waiting for news of Jimmy with an increasingly shaky Angie. "What's up?"

"Look, I thought you should know that something happened. With the laptop you gave me."

He now had Andy's complete attention. "It's been destroyed."

"Destroyed? Since I called you last night?" After what had happened to Jimmy, Andy had called to make sure that the laptop was still secure.

"There was a fire overnight. They think it was arson."

"But what was on the hard drive?"

"I didn't get to find out. We hadn't begun with it yet."

"Are you serious?"

"There's a backlog."

"Well, you have some sort of copy, don't you? Of the contents?" Joseph didn't answer.

Andy's mouth went dry. This could not be a coincidence. It seemed to mean that the Cavanaghs and their reach went further than he could have imagined.

"You must have a copy. Isn't that what you guys do?"

"Like I told you, we hadn't started on it yet. We were going to get to it this morning. I told you last night. It was safe here, I thought. I mean, nothing like this has ever happened before. The place is always locked."

"Who else knew what this was about? The case it was attached to?"

"Only two of us, I swear. Like, me and Garner. You know we are used to dealing with sensitive material. Nothing like this has happened before. I just don't understand it."

Andy understood it. Someone had got to Garner. Either that or . . .

The call.

Andy had called Joseph about it only hours before the fire.

That's how they knew. His phone was being tapped.

"Christ. This line isn't secure. I have to go," Andy said and hung up.

CHAPTER 34

Makedde Vanderwall looked at the pads of her fingers, wrinkled from a long soak in the cramped bath of her hotel. *Curious*, she thought, *how a little thing could change so much*. She cast a sideways glance at the object on the edge of the bath—a thin and fairly flat object about five inches long, housed in plastic.

Such a tiny little big little thing.

She'd woken in Andy's hotel bed before sunrise, barely believing where she was. And when the queasiness hit once more, the penny had finally dropped.

A thin line. Such a tiny little big little thing.

Mak swallowed with a mouth that was dry and ran a wet hand over her face, smearing her fingertips with the smudged mascara she'd slept in. Her black-streaked hand came to rest on her stomach, just beneath the surface of the soapy water. She looked down at her slim but still curvaceous body, observed the blackening bruise on her left hip, and her round breasts, which were sore and full—had been for a while now. Having never had a terribly predictable cycle, she'd imagined it was a sign her period was coming.

Not so.

Makedde was pregnant.

The test on the edge of the bath had been there for thirty minutes now. She'd looked at it many times. Within herself she'd already known what it would tell her. Still, when the tell-tale double lines appeared in the viewing window, she'd found it a shock. She'd been on the pill when she broke up with Andy months earlier—before their unexpected erotic reacquaintance last night—and her time with Bogey had been all too tragically brief. Could she really be pregnant? Apparently she could, and the real question was for how long. Now that the little test on the side of the bath was speaking to her with that one devastating, wonderful, mind-altering extra line, the line that changed everything, it was obvious that she'd had morning sickness for some time. Had the nausea started in Barcelona, or before then? Morning sickness usually happened in the first trimester, didn't it?

Mak took a breath and submerged herself.

A baby. God.

She blinked under the water and her eyes stung. With slippery hands she gripped the sides of the tub.

A baby?

They could have conceived before Andy left for Quantico. That would put her in the second trimester, wouldn't it? Or the end of the first trimester? Didn't they chart the number of weeks from the start of the cycle, before conception? She had no idea about these things. Yes, it could be Andy's. It couldn't be the assassin Luther Hand's, thank God, because she had escaped his clutches before . . .

And then another answer hit her.

Bogey, she thought.

My God. It could be Bogey Mortimer's child.

Heart pounding, Mak sat up, the water's surface resisting her.

She gasped for air and let out a small cry as bath water hit the tiled floor in small waves.

A terrible thought occurred to her.

The fall at the construction site. Would it have endangered her baby? She stepped out of the bath, shaking now, and stood before the mirror, dripping wet and running both hands over her belly, back and forth, wishing she could see inside herself, wishing she could see her future, see the future of the little creature in her belly, the baby announced by those two tiny lines. Growing up, she'd always wanted to be a mother one day, and had always somehow assumed she would be. But then she'd lost her own mother, and her personal world had sunk lower and lower. *Violence. Abduction. Murder.*

Now motherhood was hard to imagine, or at least very different to imagine.

Would she raise a child in this world? A woman on the run?

Could she?

Mak found the address of a clinic without difficulty. It was walking distance from the hotel and the receptionist said they could squeeze her in between appointments if she came straight over. Mak thanked her, put the hotel receiver down and ran an unsteady hand over her bare, clean-scrubbed face.

Pregnant?

She sat naked on the bed for another minute, wondering.

Makedde dressed in a T-shirt and dark jeans, marvelling at the fit of the waist, the way her lean stomach had begun to bow forwards with the slightest curve, just above the button. And again she noticed that her breasts had grown heavier week by week, pushing out from the confines of her bra. For the first time she saw that her changing physique pushed her T-shirt higher at the front, so that it did not quite cover her when she moved. She gripped the bottom of the fabric and pulled it down; as she stood before the mirror, brushing her damp hair into a knot on her head, she saw the edge rise again, exposing that thin strip of pale flesh across her belly. A skilfully applied slick of red lipstick made Mak feel less vulnerable and dishevelled somehow, and then she was ready. She pulled her shirt down one final time, slipped on her boots and a pair of mirrored glasses to shield herself from the world, and she left her small room.

Outside the cool air-conditioning of the hotel, the streets of Sydney seemed suddenly different. Smaller. More confined. More confronting. The city traffic hurt her ears, honking and screeching. How could there be so many people? The streets were chaotic. *It's only rush hour*, she thought, trying to remain calm as she struggled against streams of bodies on the packed sidewalks. Most people were shorter than her, some were taller, but all were seemingly keen to be somewhere else, fast. A tall man in a suit and tie brushed past her shoulder, turned his head and caught her eye. He was clean-shaven and handsome, and as she watched he looked her up and down. The lasciviousness of his gaze made Mak hunch her shoulders forwards, frowning. After a beat she realised she was holding her stomach, walking faster. A second man bumped straight into her—or her into him—and the impact shocked her so deeply that she fell sideways on the pedestrian crossing before catching herself and rushing on, tears gathering in the corners of her eyes.

A sign for the medical and dental centre on Pitt Street came into view just as her head began to ache. Her heart was beating too quickly, she realised. Beneath the shield of her sunglasses she'd started to cry again for no reason. *Calm yourself. Calm.* She followed the signs past a busy coffee shop and up a flight of stairs and down a corridor through a small waiting area to a reception desk, walking with deliberate movements, trying to be slow and composed. The waiting area was quiet. Only one person was waiting: an older man.

Two women were manning the desk, one busy with a call. The other woman looked up and offered a formal smile. "May I help you?"

"Yes, I called earlier for an appointment. I was told there might be time between other patients?"

"Petra?"

Mak nodded.

"We spoke on the phone. You said you hadn't been here before? Please fill out this form and get it back to me." She handed Mak a pen and a stack of forms attached to a stiff clipboard. "Shouldn't be too long before we can get you in."

Mak thanked her, clutched the clipboard to her chest and took a seat. The man in the chair opposite looked up at her, did a quick scan, tapped his foot and went back to reading the *Tribune*. Mak wondered about the journalist Richard Staples and whether she should call him to get some kind of explanation. What had happened exactly? Had he called the cops on her? To what end? Had his hand been forced? *You have other things to think about now, Mak. Choices to make.* She turned her attention to the form. She used Petra Blackman's name, and wondered fleetingly if the woman would be shocked to discover she was pregnant and that she owned a used car and a new motorcycle.

Mak filled out as little information as she thought she could get away with and handed the clipboard to the receptionist. She looked it over, then handed it back across the desk. "You didn't fill in your Medicare number." The woman pointed at the blank space with one unmanicured finger.

"Oh, that's right." Mak felt her cheeks flush. She dug through her purse and handed over Petra's driver's licence.

"Medicare card?"

She made a show of checking her purse again. "Oh, I've forgotten it. I can just pay and claim it later, can't I?"

"Of course. No problem."

"Sorry, I'm a little flustered."

"Take a seat and the doctor will see you shortly," the receptionist told her, something pitying in her expression. Mak had taken her glasses off when she'd walked in, and now she wondered if it was obvious she'd been crying.

She returned to her seat and ran fingertips under her eyes, taking a breath. She'd left her makeup at the hotel and she didn't have eye drops. Did she look a mess? Suddenly she realised that the man in the chair across from her was staring. He looked down when she caught him, and then looked up again, his puffy face animated with intense interest. After a moment he went back to his paper, but a creeping feeling of unease took hold of Mak. Instinctively, she put her sunglasses back on and crossed her arms. Was she becoming paranoid, or had he really been staring at her? Why? She got up and fetched herself a cup of water from a cold-water dispenser. There was another copy of the *Tribune* on the coffee table in the centre of the waiting room, and she picked it up and placed it in her lap when she returned to her seat. Urging herself to breathe slowly, she took a sip of cold water from the little paper cup and turned over the paper to the front page.

What she saw made her stomach flip.

I AM ON THE FRONT PAGE OF THE PAPER. JESUS CHRIST.

A journalist named Robin Harcourt had penned a sensational piece on the shooting of Detective Jimmy Cassimatis—a shooting for which one Makedde Vanderwall was the primary suspect. Mak had known that she was a suspect after her talk with Andy, but seeing it in print was an altogether different thing. And on the front page? Of the *Tribune*? The same paper Richard Staples worked for? Mak read the story like a woman reading her own obituary. It was incredible stuff. Her eyes raced over the words, head spinning. It continued on page seven, with a large photo of her infamous exit from the Cavanagh mansion at Damien's thirtieth-birthday party, a shot not dissimilar to the one she'd seen along with the price for her head, back in Luther Hand's Barcelona apartment. Mak was labelled a "model and socialite," who had done "some work as a private investigator." She was "considered armed and dangerous" and was alleged to have shot Jimmy Cassimatis, "well-loved, long-serving police officer" and "loving husband and doting father of four young children."

Model and socialite? I'm a goddamn socialite *now?*

Somehow, irrationally perhaps, her eyes drifted back to that word. Being labelled a socialite, with that photo of her at the Cavanagh mansion as unspoken proof, meant Mak was instantly associated with precisely the people she despised—the champagne-sipping Cavanagh set. It seemed the final insult. One glance at the article told Mak the tale of a greedy bimbo gone mad on too many parties and too much coke. Unethical, unlawful and perhaps even psychotic, probably motivated by money and drugs. It did not seem coincidental that her PI work was mentioned as an afterthought, and her work and schooling as a forensic psychologist was not mentioned at all. The word "alleged" was used in all the right places, but the message was clear—Mak was an unhinged party girl, worthless and highly dangerous. Every negative model stereotype was in play, and there was no other side to the story. Staples could have won a Walkley for breaking the case against Jack Cavanagh, and instead the paper he worked for was playing right into Cavanagh's hands. She'd thought they were better than that.

How naïve you were to come all this way for Richard Staples, believing he could help, she thought. And what could Andy do, now that the entire police force was gunning for her?

With great willpower Mak placed the paper back on the table, upside down. Rage gathered in her like a violent storm. She was not safe. Not here, and not anywhere. Would someone at the clinic recognise her? If the old man hadn't already. Now she was wanted by both sides of the law. Could she even leave the country without being stopped? How long could she survive like this?

"Petra Blackman? Dr Green will see you now."

Mak snapped a look in the receptionist's direction. *Oh. The appointment.* She stood up, unsure what to do, and after a beat decided to follow the receptionist's directions. Without a word she walked down the narrow, well-lit hallway to a small office, skittish and paranoid. It was quite possible that Mak looked sufficiently different from the photos in the paper that she had not been recognised. She had not used her real name. It might still be okay for now.

Maybe.

The doctor was waiting. She welcomed Mak and closed the door, giving her an added jolt of claustrophobia. Dr Green was an attractive woman in her late fifties, fashionably dressed and groomed. No spectacles or doctor's scrubs. Mak wasn't sure why she should be surprised by the woman's chic appearance, but she found that she was. Perhaps she harboured some stereo-types of her own.

"Ms Blackman," the doctor said, looking at her form. She indicated a metal-backed chair next to her desk. "Take a seat. How may I help you?"

"You can call me Petra." Mak smiled nervously and sat down. Nothing about the doctor's manner was suspicious.

"What brings you in today, Petra?" the older woman asked.

"I think I'm pregnant." Mak's voice wavered a little. Saying the words out loud felt entirely unreal. "But . . . I don't know."

"Have you taken a home pregnancy test?"

"Yes," Mak admitted.

"Most of the store-bought tests are quite accurate these days," the doctor advised. Mak absorbed that bit of info with a slightly increased internal panic. *So it's for real then.* "Let's take another look, shall we?" Dr Green handed Mak a cup. "Urinate into this and bring it back. The toilets are just down the hall."

Fantastic.

Thankfully, the toilets were the opposite direction from the waiting room and she didn't have to walk past the man who might have already recognised her. She did what she had to, undisturbed, and when she returned minutes later the doctor did another test, right in front of Mak, using a dropper. The test she used operated no differently from the one Mak had taken herself. After perhaps thirty seconds the double blue line showed and Mak felt her stomach tighten.

"You are pregnant. Congratulations," the doctor said.

Mak smiled in response, but felt shaky. The doctor must have noticed it.

"Is this the news you were hoping for?" she asked.

"I don't know. I wasn't . . ." Mak wasn't sure how to finish that sentence. *I wasn't planning a baby. I was on birth control. I wasn't thinking this was possible.* It was a surprise, yes, but now that it appeared she really was pregnant and it wasn't some error, she found she was hopeful. And worried.

"I took a major fall. Do you think I'm still . . . that the baby is okay?" Her eyes stung, and the room started to blur. Tears had welled up again. She realised she wanted the baby. Really wanted it to be okay.

The doctor offered her a box of tissues. "I see. Is that how you hurt your wrist?"

"Yes." Mak noticed it was visibly red and swollen. "Have you experienced any pain or bleeding?"

"Bleeding? No. Nothing like that."

"Good. The foetus is quite well padded in there. You'd be surprised. How did you fall exactly?"

Being chased by cops. "How do you mean?"

"Backwards, onto your wrist?"

"Essentially."

"Let's take a look." Mak extended her arm and Dr Green examined the swollen wrist. "It will be fine," she announced. "Nothing broken. Some ice will help with any bruising. Was there any blow to the stomach?" she asked.

To the stomach? Mak shook her head.

"If you weren't too badly hurt yourself, it's very likely everything is fine. An ultrasound will be able to tell us more." She opened a drawer and got out a slip of paper. It was a form of some kind and she began filling it out. "Now, when was your period due?"

"I don't know actually. I've never really kept track of things like that. I know that sounds silly." Her face grew warm. "It's been a pretty, um, hectic few months." She swallowed.

"The ultrasound will tell us how many weeks you are and they should be able to check that everything is normal. Call them today and hopefully they will be able to get you in in the next week or two. They tend to be quite busy this time of year. Do take it easy the next few days and, if you have any bleeding at all, call me immediately. We have an after-hours number."

Mak accepted the referral.

"Are you okay?" The doctor was watching her.

Mak managed a smile. "I'm okay. I just have a terrible

headache," she said. The headache was real, but certainly the least of her problems. She didn't know if she could wait a week to learn how far along she was. Where would she be in a week? Truthfully, she didn't know if she would live that long.

"You can take paracetamol for it. Panadol is fine. No aspirin," Dr Green said, and it took a moment for Mak to realise what she meant.

"Oh yes. Of course." Not all medications were safe. "You think . . . that I might be okay if there is no bleeding?" Mak ventured.

The woman smiled gently. "Yes. I'm sure you'll be fine."

She stood and thanked the doctor, holding the referral she doubted she would use.

The doctor smiled again and then tilted her head. "Have you been here before?" she asked. "It's just that you do look familiar."

Mak felt a rush of adrenaline. "I get that a lot," she said. "There's an actress on *Home and Away*, you know the one? We look a bit alike. It's not me. I'm not her . . ."

The doctor squinted. "No, I don't think that's it."

"Thanks again," Mak said and hurried out.

She paid and left, relieved the man from the waiting room was no longer there. She rushed out into the sunlight, her sunglasses hiding fresh tears.

What kind of world was this? What kind of world would she be bringing a child into?

CHAPTER 35

Bradley Hunt sat in the office of his commander, who looked tense. It was easy to see why. On his desk were copies of the *Tribune* and *Daily Telegraph*.

"Did I say no press?" he said and pushed the papers across his desk towards Hunt.

"I was as surprised as anyone," Hunt said and swallowed. He needed the commander on side, for a couple more years, anyway. "I guess news travels."

"This makes us look bad. At least no one is quoted." Hunt nodded.

The commander watched him so keenly he felt the urge to push his chair back. "I saw your report," he said. "Why don't you take me through it again?"

Hunt had to be very careful now. He had to be very careful what he said, how he acted. A lot was riding on the way this all panned out. "Our intel was good," he began. "She did show and she was armed. There were a couple of uniforms in the area, so they came as backup. I suspected she was dangerous."

"You suspected she was dangerous, but you sent Jimmy in alone?"

He hesitated. "We felt it was best to send Jimmy in alone, so she wasn't spooked. They have been on friendly terms in the past, when she was dating Andrew Flynn, the former—"

"I know who Flynn is," the commander cut in impatiently. Hunt paused. "We certainly didn't, um, see this coming. I could not have imagined she would shoot him. I guess we underestimated her."

"I'd say that much is certain."

Hunt absorbed the verbal jab without comment. "I was just outside the entrance, listening," he went on. "Jimmy went in and tried to get her to come in peacefully, but they got into an argument. She resisted and pulled a firearm. She shot Detective Cassimatis before any of us could do anything. I went after her, but she ran up some stairs and jumped out a window."

"And where were these backup officers, uh, Granger and Wosley?" He glanced at the report and back again.

"I had them near the entrance, in case she tried to escape. One of them called for assistance and the other helped me give chase, but like I said, she ran up into the building, to some kind of mezzanine level, and then leaped out. We lost her. I didn't predict she would jump out the window, sir. It was quite a drop."

"And she couldn't be found in the area?"

He shook his head. "From the way she was dressed, we are guessing she had a motorcycle or scooter nearby. I heard a bike. I think that was how she got away."

"And you didn't get a numberplate, a model or make? Nothing?"

"No, sir. She just vanished," he said weakly.

"People do not vanish."

"Yes, sir. She's armed and dangerous. As I've said, we've checked with customs. She didn't come into the country legitimately."

"Has Mr. Cavanagh been made aware of what occurred?"

"I think he should be warned. She could be going after him."
He'd recommended a bodyguard for Jack Cavanagh—a friend
of one of his cousins—as a way of getting into the inner circle,
but Cavanagh had organised someone else. The commander did
not know about that exchange, of course. It wouldn't look good
to be too involved when an investigation was underway into
Cavanagh's dealings. Not that that investigation was going to get
anywhere. Neither would Mak. When the smoke cleared, Hunt
felt sure he would be generously rewarded.

The commander clenched his jaw, eyes unreadable. "You'll
have whatever resources you need to bring her in. There can't be
any more mistakes. Get this woman."

"Yes, sir," Hunt said.

Makedde Vanderwall stopped at a payphone in Kings Cross.
Her hand hovered around the keypad.

Dammit. What's the point?

Richard Staples had ratted her out. Or he'd been intercepted. They'd probably had him watched since his feature
on them was first published, she realised. They were probably
trying to find ways to discredit him, take away the threat to
them his interest caused. Their tentacles were far reaching. She
wondered if Richard was in actual danger as well? What would
the Cavanaghs do to him if he tried to write about them again?
Would he find himself out of a job or worse? Would he have an
accident? Did he sense he was in danger?

And now that Mak was on the front of the paper her time was
numbered, no matter how many disguises she used and wigs
she bought.

Enough.

She had a disturbing thought. She'd been careful, but what if
they could trace her iPhone? She still hadn't got rid of it.

Instinctively, she cracked it against the edge of the metal phone box. She smashed it again and stepped out of the booth, head down, and dumped the damaged phone in the garbage bin, where it sat on top of discarded fast-food trays and Coke bottles before sliding down and disappearing. She had the footage of Jimmy's shooting in online storage and could easily download it at an internet café: it wasn't worth the risk to keep the phone. Especially now. Especially now that she had another reason to live.

Mak spotted a punkish young woman, a backpacker, and followed her. She was at least five foot eleven and perhaps twenty-five. Even features. Blue eyes.

She would have to do.

The door was opened for her with a small key with a rusted edge. The room inside was the colour of faded photographs. It smelled of salt air and faintly of smoke, and had a small seventies kitchenette, a sagging double bed, a television with an old cathode-ray tube and a single window with a view of the dark waters of Palm Beach. Mak pulled her boots off and walked across the multicoloured carpet to inspect the bathroom, feeling the remnants of sand under her feet.

It was a far cry from the luxurious hotel she'd enjoyed. Small but adequate. The tiles around the bath were highlighted with green-tinged grout. Mak popped her head around the wall and smiled. "I'll take it!"

The landlady—an elderly woman who'd already put her hair in curlers when Mak showed up, answering the ad—looked delighted. Even more so when Mak provided her with the first week's rent in cash, not that she planned to be there that long. It had a private entrance from the rear. She was promised privacy and a place to garage her motorbike. That was enough.

Mak didn't own a lot of things. What clothing she had she hung on wire hangers in the tiny upright closet. She stepped into the bathroom and sized herself up in the mirror.

It was certainly too late for witness protection, not that she had ever seriously considered it an option. Now it was clear there was nowhere left for her to turn, and with her face on the front page of the most read newspaper in Sydney, it wouldn't take long for a well-meaning member of the public to recognise her and dob her in, if an enterprising killer didn't get to her and her unborn baby first. She doubted she would survive police custody while Cavanagh had corrupt cops in his pockets. She doubted she could survive being on the run much longer.

As she saw it, she only had one option left.

In the aged patina of the bathroom mirror she looked substantially different from the woman on the front of the paper, but not different enough. She picked up a pair of scissors and ripped them out of the plastic pack. She gave them a trial snip and grabbed a section of her thick hair. After years spent as a model she'd learned about makeup, but she'd never really learned how to cut hair. A hairdresser, she was not. She pulled a section up and snipped, watching with strange fascination as it fell into the basin. The second piece was easier. She snipped and snipped, locks of dark hair falling to the basin, to her feet.

When she was done Makedde looked at the driver's licence she'd stolen, then back at her reflection. "Hello, Kristi," she said.

CHAPTER 36

Mak found herself on Davoren Lane.

It was a narrow, grey two-level terrace, barely four metres wide. It would have been built in Victorian days, but the ironwork was gone. No plants in the barred windows. No welcome mat. Mak knocked on the front door, a smile pasted on her features. When no one answered she held her ear to the timber for a moment, looked both ways down the narrow lane and resolved to pick the lock. It was an old five-pin tumbler—easy. She quickly let herself in and closed the door behind her. She flicked a switch and a bare light bulb illuminated the space. She frowned. It was tiny. A real dive. Scratched and patchy paint job. She pulled on a pair of latex gloves, wiped her prints off the light switch and door with the corner of her shirt, and looked around. The lounge room contained a threadbare couch and a bunch of sagging cardboard boxes, stacked up. They were dusty and looked like they'd been there for years, perhaps from the move. She walked through an open doorway to discover a small kitchen. It was no larger than the one in the flat she'd decided to rent, only it was walled in. She literally could not turn around. It was depressing, and she left it immediately. There was a steep staircase a few feet inside the front door and now Mak crept up the steps to examine the upstairs. She found herself in a living room with another threadbare couch, this one heaped with unwashed clothes. Boxes of DVDs. A small flat-screen television. A makeshift office in the corner.

The terrace was a one bedroom. She could see the bed from where she stood. She moved towards the cluttered and cramped desk in the far corner of the room. It had a standard office computer chair tucked under it. An old nineties PC sat in the centre, surrounded by stacks of papers and magazines: *Australian Hunter Magazine, ASJ—Australian Shooters Journal, Australian & New Zealand Handgun.* Mak sifted through the stacks and picked up a piece of unopened mail.

Mr. John Dayle. Bingo.

Plastic slat blinds hung over the window above the desk. She pulled them back and saw, leaning in the window, a framed photograph of a skinny man in his early twenties, proudly holding a caught fish. "Hello, John Dayle," Mak said quietly and coughed. *God, it's dusty.* The photo looked as old as the computer.

Dayle had left some bags and clothes heaped on the floor. Some shirts were on hangers and some tossed on the couch. Looked like he didn't have a closet, or he didn't use it. His bed was a twin and unmade, she noticed. The bedroom door was ajar and now Mak reluctantly walked into the room, leaned over the side table and lifted the slats off the window—again the slats were so dusty she covered her mouth with the crook of one elbow to avoid sneezing. Peering out into the darkness between the terraces, Mak tried to get a sense of the man who inhabited this sad little space. This John Dayle seemed lonely, untidy and far from rich. And he might come back at any time, she reminded herself. Mak let the slats down, paused and lifted them again, eyes brighter. This window had a view of the same small courtyard the one over the computer did. The courtyard appeared to belong to the house behind. She squinted, tilted her head. She hadn't noticed it before.

It's the victim's home, Mak thought suddenly as she spotted the crime-scene tape across the back doors, rippling slightly in the moonlit breeze. It was a view of his murdered neighbour's courtyard, and her back windows. She wondered if he'd watched her often.

Mak shivered.

Well, let's see if Andy's right about you, John, she thought and let the slats down. The Glock felt reassuring against the small of her back as she flicked on the light of the small bedside table lamp and got on her knees. Her gloved hand wandered across the filthy carpet under his bed like an inquisitive spider, moving carefully around tangled fishing line, a rod and reel, crumpled tissues and several well-fingered magazines. She squinted at the magazines, lip curled in distaste, and flipped each one open to search for notes or photographs. Nothing. Mak pushed aside a revolting pair of dirty men's underwear and pulled out two black rectangular boxes. She tilted her chin, opened the first one. What she saw made her eyes narrow. A pair of standard-issue handcuffs, easy enough to buy online. She examined them with her gloved hands, feeling the weight and checking for the telltale quick release latch of novelty cuffs. No. These were the real deal. Also in the box was a length of climbing rope, looped neatly and tied off with a piece of string. A clean hunting knife sat in its leather sheath looking new and unused. A mouth gag with a red ball. It was an intriguing series of items to have stored together, she thought, and when she pulled the last item out her mind began to pull unwanted memories to the surface. *A scalpel.* Why would this man have a scalpel? That's what it was, wasn't it? Mak placed the steel blade on the carpet, eyeing it with suspicion as if it might move on its own, and opened the second box, pulling back a folded handkerchief, the significance of which escaped her.

And beneath the handkerchief she saw. The clippings.

With a sickening jolt of recognition she found herself looking at the familiar face of Ed Brown, the "Stiletto Killer," in grainy newsprint.

After a moment of shocked stillness, she dug deeper into the box and pulled out layers and layers of clippings. SYDNEY SERIAL KILLER, POLICE CLUELESS, one headline shouted. STILETTO KILLER STRIKES—BECKY ROSS MURDERED, another said. She read one more: SOAP STAR MURDERED—*Television star Becky Ross, who went missing after the launch of her own fashion label on Thursday, was found murdered in Centennial Park yesterday . . .*

Words and images of Ed Brown's horrendous crimes, lovingly collected and pored over. It was all in there. And amongst it all was a picture of Makedde's closest friend, Cat Gerber, smiling innocently in a flattering dress. She was the reason Mak had first visited this country. Cat had always raved about Sydney. And then Mak had found her dismembered amongst the tall, swaying grasses of La Perouse beach on the day of her first modelling job in Australia—the day she met Detective Andy Flynn.

CANADIAN MODEL—THIRD VICTIM OF STILETTO KILLER, the headline above Cat's face said.

Makedde lifted the image tenderly, took in her friend's face in the tiny dots of newsprint and felt a tear escape her. *Cat.* It had been more than five years since she'd laid eyes on her friend. Mak took a breath, turned the clipping over and placed it face down on the carpet. And there in the box beneath her slain friend's image was one of Makedde herself.

MODEL WITNESS FLEES TO HONG KONG.

It was a blurry photograph of Mak boarding a flight to Hong Kong, only one of many more clippings relating to the Stiletto Killer case. Some showed Andy, hand out in front of the lens, trying to shield himself from the flash glare. Many showed Ed's victims, all attractive women, some models, the earliest victims allegedly prostitutes. Mak had nearly joined their number. What she'd suffered at the hands of Ed Brown was unthinkably horrific. He'd tied her up, he'd . . .

No.

She pushed the memories firmly out of her conscious mind, but her toe began to tingle right where Ed Brown had severed it with his scalpel and the microsurgeons had expertly sewn it back on. It sometimes did that—tingled when she was distressed. Seeing these clippings made her sick inside. They made her angry. But Ed Brown wasn't going to hurt her any more. He was dead now and Mak was alive—the only known survivor of his twisted obsession.

And this fucking guy idolises him, she thought, the clippings laid out around her like puzzle pieces.

John Dayle idolises the Stiletto Killer. He wants to be him and he used his neighbour to practise . . .

CHAPTER 37

What are you doing here, Dana?

Young Federal Agent Dana Harrison sat on the stool with a drink in her hand, nursing a crick on the left-hand side of her neck. She used her left hand to change gears in her old RAV4 and the gearbox was sticky—after three hours of driving it had given her a headache.

She was in Sydney, which in itself was not so unusual for her, but in a way she still wasn't sure what she was doing at this bar, with her dark hair worn in curls at her shoulders, and the only pair of stiletto shoes she owned on her feet. She was off duty and she could do what she wanted to, she supposed. This, it seemed, was what she most wanted to do.

You fucked up. You fucked up with Flynn, she thought.

She was still embarrassed by the exchange. Why did she have to ask him for that drink? Why? It had been a stupid slip. She hadn't meant it to come across so unprofessionally. She'd thought it would sound casual, but it hadn't. She could tell by the look on his face the moment the words had left her lips, and she'd wished she could take it back. There was sexual tension between them. She hadn't accepted that until it was too late. She should have noticed how much she wanted him to like her. She'd wanted it a bit too much. What kind of psychologist was she if she couldn't even see these obvious things in herself?

She and Flynn had barely spoken on the drive back to Canberra. And now she was back here, alone.

What are you doing, Dana?

On the drive up she had told herself it had been too long since she'd come to Sydney to see her interstate friends. Too long since her last visit. She'd needed to get some distance from work, after the awkward exchanges with Andrew Flynn, a man she admired, and yes, found attractive, in a hard, brooding way. But as she'd checked in to her hotel, and dressed and hailed a taxi to Surry Hills, she'd had to face her true intentions, the idea she'd been toying with since she'd slipped into the driver's seat of her car. And now she sat on the bar stool, restless and coiled, and feeling an unfamiliar, seething rage. And she knew why she'd come to this bar where she knew no one.

No one except a man named John Dayle.

Someone has to keep an eye on him.

The surveillance team had been pulled, not because of lack of suspicion but lack of resources. Lack of resources, of all things. And he'd quite possibly murdered that poor woman. Tortured her. Done unspeakable things to her. It was a nightmare. She had not joined the cops to be useless. She could not just sit in her flat in Canberra waiting to hear news. *No.* If Dayle came and acted suspiciously, she could do something about it, at least. Maybe even help crack the case. Maybe even help someone, which was why she'd joined the police in the first place. Maybe even get herself noticed for all the right reasons. Not just for the scholarship but for what counted. The real work.

She was tough enough for this.

CHAPTER 38

Mak heard a key in the lock. She'd been in wait for John Dayle for over an hour now, sitting at the base of the staircase in his narrow, filthy terrace, rage coiled in her. Luther's Glock tingled at her lower back.

Quiet as a shadow, Mak stood up on the bottom stair and leaned her back to the wall, listening as the front door creaked open. She heard a single set of footsteps, an unintelligible muttering and the click of the door as it shut. Again, he didn't throw the dead bolt. There was something like the rustle of bags and the main light came on, illuminating the filthy lounge room. She heard the thud of rubber-soled shoes—one step, two—and a shocked yelp of surprise as the man fell forwards, tripping on the thin fishing wire she'd set up to catch him. He landed on his knees and palms, something spilling heavily on the wooden floor with a thud. Mak emerged in a swift blur and pushed herself on top of him, seizing his wrists and pulling them behind his back. In seconds the cuffs were on him and she had him flipped over and wriggling on the floor at her feet, the gleaming scalpel at his face.

And then Makedde Vanderwall saw that he was not alone. She took her eyes off Dayle to see that he had carried with him a young woman in a skirt and stiletto shoes. She was on the floor next to him. She wasn't speaking.

"Holy shit! What the fuck?" the man said, legs flailing. He was pale and insubstantial and he smelled like old sweat.

"I wouldn't move if I were you. Tell me your name," she said.

"What?"

She pressed the scalpel blade to the skin of his unwashed cheek. "Your name."

"John. John Dayle."

So she had the right man. And Andy had picked it. Mak's eyes flickered to the woman again. Her eyelids moved. She made a groaning sound. She was alive. Was she drunk, or. . . ?

"We need to chat." Mak pulled Dayle up by his T-shirt with a yank and led him to the computer chair she'd brought down from upstairs. She spun the chair around. "Sit down."

He didn't. He just stood in front of her, panicking, his red-rimmed eyes flitting about the room as he tried to decide what to do. With a single shove she pushed him into the chair, and the metal of the cuffs clacked on the hard plastic of the seat. Mak pulled the rope out and looped it around his puny chest and arms, tying it over until it was nice and tight and she was good and satisfied. She tied the ends off at the back in a neat square knot. His legs were free, but that didn't seem to be a problem.

"There we are," she said, standing before him.

"What the fuck is this?!" he shouted, and she calmly leaned in and moved the scalpel under his nose. She shook her head silently from side to side and he grew quiet again, his breathing rapid. Mak saw a glimpse of her own reflection in the blade and it was something from a nightmare—a grinning creature with shorn hair and white teeth, and death shining in its eyes. She retracted the blade.

"What did you do to her? Did you drug her?" He looked away and swallowed.

"Roofies? Rohypnol?"

He didn't answer. She pushed the scalpel against the sensitive flesh of his nostril.

"Yeah," he said quietly. "I slipped her a roofie, okay? Big deal."

Mak licked her lips and took a deep breath. She was so angry. So angry. She needed to stay calm, to think. Mak left Dayle tied to the chair and she crossed the small room to kneel by the woman's side. She was attractive and healthy, with dark hair. Her breathing and her heartbeat were regular.

What could Mak do?

She realised she was still holding Dayle's horrible scalpel, so she put it down, put her arms around the barely conscious woman's torso and lifted her up. It took her a moment to balance the weight of her, then she carried the petite woman across to Dayle's couch and lay her down on her side to make sure that her airway was clear. She would have to sleep it off and when she woke, it was likely that she wouldn't remember anything that had happened after the drug was slipped to her. It was the infamous "date rape" drug. Mak wondered how often Dayle had used it.

"It's okay. You are safe now," Mak whispered to the woman, unsure if she could be heard. The eyes fluttered and closed again. Her breathing was slow and heavy, but she was okay.

Mak returned to Dayle, who had gone very quiet. "So, you are a rapist. And a killer now, too. Congratulations."

He opened his mouth to protest, but nothing came out. "You know, John, you are nothing like him."

"What? Who?" He struggled in his binds again, the initial shock of the situation starting to wear off.

She leaned in again, letting the sharp tip of his scalpel sit just inside his nostril once more. "The Stiletto Killer," she said.

"The. . . ? I don't know what you mean," he said, quivering and seeming to grow yet smaller.

Mak smiled. "He was much smarter than you. And much, much tidier." She looked around the flat disapprovingly. "He was a neat-freak actually. And quite precise about everything he did. He'd never do something quite so stupid as kill his own neighbour."

"Kill my. . . ? Uh, uh . . . Ms. Hempsey? No! I . . . I . . . couldn't do that."

He was a terrible liar. And Mak had nothing left for him but rage and impatience.

She flicked the scalpel blade and his nose opened up, blood spilling down his face. He cried out and she put a finger to his lips to hush him, his blood staining her latex gloves. He quickly shut up again.

"Every time you lie to me, I cut you," she told him.

In addition to having his rope, knife and scalpel ready, she had placed a few key items she'd found in his bedroom on the staircase, ready for their discussion. Now she left him struggling uselessly in the binds as she plucked the first item from the stairs. When she returned he'd kicked the chair over, but she righted it again with ease.

"Okay. Why don't you tell me about this?" She held up a clipping about Ms. Hempsey's death. It was a small article from several pages into a *Tribune*, published the previous week. Mak had read it online after the discussion with Andy.

"It's . . . it's just a news clipping."

"Of ?"

"My neighbour died recently," he said cautiously.

"Died? No. She didn't die. She was raped and murdered," Mak corrected him.

He nodded and looked to his knees. By now he would know that she'd looked under his bed and found the other clippings. They'd all been in the same box.

"So, did you enjoy your correspondence with Ed Brown?" Mak said. She smiled joylessly and held up a well-worn letter from the Stiletto Killer. His handwriting repulsed her. His words, even more so.

John Dayle looked at it with wide eyes, but said nothing. "You must have found him quite inspiring," she said, without a trace of emotion in her voice. "He seemed to really appreciate your letters. What does he call you here?" She unfolded one of the pages. "*My comrade.* Comrade? Interesting choice of words." Dayle said nothing. She supposed the correspondence would have been read by the warden. It was a wonder that it hadn't pegged Dayle as a person of interest to the police. Then again, a lot of prisoners received letters. Especially high-profile prisoners.

"Anything you want to tell me about your correspondence?" He kept his head down, saying nothing. "No? Okay, let's move on then."

She calmly placed the letters on the floor, displaying them in a semicircle, and she walked to the staircase and returned with the jar, the final damning piece of evidence. Floating in the sloppy formalin was a severed toe, the nail painted with red polish. Mak had been sick when she'd first discovered it. She'd thrown up in Dayle's filthy bathroom, vomiting what little food she'd managed to keep down earlier. Now she only felt rage.

"And what about this?"

On seeing it in her hands, John arched backwards and struggled again, trying to get away. He screamed and she put a hand over his mouth to muffle the sound.

"Now, John, we don't want company, do we? You don't want company, do you? You and your souvenir from Ms. Hempsey would make quite a sight."

She removed her hand and he watched her with wide eyes. "Who are you?" he asked.

"Me? I'm Makedde Vanderwall. I thought you might have recognised me by now. Oh, it's the hair, isn't it?" She ran a hand over her short locks, feeling the weightlessness, the tingling sensitivity of her scalp. He only stared, but she could see in his eyes that he knew who she was now. His mind struggled to piece it together. Her here, in his terrace. And she was sure by now he suspected he was going to die.

"Now, I'm going to have to gag you for this next bit," she explained and placed his red ball gag in his mouth. She tightened the straps around the back of his head, then picked up the hammer.

"Ed Brown used to bludgeon his victims with a common household hammer. Like this one I found under your bed, wrapped in plastic. He didn't like them to die that way. He liked to keep them alive while he did horrible things to them." She looked at the hammer inquisitively. "Doesn't look like you cleaned it terribly well. The police would like this, I think."

He tried to speak, but with the gag, not much came out. "Now, I'm a reasonable woman, John. I don't want to bludgeon you to death. I don't want to rape you, torture you, do to you what you did to poor Victoria Hempsey. So I'll give you another option. Would you like another option, John?"

He nodded emphatically.

She pulled the knife out and waved it in front of him. "I can either bludgeon you to death, or you can just cut your own throat, now, with your knife and have it over with."

He struggled and started to cry, his face turning red.

"Don't be like that, John. You'll get no sympathy from me. You killed that woman—you made her suffer horribly—for no other reason than because you wanted to, and now you are going to die here, tonight. Be grateful you have a choice at all. Victoria didn't have a choice. Ed Brown's victims didn't have a choice. I didn't have a choice.

"So what will it be, John?"

Makedde removed the gag and let him drink from a bottle of vodka from the freezer, holding it to his lips for him. Once he said he was ready, she untied him and gave him the knife. Under her watchful eye and the sight of Luther's compact Glock, she witnessed him slit his throat. It took him three tries, hesitating again and again before he got a deep cut. It was not an easy way to go. You had to really mean it. She made sure he meant it.

It took longer for him to die than she'd hoped. But she was patient. To her amazement and dismay, she didn't feel a thing, watching the man kill himself. Not a thing.

Mak arranged the clippings and artifacts around him—a shrine of horrors. The knife had fallen from his hand and she left it where it lay. The hammer and scalpel were lined up at his feet with the formaldehyde jar, like the ones found in Ed Brown's flat and widely reported in the papers at the time of the Stiletto Murders. Victoria Hempsey's killer was himself the grim centrepiece. On the couch was the woman who would have been his next victim. She would wake to a terrible shock, but hopefully that would be in a hospital, not here, with this gruesome display in front of her. No, Mak had no choice. She had to call for medical help for this woman. Her hands still cased in latex gloves, Mak dragged Dayle's phone over to the couch and put the receiver in the unconscious woman's hand. She dialled Triple 0 and when the operator answered, said nothing.

Mak left the terrace unlocked and stepped out into the dark, rainy streets of Surry Hills.

She walked to the nearest payphone and again dialled Triple 0. "I saw a man drag an unconscious woman into his terrace on Davoren Lane," she said, using the Spanish accent she'd been working on. "He was white male, around thirty years old, wearing a red baseball cap. I think she was drugged. I am really concerned for her safety." Mak refused to give a name, but gave Dayle's address and hung up. Once Dayle and the woman were discovered, that recording would be played and replayed many times, she knew.

She hoped she was not recognisable. Or perhaps by then it wouldn't matter.

Benumbed, Mak left the payphone booth, and climbed on her waiting motorbike.

And she rode for hours. To forget.

CHAPTER 39

Early Friday morning, Andy's phone rang. *It's Jimmy*, was his first thought on coming violently into wakefulness.

He sat up and brought his mobile to his ear. "Flynn," he croaked.

"How fast can you get to Davoren Lane?" Inspector Kelley asked him abruptly.

Davoren Lane?

Andy looked at the hotel clock. It was five-thirty. "By six," he said, with a mouth that had instantly been drained of all moisture. "Another victim?"

"Just get here," Kelley said sharply and hung up.

When Andy pulled into Davoren Lane there was no question where the action was. John Dayle's terrace was cordoned off with police tape and the whole narrow alley was crawling with cops. He recognised two of them instantly: Mak's friend Detective Karen Mahoney—and Agent Dana Harrison.

Andy parked his car carelessly just beyond the action and stepped out, confused by what he was seeing, his AFP badge displayed for the benefit of a constable who waved him through as he ducked under the barrier. Andy's eyes were fixed on Dana's slumped figure. She turned her head slightly and he caught a glimpse of her puffy face in the early morning light. His heart constricted. Had she been crying? Oddly, she was wearing clothing that seemed not to fit. Denim jeans and a sports jacket, both too big? What the hell was she doing in Sydney? Doing *here*?

Detective Mahoney had an arm around her. She seemed to be comforting her.

"What the hell's going on?" Andy blurted, feeling himself panic. He strode towards them, and Karen met his eyes with a look that told him to cool it. "What's going on?" he said, looking from her to Harrison.

Dana flicked her bloodshot eyes in his direction and then quickly looked to her feet. She appeared as white as paper. "Sorry, Andy," she said, and before he could ask her why she was there and what she was sorry for, Inspector Kelley emerged from the terrace.

Kelley waved Andy over. "Flynn. I need you over here." His eyes went from Andy to Dana and back again. "Now, please."

Disoriented by Dana's presence, Andy walked towards Dayle's threshold, where Kelley pulled him to one side of the entrance. "Please tell me you don't know anything about this," he said quietly before they went inside.

"About what? What the fuck is going on? What is Agent Harrison doing here?"

Kelley watched him. "So you don't know?"

"I don't know what?" Andy thought he might punch the brick wall.

"Dayle is dead," Kelley explained.

All things considered, the news was welcome. "What happened? *Why is Harrison here?*" Andy asked.

"Your agent is talking us through everything she remembers,

which isn't much. She was found here, unconscious, after a call to Triple 0 last night."

Andy's face froze for a moment, gaping. "She was taken to St. Vincent's."

St. Vincent's. His mind flashed to Jimmy and for a moment he tried unsuccessfully to piece together what had happened to Jimmy and what he was seeing now.

"She was released half an hour ago," Kelley continued. "She says she's fine. They did a rape kit and thankfully found no obvious evidence of any sexual assault. They kept her clothing to be tested, anyway. Blood tests haven't come back, but it looks like she may have been drugged."

Holy fucking hell.

Andy had to work hard to keep himself calm. "I don't . . . understand. What was she doing here? Did he track her down? He *drugged her*?"

"Your agent spent the evening at the White Cockatoo, Flynn. She was spotted being dragged here afterwards, according to an anonymous call."

Andy's mind scrambled to make the connection, and when it hit, it felt like a kick to the stomach. He recalled how Dana had reacted when she'd heard the surveillance team had been called away. How livid she'd been. Her reaction had given him pause, but he couldn't have imagined she would do something like this. Just exactly what had she done?

"This is the scene of a suspicious death now. Though it appears your agent was drugged—was a victim here—technically she will need to be cleared as a suspect."

Andy's head swam.

Kelley caught Andy's eye and spoke in a low, steady voice. "You were right about Dayle. He's our guy. There's no question now. Your agent has been through a lot, so whatever her reasons for being at the White Cockatoo, take it easy on her, okay?"

Andy nodded. "Show me what we have."

Kelley turned his back and stepped inside the terrace. Andy followed. "You've been in here before, yes?"

"Yeah."

They walked along the short hallway, past the base of a steep staircase, and stopped. Dayle was in front of them, surrounded by a small milieu of officers recording the scene. He was seated in his computer chair in the middle of the small lounge room. There was a lot of blood, all in the one area, soaking Dayle's T-shirt, his pants, his shoes. There was a crimson pool under the chair.

His face was slack, eyes open, looking upwards.

The weapon, a knife, was on the floor, his right hand dangling above it. Thousands of Australians took their own lives each year, and many more attempted it, but it took a certain amount of dedication to open your own throat with a blade. It happened practically every year, even in Sydney, but it was quite rare compared with hangings, fatal jumps and intentional overdoses. Quite rare. Investigators had to consider it suspicious until fingerprints were taken and the angle of the cuts closely analysed. A quick glance told Andy that at least there had been no real struggle. No blood had hit the walls.

But the way Dayle had seemingly topped himself wasn't the most interesting part. The most interesting part was the display that surrounded his blood-soaked figure. In a semicircle around his thin corpse was a visual confession of his crimes. Weapons. A gag. News clippings. Souvenirs. Andy stepped towards the corpse and its grim accessories and bent to look at what was there, hands folded behind his back.

Yes. By all accounts Dayle appeared to be their man. And rather than be arrested he did . . . *this*?

"So what do we know so far? Dayle was at the bar. He brought Harrison here and then. . . ?" Andy trailed off. "Intended to assault her but had a fit of remorse? Changed his mind about attacking her and instead attacked himself? Or maybe he'd intended her to witness his suicide? He recognised her from the police canvass and knew it was over?"

"But why abduct her?"

"Why set up this whole confessional scene? He wanted her to see it? To witness it?" Andy theorised.

"She doesn't seem to think she witnessed anything. She told me she was at the bar and he came in, and then she started to feel very intoxicated and she blacked out."

Rohypnol possibly, or GBH, Andy thought. *Jesus, Dana.* He inhaled sharply. She was lucky to be alive.

"Be easy on her," Kelley said again.

A uniformed constable opened the door for him and Andy saw a rainstorm had hit. Within Dayle's dark house he hadn't noticed the thunderous din of the rainfall outside. He could see Dana's profile as she waited in a car in the lane, staying out of the downpour.

He paused before ducking under the police tape. "Are you finished with my agent for now?"

"Yeah. I'd like to speak to her again this afternoon," Inspector Kelley said. "Or tomorrow, depending on how she's doing."

"I'll give you a call and we'll come to your office."

Andy ran over to Mahoney's unmarked car, hands shielding his eyes from the wet. He knocked on the window and Karen opened the car door.

"Quite a mess in there," she remarked and stepped out with

an umbrella. She opened it and struggled to avoid jabbing him in the eye.

"Thanks for your help, Mahoney. I'll chat with Harrison now. Come on. Let's go for something to eat," he told his junior agent. She walked with him to his Honda in a bleak march, shrugging off Mahoney's umbrella and not even attempting to keep the raindrops off her own face. She slid into his passenger seat without a word and Andy started his car.

"Okay, let's have it," Andy said.

Agent Flynn and Agent Harrison sat at a small table in a mostly empty café in Darlinghurst. Before them were plates littered with the remnants of breakfast—scrambled eggs and scraps of toast. They were not far from St. Vincent's— the hospital where Andy's agent had been treated overnight without his being told, and his closest friend, Jimmy, was, according to Angie, being prepped for further surgery for complications from the gunshot wound inflicted, some believed, by his ex-girlfriend Makedde.

It was not a good day and Andy was not feeling particularly patient.

"I'm deeply sorry I've let you down. That's all I can say," Agent Dana Harrison told him. She looked up at him with puffy red eyes, then looked to the table again. She gripped her ceramic coffee cup as though it were a lifeline.

"No, that's not all you can say," he countered, his voice low. "You can tell me what the hell you were thinking. I mean, what were you doing at the White Cockatoo?"

She hesitated, probably trying to decide what story to give. "I went out. I was having a drink," she said, cagey.

He crossed his arms and leaned back. "Any particular reason you picked that bar, in Sydney, to drink alone?"

She stared down at her plate. She'd barely eaten, he noticed.

Andy let it go for a minute, let his question hang in the air. And then he couldn't leave it be any longer.

"Would I be safe in assuming that your gun is in your gun locker at AFP, locked away where it should be?"

She swallowed.

Fuck. "Please tell me I won't find that you were at a bar, off duty, carrying a loaded gun?"

"I fucked up," she said so quietly he could have missed it.

"Dammit," he muttered. "You weren't authorised. You didn't have authority to go after him, Dana."

"I wasn't really going after him. I was just . . . I was just going to see—"

"You didn't have authority to follow him. Or use yourself for bait, goddammit, if that's what you were thinking. He could have killed you. He drugged you and he could have done anything. He could have used your own weapon on you."

She raised her cup to her lips, hands shaking slightly.

Take it easy on her, Inspector Kelley had said. Andy tried to calm himself. She had a promising career, but she'd shown poor judgement. Very poor judgement. She'd nearly got herself killed.

"We'll get through this. So what happened? What really happened?" he pleaded softly and waited for her to answer in her own time.

"I went to the bar and ordered a drink. A virgin cocktail," she explained. "I'm not stupid. Yes, I had my firearm on me, but I was *not* drinking. After a while I spotted him. I was on my third cocktail by then, I think, and I swear none of them were alcoholic. You can ask the bartender. I noticed Dayle notice me and he walked past close and sat nearby. I was nervous and thirsty so I guess I drank my glass pretty fast after that. It didn't taste different and I didn't realise what was happening until it was too late. When the drink was nearly finished, he still hadn't approached me again, but my head wasn't right. I was feeling intoxicated, a bit light-headed. Before I knew it, he was right there next to me and I couldn't . . . couldn't . . ."

Andy leaned forwards, placing a hand on hers. "You're okay. You're okay now," he said.

Maybe he didn't have to check into the firearm. She hadn't discharged it. Dayle had not been killed with it. It might not come up as an issue, and if it did, he could say she had been on call and might have needed it. He could do that to cover her, couldn't he?

"So you weren't drinking and the blood tests will show that?" he pressed.

"Yes," she said with conviction. That was a small mercy.

"Because if you were found to be out drinking, off duty, with your gun, I might not be able to prevent you from being charged."

She nodded. "I was not drinking."

"Okay, then what happened?" he prompted her.

"Things seemed to go quickly. I was sweaty and . . . and I couldn't think straight. Like I was disoriented and couldn't focus on anything. And Dayle, whom I'd been watching, was suddenly very close, as I said. There were other patrons in the bar, and I think I tried to call out but realised I couldn't speak, and then I was just going out the door. I remember the fresh air on the street for a moment. I remember seeing the cars passing. He had me under the arm, I think. He seemed surprisingly strong. I don't even remember walking, or how I got inside his house."

Fuck. Anything could have happened to her. Anything. "And then what?" he said.

"I woke up at St. Vincent's. I was on a drip for hydration. I don't know how I got there, but apparently paramedics took me. I don't remember anything else except . . ."

"Except?"

"Well, this doesn't make sense, but there was a woman's voice telling me I would be okay."

"At the hospital?"

"No. Before then. When I was in the house," she said.

"You told Kelley this?"

"I told him. I remember fragments, I think. But it's confusing. I'm not sure what's real and what isn't. Something about my being on the floor and there being a conversation of some type. There was some talking, I think, between a man and a woman."

"Dayle was talking to you?"

"No. Someone else I think." She frowned and took a moment to gather her thoughts. "I don't know, Andy. I really don't know."

He rubbed his chin, which was rough with stubble. "Can you remember anything else?"

"That's it right now. There was basically nothing from about ten-thirty last night to five o'clock this morning at hospital. Nothing but these kind of impressions, like I said."

He thought about that. "I want you to write down everything you remember, or think you remember, even if you aren't sure, okay?"

She nodded.

"You never know what might be important. Now, tell me, did you have anything to do with what happened to Dayle?" He watched her carefully.

"What? No." She shook her head. "Like I said, I don't remember getting to the terrace or leaving. I don't remember anything like what happened to him."

"Do you know what happened to him? Did Mahoney or Kelley take you through the crime scene this morning?"

"No. Kelley didn't want me to see. All I know is that he's dead. They were trying to get me to describe what had happened, but like I said, I couldn't remember anything, not even getting to the front door. They had me identify my shoes, which were found at the flat, but Kelley didn't want me to see the body. I saw a bit, though. I saw that he was in the same room where I was found. He was in a chair."

"Your shoes were there?"

"Yes . . . stilettos," she said reluctantly and Andy closed his eyes for a moment. *Jesus. She wore stilettos. She* did *use herself as fucking bait.*

Until the blood tests and the crime-scene analysis proved that she could not have done anything to Dayle, she was still to be cleared of any involvement in Dayle's death, but obviously Kelley didn't suspect her, and neither did Andy. Still, her actions could reflect very badly on the unit if he wasn't careful.

"Now, this is what I'm going to do," Andy said. "I'm going to say that I gave you authority to have your gun with you in case you were needed at short notice, okay? I was in Sydney, so were you, and I asked you to be on call."

Her face lit up. She nodded.

"But if you've lied to me about not drinking, I can't help you."

She gave him a hard look. She'd been telling the truth about the booze: that was clear.

"And what were you doing at the White Cockatoo?"

She watched his face, judging how to respond. "Meeting a friend," she said.

"And Dayle got to you before your friend arrived." She nodded again.

"He probably recognised you from the canvass. You were at the wrong place at the wrong time and you were unlucky."

"Thank you, Flynn."

"Second chances are rare, Harrison. I don't want the SVCP to lose you. We need you, okay? That's why I wanted you on board. That's why I wanted you on the Hempsey case. You are a valuable member of our team. Now they'll be watching you. You can't fuck up again. I want them to see that you are the switched-on, serious profiler I believe you to be. The profiler you *are*. You are bloody lucky you didn't get killed by that sick fucker last night, Harrison. I think you know that."

Her beautiful mouth was set in a hard line. He could see that she knew.

Andy downed the rest of his lukewarm coffee. "Well," he said and exhaled, glad at least that there could be a way to resolve Dana's involvement without her being too harshly disciplined for her rash mistake. "Whatever the circumstances—and the scene in there is pretty fucking bizarre by my reckoning—we can all be grateful Dayle is dead," he said. "We can all be bloody grateful for that."

CHAPTER 40

A couple of hours later Andy broke from the hospital doors and breathed the air on the sidewalk. A bus moved away from the kerb with a low roar. He felt like a man who'd been held under water by a wave.

The day had started rough and hadn't got much easier.

Just a decent coffee. A decent coffee and I'll be okay.

The stench of grief clung to the corridors of St. Vincent's and two hours of it had been almost enough to kill him. The grief of worried loved ones. The pain. The ordered violence of surgeons. Jimmy was still in theatre. Angie wouldn't leave the ward. She'd spent another night in a cot next to the bed, her mother bringing Edmond in for feeds.

Stop thinking about it. Just get a coffee.

He walked off towards the bustling crowds at the cafés on Victoria Street, feeling lost and somehow unable to decide what to do, where to go, how to approach that simple task of finding sustenance and caffeine. He was missing the company of his former police partner Jimmy perhaps more than he ever had in his life. For all his faults, Jimmy was someone who would have truly understood what all this meant—Hunt, Mak, Jack Cavanagh. Jimmy, whose life was ebbing away before their eyes.

Jimmy had been put in this situation by Bradley Hunt, someone he deeply mistrusted. He had always joked about Hunt, what a prick he was, how he thought he was in Jack Cavanagh's pockets. And Andy had dismissed it as jealousy. Just because Hunt was a bit of an annoying dick didn't mean he was crooked. He had risen the ranks and Jimmy's lack of political nous saw his career in a stall. Andy hadn't really listened to Jimmy's complaints and now it seemed Jimmy had been right about Hunt, had even underestimated how crooked the man was. What else could be made of the footage Mak had brought to Andy's room? Hunt was lying. Why? He was wound up in this somehow.

Jimmy was dying, Mak was on the run and there was something in it for Inspector Hunt.

Andy felt something brush his side and his thoughts were suddenly pulled back into the moment.

"Hey—"

Instinctively, he grabbed the wrist of a pickpocket dipping into his right suit-jacket pocket. The pocket was empty, he realised. His wallet was in his breast pocket. A small note was folded between long, slim fingers, but in a heartbeat the note had disappeared again, behind the person's back.

He saw motorcycle boots and looked up, his gaze meeting a familiar face. It was a tall woman with brunette hair, cut in a messy style and coloured with streaks that didn't quite suit the beautiful face it half covered. The woman wore motorcycle pants and a singlet top, a hint of dark lace peeking out. Her eyes were hidden behind mirrored aviators. He retracted his hand.

"Meet me at the café with the umbrellas, on Oxford Street, just around the corner, in about five minutes. There are no CCTV cameras around there," the woman said, barely moving those familiar lips. She walked past him in the opposite direction. Just two strangers bumping into each other.

Andy stayed where he was for a moment and absorbed what had just happened. A couple of metres away was a bank ATM, he noticed. He was indeed on camera. He looked at his watch, not really seeing the time, then scanned the strip for any of the other officers who might be trying to visit Jimmy. No one familiar. Hands in his pockets, Andy entered a newsagent, bought a newspaper and, a few minutes later, wandered up to Oxford Street and entered a small café with dirty white umbrellas, to find Makedde Vanderwall, under a shaggy brown wig, waiting in the corner with a glass of water in her hand.

"Are you okay?" he asked quietly as he sat down.

She nodded. He didn't mention the hair. "How is it exactly that you know where I am all the time?"

Mak offered a sly smile from under the long fringe. "Is it so awful?"

He shook his head. "No, it's only—"

"How is he?" she cut in.

Andy shook his head again. "Not good."

Mak took a breath and it caught in her chest. "I'm sorry, Andy."

He looked at her, looked away, looked back. "I've been worried about you. I don't think my mobile phone is secure. I had no way to reach you to tell you. I had to get a new phone, to be safe. The . . ." He hesitated, knowing this would be a major blow. "The laptop you gave me. The one you said belonged to the man who tried to kill you. It's been destroyed. I found out yesterday. There was a fire at the Electronic Evidence Branch. It can't be a coincidence, and I trust the guy I gave it to."

Mak was nodding her head as he spoke. She didn't take her glasses off.

"I'm so sorry, Mak. I couldn't have foreseen this."

"I posted the Lacie and the footage to Inspector Kelley this morning, just as you suggested," she said softly, her gaze averted. "Express Post. Should arrive on Monday, I guess."

"Good." That way Andy could maintain a distance and the police still had the evidence. "I just don't know what to say about the laptop going missing, Mak," he added and shook his head. "I know how much you risked to get it to me. I'm so sorry."

"It's okay. You did what you could." She seemed calm about it. Strangely calm.

"I'm sure you saw the paper yesterday. What are you going to do?" Andy asked. "Where have you been?"

She didn't answer his questions.

"Was that a note you were trying to slip me before?" he asked.

"Andy, I have something to tell you. It's not easy," she replied and hesitated, looking around the café and at the passersby on the sidewalk.

He braced himself. "I'm not having a great day, to be honest. If it's bad news, I'm not sure I want to hear it."

She sat forwards a touch. "I'm pregnant," she said quietly and took a sip of water.

The breath went out of him. "My God, Mak," he said after a moment.

She crossed her arms over herself and watched him. He felt unable to speak. "It's true," she said.

"Are you okay—what can I do—how do you know?" All these questions poured out in a jumble, without punctuation. He was aware of the public setting, aware that he shouldn't raise his voice. Why had she chosen to tell him here? Why now? Couldn't she have waited until they were alone?

"I'm okay, and I'm not asking for anything from you or anyone else. I just needed you to know."

His eyes went to her stomach and back to her face. He had a question. *The* question.

She followed his gaze and then looked him in the eye. "Are you the father? I don't know, Andy," she replied. "That's the truth. I only found out yesterday. I went to see a doctor and she confirmed it. Until I have an ultrasound I can't be sure how many weeks I am. I can't be more than three months, I shouldn't think. Maybe somewhat less."

Before he left for Quantico or after? That's what he wanted to know. "So it could be . . ." he said cautiously.

"Yours." She paused. "Or Bogey could be the father."

Andy went quiet as his head filled with white noise. He turned away from her as she continued to speak, not hearing. The rage was almost overwhelming. Slowly sound came back, and he heard her words.

". . . shortly after I moved out," she was telling him in a neutral voice. "A few weeks, maybe five or six weeks after I'd seen you last."

So, she'd started dating someone else. He'd known that. He'd imagined she screwed him. He'd come to terms with that. She'd had sex with this younger man six weeks after Andy. That's what she was saying. And now it meant she might be pregnant with that man's child. A man who, according to Mak, was dead.

Andy wanted to punch the café wall. With some effort he kept himself in check. His temper wouldn't help anything. His temper had been part of the problem. He wanted to be angry with Makedde, but the truth was he had found solace in Carol's bed when they'd broken up years before, soon after Mak had left him the first time. He hadn't been able to really consider being with someone after she went missing in Paris, though. He'd not been seriously tempted by Dana's attraction to him, though she was beautiful and independent and smart as hell, and she looked at him like he *was* someone. He just couldn't do it. But still, how could he judge? He couldn't blame Mak if she'd found someone to help her forget. God knows there would have been a lot of offers.

But it hurt. It really goddamn hurt.

Mak was leaning against the wall, arms and legs folded tightly. He glanced down at her belly beneath the singlet. It looked flat. He hadn't noticed a baby bump when they'd made love. But she had seemed different—in so many ways that were beyond the physical.

"You've been to a doctor? You're sure?" he asked.

"Yes," she said flatly and pulled away from him a touch.

A thin waiter emerged with two plastic menus. "Breakfast?"

"Just . . . um, two lattes," Andy responded, flicking his eyes to Mak to see if she had something else in mind. She kept her eyes on the tabletop and didn't open her mouth. The young man disappeared. He didn't bother to wipe down the sticky table. "Why tell me now?" Andy asked. "Here?"

"You don't like seeing me?"

"Of course I do. Jesus, the other night was . . ." It had been amazing. "I'd hoped you would be there when I woke up. Where'd you go? It drives me nuts not to have a way to reach you. I haven't been able to stop thinking about you. You have no idea . . ."

How much I love you.

Mak crossed her legs the other way, leather creaking. She pulled one boot-shod foot up under the table. She didn't take the aviators off and he wished he could see her eyes.

"Have you ever been to Spain, Andy?" she said.

"What?"

"Have you ever been to Spain?" she asked again in a neutral voice.

"No. Why?"

"There's a great little village called Peratallada, not too far from the Costa Brava. Tiny population. It's a medieval town. Everything carved in stone. I stayed there when I was driving down from France. It's trapped in the twelfth century, Andy. Just beautiful. You'd love it."

"*What are you talking about?*"

"Keep your voice down." She pulled those aviators down a touch and he could see that her gorgeous blue-green eyes were bloodshot. They slid over the crowd around them and then settled on his, seeming brighter than usual. "Are you happy, Andy?"

He was blind-sided. "Happy? Happy about you being wanted for shooting my partner? That you were on the front page of the paper and everyone's looking for you?" He felt the anger rise in him. He was supposed to arrest her. His job was to arrest her. And she was asking him if he was happy?

"No, I mean, are you happy? Because I'm not," she continued. "I don't want any more of this. If I never see another dead body in my life, if I don't see any more blood, if I'm never chased or stalked again, I'll be happy."

He reached out instinctively for her hand and took it in his. It felt cold. "I'm sorry you've been through all this, Mak." With his other hand he ran his fingers over his hair. "Fucking hell. How did everything get so crazy? What are you going to do? What are *we* going to do?"

Mak smiled, though her eyes were strange. Not cold, exactly, but distant. She pushed the glasses up her nose again and pulled back. "The assassin who tried to kill me in Paris had money. A lot of money. Yes, blood money, but I'm no martyr, as it turns out. I've had enough of doing the right thing. I have a chance at freedom, Andy. One chance. I'm going to enjoy what I can of life now." She nodded to herself as if she still needed convincing. "What about you?" she asked him.

"What *about* me?" Andy replied, flummoxed. "Why don't you come with me?"

His chest tightened.

"No promises, no vows, just a chance. But only if we leave all this. We can change our lives, change our names, be anyone we want to be." She looked around furtively. "I don't want to be Mak any more."

Andy thought of how much he'd always wanted her. He thought of all the things that had got in their way. He thought of her on the beach at La Perouse when they'd first met—her devastated by the murder of her friend, him the detective in charge. And he thought of her now. Wanted. And he couldn't help her. Couldn't arrest her. *Couldn't.* What did that make him?

"If you want me—*us*—come find us," Mak said and smiled gently. Her hand strayed to her small belly. Fugitive and lover. And mother? He didn't know what to make of the woman he was looking at, a woman who now kept a gun on her at all times, who set up clandestine meetings and secret cameras, and disguised herself to walk the streets.

Mak leaned in, pressed herself against him, and he felt the crush of her swelling breasts—the one sign of her pregnancy he might have noticed—and he felt her strong, thin arms around him, and he wanted her again. God, he wanted her. He wanted *both* of them. He didn't care if it wasn't his child. For a moment that hurt no longer seemed to matter. She ran her hands over his back and the rough stubble of his face, and gave him a brief, devastating kiss with a mouth as sweet as strawberries, then she just stood, turned and walked out of the café. Andy resisted reaching out to her as she went. He didn't follow. He didn't call out. He just sat and watched with a feeling of terrible conflict and helplessness as she walked off into the shifting crowd of Oxford Street pedestrians. In seconds he'd lost sight of her.

A minute later the thin waiter returned to the table with two lattes.

Andy, shell-shocked, said nothing.

He leaned heavily on his elbows and sipped his coffee. It tasted tart. He fished in his pocket idly, wondering what to do, checked his phone and sat up. There was an SMS from Angie. He hadn't heard it come in. It was an hour old. Where had that hour gone?

COME TO HOSPITAL was all it said. His heart constricted.

Andy threw a ten-dollar bill on the table and rushed out.

Andy only needed to see their faces to know.

Jimmy's family stood in the hospital corridor. His wife, Angie, was flanked by her mother and three of her sons who stood, as it happened, in order of height, ages diminishing. The youngest, Edmond, was cradled in his grandmother's arms, limbs dangling, evidently asleep. Andy walked towards them and Angie opened her arms. He shut his eyes tightly as she gripped him and convulsed with tears, body warm, the grief clinging, infectious.

"I'm so sorry," he whispered and kissed her forehead.

No. No . . .

Jimmy had had close calls before and somehow he'd always made it through. He'd smoked and drunk and eaten to excess at every opportunity. He'd been reckless. He'd been selfless and selfish and a cheat and an honest, loyal fool. Was this it, here in this hospital—the end? It seemed impossible.

"Is there anything I can do?" he asked, to the top of Angie's hair.

She pulled back, and he saw the anger in her pain. "You can get the—excuse me—but *bitch* who shot him."

He cringed. Now Jimmy was dead and Mak, of all people, the woman he'd just seen, the woman who might be pregnant with his child, was wanted as Jimmy's killer. A cop killer. Cops looked after their own. Every police officer in the country would want to see her go down. If convicted of his murder, she would get mandatory life imprisonment. He wondered what Angie had been told, and by whom.

"We'll get whoever is responsible for this, I promise you," he said, holding her gaze. "I'll see to it that Jimmy gets his justice." He kissed her gently again on the forehead. "We don't know who did this or why, but we will. We'll get his killer, I promise you."

He left his ex-partner's grieving family in the presence of hospital staff and went in search of a doctor who could give him answers. That was the only way forwards. Answers.

Action. After fifteen frustrating minutes he was put onto the right person—Dr Richard Hutton, a short, tidy man with greying hair and the scent of disinfectant about him.

"I'd like to speak to you for a moment about your patient Mr. Cassimatis," Andy told him.

"Are you family?" He was a bit cagey. *A dead cop. Questions.* Andy showed his ID. "Agent Andrew Flynn, Australian Federal Police. And a close friend of the deceased."

Dr Hutton hesitated, then shook Andy's hand. He had the cleanest, most elegant hands Andy had seen on a man. He could have been a pianist. "All right. Come with me. I have a few minutes before I'm needed," the doctor told him.

Andy followed him down the corridor and into a small office. He closed the door behind them and the blinds across the office window rattled. The doctor sat on the edge of a small desk, arms folded. "I assure you we did everything we could. He came in with a chest wound. He'd lost a lot of blood—"

"He was on blood thinners," Andy cut in, standing against the closed door. "He had AF." *Atrial fibrillation.*

"Correct. When the atrium," the doctor gestured to the left-hand side of his chest, "the top two chambers of the heart—fibrillate, they do not expel all the blood into the ventricles with each beat. Unfortunately, blood-thinning medication, like the Warfarin your friend was on, is not good when there is an injury like he had. They got him here fast, but he had already lost a lot of blood. We used FFP—um, fresh frozen plasma—and Vitamin K to reverse the effects of the Warfarin. The initial surgery was successful. Unfortunately, he developed a haemo-thorax, post-op. We performed a thoracotomy this morning, to drain the haematoma and find the source of the bleeding, but he suffered a myocardial infarction."

Andy grimly took all of it in. Myocardial infarction. Jimmy had suffered a heart attack. It wasn't his first.

"Unfortunately, anticoagulants are contraindicated under the circumstances," Dr Hutton explained. "Giving them might have saved his heart from ongoing damage, but he risked bleeding to death in the process. We tried to open the heart artery with a stent, but the damage to the heart, along with the strain from the gunshot wound and the ongoing bleeding, were too much. We did everything we could."

"Thank you, doctor." Andy took a breath. "Can I ask about Jimmy's initial wounds?"

"The gunshot wound?"

"Yes."

"It missed his heart and major organs. The police have all that information already."

Andy shifted from foot to foot. "Was there an exit wound?"

"I think so. I did not perform the initial surgery," Dr Hutton explained.

"Where is he now?"

"He was brought to the hospital mortuary. I think he's

being transferred to Glebe now." The Department of Forensic Medicine. "Perhaps they will be able to help you with any further questions you have."

Andy thanked the doctor for his time and set out for the city morgue.

Mak dismounted her Speed Triple in the residential cul-de-sac, propped it onto its kickstand, flipped her tinted visor up and looked around.

There was a late-model Mercedes parked down the road and a family wagon in the driveway of the house across the street, but otherwise the area was empty on this weekday afternoon. Through the mesh of family homes along the shore, boats bobbed up and down on the blue waters of Pittwater. Beyond a low picket fence, a child's tricycle lay on its side, resting on green, neatly mowed lawn. A row of bare roses was lined up along the fence, the heads clipped off, thorns sitting up like tiny knives. Next door, though, the lawn was slightly overgrown, the fence broken in one spot. A little less cared for. No high-maintenance rose garden. A holiday rental, perhaps? This was as good a place as any. She pulled her helmet off and slung the canvas bag and purse off her shoulder. It felt good to get her motorcycle jacket off. She left it slumped over her helmet on the kerb for a moment, the stiff leather arms slowly deflating in the sun.

Mak stood in her tank top and leather pants, a line of sweat snaking down from her temple. She put her aviators on.

This is the day.

She gave another swift glance over her shoulder, paused for a second of contemplation, then hopped the picket fence and crouched behind a tall, unkempt shrub to strip off her pants. She put on a pair of new khaki shorts and simple white sneakers, and stuffed her motorcycle leathers, helmet and wig into the canvas bag, zipped it up and shoved it under the bush where it could not be easily seen. She stood and ran her fingers through her freshly shorn, spiky hair. A breeze tingled against her legs, and she could feel herself begin to cool. Patting herself down, she found a swing tag on the back pocket of her shorts and a price tag on the bottom of her sneakers. She pulled them off. Satisfied, she threw her leather handbag over her bare shoulder and set out on the walk towards the nearby strip mall, back up on the main road.

Twenty minutes later Makedde had reached her destination, and she watched, strangely wide-eyed, as two mums with strollers walked past, caught up in conversation, bags of groceries hanging off every available surface and children sleeping soundly with their tiny, floppy legs hanging out into the sun. For a moment Mak tried unsuccessfully to imagine their roles reversed. *Her* with the pram. *Them* with this plan.

She couldn't quite imagine it.

Mak had never been very domestic, but then, not all mothers were. Mothers were criminals, too. Killers even.

She crossed the road and headed towards the entrance of Sanctum Spa, a one-level building at the end of the small strip mall, next to a half-empty car park. The glass display front was decorated with hanging white baubles and crystals, along with ads for a line of French beauty products, each featuring the same beautiful young model stretched across white sand and covered only with pearl-like white stones. *Discover a New You*, the ads invited.

Mak stepped inside the spa and was immediately hit with cool, air-conditioned air, dreamy instrumental music and the scent of jasmine coming from an aromatherapy oil burner. The shift was jarring.

"Welcome to Sanctum Spa. How may I help you?" the

receptionist said primly, looking Mak up and down and taking in her appearance. The austere woman had the prescribed ponytail and neat white uniform of the modern spa. Thankfully, nothing in her demeanour indicated that she recognised in the brunette before her the blonde socialite cop shooter from the front of the paper.

"What kind of treatments do you have available?" Mak asked. She took in the small water fountain and plush white lounges.

Treatment rooms stretched down a hallway, each labelled with a different name on the door—*Calm, Relax, Refresh* . . .

"We have a variety of masseuses available for relaxation, deep-tissue, Swedish, Hawaiian and hot-stone massage. We also do facials, manicures and pedicures."

Mak picked up a brochure and flipped through it idly, aware that with her bare nails, tomboyish attire and DIY haircut, she might seem an unlikely patron. "I'd like to book in for a massage next week. Would that be possible? Something deep tissue. The masseuse has to be really good. Really strong. And do you do oxygen facials?"

"Absolutely," the receptionist said earnestly. "I'll just see who is available."

"May I use your ladies' room?" Mak asked.

"Of course. It's just that way." She pointed down the hallway distractedly. "Fifth door on the right."

"Thanks." Mak walked off in the direction the receptionist had indicated.

She passed the doors of the treatment rooms and the bathroom and stopped. She looked both ways, saw the security camera in the corner of the ceiling and decided she didn't care. A lot of shops now had security cameras, yet no one checked the tapes unless there was an incident, and shops commonly used the same tape over and over, recording over one day with footage of the next. By the time anyone thought to look, it would likely be too late.

Mak tried an unmarked cupboard, found that it was open and scanned the shelves.

Perfect.

She swiftly stuffed what she needed into her handbag—a uniform cap, vest and polo shirt—and walked back to the front, her bag a touch overfilled. Mak leaned on the counter, smiling. The receptionist was still checking her computer.

"I can give you Penelope on Thursday, two p.m. for the massage." She stared at the screen for another minute. "Emily can do your facial afterwards," she concluded.

"That's great. Thank you."

"We need a deposit to secure the booking," the woman said, smiling and giving no sign that she knew what Mak had just done.

For her part Makedde smiled in return, wondering fleetingly if that was always the policy, or if there was something about her that seemed suspicious. "I can pay with cash if you like." How ironic that this woman might be worried Mak would flake on a spa appointment.

Mak was given a receipt and appointment card. She thanked the woman and walked undisturbed onto the sunny sidewalk, pleased with her haul and knowing she would never be back. She made her way to the beach shop a few stores down to buy some white towels, then turned left and made for the car park, balancing her bags of purchases. She spotted the vehicle she wanted and approached it, checking casually to see if anyone was watching her. Unobserved, she took out a mangled coat hanger, twisted it around into a wire hook and lowered it down between the window and the car door, manoeuvring it until it caught the lock.

There.

She pulled the locking mechanism up and the door obediently unlocked for her. She threw her bags in the back and got in.

CHAPTER 41

Andy parked on Arundel Street directly outside the Mortuary Office of the Department of Forensic Medicine in Glebe, the biggest mortuary in the southern hemisphere, his heart thudding with urgency. He'd sped there, and now he pushed his way inside and pressed his badge against the wall of glass at reception. It, too, was bulletproof, he knew. Not everyone was happy with autopsy results. Some relatives got quite tetchy, in fact.

"Agent Andrew Flynn, Federal Police," he declared.

He was buzzed through the security door with little hesitation.

Andy had frequently come here in his capacity as an investigating officer, required to view autopsies for major homicide cases, and now he stood in the small, familiar police area where the beige Eaglenet phone and two desktop police computers sat waiting below a bulletin board decorated with notices about SIDS procedures, drownings in private pools and instructions for P79A forms. The mortuary office was just beyond a waist-high divide, cluttered with papers and visitor logs.

"How's it going?" the woman at reception asked him. Behind her, a round, white clock ticked loudly. She had a black fringe and a nose ring and he realised that he recognised her.

He leaned over the divide. "Good. I need to see Jimmy Cassimatis. Detective Jimmy Cassimatis. He just came in here."

There was a short hesitation and then a flicker of recognition as she noted he was talking about a deceased detective, not one wandering through the morgue. "Well, he's just being checked in, I think." She sat at her computer to look at the database nick-named "The Deadbase." She pushed a few keys.

"Thanks, that'll do," Andy said and pushed on the swinging doors to the morgue.

"Hey, wait. You've gotta sign in!" she insisted and he sloppily signed the blue visitors book and headed for the doors again before she could stop him.

The peculiar smell of the morgue hit him like a slap. Andy never quite got used to it. The wet tiled floors, like a fish market, only with human bodies gutted on the rows of stainless-steel trays. Organs weighed and bodies disassembled. The low, nervous jokes of staff and the long, heavy silences—coping mechanisms in the dominion of the dead. There was no denying death here, where the dead so outnumbered the living. Andy stood next to the collection of wellie boots shelved after a day of use, some plain, some hot pink or decorated with skulls. A small wicker baby basket fitted with pretty blankets sat atop a neat stack of clean white gowns, a reminder that death cared little for age and nothing for promises.

All was quiet. Jimmy had obviously already passed through.

He could see the loading dock was empty.

The swinging doors of the fridge opened and the mortuary clerk walked through in her black pants and a white collared shirt, security tag swinging. She'd been working there for years. Her first name was something like Phyllis, he thought. Yes, that was it. Phyllis. Behind her, Andy caught a brief glimpse of the rows of blue plastic body bags on their trolleys, stored two shelves deep.

And a trolley that hadn't been put away yet. One arm hung out of the side of the body bag. Curly black hair. Hospital wristband.

Jimmy.

She recognised Andy and he managed a smile. "How are you, Phyllis?" he said.

"Good. You?" She waited.

"I need to take a look at Detective Cassimatis. I can see him right there."

She turned around and looked where he was indicating. "You want to . . . go to the viewing room?" she asked after a pause.

If Andy was here as a friend of Jimmy's, Phyllis would have to get him an appointment with an on-call counsellor and he'd have to wait in that grim room out front, breathing the air of a thousand weeping relatives and that stifling plug-in aroma-therapy perfume which tried unsuccessfully to mask the odour of death. And when the allotted time came he'd witness Jimmy, dead, in that same horrible viewing room they'd both stood in a thousand times together for homicide cases, with the bouquet of plastic flowers and the boxes of tissues, only this time some social worker would be outside the door, keeping watch, waiting for *Andy*, waiting to offer him the same words, designed for comfort, that he'd offered a hundred times before, the silent orange lights spinning round and round throughout the mortuary, telling everyone not to be too loud, not to shout, not to laugh amongst themselves because a loved one was in the viewing room in the throes of their grief.

Fuck that.

"No need. I can do it here. I need to ID him," Andy lied. Phyllis looked uncertain. "Is there a problem?"

"Let's find out," he said, pulling a white gown on over his jacket and blue disposable shoe covers over his leather shoes.

He pushed his way inside, striding across the wet tiles as she trailed behind. He wondered if she would call someone, the general manager perhaps, or if she'd let Andy do what he had to. The fridge was damned cold inside and he walked along the sets of trays inhabited by silent blue plastic body bags, some sagging where they ought not, others suspiciously bloated, each telling a different, dark story. A few bags were yellow. The infectious bodies. He walked up to that stray arm hanging out of the blue bag and he stopped. It was the same hand that had made rude gestures behind Inspector Hunt, the same hand that had offered him another drink after dinner.

The blue plastic bag was open on the stainless-steel trolley.

She hadn't locked it with the plastic ID tag yet.

Andy pulled back the flap.

". . . thought you were with the feds now?" Phyllis was saying as Andy's head swam dangerously, filled with a shouting that only he could hear. ". . . was sure he had been identified already," he heard her continue after a moment, when the shouting became lower.

He nodded absently, staring.

"The autopsy won't be performed until tomorrow," Phyllis said.

He nodded again. "And you want to. . . ?"

Phyllis trailed off and Andy stared at his dead friend, not knowing what to say, what to feel, what to do. He'd wanted to see the trajectory of the bullet for himself, to see if Mak's story was right. He'd wanted to see where the exit wound was in Jimmy's back—if it was below the level of the entry wound because he'd been shot from a mezzanine, or if it was dead straight like she'd said it would be, because she didn't shoot him at all. That's what he'd told himself when he'd rushed here, but now he realised how absurd that was, how futile. He was no pathologist and in truth he did not doubt Makedde in the slightest. This was not the place for Andy to be. This was not the way. His friend Detective Jimmy

Cassimatis lay naked on a cold, stainless-steel tray before him, filled with stitches and tubes and stents, his back already discolouring with the deep purplish bruises of post-mortem lividity. The hospital had patched up the original bullet wound as best they could, but the internal injuries had been catastrophic. They'd left everything in place as it was in theatre when his heart had given up. His eyelids were closed with the sleep of anaesthesia and his face was slack, tubes hanging out of his nose and from between his lips. His chest was open in a terrible red yawn, arteries clamped, organs visible.

"Andy?"

Death cares nothing for promises.

"Are you okay?" He nodded.

"Is this the man? Detective Jimmy Cassimatis?"

He nodded again. "It is." Andy snapped himself out of his trancelike stare. "When is the autopsy scheduled?"

"He's only just come in. The duty pathologist will assign him a senior specialist in the morning. He'll get the best possible care," Phyllis added, obviously by now sensing this was more than a professional visit. She quietly pulled the plastic flap of the body bag shut and led Andy towards the arrival bay, her fingers at his elbow.

He pulled off his shoe covers and gown and threw them in the bins. He washed his hands. Once. Twice. Three times.

"Andy . . ." Phyllis said, but he was gone.

Andy Flynn sat in his car at the kerb, numb with grief and impotence. Now that his tears had finally started he worried they wouldn't stop. The steering wheel was wet. His hands were wet. *Goddammit, Jimmy. Goddammit. Goddammit . . .* With all his physical strength he slammed his open palms hard against the wheel for the second time, and he shouted a madman's cry—the angry wail of the bereaved, one he'd heard before from others—as his palms stung from the force. It was a brief and terrible sound and when it stopped so did the shouting in his head. So did the tears.

He fell silent, slumped in the driver's seat.

"Fuck!" he yelled as another spasm of grief hit him, and he struck the wheel with a closed fist, opening his knuckles in a red line.

Hunt.

If Inspector Hunt was responsible for this, he would pay.

Andy would *make him* pay.

He swiped his bloodstained hand on his dark pants and felt something in the suit pocket, the edge of something in there. He shifted in his seat and pulled it out.

A folded piece of paper.

Andy stared at it and blinked. He wiped his eyes and then turned the piece of paper over in his hands, mystified. He unfolded it to find handwriting. Mak's handwriting.

Dear Andy, the note began . . .

CHAPTER 42

Makedde Vanderwall leaned in to the intercom. "Sanctum Mobile Massage."

She waited outside the large wooden door of the Palm Beach home of Jack and Beverley Cavanagh, clutching a mobile massage bed and folded towels, purse tucked over her shoulder. Behind her, the Mazda hatchback was neatly parked, the words SANCTUM MASSAGE printed in big letters along the side.

It's now or never.

There was an audible buzz as the door released and Mak pushed it open, smiling sweetly. A bodyguard dressed in dark denim and a black polo shirt was waiting on the other side, iPod earphones dangling down his neck. His bulging biceps were tanned and his face was pockmarked and brown. Above his collar was the barest suggestion of a neck. Ropey, over-sized thighs were visible beneath the slightly strained edges of his khaki shorts, which were similar in style to her own, but looked entirely different. He appeared younger than she was—perhaps in his early to mid-twenties. He wore his gun in a bare holster—a semi-automatic handgun Mak guessed was a Czech CZ 75 or one of its many copies. She'd seen him during her recon. He was bigger up close.

"Sanctum Mobile Massage for Mr. Cavanagh. Beverley sent me," Mak said, with just the faintest hint of flirtation in her voice. She tilted her head to one side and looked up into his broad face, smiling.

He took a step towards her and looked her over.

Behind Mak's cheerful demeanour, panic went through her like an electric shock. At over six feet tall, she was no wraith, but this creature dwarfed her, thanks to some scary genetics and an obvious dedication to steroids. Frankly, he was intimidating. She'd seen this guy come and go and she'd eventually accepted that he would be there. If she'd paid better attention to Pete Don's lessons in her private investigator course, if she hadn't been in such a hurry, perhaps she'd have been able to find a window when he was not there, but she hadn't. She would be murdered in a matter of days if she didn't do something now: she was certain of it. She could not rely on the police. She could not rely on a public outcry to bring the Cavanaghs to heel. The time to wait was over, she'd decided. This was the time for extreme measures. She had no choice.

And there was certainly no turning back now.

The guard looked her up and down. Mak had scrubbed her face free of makeup, except for some pencil to darken her naturally blonde brows. She wore her freshly shorn hair under a white baseball cap emblazoned with the Sanctum logo, and she was clothed in her new shorts and white sneakers, along with an unzipped black fleece vest and white, short-sleeved polo shirt, both stolen from the spa and bearing the same logo. The top showed off her newly muscled arms, which seemed insubstantial next to his. As a final touch she'd worn Bogey's black-rimmed glasses—a part of her physical transformation, but also a talisman of sorts. It seemed fitting to wear something of Bogey's as she faced the man responsible for his murder.

For a moment Mak wondered what the guard might say, but he only nodded and closed the door behind her. He didn't offer to help carry her towels or the folded massage bed, and she felt small next to him as she followed him through the stunning, open-plan beach house. It had dark polished timber floors and was decorated with stylishly minimalistic modern furniture and abstract oil paintings in muted tones. When they reached the base of a timber staircase the guard asked her to wait. He climbed the stairs and disappeared.

She was in.

Jack Cavanagh's beach house was soundless and tranquil. Sliding floor-to-ceiling glass doors at the back were pulled open to the beautiful outdoors, giving the effect of a living area that extended all the way to the water's edge. There were no fences or walls to obstruct the idyllic, panoramic view. There wasn't even a garden, she had noted in her earlier reconnaissance. The house opened onto a lush green lawn and stretch of white beach with a small jetty. A boat was moored there, bobbing up and down with the placid tide—the Cavanaghs' house was on the western beach, facing into Broken Bay, not on the ocean coast. The vessel was sleek and wood-panelled and it shone on the glittering water. Mak knew nothing about boats, but she didn't need to know about such things to see that this was a very expensive one indeed. She could hear the water lapping gently at Jack Cavanagh's beautiful boat, and a bubble of rage surfaced at the sound of it, the sight of that white, pristine shore.

Mak suppressed her rage. She had to remain emotionless to do what she had to do.

So this is a view worth killing for, she thought calmly.

She placed her supplies on the floor and scanned her surroundings, spotting interior motion sensors for an alarm system, and taking in the potential escape points at her disposal.

No surprises. The configurations were as she had imagined. Yes, she'd been a little rushed in the end, but truthfully, she felt she was as prepared as she could be considering the pressing time constraint of knowing that every hour she waited could bring the moment an assassin found her and ended her. Why wait for death, when she could bring it, could control some small part of the violence that was inevitable?

Mak heard footsteps approach. She straightened, standing with her feet shoulder-width apart, her fingers laced behind her back. With this stance came new stillness. She felt strangely compact and dense on her feet, ferocity waiting inside her like a coiled snake. Luther's nine-millimetre Glock semi-automatic itched at her lower back. It felt hot, as if she might have already discharged it. She couldn't take the loose-fitting black zip-up fleece off, or the shape of it would show. The weapon was just there, fitted with its silencer. Within seconds she could have it in her hands.

The guard appeared. He was alone. His gun was still holstered.

"You can set up here," the huge man said simply, pointing to the living area. "Stereo's there," he added, gesturing to a high-end entertainment system in a glass cabinet along the wall.

Stereo?

Ah, yes, for relaxation music.

She hadn't thought to bring any. Perhaps there'd been a CD case full of Enya in the boot of the car, along with the massage bed. If so she hadn't noticed it. But noise could be a good idea, she supposed, all things considered.

Mak smiled. "Thanks." She batted her naked lashes from beneath the glasses Bogey wore when he was murdered.

The guard turned and wandered back to the front half of the house, leaving her alone again. Nothing in his face had betrayed an awareness of who she was. Nothing in his demeanour had given her any sense of there being a problem. So, Jack Cavanagh was not all that paranoid about his personal safety, it seemed. Not like Mak herself was. Perhaps Jack felt invincible, she reflected. Privilege could do that. Or perhaps the sheer madness of her plan also held the key to its success? Why would she come to him? Why, except to die?

Mak kneeled by the stereo and flicked the dial until she found a station playing jazz. A new track started and a smooth announcer's voice came on briefly over the sound of piano. "And now a little Miles Davis." The announcer went on to say she would play the full track, running for nine minutes and twenty-two seconds. "'So What', from the 1959 album *Kind of Blue* . . ."

Mak placed her handbag on a waist-level shelf of the entertainment unit and turned the keyhole camera in the direction of the room. It was already recording. With some awkwardness she unfolded the massage bed and clicked the legs into place. She carefully laid a towel across the top and rolled one into a neat ball, placing it near the end. That's how they did it, wasn't it? She wished she had Bogey to guide her, to make it look more convincing. He'd worked as a masseur briefly, he'd told her. He'd worked as a coffin maker, too, and he'd played in a band, all before being needlessly slaughtered before the age of thirty. Because of Mak. Because of Jack Cavanagh.

For Bogey. For my baby, she thought as the sound of Miles Davis's trumpet filled the room.

She listened and waited.

Finally, a single set of footsteps could be heard on the wooden staircase. She turned in the direction of the staircase, saw at a glance that it was Jack Cavanagh, and she gave a little nod of acknowledgement to him. He was instantly recognisable from the many photographs she'd seen of him in the press, though she thought he seemed smaller. He was shorter than Mak, and he wore a Ralph Lauren T-shirt and neatly pressed denim jeans.

Her heart did not speed up. She did not flinch. She was steady.

Without meeting Jack Cavanagh's eyes, Mak said, "Please disrobe down to your underwear and make yourself comfortable on the table, face down." She turned away from him, hands laced behind her, and stepped up to the edge of the folding glass doors. They were open, the panels folded up, and she could see his reflection in the angles of glass, illuminated by a beam of sunlight. He wasn't disrobing, she noticed. He wasn't even moving.

Fuck.

"You say my wife sent you?"

She turned but kept her head down as she spoke. "Beverley— Mrs. Cavanagh sent me. Is now not a good time?"

He hesitated. "I thought you were coming on Sunday?" he said.

"Perhaps it was meant as a surprise? They just told me to say that Beverley sent me. I can certainly come back at a later time."

He frowned. "Are you new there? What accent is that exactly?"

Mak looked up and smiled, and despite her changed appearance, despite Bogey's spectacles, the uniform, the hair, the recognition hit him with a jolt. His face contorted.

Okay, it's going to be like that.

"Good. You recognise me," Mak said immediately. "That makes this simpler."

He gave a worried glance behind him, but the guard was nowhere to be seen.

"Don't call him back. Let's just have a chat first, okay?" She held both palms in the air. "I'm here to tell you to call them off. I no longer care what you've done. I'm not after you or your family. Just call off your people and I promise I will leave you alone."

Jack Cavanagh didn't speak or move. Now that she was really looking at him, she noticed he looked a little unwell beneath his tan. There were bags under his pale blue eyes. He looked much older than the photographs she'd seen.

Seconds ticked by. "You're mad to come here," he finally said.

Yes, I am. "Mad is a good word," she agreed. "Mad, yes, but willing to let things go."

"Oh?"

She knew she would not have long. The guard would be back to check on things, and then she'd have to deal with all that bulk and that semi-automatic of his. "Please leave me be now, Mr. Cavanagh. Promise me you will leave me alone and I will leave here, no harm done." Mak felt a strange flutter in her stomach, and for a moment her composure wavered. There it was, her reason for taking this drastic step. The reason she could wait no longer. She felt an unexpected sting in her eyes as they threatened to well up. With significant effort she suppressed the ill-timed swell of emotion. This was not the time or place to wonder if the flicker of life in her belly would survive her troubles to one day be safely born, or if that child would be born in a prison, or to a life on the run.

Jack watched her carefully.

"Please," Mak continued, managing a steady voice. "Leave me alone and I will leave you alone. I am pregnant. I want to live. On my mother's grave I promise I will leave you alone forever." She raised her palms again, as if to show she wasn't armed. For a moment the gun in the small of her back no longer itched. She felt ill, imagining she might have used it. She wanted so badly to be human again, to have this all go away. She wanted to see his humanity. She wanted to see that he wasn't to blame. That it was all a mistake. A misunderstanding.

"I don't know what you mean," Jack Cavanagh said and

rubbed his nose. He shifted on his feet. He looked to her stomach and back to her face.

Liar.

A line of rage bubbled up and her hopeful emotions left her as quickly as they had arrived. She took a deep breath and shook her head. "Yes, you do, Mr. Cavanagh. I can see that you do. But I wonder if you do know that I was already gone? That I wasn't ever going to return to this country? If you, or your advisors, had not sent men to kill me, I would not be in your living room right now. I don't want to be here, believe me. And I'll be happy to leave here and never, ever return if you can ensure my safety."

"So you come here under false pretences, posing as a masseuse? You know I could have you shot. I'd be well within my rights."

"I don't know about that," she countered. "But I do know that this is the only way I could speak to you face to face. Maybe you really aren't so callous about human life, Jack? Maybe you didn't mean to unleash all this violence? If you are telling the truth, and you really don't know about the contract on my head— which I seriously doubt—I fear your advisors are doing things you are not aware of."

Cavanagh folded his arms. His eyes narrowed. "Have you got a wire on or something? Is that what this is?"

She shook her head, pulled the unzipped fleece back and lifted the white polo shirt a touch to reveal a stretch of her stomach. As it happened, she wasn't wearing a wire, but the bag she'd brought with her was recording everything in that living room, all for naught if he did not admit anything. After everything, a clear, indisputably authentic video of the Cavanagh patriarch admitting his own guilt might finally be enough to push the case against him over the line, to erode his corrupt power and see him properly investigated. Especially if it was posted online. "I guess it doesn't matter if you are. They'll take it off you," he said.

They. The people who protected Jack. The people who killed Jimmy for nothing. The people responsible for killing Bogey.

"I don't want to die. You don't have to have me killed. I will leave you alone," she reiterated. "Please call your security man, The American, and tell him to leave me alone."

Inside, she was growing impatient. But she had to do this right, had to say the words.

His eyebrows shot up. He was perhaps surprised she knew of the man.

"The American? Tell him yourself. He'll be here soon," Jack responded.

Mak swallowed. *Is he bluffing?* she wondered and nodded to herself, trying to take the news calmly. She'd already known the clock was ticking. "And you didn't call the cops?"

He didn't respond.

No, he wouldn't want them coming too soon. Not until things are finished and I'm dead.

"I need you to think about the fact that people are being murdered on your behalf. People like that girl who overdosed with your son and the friend of your son's who witnessed her death and was murdered because of it. People like Bogey Mortimer." Jack simply continued looking at her, silently. "You need to put an end to this or more people will die. People like me and my unborn child."

His pale eyes flickered to her stomach again.

"My offer is sincere," she said. "I will leave you alone if you stop pursuing me. Maybe justice will finally catch you, but it's not my fight any more. I want nothing to do with it. Let me go. *Please. Let me live.*"

As she spoke the words she'd rehearsed again and again

in her mind, she realised that some tiny, naïve part of her had actually hoped her words would have an impact, could make a difference to the hard reality of things. She found that same naïve part of her had actually longed to look into Jack Cavanagh's eyes and find innocence—not a man used to sitting in his mighty high-rise office ordering death and corruption, but a man unaware of what was being done in his name.

But this was not a fairy tale. She knew what she had to do, what she'd come here to do.

Jack Cavanagh stood before her, and the corners of his mouth turned down into a sneer. "Honestly, woman, did you think this would work?" he said and took an unwelcome step towards her, his blue eyes glittering darkly, hard as diamonds. "Did you think you could win my sympathy by getting yourself knocked up? If you even are? By coming here to show yourself? This is larger than you. You should be fucking dead." *Ah. There you are.* This was the other side of Jack Cavanagh.

The ruthless side his spin machine worked so hard to hide. The side she'd known was there.

Mak shook her head. "You make me sad, Jack. You're doing all this so you can keep your son's precious secrets while he parties it up in Monaco—with, I'm guessing, your money—and leaves you here to clean up the mess? Tell me, has it been worth it? Worth your marriage?"

His mouth tightened like he'd sucked a lemon.

"Oh yes. Your wife wouldn't send you a surprise massage because you aren't on speaking terms at the moment, are you? And your son? Have you spoken to him lately?"

Jack's face reddened. "Jayden, get this woman out of my sight!" he shouted and stepped back. "You've signed your own death warrant," he spat and folded his arms, as if he was done with their exchange and she would simply disappear now that he'd ordered it.

"*Fucking bitch.*"

It was not Jack who spoke.

The voice came from behind him.

From the base of the stairwell.

Not the bodyguard she'd been expecting, but someone else.

Someone familiar.

Damien Cavanagh?

Jack's son was sullen and dark-eyed, his hair askew. He wore a black silk robe draped loosely over the angles of his long, lean, deeply tanned body. Despite the time, Damien appeared to have been woken from slumber. *My God, it's really him.* Mak had not seen him during her reconnaissance of the house. Andy had not mentioned his return. *How could I have missed that Damien was in the country?* Makedde wondered in the stunned instant it took to realise that he was there and to see that he was raising his right arm.

Something was in his hand. Something that flashed silver, reflecting the sunlight.

A gun.

He has a gun.

He held it out towards her, his mouth turned down into a scowl. "Bitch," she heard him say again.

"Damien! Get back!" his father yelled, but Mak was no longer focused on him.

She pulled up the back of her shirt, took the loaded nine-millimetre Glock out from her waistband and aimed it at the Cavanagh heir, one hand cupped around the other, thumbs locked down. Her heart quickened. Her vision constricted. All she could see was Damien Cavanagh, holding a gun on her—his face, his hands on the gun—and everything else had somehow disappeared. She had tunnel vision. The adrenaline was causing it. The fear. In her ears was a kind of buzzing. It was her blood.

"Jayden!" Jack yelled, calling for his bodyguard.

Mak took a slow, deliberate breath, squinting with her left eye and shutting the other entirely. She looked down the barrel and the silencer, and now the world seemed to slow with her breathing. She squeezed her trigger finger just as she had practised so many times, and there came the sound of two blasts— one muffled and close, the other loud and metres away. There was an explosion of red around Damien's head and he dropped like a stone. Behind her, a pane of glass shattered.

Damien had fired at her. He'd missed. "Drop your weapon!"

Mak spun and squeezed off a second shot, missing the tall security guard as he ran across the lawn with his iPod earphones dangling from his shorts, dwarfed by his enormous, muscled thighs. He'd already unholstered his CZ 75 and now he let off two quick rounds, both hitting the wall behind her as she ran full tilt towards the designer leather lounge and dove behind it.

Damien. Damien is dead.

Had Damien been a decent aim, she would be as dead as he was. And she had been too absorbed in her exchange to notice the guard's approach. She'd not even been able to see her periphery. Now the bodyguard was there. Armed.

Get yourself steady.

Get yourself steady, Mak.

She stayed crouched behind the lounge, panting, and pulled off her cap and Bogey's glasses, then sat up and peered over the edge of the lounge to see the armed guard move past the open living-room doors in his lumbering sprint. He disappeared for a moment and reappeared in the open-plan kitchen, framed by hanging pots and pans. She clocked him in her sights, took a breath and squeezed off a shot. He ducked behind the stainless-steel counter and her bullet hit a blender, which switched on for a moment, losing its lid before shorting out.

"Damien! Damien!" Jack was yelling, weeping. He'd gone to ground, stretched out on his stomach.

"Drop it or you die, Jayden!" Mak shouted from behind the lounge.

She peeked around the edge again and saw that the guard was still creeping around the kitchen. His aim gave her hope that he was not up on his practice. Had he discharged his weapon in a gunfight before? Perhaps not. A lot of long-serving cops never discharged their weapons. Mak was not so lucky.

While she stayed down the guard took two further shots. They hit the cushions on the lounge she was hiding behind, the sound muffled.

His CZ 75 was set on double shot.

"He's not paying you enough. Drop it," she called out. He didn't respond.

In the reflection of the stereo cabinet she saw Jack crawling towards the glass sliding doors on his hands and knees. *Dammit.* She didn't want to chase him across the lawn. Makedde peeked around the leather lounge to see the guard coming towards her, gun drawn. He had a lot of bullets left.

So did she.

Mak lined up her shot and fired at the pots and frying pans hanging over the guard's shoulder, causing a clangour as they rocked and leaped off their hooks, some falling to the tiles below. As they fell she surged upwards and the guard, taken by surprise, tried another two shots—which zinged into the wall just above her. Mak plugged him square in his enormous chest with a single shot. She ducked back down, unsure of her aim. When she peered over the edge again she saw him stumble backwards. He clutched himself, took two steps forwards, puzzlement etched on his young face. He made it three more steps before sinking to his knees only a few metres away from her. His weapon clattered to the floor and finally he went down like a speared bull, chin first, right in front of the lounge.

A stainless-steel pot, having fallen from its hook, rocked one way and the other on the tiled floor, back and forth, back and forth, until it eventually, mercifully became still.

Mak stepped out from behind the leather lounge, picked up the guard's CZ 75 and pocketed it. She couldn't tell whether he was breathing and she didn't bend down to check. She turned her head and at a glance saw that Damien was still at the base of the stairs, lying in a growing pool of blood. She turned her gun on Jack, who had flipped onto his back, and was making strange motions, like a fish out of water. His expression was one of naked loss and fear and confusion—and of rage. His mouth kept opening and closing. A dark stain spread out across his jeans. Urine. She aimed the gun at Jack Cavanagh's head, both hands on the grip and her index finger placed lightly on the trigger. The weapon was disproportionately long with the addition of the dark, cylindrical silencer. She squinted, looking down the long barrel into Jack's widening eyes, and swallowed back any remaining fear. She found there wasn't much fear left in her. She was simply empty.

"Just look what you've made me into," Makedde said, more to herself than anyone. "Look at me."

She thought of Luther Hand. Of John Dayle. Of Damien. Of the nameless men who'd come after her. Jack could not possibly understand what it was like to become a killer against your own will. To be perverted like that by trauma and by horror. To be forced to kill. And she realised in that moment that she was grinning again. That maniacal grin she'd seen reflected in the handle of John Dayle's scalpel.

"I didn't want it to be this way, but you leave me no choice. Damien left me no choice," she said. She touched one hand to her stomach. "If we're going to die, we may as well take you with us."

Jack backed up across the floor. He looked from her horrible grin, down to the barrel of the gun she had pointed at him and back again. She had the gun aimed at his head, and now his eyes flickered away. She imagined that he wished he had a better bodyguard. Or that he really had called "The American."

"Fuck you. You should have died in Paris," he spat.

"There. That was an admission, wasn't it? I should have fucking died in Paris, right? *Stand up,*" she ordered, and he got up shakily. "You've lost your son. You caused all that death for him, for nothing. And now it's over."

"You fucking bitch!" he shouted—*Like father like son*—and he lunged clumsily for her Glock, red-faced, his fingers spread like claws.

Mak squeezed the trigger and everything seemed to stop.

A single hollow-point bullet exited the muzzle, the sound muffled by the silencer, and penetrated the centre of Jack Cavanagh's forehead, entering his skull and mushrooming out through the brain tissue. The impact threw Jack Cavanagh's head back with a whiplash effect, propelling his body backwards into a designer chair that slid on wheels across the timber floor to hit the stereo cabinet with a crack.

Then all was quiet save for the stereo. No screams.

No choking.

No more conversation.

Jack Cavanagh's pale blue eyes were open and unseeing—or perhaps seeing whatever there was to witness beyond the threshold of life. He would have looked like he was sprawled out in the seat, resting in beams of sunlight, except his brains were across the stereo cabinet up the wall. Behind him, his son lay in a pool of blood. By the lounge, his bodyguard lay dead.

On the radio Miles Davis was still playing "So What."

The men who could not have her live were gone. And Makedde Vanderwall was a murderer. For the first time in her life she'd killed someone in cold blood. She'd killed a corrupt billionaire, a man, a human being, a husband, a son, a father. Damien had fired on her, but Jack had been unarmed. She'd murdered him.

She caught sight of motion as a figure appeared from behind her, across the lawn.

Fuck . . .

Mak crouched behind the edge of the stereo cabinet, gun extended. Had the guard called for backup? No, this was a neatly dressed older man with a full head of white-grey hair. She knew instinctively that this must be The American Andy had told her about. Cavanagh's security man. He was capable and highly dangerous, Mak knew. Jack had phoned him, just as he'd said. He must not have been far away, or he'd already been on his way over. What were the chances? From the look of his quick breathing the man had been moving quickly, perhaps even running, but now he stood a few metres away from Mak, stock still, his gun trained on her. The air between them seemed to thicken.

Mak did a quick count. She'd only used seven bullets—two of them on the pots and pans. Eight left. And she had a second fifteen-round magazine ready in her thigh pocket.

"Drop it," she said, keeping her gun steady on him.

He didn't. His weapon, a Beretta, remained pointed at her, but his eyes strayed to the motionless guard on the floor, then to Damien at the base of the stairs, and finally to Jack, who was slumped in the chair, arms at his sides, head thrown back at an uncomfortable angle. The man they called The American moved slowly through the open doors into the living room towards his client, not wanting to alarm Mak with any sudden movements. With his left hand he held two fingers to the side of Jack's neck and waited a couple of beats. It was clear to Mak that Jack Cavanagh was not breathing and would never breathe again. He stepped away and looked Mak up and down. He seemed what . . . impressed? Surprised? She could see no fear in him.

"*Sanctum Massage?*" he said in a rich American accent, reading her uniform and nodding his head. "He didn't fear you, you know. Maybe I should have convinced him you were dangerous."

"See, now that surprises me," Mak said, her Glock still trained on him.

"Dangerous in that you could make his life difficult, Makedde Vanderwall, he knew that," he said, pronouncing her name correctly. "But not . . ." He glanced towards the spray of blood and torn flesh dramatically colouring the cabinet and wall behind his boss. He did not need to say more. "He thought he could hold you off. What now?" he asked her.

"Now you drop your weapon," she ordered. He kept the Beretta pointed at her.

"You won't shoot me unless you have to," he said, with a confidence that was jarring. But he was, of course, correct. "You're not a killer."

"I've just killed three men," she said coolly. "So you can save your psychology for someone else."

He absorbed her response without comment and kept his gun out as he visited the bodyguard to check for a pulse. He put his finger to the man's throat, waited a beat and then stood. Jayden was evidently dead, as he made no attempt to help him. "Jack didn't want a guard at all. I couldn't convince him to get a better one," he told her. "I'd have insisted on more, but even I didn't imagine you would come here."

"And you are Jack's security advisor, I assume?"

"Something like that," he said quietly. "So, what will you do? They are dead now. The Australian authorities don't appreciate vigilantes. You're already wanted for the murder of a cop."

Murder? Jimmy's dead?

Mak felt her concentration waver again. *Was it true?* "I need the contract on me cancelled. I want to be left alone. If I'm not left alone, I will do whatever is necessary," she told him. "I'm not going to live on the run."

He nodded. "You'll be left alone," he assured her. "By me and my people, anyway."

Mak squinted at him. "You'll excuse me if I don't so easily believe that right now." She licked her lips. "Why don't you go ahead and convince me exactly how that is going to be possible. What about the Cavanagh empire?"

"There is no Cavanagh empire, Makedde Vanderwall. Not any more. The investors will be gone the moment news of Jack's death breaks. It's over."

He was probably right.

"It's been heading this way," he said. "It was a good run for me, but this was signposted months ago. If it wasn't you, my guess is it would have been someone else. Or Jack would have done it to himself."

The sound of choking interrupted the moment. They both turned towards the kitchen. Jayden—the bodyguard who had so failed Jack—was alive. He rolled onto one shoulder, curled in the foetal position. Mak kept her gun on The American as he walked over to the giant man on the floor and observed his soft, ragged breathing and the large exit wound inflicted by her hollow-point. Just when she expected he might offer help, he lowered his Beretta and discharged it into the side of the man's head.

Mak looked away.

"He would not have survived the night," The American said simply.

No witnesses, she thought.

A hand twitched and stopped. Mak swallowed.

The American caught Makedde's gaze and lowered his gun again, inch by inch until it was at his side.

Her aim remained fixed. "So, you aren't going to shoot me?" she said.

"For whom? It's over, Makedde."

It's over. She felt a sting in her eyes and this time she didn't fight it, had no intention of fighting it. She slowly lowered her Glock, letting hot tears pour freely down her cheeks. "It is over," she repeated back, genuinely flooded with emotion.

"It's over."

As the muzzle was aimed closely at The American's right knee, she squeezed the trigger.

The shot came out with a dull thump, and The American cried out as his kneecap exploded, blood and bone spraying them both. He collapsed to the floor, cradling his wounded leg. Face twisted with pain, he raised his Beretta and it went off as Mak knocked it from his hands, the bullet hitting one of the glass sliding doors behind her and shattering it with a thunderous crash. She kicked his gun away across the floor.

"You know you have no hope of getting away with this," The American said through gritted teeth, holding his devastated knee and bleeding out onto the floor.

"I never planned to," she said. Her vision was blurry with tears. She stood over him, her gun aimed at his face.

"I'd rather die than raise my child behind bars," she told him. "But you're right. I'm not cut out to be a killer."

She opened her mouth and put the muzzle inside, one trigger

squeeze away from a quick and bloody death. The feel of the hot steel made her heart pound. It burned.

The man at her feet opened his lips to speak, but nothing came out. He watched with wide eyes as Mak held the gun in her mouth for a tense stretch of time, feeling the hard steel of the silencer against her lips, against her tongue.

It's over, she thought.

It's finally over.

And as quick as she'd put it in, she pulled the Glock out of her mouth and threw it across the room, tossing it far from where The American lay.

"It's over," she repeated aloud in a voice choked with tears, and walked to the kitchen, stepping around the feet of the dead guard. She pulled a large kitchen knife from a block next to the stove and walked back to The American, barely noticing the way her hand shook as she held the keen blade. By the time she returned, he had crawled a couple of feet, evidently going for his gun, or the telephone to call for help. There were streaks of his blood across the floor.

Mak seized the phone cord and cut it with the knife. "Don't try to stop me," she warned him and kicked his Beretta further away. She pulled the mobile right from his belt and tossed it, and he didn't attempt to stop her.

She left The American on the ground unarmed next to his very rich and very dead client, who lay back in his designer chair in a beam of sunlight, haloed in blood and precious brain tissue. Jack and Damien Cavanagh were both dead. The American's career was over. He would have to live with his failure.

It's over. It's all over.

Makedde stepped through the sliding doors, shoes crunching on glass, and walked to the shore with the knife in her hand.

CHAPTER 43

Detective Inspector Hunt watched the grainy footage on the monitor, barely able to see for the cloud of anger and fear hanging over him.

"Play it again," he said in a voice that sounded foreign to his own ears.

Detective Walsh pressed "play."

The officers of the newly formed Strike Force Alpha focused once more on the monitor as it gave them the view from a single CCTV camera. Hunt squinted, trying to stay calm as the camera watched a woman's back with its unemotional, electronic eye. She walked down to the beach, dressed in a polo shirt and khaki shorts, a lone figure in washed-out, grainy colour, growing smaller as she moved towards the shore. The shape of a long kitchen knife could be seen in her right hand, known to be the same one that was missing from a knife block next to the stove in the Cavanaghs' kitchen. The woman in the footage stopped at the shoreline and sat down on the sand. It was hard to see what she was doing until she stood up again, stripped down to her underwear.

The figure raised something that looked like the knife and made a couple of quick movements.

Detective Inspector Hunt shook his head. "Again," he said.

His world had changed dramatically in the course of a single phone call; and now, as he sat with the team of homicide officers going over what they had on the triple murder of Jack and Damien Cavanagh and the security guard at the Cavanagh house in Palm Beach, he felt disoriented, his mind racing to catch up with this new reality and what it could mean for him. This investigation would go to the very top. It would be closely monitored by the police commissioner, the international media—even the prime minister. Beneath the surface of his every action, his every statement and command, he wondered how this sudden turn of events would affect him and his future. He wondered if anyone knew about his involvement in blocking the progress of the trial against the Cavanaghs. Discrediting and removing witnesses. Disposing of evidence. He wondered if anyone knew about his involvement in the shooting of Detective Cassimatis, whom he'd known was conspiring against him. Who would protect him now, if his actions were discovered? What assurances did he have? He had none.

The footage was stopped and rewound.

The woman—now positively identified as Canadian national Makedde Vanderwall, the prime suspect in the fatal shooting of Detective Cassimatis—had evidently infiltrated the luxury beachfront home of Jack Cavanagh and murdered him, his son, Damien, and a man who had apparently been hired by Damien Cavanagh for protection and did not have a current security licence. Neighbours reported the sound of gunshots and, when a couple of uniformed police nearest to the area arrived, they discovered the bodies of Mr. Cavanagh, his son and Jayden Tully in the living area. None could be revived by paramedics and all were pronounced dead at the scene. Three handguns had so far been recovered—a CZ 75 found on the shore, an unregistered Glock on the living-room floor and a unique, silver-plated Smith & Wesson, engraved as a gift to Mr. Cavanagh. All had been recently discharged. The house was fitted with CCTV cameras, but the hard drive recording their footage had been intentionally destroyed. Multiple gunshots had damaged the platters inside. No data could be recovered. Ballistic fingerprinting had yet to establish whether the bullets that damaged the hard drive were fired from any of the three recovered weapons.

But the neighbours also had security cameras. "There. Stop there," Hunt ordered.

The group of officers sat forwards on their metal chairs, as if the extra six inches would somehow make it all clear. The figure on the tape appeared to walk out alone from the direction of the Cavanaghs' back door, then strip down, cut herself with the knife she'd taken from the kitchen and swim out into the water. *Straight out.* Past the boat, which was still at the jetty. Past the point of visibility. Makedde Vanderwall had abandoned the weapon used to kill Jack and Damien Cavanagh and a car she had stolen from the nearby mall, both covered in prints. She had even left her handbag behind, fitted with a keyhole camera that held a video of the murders, a device she would have become familiar with in her work as a private investigator. The footage, which was still being analysed, proved her unequivocal involvement in the killings, but also indicated the presence of a fourth person—a man who was also wounded at the scene. A trail of blood had been found leading to the security system and out to the driveway, suggesting that this man knew his way around the house and its security features and had been the one to intentionally destroy the CCTV footage.

The strike force was still working on leads to identify the man and already one Cavanagh employee, Joy Fregon, had said he was a Mr. Robert White, a consultant for Cavanagh Incorporated on international security issues. No one by that name existed on the company databases, however, and Hunt had no intention of divulging what *he* knew. The man in the footage was indeed the man he'd known as Mr. White, "The American." Hunt was fairly sure he had never been recognised in public with him, but he could not be one hundred per cent certain. If it was found that he'd met with The American, his career would be over. Even more worrying though, Hunt wondered if Mr. White considered him a threat. He was not a man who liked to leave loose ends.

"Go back again. Go back," Hunt ordered.

If only he'd managed to destroy the footage from Makedde's handbag showing Mr. White, so he could not be identified. Surely that was White's intention in destroying the CCTV footage in the house? He must not have been aware of the device in the handbag. Yet without that tape they would not have the footage showing Makedde Vanderwall murdering Jack Cavanagh in cold blood. He'd been unarmed, and the murder certainly helped the case against her for the Cassimatis shooting. Hunt continued to move the facts around like squares on a Rubik's cube. Every possible move seemed to bring him closer, and further away, from what he needed to survive the bloody turn of events.

Again the team watched as the woman in the neighbour's CCTV footage appeared to hold the knife out, then move it in two quick arcs before dropping it to the sand.

"She's cutting her wrists."

"We can't be sure," Hunt protested.

"There's blood on the knife," Walsh pointed out.

The knife and her bloodstained clothing had been found on the edge of the water. The blood was being tested against that of the murder victims.

Fuck.

A triple homicide and suicide? That was how his career trajectory ended? Hunt held a hand over his mouth as the grainy figure in the footage waded into the waves again, disappearing from view.

CHAPTER 44

Dear Andy,

I can't seem to do anything right. Just know I always loved you and I never meant to hurt anyone.

    Forgive me.

—Mak

Andy Flynn sat in the interrogation room with his head filled with darkness, regret and rage. He was on the other side of the table this time. The interrogated, not the interrogator. A glass of water had been placed on the Formica tabletop in front of him. It wasn't quite what he had in mind to drink.

"For the tape I require you to answer, Agent Flynn," Detective Inspector Hunt prodded again. "Is this the note you found in your pocket?"

Under the table, Andy clenched his hands into fists. "Yes," he said.

That was the note. He could see Makedde's devastating words from where he sat. She'd slipped the note into his pocket somehow, probably when she'd kissed him goodbye at the café, he realised. Now the note was spread open inside a plastic evidence bag. A fucking suicide note, and he'd found it in his pocket too late.

How could you do it, Mak?

Andy could not keep himself from replaying every second of their last encounter. How she hadn't taken her mirrored glasses off. How she'd seemed resigned about the laptop being destroyed, the corruption. How she'd looked as she'd walked away for the last time, leaving him in that Darlinghurst café. How could she have calmly talked to him the way she had, told him she was pregnant, and then set out on a mission of murder? One she had a slim chance of surviving and no hope of getting away with? Had he reacted so badly that she'd felt she had no choice? Could he have said something different? Followed her instead of letting her walk away? How had he so misjudged the situation? Misjudged her? God knows she'd had to defend herself before. Maybe she'd only meant to entrap Cavanagh, get a confession on her recording device? Maybe she'd just meant to threaten him and it had all gone horribly wrong? Yet she'd slipped him that note, a note she would have written before they even talked. Had she really known how it would end before she'd even said goodbye? That it was a suicide mission? That she'd never see him again? Andy knew he would be asking himself those questions for a long time to come.

She's dead. And you didn't stop it. You couldn't save her. "You did not see her?" Inspector Hunt pressed.

"No," Andy said, feeling the sting behind his eyes.

That was half true, at least. He hadn't seen her give him the note.

"But you identified her writing. You knew Makedde Vanderwall was a person of interest in your own ex-partner's death and yet by your own admission you took your time calling in this vital piece of information. Why is that?"

That Andy had to deal with an interrogation by Bradley Hunt, of all people, was almost too much to bear. He might not have killed Jimmy himself, but Andy knew he was indirectly—or even directly—responsible for his death. And now Mak had been pushed to suicide because of men like Hunt and all the others who had been under Cavanagh's thumb. Andy would not be satisfied until Hunt was out of a job and into a cell, but it would do no good to admit now that he *knew* Hunt was lying when he claimed Mak had been the shooter, that he knew without a doubt that Hunt was corrupt, that he'd seen the footage from the construction site himself in his hotel room, that he'd spent the night with Mak after Jimmy was shot . . .

Wait until Mak's footage arrives. Just wait.

It was Monday. It had to be there on Kelley's desk.

He had to believe she'd posted it, like she said she had. Mak wouldn't lie to him. She would keep things from him, perhaps, but she wouldn't lie. Even if he could not comprehend what she had done at the Palm Beach house—could she really have been responsible for all that bloodshed and violence?—he had to believe that she would not lie to him.

Andy turned his neck on an angle and it clicked, the muscles releasing. "I was distracted. Get it? Jimmy . . ." He trailed off. "I got the news about Detective Cassimatis and I didn't notice the note. Maybe I would have on any other day? Who knows? Who knows how long it had been in my pocket? An hour? Two? When I found it I called it in. You think she would leave a note like this and wait around? She was long gone, if she was the one who put it there at all."

"If not her, who else do you think would put it there?"

"How should I fucking know?"

"There is no need for hostility, Flynn," Hunt said.

Oh yes. Oh yes there is, you fucker. Andy gritted his teeth.

"I think you delayed imparting this vital piece of information," Hunt said, pointing at the note, "to aid her."

"You think I *aided* her? In her suicide? Christ!" Andy stood up suddenly in his chair, toppling it over. He wanted so badly to punch Hunt that he could feel it. Could feel his knuckles make impact, could hear the jaw breaking.

She was pregnant. SHE WAS GODDAMN PREGNANT, he thought.

"Take a seat—"

"This is bullshit, Hunt. You know this is fucking bullshit . . ."

Flynn felt eyes on him. Kelley was probably watching. How long would he let this charade go on for?

Andy had told Les Vanderwall himself. Though he couldn't deliver the terrible news in person, he'd felt he owed Mak's father that much. He had not told him his daughter was still alive when she'd appeared in Australia—had not done the right thing there, despite promising him he would. Andy would always feel guilty for that. But he'd told him what had unfolded at the Cavanagh house, over the phone, as Canadian police officers, the man's colleagues before he retired, were gathered around him at his home in Canada, to console him. Vanderwall had wailed down the line—wailed like a wounded animal. First his wife, lost to cancer, and now his daughter gone forever. He was inconsolable. Andy could not stand to tell him Mak had also been pregnant. In a way, if her body never washed up, it would be better for everyone. Les would never have to know about the baby. And Andy would never have to know if it was his own. He'd never have to think about the child he wouldn't have.

"We don't know that she suicided," Hunt reminded him. "It's on the neighbour's security footage for fuck's sake. And she didn't kill Jimmy. You know that, too, you slimy piece of shit."

Fucking Hunt, of all people. Hunt has to be the one to grill me about the note? Jesus. Andy had little patience left for this, particularly with Jimmy's funeral only hours away. He had to believe Hunt's brief reign was nearly over. He had to believe that now Jack Cavanagh was dead, it would all come out. The bribes. The corruption. Everything that had pulled apart a good, honest police force. The taint of the Cavanaghs stretched from the politicians to the media to the police. Yes, even the police. Hunt, and God knew who else. It was unthinkable. But there was no one left to pull the strings now. What Mak had done couldn't be for nothing. It just couldn't.

"What are you accusing me of?" Hunt said cautiously.

With some effort Andy contained himself. He sat down, crossed his arms and kept his mouth shut.

Perhaps a minute passed in tense silence. Andy half expected the door to open, but it didn't. Hunt changed tack. "Well, you may not think she'd kill your friend Detective Cassimatis, but she certainly killed Jack Cavanagh. It's on tape." There was a hint of triumph in his tone.

"Yes," Andy admitted in a low voice.

It was on tape. On the tape she'd left behind. And her prints were all over the place. On the note. On the stolen car. On the murder weapon. On the knife she'd cut herself with. How could she do it? Had the police let her down—had Andy let her down—so badly that she had to kill Jack Cavanagh and his son for all to see and then kill herself while there was a child growing in her belly? God knows he would have loved that baby, taken it on, even if it wasn't his. It would have hurt, yes. It would have taken him a little while to get over it if it had turned out to be the child of that man she'd screwed so soon after leaving him, but he'd have got over it eventually. He'd have been able to get past it. But now they'd never have the chance to work things out. She was dead. She and the baby in her belly.

He felt a hot tear roll down one cheek.

Great. I'm fucking crying now. Arsehole.

Andy wiped the tear and spoke. "Yes, it's on the tape. So is his admission that he'd tried to have her killed in Paris. She was being *hunted*. Can you imagine how pressured she must have been to resort to this? And you know what, you're right that I fucked up. You're absolutely fucking right to bring me in here and grill me. Yes. If I could do it again, I would have reached in my pocket and read this scrap of paper and understood what was going on. I would have found the surprise note in my pocket when I was at the hospital with my partner dead and I would have read it and recognised the writing and thought, Jesus Christ, I'd better call my mates at the New South Wales police. Who knows, maybe we could have found her and stopped her? Maybe she'd still be alive?"

Hunt frowned. "We don't know that she is dead—"

"Jesus, mate, did you see the way she stuck that fucking gun in her mouth? Do you think she'd leave video of herself murdering Jack Cavanagh if she'd planned on sticking around? You think she'd just leave the murder weapon there with her prints on it?"

"How did you know about—?"

"Don't insult me, Hunt. I've still got mates here." He'd seen it. He'd seen it all. And it made him sick inside. "My ex-girlfriend killed herself and saw fit to give me the suicide note. No, I didn't find it right away. We lost an hour because of me. Maybe two. That's true. I'm going to have to live with that."

Hunt was silenced.

"I've got a funeral to go to," Andy said. "Are we done here?" He stood.

They all had to go and die on him, didn't they? Cassandra and Jimmy and now Mak. He had no one left.

All dead. They're all dead. Everyone you ever truly cared about.

"Just a couple more questions—" Hunt began and his sentence was stopped short by one sharp punch to the face. Andy walked out of the interrogation room, pulling open the door for himself as Hunt stood shocked, holding a broken nose which bled freely between his fingers. Two officers rushed into the room to aid him.

Detective Inspector Kelley was waiting outside the commander's office, arms tightly crossed. His slate-grey eyes were full of disappointment, but he patted Andy's shoulder. For a man like Kelley, a gesture like that was akin to an embrace. "Sorry about that nonsense," he said quietly, not mentioning his violent outburst. "I'll see you at the funeral."

Kelley flicked his eyes to Hunt, who had emerged from the interrogation room, bloody and flushed. "Hunt, the commander and I would like to speak to you," Kelley said as Andy walked away. The door to the commander's office was ajar. An Express Post package was ripped open on the desk.

Mak's package for Kelley had arrived.

You did it, Mak. You did it.

Agent Andy Flynn was the last to leave the wake at the Cassimatis house. It was near ten o'clock when he finally stepped from the clinging grief of the small suburban house and walked out to his car, leaving Jimmy's widow in the kitchen with her elderly, widowed mother, the two women making themselves busy with the domestic needs of a household that would need to keep on keeping on, without its patriarch.

Four fatherless boys to raise. There would be dark days ahead.

As Jimmy's closest friend, Andy had been asked to speak at the funeral. He'd managed to keep it together, even when they'd played a video with photographs of Jimmy over the years. As a toothless, smiling baby. Fresh-faced in uniform for the first time.

Holding his first baby boy, Dominique. Playing ball in the back-yard. Posing as a dubious Santa in board shorts at Christmas. He'd been so young and slim once. Andy had almost forgotten.

Jimmy was buried with full honours. Killed in the line of duty. No one mentioned Makedde or the Cavanagh murders to Andy. If it was a topic of speculation amongst the family, they kept it to themselves.

What a fucking mess.

Andy unlocked the door of his car. He'd remained sober out of respect for Jimmy's family, but he'd soon fix that. He'd stop by the liquor store on the way to the hotel. The interior light came on and he slid himself inside, feeling hollowed and bare.

What's this? There was something on the driver's seat. He picked it up and turned it in his fingers.

Strange.

A business card. It was bent at the corners, as if it had trav-elled in his wallet for months, only he didn't recognise the card at all. He examined it under the glow of the interior light and his eyes widened.

Holy shit, Mak.

His brain scrambled with this new information, what it meant. He thought of the video footage Mak had left at the scene, that horrifying image of her putting the gun in her mouth, nearly pulling the trigger. He thought of the blood they'd found on the knife at the shore. It would be her blood, he knew. Only it wouldn't be from slitting her wrists. She faked it. She faked her own suicide to survive. The note. The tears. All of it. She'd known what she was doing.

Makedde . . .

HOTEL MIRALLUNA, PERATALLADA, SPAIN, the card said in big letters across the front.

Have you ever been to Spain, Andy?

EPILOGUE

They made a striking trio, backlit against the Mediterranean sunset: the tall, handsome man with his full head of salt-and-pepper hair, the statuesque blonde woman and the small, smiling, spectacled boy.

The man stood on the edge of the shore, cupped his hands to his face and shouted something in Spanish, and she, ahead of him, turned to smile in his direction. She had the even features of a model, with full lips and an even fuller mane of dirty blonde hair she was growing out, currently shoulder length and worn loose with a natural wave. What he'd said had pleased her and her eyes crinkled up, and she flashed a broad, dazzling grin as she bent at the waist in her white swimsuit and sarong to whisper something conspiratorially to the child at her heels. And then in seconds she was off, dashing up the beach on long, tanned legs, the sarong flapping behind her like a white flag and the young boy screeching with high-pitched laughter as he chased her, holding his black-rimmed glasses to his face and giggling madly. The man who had been Andy Flynn ran after the woman and the boy making fresh footprints on the unmarked, pale sand. And then he stopped and shook his head, the salty sea foaming around his bare ankles as he caught his breath. It was time for dinner and they were close to home now. Her father and stepmother would be waiting inside. He watched as his girl-friend scooped her son up further down the beach they called their own. She held him to her chest, his small legs flailing and kicking, and his laughter drifted back on the wind. Four years he'd been here. *Four years.* Day by day the past was fading like the paint on their beachside house, seasoned by laughter and sun and salt air. He'd lost himself and gained a future. They all had. Beneath the crimson rays of the setting European sun, they fit in, their scars invisible. Just a man, a woman and a beautiful boy.

Nameless and wanting for nothing.

ACKNOWLEDGEMENTS

Makedde's full story has been a long time in the making. I've had some valuable support over the past thirteen years to see me through the ups and downs of Makedde's changing fortunes—and my own. I would especially like to thank my agent Selwa Anthony for her guidance and both Selwa and Brian for making me part of their family. Thank you also to the team at HarperCollins for taking the chance on me when I was a young, unpublished author.

I have experienced some fascinating research for this novel. I'd like to thank Mark Patterson, General Manager, Department of Forensic Medicine, Glebe, and all the staff there who do such an important job in helping to answer questions of cause of death. I would also like to acknowledge the wonderful research assistance of NSW Homicide Commander, Detective Superintendent Michael Willing, DCI John Lehmann and the homicide and unsolved squads, Peter Moroney of Nemesis, Detective Senior Sergeant Mick Garrahy, Digital Scientist Allan Watt, Digital Forensic Examiner Kevin Clayton, Senior Constable Mick Samson, Senior Constable Michael Dunn, Chris Allen and Charles Stingel. I'd also like to thank St. Vincent's Hospital and my friend, fellow author Dr Kathryn

Fox, for the fictional thoracotomy. I should also like to mention that Geoff Rosamond, who is named in this book, is not actually an assassin of any kind, but was good enough to bid on being named one in this novel, with his generous donation going to UNICEF Australia to help some of the world's most vulnerable children. Hans Reichhold of Townsville, who is mentioned in this novel as a fine constable, bid generously to help rebuild a much needed maternity hospital in Minova, in Democratic Republic of Congo. Your generosity has made such a difference. Thank you.

I am blessed to enjoy the company of some inspiring and diverse friends, including Miss J, Alison, Emma, Helen, Caroline, Catharine, Mindi, Tracey and little Charlie, Jacinta, Sarah, Marianne, Linda, Liz, Desi, Amelia, Dominic, Martin, Penelope and Karim, Tessa and Shane, Jody and Simon, Lauren and Josh, Kelly and Mick, Lisa and Julian, Jack and Venetia, and Adam and Susie. Thanks to all my patient friends and the gang at Sisters in Crime, the Stella Prize, Chadwicks, Foxtel, 13th Street, RIDBC, BFHI and UNICEF for your support and camaraderie.

To my brave childhood friend Alana, be well.

To my cherished father, to Lou and Jackie, Dorothy, Nik, Annelies, Maureen, and my extraordinary husband, Berndt, and our girl Sapphira, I love you all. Thank you for your unfailing love and life support. And the patience. Goodness me, the patience.

Mum, I never forget you.

ABOUT THE AUTHOR

Tara Moss is an international bestselling author, documentary host, and human rights advocate. She is the author of fourteen books, published in nineteen countries and thirteen languages. Moss is an advocate for the rights of women, children, and people with disabilities, and has published two bestselling nonfiction books, *The Fictional Woman* and *Speaking Out: A 21st Century Handbook for Women and Girls*. She is a UNICEF Goodwill Ambassador and Australia's National Ambassador for Child Survival. In 2015 she received an Edna Ryan Award for her significant contribution to feminist debate, inspiring others to challenge the status quo.

THE MAKEDDE VANDERWALL THRILLERS

FROM OPEN ROAD MEDIA

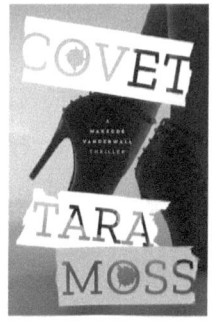

OPEN ROAD
INTEGRATED MEDIA

INTEGRATED MEDIA

Find a full list of our authors and
titles at www.openroadmedia.com

FOLLOW US
@OpenRoadMedia

www.ingramcontent.com/pod-product-compliance
Lightning Source LLC
Chambersburg PA
CBHW020636030726
47498CB00002B/243